Kathy Acker is now in her thirtie[...] the early seventies, principally w[...] publishers. She has taught in the [...] Francisco Art Institute in recent years and has given many readings and performances in San Francisco, Seattle and New York.

Kathy Acker

Blood and Guts
in High School

plus two

PICADOR
published by Pan Books

First published in Great Britain 1984 by Pan Books Ltd
Cavaye Place, London SW10 9PG
9 8 7 6 5

Blood and Guts in High School © Kathy Acker 1978
Great Expectations © Kathy Acker 1982
My Death, My Life © Kathy Acker 1983
ISBN 0 330 28186 0 paperback
ISBN 0 330 28326 × hardback
Printed in Great Britain

Blood and Guts
in High School

Contents

Inside high school

Parents stink

Never having known a mother, her mother had died when Janey was a year old, Janey depended on her father for everything and regarded her father as boyfriend, brother, sister, money, amusement, and father.

Janey Smith was ten years old, living with her father in Merida, the main city in the Yucatan. Janey and Mr Smith had been planning a big vacation for Janey in New York City in North America. Actually Mr Smith was trying to get rid of Janey so he could spend all his time with Sally, a twenty-one-year-old starlet who was still refusing to fuck him.

One night Mr Smith and Sally went out and Janey knew her father and that woman were going to fuck. Janey was also very pretty, but she was kind of weird-looking because one of her eyes was lopsided.

Janey tore up her father's bed and shoved boards against the front door. When Mr Smith returned home, he asked Janey why she was acting like this.

Janey: You're going to leave me. (*She doesn't know why she's saying this.*)

Father (*dumbfounded, but not denying it*): Sally and I just slept together for the first time. How can I know anything?

Janey (*in amazement. She didn't believe what she had been saying was true. It was only out of petulance*): You ARE going to leave me. Oh no. No. That can't be.

Father (*also stunned*): I never thought I was going to leave you. I was just fucking.

Janey (*not at all calming herself down by listening to what he's saying. He knows her energy rises sharply and crazy when she's scared so he's probably provoking this scene*): You can't leave me. You can't. (*Now in full hysteria.*) I'll . . . (*Realizes she might be flying off the handle and creating the situation. Wants to hear his creation for a minute. Shivers with fear when she asks this.*) Are you madly in love with her?

Father (*thinking. Confusion's beginning*): I don't know.

Janey: I'm not crazy. (*Realizing he's madly in love with the other woman.*) I don't mean to act like this. (*Realizing more and more how madly in love he is. Blurts it out.*) For the last month you've been spending

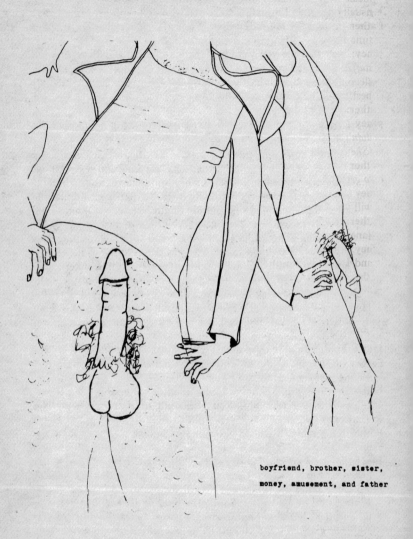

boyfriend, brother, sister,
money, amusement, and father

every moment you can with her. That's why you've stopped eating meals with me. That's why you haven't been helping me the way you usually do when I'm sick. You're madly in love with her, aren't you?

Father (*ignorant of this huge mess*): We just slept together for the first time tonight.

Janey: You told me you were just friends like me and Peter (*Janey's stuffed lamb*) and you weren't going to sleep together. It's not like my sleeping around with all these art studs: when you sleep with your best friend, it's really, really heavy.

Father: I know, Janey.

Janey (*she hasn't won that round; she threw betrayal in his face and he didn't totally run away from it*): Are you going to move in with Sally? (*She asks the worst possibility.*)

Father (*still in the same sad, hesitant, underlyingly happy because he wants to get away, tone*): I don't know.

Janey (*She can't believe this. Every time she says the worst, it's true*): When will you know? I have to make my plans.

Father: We just slept together once. Why don't you just let things lie, Janey, and not push?

Janey: You tell me you love someone else, you're gonna kick me out, and I shouldn't push. What do you think I am, Johnny? I love you.

Father: Just let things be. You're making more of this than it really is.

Janey (*everything comes flooding out*): I love you. I adore you. When I first met you, it's as if a light turned on for me. You're the first joy I knew. Don't you understand?

Father (*silent*).

Janey: I just can't bear that you're leaving me: it's like a lance cutting my brain in two: it's the worst pain I've ever known. I don't care who you fuck. You know that. I've never acted like this before.

Father: I know.

Janey: I'm just scared you're going to leave me. I know I've been shitty to you: I've fucked around too much; I didn't introduce you to my friends.

Father: I'm just having an affair, Janey. I'm going to have this affair.

Janey (*now the rational one*): But you might leave me.

Father (*silent*).

Janey: OK. (*Getting hold of herself in the midst of total disaster and clenching her teeth.*) I have to wait around until I see how things work out between you and Sally and then I'll know if I'm going to live with you or not. Is that how things stand?

Father: I don't know.

Janey: You don't know! How am I supposed to know?

That night, for the first time in months, Janey and her father sleep together because Janey can't get to sleep otherwise. Her father's touch is cold, he doesn't want to touch her mostly 'cause he's confused. Janey fucks him even though it hurts her like hell 'cause of her Pelvic Inflammatory Disease.

The following poem is by the Peruvian poet César Vallejo who, born 18 March 1892 (Janey was born 18 April 1964), lived in Paris fifteen years and died there when he was 46:

September

This September night, you fled
So good to me . . . up to grief and include!
I don't know myself anything else
But you, YOU don't have to be good.

This night alone up to imprisonment no prison
Hermetic and tyrannical, diseased and panic-stricken
I don't know myself anything else
I don't know myself because I am grief-stricken.

Only this night is good, YOU
Making me into a whore, no
Emotion possible is distance God gave integral:
Your hateful sweetness I'm clinging to.

This September evening, when sown
In live coals, from an auto
Into puddles: not known.

Janey (*as her father was leaving the house*): Are you coming back tonight? I don't mean to bug you. (*No longer willing to assert herself.*) I'm just curious.

Father: Of course I'll be back.

The moment her father left the house, Janey rushed to the phone and called up his best friend, Bill Russle. Bill had once fucked Janey, but his cock was too big. Janey knew he'd tell her what was happening with Johnny, if Johnny was crazy or not, and if Johnny really wanted to break up with Janey. Janey didn't have to pretend anything with Bill.

Janey: Right now we're at the edge of a new era in which, for all sorts of reasons, people will have to grapple with all sorts of difficult problems, leaving us no time for the luxury of expressing ourselves artistically. Is Johnny madly in love with Sally?

Bill: No.

Janey: No? (*Total amazement and hope.*)

Bill: It's something very deep between them, but he's not going to leave you for Sally.

Janey (*with even more hope*): Then why's he acting this way? I mean: he's talking about *leaving* me.

Bill: Tell me exactly what's been happening, Janey. I want to know for my own reasons. This is very important. Johnny hasn't been treating me like a friend. He won't talk to me anymore.

Janey: He won't? He feels you're his best friend. (*Making a decision.*) I'll tell you everything. You know I've been very sick.

Bill: I didn't know that. I'm sorry, I won't interrupt anymore.

Janey: I've been real sick. Usually Johnny helps out when I am, this time he hasn't. About a month ago he told me he was running around with Andrea and Sally. I said, 'Oh great,' it's great when he has new friends, he's been real lonely, I told him that was great. He said he was obsessed with Sally, a crush, but it wasn't sexual. I didn't care. But he was acting real funny toward me. I've never seen him act like that. The past two months he's treated me like he hates me. I never thought he'd leave me. He's going to leave me.

Bill (*breaking in*): Janey. Can you tell me exactly what happened last night? I have to know everything. (*She tells him.*) What do you think is going on?

Janey: Either of two . . . I am Johnny. (*Thinks.*) Either of two things. (*Speaks very slowly and clearly.*) First thing: I am Johnny. I'm beginning to have some fame, success, now women want to fuck me. I've never had women want me before. I want everything. I want to go out in the world as far as I can go. Do you understand what I'm talking about?

Bill: Yes. Go on.

Janey: There are two levels. It's not that I think one's better than the other, you understand, though I do think one is a more mature development than the other. Second level: It's like commitment. You see what you want, but you don't go after every little thing; you try to work it through with the other person. I've had to learn this this past year. I'm willing to work with Johnny.

Bill: I understand what's happening now. Johnny is at a place where he has to try everything.

Janey: The first level. I agree.

Bill: You've dominated his life since your mother died and now he hates you. He has to hate you because he has to reject you. He has to find out who he is.

Janey: That would go along with the crisis he was having in his work this year.

Bill: It's an identity crisis.

Janey: This makes sense. . . . What should I do?

Bill: The thing you can't do is to freak out and lay a heavy trip on him.

Janey: I've already done that. (*If she could giggle, she would.*)

Bill: You have to realize that you're the one person he hates, you're everything he's trying to get rid of. You have to give him support. If

11

you're going to freak out, call me, but don't show him any emotion. Any emotion he'll hate you even more for.

Janey: God. You know how I am. Like a vibrating nut.

Bill: Be very very calm. He's going through a hard period, he's very confused, and he needs your support. I'll talk to him and find out more about what's going on. I have to talk to him anyway because I want to find out why he hasn't been friendly to me.

Later that afternoon Mr Smith came home from work.

Janey: I'm sorry I got upset last night about Sally. It won't happen again. I think it's great you've got a girlfriend you really care about.

Father: I've never felt like this about anyone. It's good for me to know I can feel so strongly.

Janey: Yes. (*Keeping her cool.*) I just wanted you to know if there's anything I can do for you, I'd like to be your friend. (*Shaking a little.*)

Father: Oh, Janey. You know I care for you very deeply. (*That does it: Janey bursts into tears.*) I'm just confused right now. I want to be my myself.

Janey: You're going to leave me.

Father: Just let things be. I've got to go. (*He obviously wants to get out of the room as fast as possible.*)

Janey: Wait a minute. (*Collecting her emotions and stashing them.*) I didn't mean it. I was going to be calm and supportive like Bill said.

Father: What'd Bill say? (*Janey repeats the conversation. Everything comes splurting out now. Janey's not good at holding words back.*) You've completely dominated my life, Janey, for the last nine years and I no longer know who's you and who's me. I have to be alone. You've been alone for a while, you know that need: I have to find out who I am.

Janey (*her tears dry*): I understand now. I think it's wonderful what you're doing. All year I've been asking you, 'What do you want?' and you never knew. It was always me, my voice, I felt like a total nag; I want you to be the man. I can't make all the decisions. I'm going to the United States for a long time so you'll be able to be alone.

Father (*amazed she's snapped so quickly and thoroughly from down hysteria to joy*): You're tough, aren't you?

Janey: I get hysterical when I don't understand. Now everything's OK. I understand.

Father: I've got to go out now – there's a party uptown. I'll be back later tonight.

Janey: You don't have to be back.

Father: I'll wake you up, sweetie, when I get back. OK?

Janey: Then I can crawl in bed and sleep with you?

Father: Yes.

Tiny Mexican, actually Mayan villages, incredibly clean, round thatched huts, ducks, turkeys, dogs, hemp, corn; the Mayans are self-contained and thin-boned, beautiful. One old man speaks: 'Mexicans think money is more important than beauty; Mayans say beauty is more important than money; you are very beautiful.' They eat ears of roasted corn smeared with chili, salt, and lime and lots of meat, mainly turkey.

Everywhere in Merida and in the countryside are tiny fruit drink stands: drinks *jugos de frutas* made of sweet fresh fruits crushed, sugar, and water. Every other building in Merida is a restaurant, from the cheapest outdoor cafés, where the food often tastes the best; to expensive European-type joints for the rich. Merida, the city, is built on the money of the hemp-growers who possess one boulevard of rich mansions and their own places to go to. Otherwise the poor. But the town is clean, big, cosmopolitan, the Mexicans say, un-Mexican.

Mexico is divided into sections: each has its specialty: Vera Cruz has art. Merida has hemp, baskets, hammocks.

Uxmal: Mayan ruins, huge temples, all the buildings are *huge*, scary, on high. Low low land in centre. Everything very far apart. Makes forget personal characteristics. Wind blows long grass who! whoot! Jungle, not Amazonian swamp, but thick, thick green leafage so beautiful surrounds. Hear everything. No one knows how these massive rectangular structures were used. Now birds screech in the little rooms in the buildings, fly away; long iguanas run under rocks. Tiny bright green and red lizards run down paths past one tiny statue, on lowish ground; on a small concrete block, two funny-monkey-hideous-dog-jaguar faces and paws back-to-back. Janus? The sun?

A small Mayan village in the ruins of an old stone hacienda; church, factory, the whole works. Huge green plants are growing out of the stones; chickens, lots of dark-brown feathered turkeys, three pigs, one pink, run around; people, thin and little, live in what ruins can still be lived in.

And further down this dirt road, another village. On Sunday the men, normally gentle and dignified, get drunk. The man driving the big yellow truck is the head man. All the male villagers are touching his hand. They're showing him love. He will get, they say, the first newborn girl. In return, he says, he will give them a pig. All of the men's bodies are waving back and forth. The women watch.

By the time the clock said five (a.m.) Janey couldn't stand it anymore, so, despite her high fever, she walked the streets. Where could she run to? Where was peace (someone who loved her)? No one would take her in. It was raining lightly. The rain was going to increase her infection. She stood in front of Sally's house. Then she made herself walk away.

She walked back into her father's and her apartment. She hated the

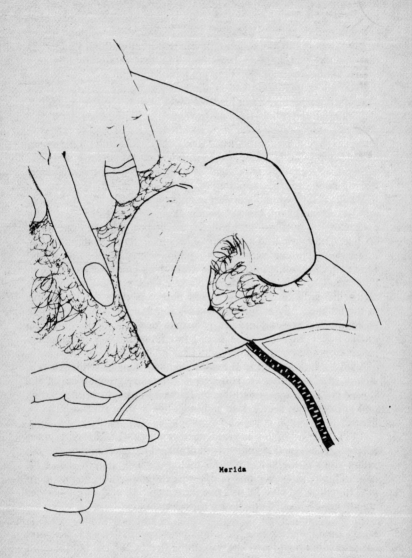

Merida

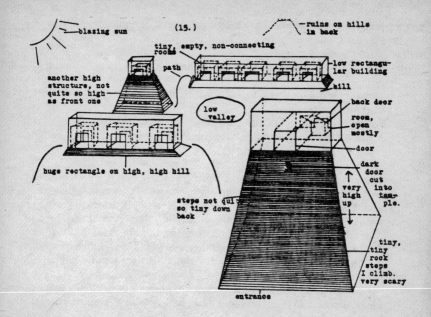

apartment. She didn't know what to do with her hateful tormented mind.

At 7:30 a.m. she woke up in her own bed. As she walked by her father's bed to get to the toilet, she saw her father and spontaneously asked, 'You must have gotten home late. How was the party?'

Father: I didn't go to the party.

Janey: You didn't go to the party!? (*Realizing the truth. In a little girl's voice.*) Oh.

Father (*reaching for her*): Come here (*meaning: into my arms*).

Janey: No. (*She jumps back.*) I don't want to touch you. (*She realizes her mistake. She's very jumpy.*) Just go to sleep. Everything's fine. Goodnight.

Father (*commanding*): Janey, come here.

Janey (*backing away like he's a dangerous animal, but wanting him*): I don't want to.

Father: I just want to hold you.

Janey: Why d'you lie to me?

Father: It got late and I didn't feel like going to the party.

Janey: What time d'you get home?

Father: Around seven.

Janey: Oh. (*In an even smaller little girl's voice.*) You were with Sally?

Father: Come here, Janey. (*He wants to make love to her. Janey knows it.*)

Janey (*running away*): Go to sleep, Johnny, I'll see you in the morning.

Janey (*a half-hour later*): I can't sleep by myself, Johnny. Can I crawl into bed with you?

Father (*grumbling*): I'm not going to get any sleep. Get in. (*Janey gives him a blow job. Johnny isn't really into having sex with Janey, but he gets off on the physical part.*)

Three hours later Johnny woke up and asked Janey if she wanted to have dinner with him that night, their farewell dinner, and then she would leave. Janey said 'No' in her sleep because she felt hurt.

As soon as Janey woke up, she called Bill, desperate. 'Everything's even worse, Bill,' she said. 'Johnny's trying to hurt me as badly as he can.' How? He told her he'd spend the night with her and then he spent it with Sally. Then he told her he felt about Sally the way he had never felt about another girl.

Bill tells Janey Johnny doesn't love Sally: he's just using Sally to hurt Janey as much as possible. Johnny has become very crazy and Janey'd better stay out of his way.

Janey: Do you think he'll want me again?

Bill: There's always been a really strong connection between the two of you. You've been together for years.

In the Merida marketplace there are beetles about an inch to two inches long crawling in a box, their backs covered by red or blue or white rhinestones.

Outside the church a woman sells all sorts of tiny cheap silver trinkets. People buy the appropriate trinket (an arm is a broken arm, a baby is problems with baby, a kidney, a little worker . . .) and take the trinket into the big church to give to the Virgin.

Monumental ruins.

Lost in the grass. Huge buildings that are staircases, staircases to the heights, steps of equal height so high legs can hardly climb. Some buildings are four walls of hundreds and hundreds of steps. On top is nothing, nothing but a small stone rectangle containing an empty hole. Every now and then a huge monster rattlesnake sticks its head out. The stones are crumbling. The oldest buildings are so ruined you can hardly see them.

The next mass of buildings. The architecture is clean, the meaning is clear, that is, the function. A habitation. Hiding tunnels run through each horizontal layer of the habitation. The scale is human. There are wells. There are no pictures or religious representations. A clean people who didn't mess around with their lives, who knew they were only alive once, who disappeared.

The next section contains the largest buildings, vast and fearsome. Thousands of endlessly wide steps on all sides lead up to a tiny room, eagles and rattlesnakes, outside, inside? Inside this structure, steps, narrow, steep and wet, deep within the structure a small jaguar whose teeth are bright white, mounted by a reclining man. The outer steps are so tiny, the burning white sun endlessly high. The climb. It is easy to fall.

All of the other structures are the same way. Heavily ornamented and constructed so beyond human scale they cause fear. Ball parks that cause fear. What for? Why does Rockefeller need more money so badly he kills the life in the waters around Puerto Rico? Why does one person follow his/her whims to the detriment (deep suffering) of someone that person supposedly loves?

'No one,' a booklet says, 'really knows anything about these ruins,' and yet they raise human energy more than anything else.

Don't say it out loud. The long wall of skulls next to the ball park repeats the death.

ANNOUNCE. Johnny stopped in his apartment for just a second to change his clothes. Janey told him she wanted to go out to dinner with him. Johnny replied he thought she didn't. She pleaded that she had been feeling jealous and she didn't mean to feel. She promised that she wouldn't feel jealous as long as she knew what to expect. He warned her to watch out for her jealousy, he knew all about jealousy. He had just spent the night on a rooftop with a girl who was telling him that she was madly in love with David Bowie. Janey started protesting in her head that that wasn't the point; she shut herself up, and calmly asked when and where they would be having dinner and please, before she left, could they pretend they were in love. It would be a very romantic two days and then nothing. She was better at handling fantasy than reality.

Johnny left the house so he could see Sally.

Inside Janey's favourite restaurant, Vesuvio's, the only Northern Italian restaurant in Merida:

Janey (*searching for a conversation subject that doesn't touch upon their breaking up*): What's Sally like?

Father: I don't know. (*As if he's talking about someone he's so close to he can't see the characteristics.*) We're really very compatible. We like the same things. She's very serious; that's what she's like. She's an intellectual.

Janey (*showing no emotion*): Oh. What does she do?

Father: She hasn't decided yet. She's just trying to find herself. She's into music; she writes; she does a little of everything.

Janey (*trying to be helpful*): It always takes a while.

Father: She's trying to find out everything. It's good for me to be with her because she goes everywhere and she knows everything that's happening. She knows a lot and she has a fresh view.

Janey (*to herself*): Fresh meat, young girls. Even though I'm younger, I'm tough, rotted, putrid beef. My cunt red ugh. She's thin and beautiful; I've seen her. Like a model. Just the way I've always wanted to look and I never will. I can't compete against *that*. (*Out loud*) It must be wonderful (*trying to make her voice as innocent as possible*) for you to have someone you can share everything with. You've been lonely for a long time. (*Janey trying to make herself into nothing.*)

Father: Let's talk about something else.

Janey (*very jumpy every time something doesn't go her way*): What's the matter? Did I say something wrong? (*Pause.*) I'm sorry.

BLACK. The conversation petered out.

Father: Sally's always wondering what's right and wrong. She's always wondering if she's doing the right thing. She's very young.

Janey (*apologizing for Sally*): She's just out of college.

Father: She's a minister's daughter from Vermont.

Janey (*knows from her sources that Sally's a rich young bitch who'll fuck anyone until a more famous one comes along as young WASP bitches do*): Well, you've always liked WASP girls. (*Can't keep her two cents out of it.*) They don't want anything from you. (*To herself: Like you, honey.*)

Father: She reminds me of my first girlfriend, Anne.

Janey: I remember Anne. (*Anne is a tall blonde who now plays in soap operas.*)

The conversation died. Janey to herself: Sally is the only subject we have left to talk about.

Janey: Do you think you'll live with Sally?

Father: Oh, Janey, I don't think so.

Janey: I didn't mean anything.

We went to the movies. Johnny paid for everything. As soon as the movie started, I wanted to lay my head on Johnny's shoulder, but I was scared he didn't want to feel my flesh against his. 'Are you still interested in me sexually?' I asked him. 'Yes,' and his hand took my hand. But all through the movie his touch was dead.

LASHES I FEEL. In the taxi my mood changed to lousy. I wanted to get out of the cab. Oh shit, I was ruining everything again. Just when things were going good.

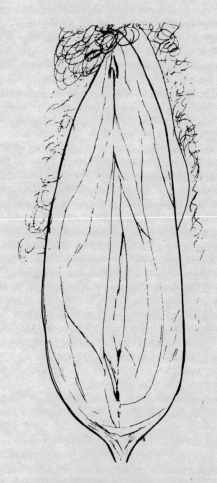

My cunt red ugh.

Johnny realized something was the matter and asked me what was wrong.

I said nothing was the matter and tried to jump out of the cab.

He replied that we shouldn't have talked about Sally.

Why shouldn't we have talked about Sally?

He didn't answer, so I realized that Sally was a sacred subject.

Once we were safe inside our kitchen, we rehashed all the times he had wanted to be close to me and I had refused; all the times I had driven him away when he loved me; all the times he had rejected my timid advances of sex, and all the times I had cut him dead, I had told him I would never care about him; how the slightest rejection from me or affair had made him turn away from me and seek someone else; how I reacted to his hurting me so badly by looking for someone more stable; how hurt causes increasing hurt; how our mutual fantasy that he adored me and I was just hanging on to him for the money actually concealed the reality that he had stuck to me all these years cause I didn't ask too much of him, especially emotionally. In this way a fantasy reveals reality: *Reality* is just the underlying fantasy, a fantasy that reveals need. I have an unlimited need of him. I explained all my lousy characteristics: my irritability, my bossiness, my ambition in the world, my PRIDE.

By this time we were both crying. A fag friend of mine just walked into the apartment and I chased him away, but he saw us crying. Then Johnny said that my characteristics that had attracted him at first now repelled him. He hinted that I'm a loud, brassy Jewess. I'm too dependent on him and that freaks him out of his mind. What makes it worse is that even though I need help, I don't know how to ask anyone for it. So I'm always bearing down on him and blaming him. I'm too macho (that's my favourite one).

I repeated all these sentences in my mind. I knew that I was hideous. I had a picture in my head that I was a horse, like the horse in *Crime and Punishment*, skin partly ripped off and red muscle exposed. Men with huge sticks keep beating the horse.

Johnny said he thought I was his mother and all the resentment he had felt against her he now felt against me. I scared him so badly he wanted to run away.

I said, 'OK. I guess it's good this is all coming out.'

LASHES MAKE ME NO LONGER MYSELF. Now I knew that Johnny hated me. I was still trying to remain calm, to be mature. My fever from my sickness rose real high, I think to 102°, and the pain in my ovaries increased.

The thought flashed through my mind that I was getting off on all this. I was a masochist. So: was I making the situation worse?

I told Johnny that I loved him deeply, very deeply. I saw now that he needed to be alone and to decide by himself what he wanted. In a little over twenty-four hours I would be going to the United States. I would not see or speak to him again, unless he asked me to see or speak to him.

Father: I have to get out of the house. I'll be back in a while. (*He had arranged to meet Sally in a bar.*)

LASHES, AS IF THE WORLD, BY ITS VERY NATURE, HATES ME.

Early that morning, a few hours before the sun was due to come up, nothing else in the world being due, Johnny returned home (what is home?) and told Janey he had been drinking with Sally.

It was very dark outside. She lay down on the filthy floor by his bed, but it was very uncomfortable: she hadn't slept for two nights. So she asked him if he wanted to come into her bed.

The plants in her room cast strange, beautiful shadows over the other shadows. It was a clean, dreamlike room. He fucked her in her asshole cause the infection made her cunt hurt too much to fuck there, though she didn't tell him it hurt badly there, too, cause she wanted to fuck love more than she felt pain.

A few hours later they woke up together and decided they would spend the whole day together since it was their last day. Janey would meet Johnny at the hotel where he worked when he got off from work.

They ate raw fish salad (*cerviche*) at a Lebanese joint and tea at a Northern Chinese place. They held hands. They didn't talk about Sally or anything heavy.

Johnny left her, telling her he'd be home later.

CAUSE OF LASHES: THE SURGE OF SUFFERING IN THE SOUL CORRUPTS THE SOUL.

Father: You have to learn not to press so hard. This wouldn't have happened if you hadn't made it happen.

Janey (*thinking hard. Slowly*): You said that before. I don't think so. I think you set this situation up. (*She doesn't say directly what she thinks: that he pretended he loved Sally so from anger she'd mention breaking up with him so they could break up.*) You know exactly how I react, and you set this situation up so I'd react this way. You wanted this to happen.

Father (*as if discovering something for the first time, slowly*): I think you're right.

A few hours later they woke up together and decided they would spend the whole day together since it was their last day. Janey would meet Johnny at the hotel where he worked when he got off from work.

cause she wanted to fuck love more than she
felt pain

They ate raw fish salad (*cerviche*) at a Lebanese joint and tea at a Northern Chinese place. They held hands. They didn't talk about Sally or anything heavy.

Johnny left her, telling her he'd be home later.

I AM NOT ME:

Janey (*sitting on her bed with Tarot cards*): Should I tell your fortune?

Father: OK (*Johnny's fortune is that he's gone through a bad time; now everything is clearing up; in the future a close friendship/marriage? with a woman; final result: a golden life.*) I'm worried about this psychic stuff of yours.

Janey: What can I do about it? It freaks me.

Father: You dreamed that night what she looked like – you hadn't even met her.

Janey: I even described what she was wearing that night. A black jacket over something white. (*Wondering.*)

Father: You said I was going to leave you before it even entered my mind.

Janey: I didn't want to provoke that. Oh God no. These things just come into my head and I say them. Don't you understand?

Father: I'm scared of it.

A few hours later they woke up together and decided they would spend the whole day together since it was their last day. Janey would meet Johnny at the hotel where he was working when he got off work.

They ate raw fish salad (*cerviche*) at a Lebanese joint and tea at a Northern Chinese place. They held hands. They didn't talk about Sally or anything heavy.

Johnny left her, telling her he'd be home later.

TINY SOUNDS, BUT SOUNDS . . . OPEN DARK DITCHES IN THE FACE

Janey: Now I'm going to tell my fortune. (*She gets a totally horrible fortune: death and destruction before and after. Her fever gets high. She wonders if she's going to die in the USA.*)

Father: Are you upset?

Janey: Yes.

Father: I am, too. These cards are weird.

A few hours later they woke up together and decided that they would spend the whole day together since it was their last day. Janey would meet Johnny at the hotel where he worked when he got off from work.

They ate raw fish salad (*cerviche*) at a Lebanese joint and tea at a Northern Chinese place. They held hands. They didn't talk about Sally or anything heavy.

Johnny left her, telling her he'd be home later.

MAKE MORE FIERCE AND MAKE SEXUALITY STRONGER. THIS IS THE TIME FOR ALL PRISONERS TO RUN WILD. YOU ARE THE BLACK ANNOUNCERS OF OUR DEATH. (BE SUCH TIME YOUNG HORSES OF ATTILA THE HUN. OH ANNOUNCERS WHO US SEND DEATH.)

Johnny and Janey lay together and didn't, as on the last nights, touch. Janey was so upset she got up and sat in the kitchen. Johnny lay there awake. Janey returned to the bed and they lay there without touching.

A few hours later they woke up together and decided they would spend the whole day together since it was their last day. Janey would meet Johnny at the hotel where he worked when he got off from work.

They ate raw fish salad (*cerviche*) at a Lebanese joint and tea at a

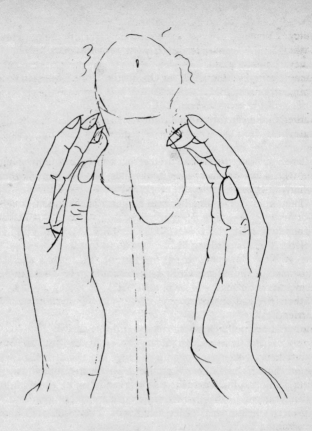

YOU ARE THE BLACK ANNOUNCERS OF MY DEATH.

Northern Chinese place. They held hands. They didn't talk about Sally or anything heavy.

Johnny left her, telling her he'd be home later.

ANNOUNCE THE RUINS PROFOUND OF THE CHRISTS WITHIN (US). OF SOME BELIEF CHERISHED WHICH FATE CURSES, THESE *LASHES* BLOODY SOUND THEIR CRACK-LINGS OF A LOAF OF BREAD WHICH IN THE VERY OVEN DOOR BURNS US UP.

Janey: Sometimes I think we're star-crossed lovers. (*Pursuing and explaining this thought.*) Each of us moves to the other at the wrong time. (*She holds the movie* Gilda *in her mind.*)

Father (*lightly, sadly*): It's just the wrong time now for you to do this.

24

Janey: I know.

Father: I do love you, Janey. (*Holding her in his arms.*) I don't want to never see you again.

Janey (*loving his arms*): I'll be OK in the United States. If you want me, write me, I'll . . . (*She stops herself from saying more. She thinks she's always saying too much.*) I've got to go now.

Father: Take care of yourself, will you?

Janey: OK (*She doesn't say that she might die in the USA.*)

A few hours later they woke up together and decided they would spend the whole day together since it was their last day. Janey would meet Johnny at the hotel where he worked when he got off from work.

They ate raw fish salad (*cerviche*) at a Lebanese joint and tea at a Northern Chinese place. They held hands. They didn't talk about Sally or anything heavy.

Johnny left her, telling her he'd be home later.

From the USA Janey called Johnny in Merida to see if she could return home. At one point:

Father: Sally and I have pretty much split. We decided we'd be just friends.

Janey: Are you going to want to live with me again?

Father: I don't know right now. I'm really enjoying the emotional distance.

Janey: I didn't mean to pry. I'm sorry. I just have to know.

Father: What do you want to know, Janey?

Janey: I mean . . . Well, how are you doing?

Father: I'm being very quiet. I'm staying home most of the time and watching TV. I really need to be alone now.

Janey: When do you think you'll know if you ever want to live with me again?

Father: Oh, Janey. You've got to lighten up. Things just got too entangled. Everything between us is still too entangled for me to be with you.

Janey: I see. That means no.

Father: Are you trying to get me to reject you?

Janey: No. No. Not that. I don't want you to decide now.

Father: Where are you staying now?

Janey: I'm in New York City. I'm not anywhere. When I settle down, I'll let you know where I am. When I settle down, I'll let you know where I am. I'm going to get off the phone now.

Father: How's your health?

Janey: I'm fine. Fine. Listen. I have to know whether you want me back or not. I can't stand this.

Father: Do you really want to know now?

Janey: I'm sorry, Johnny. I know you think it's a high school romance like you and Sally, and we're just breaking up, but it's really serious to me. I loved you.

Father (*doubting*): It's serious to me, too.

Janey: Then don't you understand? How long will I have to hang on? It's been a week since I left Merida. Do you want me to wait a month, a year while you're going eeny-meeny-miney-moe?

Father: I have to be alone, Janey. If you demand I say anything more, it'll only be to totally reject you.

Janey: I have nightmares in my head. Either I fantasize you take me in your arms again and again, telling me you love me. I don't know whether I can let myself fantasize that because if it isn't true . . . Or I have to wipe you out of my mind. There is no more Johnny.

Father: Why do you have to do that?

Janey: I have to make a new life for myself! I have to live. I can't spend all my time thinking about someone who doesn't love me.

Father: I don't know what to say.

Janey: I don't know what to think and each nightmare is pulling me backwards and forwards and I can't stop.

Father: Don't let your mind drive you crazy.

Janey: What can I do? I'm sorry. This isn't your problem. I'm going to get off the phone now.

Father (*pleading*): Look. Don't keep pushing things. You're making things worse than they are.

Janey: How can things be worse?

Father: You want to know how?

AND THE MAN:

Janey called Johnny again because she needed to hear a friendly voice because she was scared.

(*After a long silence.*)

Father (*heartily*): Hello, how are you?

Janey (*just wanting to hear a friendly voice*): I just wanted to say hello.

Father: Where are you?

Janey: I'm still in New York City. I haven't settled down yet.

Father: I'm really enjoying living alone. I'm happier than I've been in months.

Janey: Oh. (*She doesn't want to feel anything.*) That's wonderful. Who're you seeing?

Father: I'm not really seeing anyone. I'm living very quietly. I'm going to stay here till the end of September and then I'll decide what my plans are. (*He wants to say, 'My plans absolutely don't include you because you terrorize me', but he feels guilty about hurting her.*) I can't tell you anything more than that now.

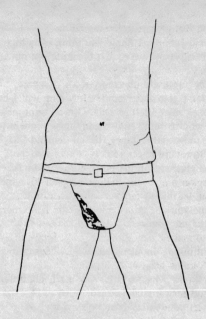

AND THE MAN:

Janey (*though she wants to keep the conversation light, she's been programmed to say it*): You mean you're not going to live with me again?

Father: Right now I just really like opening my door to this apartment and walking into my own space. I'm going to be here through September and then I'll see what my plans are. I don't think you should bank on anything.

Janey: I see. I guess that's that.

Father: What do you mean 'that's that'?

Janey: I guess it's over.

Father: I don't know.

Janey: Oh no? I don't understand. I just don't understand.

Father: I have to be alone.

Janey: OK. So you're alone. I'm not stopping you from being alone. I went off to the United States, didn't I? You said, 'Get away from me,' and I went to another land. How far around the world do I have to go?

Father: You were planning to go to the United States.

Janey: I wouldn't have gone to the United States when I was as sick as I was.

27

Father: You didn't have to go to the United States 'cause of me.

Janey: Well, I didn't know that. You said, 'Get away', and I got away. I want to give you what you want. This all doesn't matter anymore. I'd better go.

Father: Do you mean you never want to see me again?

Janey: You said it's over.

If the author here lends her 'culture' to the amorous subject, in exchange the amorous subject affords her the innocence of its image-repertoire, indifferent to the proprieties of knowledge. Indifferent to the proprieties of knowledge.

Father: I have to be alone.

Janey: I understand.

Father: I have to be alone. You've had the same thing. It's like I'm on a retreat.

Janey: I'm not protesting against that.

TURN THE EYES AS IF I SEE SOME HOPE, I think it's wonderful to be alone. But you don't know whether you love me anymore.

Father: That's true. It's really heavy, isn't it? (*As if he doesn't want to believe it's heavy.*)

Janey: Yeah. It's heavy. OK (*Sighs because she's made a decision.*) If you really want, I wait around as long as you want until you make a decision.

Father: I had to get away. I felt trapped.

Janey: Well, you're not trapped anymore. You've got everything the way you want it. There's no need to explain anything anymore. (*She's still crying.*) Whenever you make your decision, just tell me.

Father: If you need any money, Janey, you can rely on me.

Janey: What do you mean by that?

Father: If you want me to help you out monetarily, I will.

Janey (*now that she's made her decision, her emotions are gone*): You can't just say that. I have to stay alive. I can't do anything about the emotional . . . but I can keep myself alive physically. What do you mean by MONEY? I'm sorry I'm being so crude. I have to stay alive.

Father: I'll pay your rent wherever you are.

Janey: OK. I'll wait for you and you'll pay the rent. You'll have to give me a month's notice if you're going to stop paying it. I just have to know. Is that OK?

Father: Listen, Janey, will you take care of yourself?

Janey: IS THAT OK? I'm sorry it might not be important to you how I stay alive, but it's important to me.

Father (*evading*): I'll help you out however I can.

Janey: I'm sorry I'm being so hard (*she thinks she's really being a little bitch*) but I have to figure out how I'm going to live. I don't want to make a thing of it, but I'm still sick. (*She thinks she's going to die.*) The phone call hasn't really gotten bad yet.

It starts off slow, stagnant.	**Father** (*obsessed with trying to explain to Janey he doesn't want her anymore. Trying to show her as little affection as possible*): Our relationship just got too entangled. If anything is ever going to work out between us, it'll have to work out while we're living separately.
	Janey: I said I'd wait here for you.
	Father: I've been thinking everything over and I see that we were always out of phase with each other.
	Janey: I know. I was very selfish.
	Father: I don't hate you. I just dwell on how good things were between us.
	Janey: It's funny. We always had this fantasy that you were the one who was madly in love, but now it turns out I'm the one.
The energy rising	**Father:** Why don't you just dwell on the memories of how good things were?
	Janey: What? Now you want me to live in the past? That's too much to ask of me. You can't ask that. Oh God is there no end to pain? I'll do anything, anything, but Jesus Christ!
	Father: I want you to know there's very little hope.
	Janey: I got the message, Johnny.
	Father: I just don't want to give you any false impressions.
Full pain	**Janey:** You've made your point. (*Howls.*) I'd better get off the phone now.
	Father: We have to talk together. I can't talk to you over this phone.
	Janey: I can't talk either.
	Father: Maybe you'd better come home.
	Janey: You want me to come home? I'll be home as soon as possible.

Janey: I'm calling to tell you I can't come home from New York City 'cause I'm too sick. I have to rest here a few days to get my strength back and then I'll come home as soon as possible. New York is a very hard city to live in.

TURN MY EYES INSANE, WHILE BEING CORRUPTS ITSELF, AS A POOL OF SHAME, IN THAT HOPE.

Father: You don't have to come home 'cause of me, Janey.

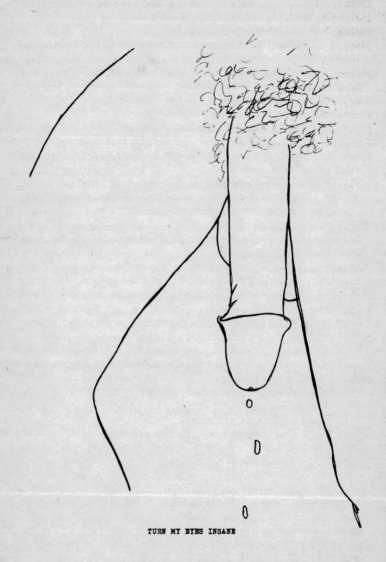

TURN MY EYES INSANE

Janey: I thought you said you wanted me home.

Father: I just said that for your sake. I thought you were freaking out.

Janey: Oh. Well, I won't be coming home soon.

Father: You should enjoy your vacation.

Janey: I am. I hate the Americans, but there are lots of French and German tourists here and they're all wonderful. (*Gossips about them.*)

Father: I wanted to apologize about how I've been acting. I think I've been too mean.

Janey: Oh, I decided you were a UBH.

Father: What's that? (*Laughing.*)

Janey (*laughing*): An Unnecessarily Brutal Horror.

Father: Well, I was confused.

Janey: And I decided I'd sue you for a thousand American dollars for child abuse.

Father: I see your mind's thinking up lots of schemes. (*They both laugh.*) We should make this phone call short. These phone calls have been costing me a fortune.

Janey: I just called you 'cause I had to give you that message. I won't call you again. By the way, if you want to come here and stay with me, I'll pay for it somehow. . . .

Father: I'm alone right now.

Janey: Well, goodbye.

Father: I never know how to say goodbye.

Janey: We never do, do we? Just say, 'Goodbye.'

Father: Take care of yourself, Janey.

Janey: Goodbye.

PLEASE
ME NO LONGER MYSELF

Mr Smith puts Janey in school in New York City to make sure she doesn't return to Merida.

Excerpt from Janey's diary:

The scorpions

I was running around with a wild bunch of kids and I was scared. We were part of THE SCORPIONS.

Daddy no longer loved me. That was it.

I was desperate to find the love he had taken away from me.

My friends were just like me. They were desperate – the products of broken families, poverty – and they were trying everything to escape their misery.

Despite the restrictions of school, we did exactly what we wanted and it was good. We got drunk. We used drugs. We fucked. We hurt each other sexually as much as we could. The speed, emotional overload, and pain every now and then dulled our brains. Demented our perceptual apparatus.

We knew we couldn't change the shit we were living in so we were trying to change ourselves.

I hated myself. I did everything I could to hurt myself.

I don't remember who I fucked the first time I fucked, but I must have known nothing about birth control 'cause I got pregnant. I do remember my abortion. One-hundred-ninety dollars.

I walked into this large white room. There must have been fifty other girls. A few teenagers and two or three women in their forties. Women lined up. Women in chairs nodding out. A few women had their boyfriends with them. They were lucky, I thought. Most of us were alone. The women in my line were handed long business forms: at the end of each form was a paragraph that stated she gave the doctor the right to do whatever he wanted and if she ended up dead, it wasn't his fault. We had given ourselves up to men before. That's why we were here. All of us signed everything. Then they took our money.

My factory line was ushered into a pale green room. In the large white room fifty more girls started to sign forms and give up their one-hundred-ninety stolen, begged-for, and borrowed dollars.

In a small orange room they explained an egg drops down from the ovaries and, when the cock enters this canal called THE UTERUS, it leaves millions of, I don't remember how many, sperm. If just one sperm out of all these sperms meets the dropping egg, the female (me and you) is in a lot of trouble. A female can use any of the many methods of birth control, all of which don't work or deform.

It's all up to you girls. You have to be strong. Shape up. You're a modern woman. These are the days of post-women's liberation. Well, what are you going to do? You've grown up by now and you have to take care of yourself. No one's going to help you. You're the only one.

Well, I couldn't help it, I just LOVE to fuck, he was SO cute, it was worth it.

We girls knew everything there was to know without having to say a word and we knew we had put ourselves here and we were all in this together.

An abortion is a simple procedure. It is almost painless. Even if it isn't painless, it takes only five minutes. If you MUST have it, weak, stupid things that you are, we can put you to sleep.

The orange walls were thick enough to stifle the screams pouring out of the operating room. Having an abortion was obviously just like getting fucked. If we closed our eyes and spread our legs, we'd be taken care of. They stripped us of our clothes. Gave us white sheets to cover our nakedness. Led us back to the pale green room. I love it when men take care of me.

I remember a tiny blonde, even younger than me. I guess it must have been the first time she had ever been fucked. She couldn't say anything. Whether she wanted a local or not. A LOCAL means a local anaesthetic. They stick large hypodermics filled with novocaine in your cunt lips and don't numb where it hurts at all. A general anaesthetic costs fifty dollars more and fills you up with synthetic morphine and truth serum. All of us gathered around her, held her hands, and stroked her legs. Gradually she began to calm down. There was nothing else to do. We had to wait while each one of us went through it. Finally they came for her.

She was the believing kind. She had believed them when they said a local wouldn't hurt. They were taking the locals first.

I'll never forget her face when she came out. She couldn't have come out of her mommy's cunt any more stunned. Her face was dead white and her eyes were fish-wide open.

'I made a mistake. Don't do it. Don't do anything they tell you to.'

Before she could say more, they wheeled her away.

I got to like that pale green room, the women who were more scared than I was so I could comfort them, the feeling someone was taking care of me. I felt more secure there than in the outside world. I wanted a permanent abortion.

They strapped my ankles and wrists to this black slab. When I asked the huge blonde anaesthesia nurse if there was any chance I'd react badly to the anaesthesia, she told the other huge blonde nurse I was a health food freak. After that I didn't ask them anything and I did exactly what they told me.

An hour later a big hand shook me and told me it was time to go. Girls were lying all around me, half-dead. Blood was coming out between my legs. Another nurse gave me a piece of Kotex, half-a-cup of coffee, my clothes, twenty penicillin pills, and told me to get out. I didn't get to talk to any of the other girls again.

Penelope Mowlard was the creepiest girl in my class. Her skin was green. She was stupid. She didn't know how to kiss. She was gangly. She was an idiot. Her face was scrunched-up, covered with snot, partly eyeless, and her hair was full of puke.

Miss Richard's was a school for nice well-bred girls. We knew better than to get visibly in trouble. For months Penelope wandered through the classrooms and hallways with a larger and larger stomach. She was too stupid to know what was going on. The teachers didn't tell 'cause they were scared or mean dykes. We didn't tell her 'cause it was fun to make her suffer.

Early one morning the janitor, an old man, found a bloody bundle in the bottom of one of the basement garbage cans. Later that day we saw Penelope's stomach had disappeared. The principal couldn't suspend her 'cause she had to do everything she could to prevent scandal.

I couldn't figure out what birth control method to use. Foams and diaphragm creams tasted so bad every time I got the chance to feel a tongue on my cunt, I chose the tongue. An IUD made me bleed and get PID again. There was a druggist in Harlem who'd slip me some pills every other month if I'd give him a blow job under the counter, but once every other month isn't enough. All the boys I fucked refused to use condoms.

I decided that if I got pregnant again, I'd stick a broken hanger up my cunt. I didn't care if I died as long as the baby died. Then I heard a story about a woman, I think it's true, who was so desperate to kill her baby she chained flatirons around her arms, legs, and stomach and threw herself down three flights of stairs. Even though almost every bone in her body broke, her baby didn't die and she gave birth in traction.

I was still desperate to fuck. Abortions make it dangerous to fuck again because they stretch out the opening of the womb so the sperm can reach the egg real easily. They upset the hormonal system: the hormones send out many more eggs to compensate. They leave gaping holes in the womb and any foreign object that nears these holes can cause infection.

I'm not trying to tell you about the rotgut weird parts of my life. Abortions are the symbol, the outer image, of sexual relations in this world. Describing my abortions is the only real way I can tell you about pain and fear . . . my unstoppable drive for sexual love made me know.

My second abortion took place two months after my first abortion.

It cost fifty dollars because it was a menstrual extraction. The differences between a menstrual extraction and an abortion are:

In a menstrual extraction the doctor doesn't dilate the cervix. The baby is still too small.

Since the doctor may or may not find the baby, menstrual extractions can be dangerous and are illegal.

Most of the doctors who perform menstrual extractions are not certified MDs.

The minute I entered the office, they doped me up with Valium.

The factory line was shorter.

I actually saw the doctor.

He was the only doctor there.

He killed 32 to 48 babies and netted 1,600 to 2,400 dollars a day.

He stuck his hand up my cunt and told me I was OK.

He stuck a little needle in my arm and tried to be nice to me.

A week after my second abortion I came down with a case of PID. When I called up the doctor to complain, he said it wasn't his fault and he had never heard of me.

I didn't know how much these abortions hurt me physically and mentally. I was desperate to fuck more and more so I could finally get love. Soon my total being was on fire, not just my sex, and I was doing everything to make the non-sexual equivalent of love happen.

The rest of THE SCORPIONS were growing the same way I was.

We started out making trouble. Early one morning we rode in a stolen van into a Connecticut town and busted into a hardware store. We threw everything in the store out of the door.

We don't hate, understand, we have to get back. Fight the dullness of shit society. Alienated robotized images. Here's your cooky, ma'am. No to anything but madness.

Broken glass lies over the floor. Gum sticks everywhere. Shit smeared in the cracks of the table. Their cash register is ash-black like a burnt-up telephone book.

We made the store into a death-house and the street look like the New York City east-side slum we had to live in.

As soon as we had accomplished our purpose, we left the Connecticut town.

We stole.

Me and Monkey were the first to steal. We were high on meth. We ripped off Bloomingdale's, a big department store in New York City.

I was going somewhere my father and his girlfriend were also going. Johnny and his girlfriend wanted nothing to do with me.

We took a taxi to Bloomingdale's so we could be straight. I was dressed in a red wool suit and a light brown wool coat. It's necessary to be straight when you steal.

I was hanging on to the end of the taxi Johnny and his girlfriend had picked me up in. Clearly they wanted nothing to do with me. The rest of Johnny's rock band were in the car.

As soon as Monkey and I got to Bloomingdale's, we separated. I checked my appearance. My dark curly hair, light makeup, and dark red suit made me look like a nice, rich girl. I wanted to stay that way. Being nice and rich is a dream. I checked my vibes. I told myself to stay guarded, slow and calm. As I entered the store, I checked out the store's vibes. No one was following me.

Daddy and I are standing in the downstairs of the Laguna Beach Hotel, which is Nixon's favourite hotel. Facing me there's a rectangular white wall. A few feet below this white wall and to its right, single stairs with no back move upwards. Further to the right, another large rectangular white wall. Set in this wall, one-third of its width further right, an absolutely black hallway. Above this white wall, empty space; above the empty space, a white hanging rectangle means a room. There's nothing around these walls, staircase, and hall.

Back east, architectural objects are connected to, hidden in each other. I move alone without daddy forwards BACKWARDS through the hotel. The hotel is now, is really large transparent squares. I glide to the final back room.

The back wall of this room is really windows. Windows are opaque. Windows through which I'm seeing a black phosphorescent ocean. None of the men in daddy's band want to be with me and daddy's with Sally. I want to go swimming I have to go swimming. The ocean is bright green, even though it's night. The ocean is glowing.

Now the window is totally transparent. Through it I see a man's body as if dead turning in the sparkling green water.

I wanted a fur coat.

Little halls surround one long black major hall. Thin white walls, almost non-existent, separate these halls.

I bought a red sweater in the Junior Department on the third floor so anyone who was watching would know that I wasn't a thief.

Then I rode the escalator upstairs to the Fur Department. Tossing my brown woolen coat across a rack, I tried on fur after fur. Stealing is luxury. Ten or fifteen minutes later the salesgirl had to run across the hall to get change.

Of course, daddy and Sally and the boys in his band are given their rooms first. My room is the room no one else in the world wants.

My bedroom is the huge white hexagon in the front left corner of the hotel. It has no clear outside or inside or any architectural regularity. Long white pipes form part of its ceiling. Two of its sides, which two is always changing, are open.

My bedroom's function is also unclear. Its only furniture is two barber's chairs and a toilet. It's a gathering place for men.

Hotel men dressed in white and black come in and want to hurt me. They cut away parts of me. I call for the hotel head. He explains that my bedroom used to be the men's toilet. I understand.

My cunt used to be a men's toilet.

I walk out in a leopard coat.

Dear dreams,

You are the only thing that matters. You are my hope and I live for and in you. You are rawness and wildness, the colours, the scents, passion, events appearing. You are the things I live for. Please take me over.

Dreams cause the vision world to break loose our consciousness.

Dreams by themselves aren't enough to destroy the blanket of dullness.

The dreams we allow to destroy us cause us to be visions/see the vision world.

Every day a sharp tool, a powerful destroyer, is necessary to cut away dullness, lobotomy, buzzing, belief in human beings, stagnancy, images, and accumulation. As soon as we stop believing in human beings, rather know we are dogs and trees, we'll start to be happy.

Once we've gotten a glimpse of the vision world (notice here how the conventional language obscures: WE as if somebodies are the centre of activity SEE what is the centre of activity: pure VISION. Actually, the VISION creates US. Is anything true?) Once we have gotten a glimpse of the vision world, we must be careful not to think the vision world is us. We must go farther and become crazier.

I didn't have enough food, so I started working in a hippy bakery. It was 1977.

Working for money is the omnipresent fact of American life.

I wasn't allowed to cook or make any decisions. My job was to hand people the bread or cookies they wanted and take their money. I also made vegetable juices, sliced bialies, dumped spreads made out of tofu and vegetables between the slices.

I am nobody because I work. I have to pretend I like the customers and love giving them cookies no matter how they treat me:

(*Inside a small East Village bakery.*)

Fat Lady: What's the ingredients in that cooky?

Lousy Mindless Salesgirl: a bit of coconut and safflower oils, all hard-pressed, wheat flour, barley malt, water, and sesame seeds.

Fat Lady: Is the wheat flour organic?

Lousy Mindless Salesgirl: All the ingredients we use are organic.

Fat Lady: What's barley malt?

(*Clammerings of ten customers in background. One grimy kid is feeling up the cookies.*)

Lousy Mindless Salesgirl (*who never has any expression*): It's a grain derivative.

Fat Lady: You don't use sugar or honey.

Lousy Mindless Salesgirl: No.

(*The grimy kid has grabbed two maple-hazelnut cookies and run.*)

Fat Lady: What's in that cooky there?

Lousy Mindless Salesgirl: That's a sunflower-cranberry cooky.

Fat Lady: Is there wheat flour in that one?

(*A thirty-year-old man is rummaging through the bialies. The salesgirl turns around and says, 'Excuse me, sir, I'll be with you in a second.*)

Thirty-year-old Man: I want this bialy.

Lousy Mindless Salesgirl: I'll be able to help as soon as I finish with this lady.

Fat Lady: What's in this cooky? (*She upsets the whole tray.*)

Lousy Mindless Salesgirl (*looking around quickly*): That's a maple-currant oatflour. (*To the thirty-year-old man*) I'll be with you in a second.

Thirty-year-old Man (*crying*): Every time I come to this bakery, nobody pays any attention to me. It isn't like it used to be in the old days when I could sit here and talk. People would take care of me. (*He walks out sobbing loudly.*)

Fat Lady: And what's in this cooky? I have to be very careful. My doctor told me I'm not allowed to eat any sweets.

Lousy Mindless Salesgirl: That's a carob fudgie.

Fat Lady: That means it has sugar.

A Rich Girl: I just want this cooky. (*Grabbing a peanut cooky and breaking the shelf.*) Here.

Lousy Mindless Salesgirl (*taking the change and returning 5¢*): that'll be 40¢. Thank you. (*To the Fat Lady*) We only use barley malt, and maple syrup in the cookies that have maple in their names.

(*The baker comes out of the kitchen and tells the salesgirl she's not working hard enough. Why are so many people still waiting to be served? He hired her to WORK. None of his other workers have these problems.*)

Fat Lady: Well, what's in that cooky?

Lousy Mindless Salesgirl: That's a peanut cooky.

Fat Lady: Does it have any sugar in it?

A Thin Young Woman: I want ten loaves of rice bread, a dozen bialies, three dozen assorted cookies, two vegetable juices, and two sandwiches wrapped to go. I need it now.

Lousy Mindless Salesgirl (*to the Fat Lady*): Would you like a cooky, ma'am?

(*While five customers are grabbing cookies, a sixth customer climbs on their shoulders to get at the cookies. All the cooky shelves collapse.*)

Fat Lady: Miss? I want that cooky over there. (*Points to a poppy-seed cooky lying under a dead – concussion due to falling shelf – body.*)

Because I work I am nobody. The bakery has many customers. Hippies have ideals and sell good cookies cheap. As soon as I dare to take the time to think a thought, to watch a feeling, usually hatred, develop, to rest my aching body, a customer enters.

It was as if he had risen before me, I read, a man who, in his wild and passionate youth, had been the idol of Madrid and a source of dismay to his parents. He had carried away, by violence, a nun from a convent, incurring the enmity of the Church and the displeasure of his

Sovereign. He had followed desire regardless of anything else and survived. To see. To see the nothingness. That is vision. He had sacrificed all his fortune in Europe to the service of his king, had fought against the French, had a price put on his head by special proclamation. He had known passion, power, war, exile, and love. He had been thanked by his returned king, honoured for his wisdom, and crushed with sorrow by the death of his young wife.

A twenty-six-year-old English-accented Parisian hippy worked the counter with the Lousy Mindless Salesgirl. The hippy never did any work because she had to spend all her time finding out from the customers what she should do with her life and how she was going to be creative. 'Why do you smile at everyone?' the hippy asked the Lousy Mindless Salesgirl while the latter was desperately trying to read just one page.

'Why shouldn't I smile?'

'You don't really like everyone, do you? You shouldn't act nice if you don't feel like it.'

'How should I act?'

'Act like you feel. You don't want to be a hypocrite.'

'I don't feel anything.' The Lousy Mindless Salesgirl wanted to kill the stupid hippy.

'Then don't smile and be nice to customers.'

'I'm being paid to smile.'

'You're acting hypocritically, Janey. It's because you're male-centred. Look at me. I don't smile when I don't feel like it and I don't go out of my way to help anyone.'

Just then a middle-aged shrivelled man walked into the bakery. 'Can I have a glass of wheat-grass juice?' he asked.

Lousy Mindless Salesgirl: Certainly, sir. (*She runs around the counter to get a paper cup, runs back around the counter, down on her hands and knees to get the juice out of the front fridge, stands to pour, down on her hands and knees to put the juice away, back to standing.*) Here you are, sir.

Middle-aged Shrivelled Man: Did you know that this juice kills all the diseases in the world if you drink enough of it? It kills cancer. In the Bible Nebuchadnezzar ate grass and cured all of his afflictions.

Twenty-year-old Whore-like Jew Lady (*entered the bakery while Lousy Mindless Salesgirl was making the wheat-grass run. Standing very close to Lousy Mindless Salesgirl*): What do you do?

Lousy Mindless Salesgirl: What do you mean 'What do I do?'

Twenty-year-old Whore-like Jew Lady: How else do you make your money? Are you a whore?

Lousy Mindless Salesgirl: No. I go to school.

A Wispy Blonde Hippy Girl: I want that cooky and that cooky and two of those and, is that one soft, I'll take that one. And a loaf of round bread. (*As the Lousy Mindless Salesgirl's climbing on the shelf to get the bread.*) Do you like your job?

Lousy Mindless Salesgirl: It's OK.

Wispy Blonde Hippy Girl: Is something the matter with this job? Are you discontent?

Lousy Mindless Salesgirl: I'm not in love with handing out cookies and taking money four hours a day. It's OK.

Wispy Blonde Hippy Girl: If you took more of an interest in the bakery, went inside to see how the cookies are made, talked to the customers more, maybe you'd like this job better.

Lousy Mindless Salesgirl: When I'm here, I'm being paid to take care of the customers, and otherwise I don't have any time. I have to do my homework.

Wispy Blonde Hippy Girl: Oh, I see. You have your own thing. (*As the wispy blonde hippy walks out of the bakery, the Parisian hippy says: 'You're rude.'*)

Lousy Mindless Salesgirl: Why am I rude?

Parisian Hippy Salesgirl: You should know.

Lousy Mindless Salesgirl (*panicking*): I don't know. Why am I rude?

Parisian Hippy Salesgirl: You're just not a nice person.

Lousy Mindless Salesgirl: Look. If we're going to work together, we're going to have to get along some minimal bit. You can't just insult me for no reason at all.

Parisian Hippy Salesgirl: You don't like playing those games, do you? (*Walks away from the Lousy Mindless Salesgirl.*)

From then on, everyone at the bakery avoided me. I was the plague and there was a huge circle of emptiness around me. if another counter girl was supposed to be working, the moment she saw me she retreated into the back room.

I had to do all the counter work. My father stopped sending me money. I had to work seven days a week. I had no more feelings. I was no longer a real person. If I stopped work for just a second, I would hate. Burst through the wall and hate. Hatred that comes out like that can be a bomb.

I hated most that I didn't have any more dreams or visions. It's not that the vision-world, the world of passion and wildness, no longer existed. It always is. But awake I was disconnected from dreams. I was psychotic.

I walked out of my crummy school. It was already night. I was running 'cause I was late for the bakery. I tripped.

'Ha ha ha.' Some boys were chuckling behind me. Fuck them.

'Just 'cause she used to be part of THE SCORPIONS she thinks she's tough,' some dumb gum-chewer snarled. 'Now she's handing dumb little cookies to dumb little people. I bet she got her cunt sewn up.'

I did. I kept running so I wouldn't be late to work.

'Cumere.'

I kept on running.

'Cumere.' Something grabbed my shoulder. 'Look at me.' As the hand turned my body around, the other hand shoved my chin up so my eyes saw a pair of grey Chinese eyes and a long nose. I couldn't see anything else 'cause of the darkness.

'Don't listen to them. They never used their cocks in their lives. I hear you make it with a lot of guys.'

'I used to. I don't anymore. Who're you?'

'Heh heh heh.' His laugh sounded like a sneer to me. 'I hear you used to not even care what the guys' names were who you made it with.'

'What do you want with me?'

'I want to stick my dick between your legs.'

'You can't.' I was back to my old hard SCORPION way of speaking. And his hand running up and down my back hard made my legs wet.

'You don' wanna. You don' wanna.' He was talking right in my ear. 'What does girlie wanna do? You gotta boy at home you gotta go and screw? You gotta boy who's a better screw than me?' The words were closer and hotter. 'You're coming home with me now.'

'I can't.'

'Why not?'

'I gotta go to work.'

'What's the bitch crying about?' 'Why don't you beat her up, Tommy?' 'Punch her in the stomach.'

'My friends like you,' he whispered right into my ear as he pushed me along. 'We're gonna be hot together.'

'Listen. I can't go home with you. I'm not what you think. I lose my job and I'll be up shitcreek. I'm not going to give up my life for a one-night fuck.'

His lips came down on mine. His tongue travelled in and covered mine. His hands ran huge insects down my back.

I guess a long time passed, but I didn't know.

'Well?'

'Uh . . .' I didn't know. 'If I come home with you, I'll ruin the friendship between us.'

His hand brought my mouth to his mouth till his mouth was fucking my mouth. It was a fountain. We shoved against each other.

He lifted his head. 'It's up to you,' he told me.

I went home with him and didn't give a shit anymore about anything else but him.

Love turned me back to crime. Tommy and I kidnapped children.

Smeared up the walls of buildings. Carried dangerous weapons and used them. Did everything we could to dull our judgement and acted as outrightly violent as possible. Shitted on the streets. Attacked strangers with broken bottles. Hit people over the head with hard objects. Kicked the guts out of people on the streets. Started fights and riots.

I could barely stand being so happy. The sex made me crazier than the crime. I started to thrash just when he touched me: just his fingers pinching my nipples made me come. I couldn't stop rushing toward him like an overloaded volcano. . . .

We still didn't have any emotions but underneath . . .

It's hard to get beyond sex:

My legs are split apart. Knees up. Fish is open. One hand on clit.

Left leg raised up. Right leg bent and horizontal. Hand under left leg; middle finger all way in cunt.

Legs spread; ass up. Third and fourth fingers, V open cunt wide.

> Tommy was a SCORPION
> He was an intellectual criminal.
> He believed his plans worked and they did.
> He couldn't see reality beyond his plans.
> He was too smart to believe his plans.
> Totally scared out of his mind in the blackness no ground SPLIT.
> All the SCORPION boys hit SPLIT.
> That's why they hated women.
> They depended on crime and crime kept them stupid.

BEYOND CRIME, DREAMS, AND SEX: DISASTER

A conversation between Tommy and Janey before disaster hit: disaster beyond SPLIT:

Tommy: Do you think there's a for ever?
Janey: Anything lasts for ever? (*Thinks.*) Sure. Everything lasts for ever.
Tommy: Huh?
Janey: Love goes away only when your mind goes away and then you're someone else.
Tommy: There're no truths anymore. Nothing stands up.
Janey: Your mind stinks, not 'cause you got all these opinions, ways of judging, but 'cause you depend on them.
You know your plans aren't real. You're a smart boy. All you see is nothing.
There's a world right in front of your eyes. It ain't money, the world of alienated action. Anyone can do absolutely anything he or she wants. It's all absolutely free. In the brilliant sunlights. Events rise

singly out of . . . I don't know what I'm saying I gotta get money. I
gotta shake hands with the death-world and death-world is killing off
human beings. . . .

We gotta get to a point where we can be together. . . .

I can't take you, Janey. I don't want to know who you are.

But if we're not together, we're not going to be able to live. This isn't
romance. This isn't about you and me being in love.

No.

NO to you language no to anything but the money-work I'm forced to
do I sit alone in this room how do you get a book to split open,
the object the event no a big flaming NO
and only because of NO do you understand
Tommy and I are together.

We pulled into the rock club about one o'clock. It looked like a war
was happening.

We had heard that this rock band called THE CONTORTIONS was
gonna play in a redneck town in New Jersey and the white head singer
thought he was James Brown. The rest of the band would be too drunk
to stop the rednecks from beating up Brown.

James Brown was crawling baby-style across the floor.

The rednecks were jerking their cocks off in a corner.

James Brown crawled up to the redneck's boot.

The redneck, confused, jumped James.

Everyone in the club started hitting each other.

I heard cops' sirens.

I ran.

The rest of THE SCORPIONS were behind me.

We piled into the van.

Green and pink lights flashed past us, neon yellow and violet lights
gleamed.

The bright lights were denser and denser.

We were moving faster.

'Hey,' Sally said, 'step on it.'

'Huh?'

'The cops're after us.'

He drove faster.

'Can't ya go faster?'

He drove even faster.

I heard the cops' sirens clearly.

'Suck my tits.' Greaso leaned over and sucked Sally's tit while he
drove.

'Watch where you're going, Greaso.'

The cops' sirens were louder.
Greaso's foot hit the accelerator all the way.
We were in a totally black section of Newark.
A tiny red light appeared in the blackness.
The red light grew larger and larger.
I don't remember the crash. Everyone died but Monkey who got brain damage and me. For a few days I floated in a dream.

The blackness I now see everywhere comes from perverted because unrealized wants. I see this. I won't be able to pretend the world isn't horrible. Overwhelming fear separates me from the want I saw. Now overwhelming fear makes me part of the death-world.

She started to run from death . . .
She left high-school and lived in the East Village . . .

Outside high school

How spring came to the land of snow and icicles

1 The Hideous Monster and the Beaver
Once upon a time . . .
there was a big ugly hideous monster. He lived in a hut below the living fountain within the long icicles. All of the land was ice. The air was almost white. Air rapidly became solid and the solid became air.

The big ugly monster kept house with a beaver. While his head was scraping against the low kitchen ceiling, he would cook for the beaver. He would bring the food to the table. Then they would sit in two huge rocking chairs and face each other across the huge round red table. They wouldn't say anything.

The beaver stood up and waddled to the upstairs of the hut. As he climbed the stairs, his tail said, 'Pad, pad'. Alone the hideous monster scraped the plastic dishes, dumped them in the sink and washed them. Then he tied up a dark-green garbage bag and dragged it outside.

The snow was falling over the ice and turning to ice. The snow was falling over the ice and hiding the ice. The poor hideous monster couldn't see anything. He started to cry and the tears turned to ice on his cheeks. He didn't know what to do. He grew scared because he didn't know what to do.

He forgot he didn't know what to do.
He just stood there.
He went back inside the hut.
You couldn't tell the difference between a snowflake and a star.

2 *How a bear tried to get into the Monster's and the Beaver's House*

A bear came sludging through the snow. The big brown bear was cold, hungry, and tired. All night he had been wandering in the falling snow looking for food. The falling snow had obscured the ice that hid the frozen fish. Falling snow had obscured the world. The bear saw the beaver's and the monster's hut.

When he lifted his paw to knock on a door almost the size of his paw, an avalanche of snow fell to the ground.

Knock. Knock. Knock.

The monster had just stumbled out of bed. He hadn't had his coffee yet. It was too early for someone to be at the door, so no one could be at the door.

Knock. Knock. Knock.

'Whatta ya want?' the monster grumbled. He was looking for the coffee. He didn't listen to the answer.

Knock. Knock. Knock. 'Please let me in,' the bear yelled in a little girl's yell.

'Why should I let you in? You might rape me or kill me or you might be one of those muggers who robbed three people down the street yesterday. We know all about you.'

'I'm not a robber. I'm a little girl who lost her way in the woods last night. I want to call my mommy 'cause she's worried to death about me. I want to tell her I'm still alive.'

'What were you doing out in the snow all night?'

'My mommy and my twenty sisters live in a horrible slum on the east side of town. Mommy has no limbs and ten of my sisters are paralyzed. The other ten are wanted by the police for bank robberies. They didn't really do them. So I'm the only one who can get the food. Every day I go out and gather weeds. Then my ten bank robber sisters make a soup out of them.

'There aren't any weeds left around our house, so yesterday I went farther away from the house than usual.

'Before I knew it, it became dark.

'It was the blackest night. Huge sheets of snow and hail and sleet suddenly fell out of the blackness. I couldn't see anymore and I couldn't hear anymore.' (The monster remembered when he was out in the falling snow with the green garbage bag.) 'Everywhere I turned was blackness. Everywhere was pure whiteness and blackness and cold, cold.'

'I know what you're talking about,' the monster replied.

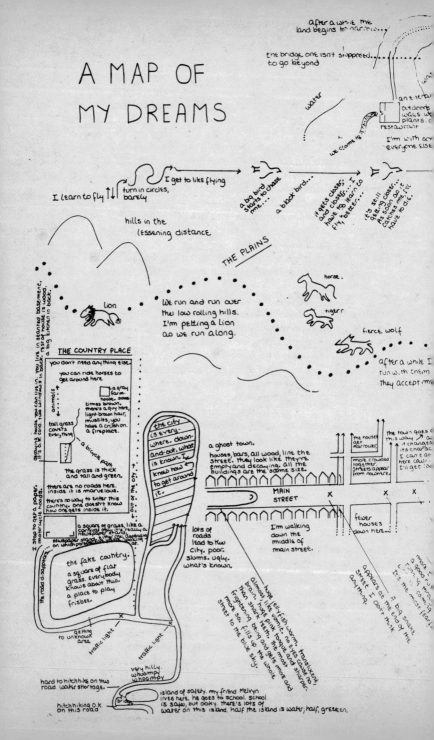

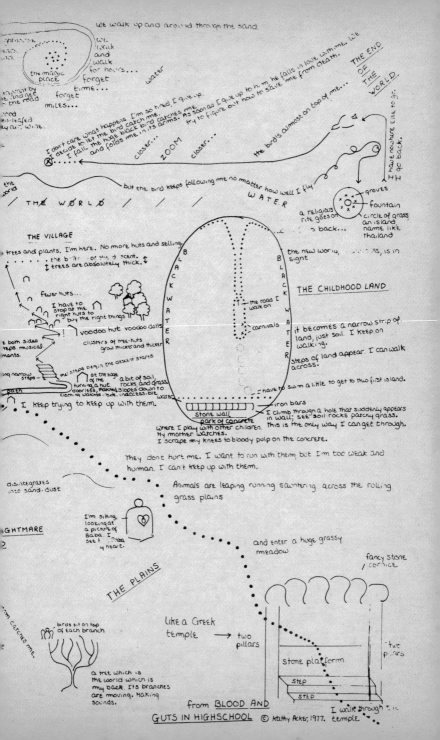

we walk up and around through the sand.

the magic place

We walk and walk for hours... forget time... forget miles...

water

I don't care what happens. I'm so tired, I give up. I decide to let the black bird catch me. I fall, the huge black bird catches me. and folds me in its arms. As soon as I give up to him, he falls in love with me. We try to figure out how to save me from death.

closer... ZOOM closer...

the bird's almost on top of me...

THE END OF THE WORLD

I have nowhere else to go.

but the bird keeps following me no matter how well I fly

THE WORLD

WATER

a religious rite goes on ... back...

groves
fountain
circle of grass an island name like Thailand

THE VILLAGE

trees and plants. I'm here. No more huts and selling.
the b... of the d scent.
trees are absolutely thick.

the new world, ...ss, is in sight

THE CHILDHOOD LAND

Fewer huts...
I have to stop at the right huts to buy the right things

voodoo hut voodoo dolls

clusters of tree-huts grow thicker and thicker

BLACK WATER

the road I walk I
carnivals

it becomes a narrow strip of land, just soil. I keep on walking.

Steps of land appear. I can walk across.

I have to swim a little to get to this first island.

e both sides teps. musical ments.
the steps begin the descent starts
at the edge of me turning a hut. a bit of soil doorless, floorless. slopes down to closing watches... back... inaccessible. rocks and grass
ong narrow steps
water

I keep trying to keep up with them.

Stone wall
park of concrete
iron bars
I climb through a hole that suddenly appears in wall; see soil rocks patchy grass. This is the only way I can get through.
where I play with other children. My mother watches.
I scrape my knees to bloody pulp on the concrete.

They don't hurt me. I want to run with them, but I'm too weak and human. I can't keep up with them.

Animals are leaping running sauntering across the rolling grass plains

disintegrates into sand-dust

GHTMARE 2

I'm sitting, looking at a picture of Baba. I see ... Baba ... y heart.

and enter a huge grassy meadow

fancy stone cornice

THE PLAINS

from catches me.

birds sit on top of each branch

a tree which is the world which is my back. Its branches are moving. Making sounds.

Like a Greek temple → two pillars

stone platform
step
step
two pillars

from BLOOD AND GUTS IN HIGHSCHOOL © Kathy Acker, 1977.

I walk through ... temple

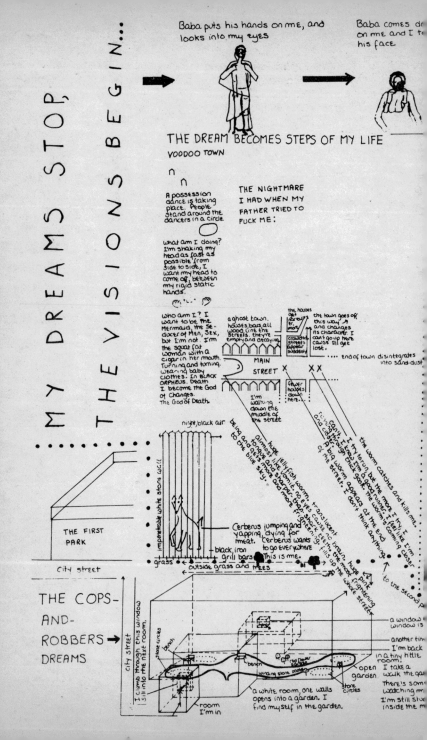

MY DREAMS STOP,

THE VISIONS BEGIN....

Baba puts his hands on me, and looks into my eyes

Baba comes do on me and I te his face

THE DREAM BECOMES STEPS OF MY LIFE

VOODOO TOWN

n
n

A possession dance is taking place. People stand around the dancers in a circle.

THE NIGHTMARE I HAD WHEN MY FATHER TRIED TO FUCK ME:

What am I doing? I'm shaking my head as fast as possible from side to side, I want my head to come off, between my rigid static hands.

Who am I? I want to be the Mermaid, the Seducer of Men, Sex, but I'm not. I'm the square fat woman with a cigar in her mouth. Turning and turning. Wearing baby clothes. In BLACK ORPHEUS. Death I become the God of Changes. The God of Death.

a ghost town. houses, bars, all wood, like the streets. they're empty and decaying.

the houses are narrower, mor

crowded streets appear suddenly

MAIN STREET

the town goes off this way → and changes its characters. I can't go up here cause I'll get lost.

.... end of town disintegrates into sand-dust

fewer houses down here..

I'm walking down the middle of the street

X X X

night, black air

imperetrable white stone wall

huge jellyfish worm, translucent, almost like those of a once more frightening teeth then once more teeth then ...

being bad dreams cause brain, huge, pink this is the most frightening worm

the worm catches me and kills me. I try. I find I have a gun. I shoot at the end of the worm's coming closer of the street. I don't think anything.

I try town but the moon. I try. I feel like I'm room, banging, I find I got a big worm appears of a big room

Cerberus jumping and yapping, dying for meat. Cerberus wants to go everywhere This is me.

black iron grill bars

grass ← outside grass and trees

bi

to the second p

to the second

THE FIRST PARK

City street

THE COPS-AND-ROBBERS DREAMS →

city street

I climb through this window & into the next room.

stone circles

bench

bench

winding stone path

open garden

stone circles

a white room, one walls opens into a garden. I find myself in the garden.

room I'm in

a window window is

another tim I'm back in a tiny little room. I take a walk the gar

There's some watching m

I'm still stu inside the m

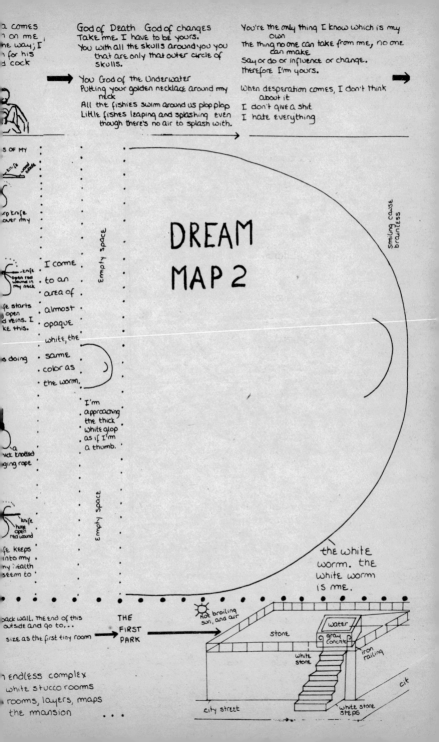

a comes
n on me,
ne way; I
n for his
d cock

God of Death   God of changes
Take me. I have to be yours.
You with all the skulls around you you
   that are only that outer circle of
   skulls.

You God of the Underwater
Putting your golden necklace around my
   neck
All the fishies swim around us plop plop
Little fishes leaping and splashing even
   though there's no air to splash with.

You're the only thing I know which is my
   own
The thing no one can take from me, no one
   can make
Say or do or influence or change.
Therefore I'm yours.

When desperation comes, I don't think
   about it
I don't give a shit
I hate everything

s OF MY

rp knife
over my

Empty space

DREAM
MAP 2

Smiling cause
brainless

nife
open red
wound in
my neck

I come
to an
area of

fe starts
open
d veins. I
ke this.

almost

s doing

opaque

white, the

same

color as

the worm,

a
rick knotted
ging rope

I'm
approaching
the thick
white glop
as if I'm
a thumb.

knife
huge
open
red wound

Empty space

fe keeps
into my
my health
seem to

the white
worm. the
white worm
is me.

ack wall. The end of this
outside and go to...

size as the first tiny room

THE
FIRST
PARK

Hot broiling
sun, and air

stone

water

gray
concrete

white
stone

iron
railing

white stone
steps

city street

cit

n endless complex
white stucco rooms
rooms, layers, maps
the mansion

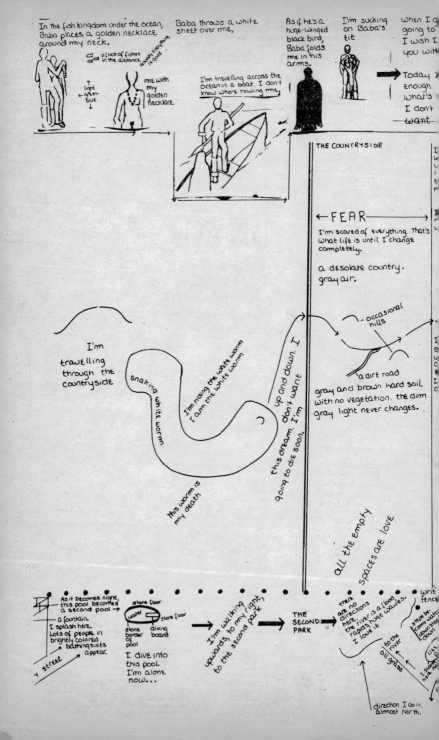

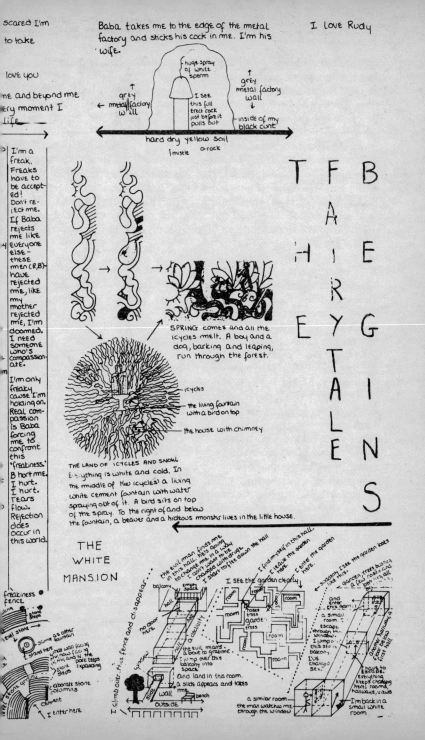

scared I'm
to take

love you

me and beyond me
every moment I
life

Baba takes me to the edge of the metal factory and sticks his cock in me. I'm his wife.

I love Rudy

huge spray of white sperm

grey metal factory wall

grey metal factory wall

I see this full erect cock just before it pulls out

inside of my black cunt

hard dry yellow soil
a rock
thistle

I'm a freak. Freaks have to be accepted! Don't reject me. If Baba rejects me like everyone else — these men (R,B) have rejected me, like my mother rejected me, I'm doomed. I need someone who's compassionate.

I'm only freaky cause I'm holding on. Real compassion is Baba forcing me to confront this "freakiness." B hurt me. I hurt. I hurt. Tears flow. Rejection does occur in this world.

T
F
B

H
A
I

A
R
E

I
Y
G

R

E
T
I

Y
A
N

L
S

SPRING comes and all the icycles melt. A boy and a dog, barking and leaping, run through the forest.

icycles

the living fountain with a bird on top

the house with chimney

THE LAND OF ICYCLES AND SNOW.
Everything is white and cold. In the middle of the icycles a living white cement fountain with water spraying out of it. A bird sits on top of the spray. To the right of and below the fountain, a beaver and a hideous monster lives in the little house.

THE
WHITE
MANSION

the evil man finds me in this hall. He's doing in this hall to change me in a way I don't want to be changed with drugs. I start to flee down the hall.

I find myself in this hall.

I leave the garden here.

I enter the garden here.

suddenly I see the garden looks like this:

I SEE the garden clearly

garden, trees bushes & a few rocks and — oh! It's all changed

and enter this room:

a small room I escape through this window.

I jump out this window. I've changed sex.

another hallway, another first hall.

balcony hall

empty space

a deadly

the evil man's about to grab me. I jump over his balcony into space.

And land in this room. A slide appears and takes me.

house trees garden trees

room

room

room

room

everything keeps changing here: rooms, hallways, views

freakiness fence

same as other fountain

stone steps

evil stone

I stand here

what was looking in now facing W, NW, and N. the gate keeps expanding

stone steps

elaborate stone columns

cement

I enter here

I climb over this fence and disappear.

no door here

a deadly

window

window

slide

tree

wall

OUTSIDE

a bench

a similar room: the man watches me through the window.

I'm back in a small white room

'I started walking to my home (I had an idea of home in my mind), but I didn't know where home was. There were just unending blocks of pure blackness and whiteness. Finally grey morning light began to filter through and as I began to see, the first thing I saw was your hut. Smoke was coming out of the chimney and lights shone through the windows.

'Please let me come in for a minute.'

'You poor baby.' The hideous monster opened the front door, saw a huge brown bear, and screamed. He slammed the front door. 'BEAVER! BEAVER!' He raced up to beaver's room. Beaver was asleep, snuggled under three layers of white satin quilting. 'BEAVER! BEAVER!' He sat on beaver's face and told him what the problem was. The beaver waddled downstairs and locked all the doors and windows securely so no one could possibly get in.

3 The Bear tries a second time to get into the House

The bear's difficulties made the house even more wonderful to the bear. He decided he'd force his way into the house with all his strength.

Sun was now pouring down, in through tiny closed kitchen windows, and flooding the kitchen.

In this light the monster was frying four eggs in a huge black frying pan. Golden pieces of buckwheat-and-rye toast popped out of an old iron toaster, hit the ceiling, bounced on to the blue-tiled floor, then on to two Dutch china plates sitting on the round red table. Tiny china bowls filled with rose-petal jam, orange-lemon-ginger marmalade, huckleberries and raspberries, chrysanthemum blossoms and guava jellies covered the remainder of the table. The beaver was taking a shower upstairs. He refused to use shower curtains so blue water was going 'plop, plop' and flooding the bathroom. The only thing beaver saw was the white morning sunlight and the only thing he heard was shower water falling like the beating of his heart.

Just as the monster was turning the eggs, the kitchen door started to shake so hard and to resound so loudly with hits and bangs, the monster decided there must be a bill collector at the door.

'Go away, you stupid bill collector!' he shouted. He was proud of himself for shouting.

The bear threw himself even harder against the kitchen door.

'Go away, you damn bill collector: I don't have any money and I'll never have any money. This world is a pit-hole and a garbage dump. It's 'cause of people like you. All anyone cares about,' the monster's voice was shaking, 'all all of you care about is getting as much money any way you can, and lying and cheating and using people, and passing this filthy paper around in devious circles, so it's all power, power power

power and I can't sleep or think or dream of anything else. I hate you and I hate your money.'

The bear raged. Foam frothed out of his mouth. He threw himself against the door as hard as he could.

That didn't work.

The bear forgot himself and threw himself against the door even harder.

'And if I had any money, I wouldn't give it to you. I'd piss on it and set it on fire, I'd bury it under all the ice in the world, I'd sprinkle oil on it and set Con Edison on fire, I'd tear it up and make some new fetishes. I'd feed it to the rats who live in my house, but I wouldn't give it to you. I hate you.'

By this time the bear's shoulders were masses of bruises, his mouth was a froth-pit, his fur was gone, and blood was streaming down his torso so he went away.

4 Betrayal and treachery

The hideous monster had a pet named Fritzy. Fritzy was a red-eyed white rat. As Fritzy was sleepily glomping around the kitchen and waiting for breakfast to get finished so she could get hold of some good crumbs, a big drop of butter leaped out of the frying pan onto her head, so just as the bear gave up and stomped into a nearby snowdrift, Fritzy ran out of her special door into the snow. 'Ah hah!' the bloody bear said. 'Food!' and snatched Fritzy up in his sharp-clawed paws.

'I'll tell you how you can trade me for some bigger game,' Fritzy squeaked as fast as she could. 'It'd be worth your while to keep me alive.'

'Oh yeah?'

'The guys who keep me are bigger and taste better than me. Rats are poison. Just tell hideous monster and beaver you've got me. They love me so much, especially that stupid monster, they'll come running through the walls to save me.'

The bear was so desperately in love with the house, he'd do anything to get inside it. 'Listen you,' he yelled at the house. 'I asked you nicely to let me in. You wouldn't let me in. Now I'm going to get you. I've got your pet Fritzy and I'm going to eat her up in one second flat if you don't let me in.'

'BEAVER! BEAVER!' The hideous monster fainted. When he came to, he stumbled, bumbled up the stairs, and dragged beaver out of the flooded shower. 'That horrible beast has Fritzy. He's going to eat Fritzy up! I'm going to trade myself for Fritzy, that's what I'm going to do, I'm going to throw myself into the bear's arms . . .'

'No!' beaver screamed. The monster raced down the stairs, but he couldn't go very fast because one of his legs didn't work and the other was knock-kneed. 'Monster, I love you. I adore you. I'll give myself to the bear!'

The monster and the beaver rushed down the stairs in a race to get into the bear's arms.

The bear had been waiting for an answer, but no one had answered him. When he lifted the rat to his mouth to eat her, she bit him and leaped into the snow.

By the time monster and beaver got outside, the bear had disappeared.

5 The Bear's defeat

The bear was defeated. There was no way he could get into the wonderful house.

He couldn't stop being in love with the house. He stared and stared at the house. He saw a white horse pawing short green grass. The magnificent horse started racing without effort, flying, across the sloping meadows, meadow-hills, tiny houses nestling in the hills, patches of all-colours flowers. A long time passed. The white horse was lying on the dirt, dying. A huge open red wound gaped in his right side. Several humans with sticks were plunging their sticks into the wound.

The bear's teeth started moving up and down. Soon these teeth were chattering so loud and fast, the bear got scared he was a chattering skull. All of his warm fur would fall off, his skin and his veins. The teeth kept chattering and biting. He got real pissed and his claws came out, but he couldn't figure out who to claw.

Bear was an elephant. Elephant rose up, mighty mighty grey, on two legs and roared. Roar of Universe. Elephant thudded down a narrow dirt road. Thud thud. Thud thud. Travelled many many miles to find water. His long trunk stuck food in his snake-shape mouth. Every now and then ROAR to tell the forest who he was.

Who am I? he asked. I'm an elephant.

A little boy who was thin and had a crew cut was sitting on the edge of his bed in pyjamas. The bed was as narrow as a cot. Someone had turned the sheets down for the night. Knees tucked under his chin, the little boy was looking directly ahead at a big being who was telling him a story. 'Once upon a time,' the big being said. 'Once upon a time there was a man who roamed the whole land. This man wasn't a giant physically, but he was a giant in every other way. The giant ate ears of corn and, now and then, the heads off of human beings . . .'

The bear's teeth started chattering again and the bear cried. Why wouldn't his teeth stop? Why was he shaking like this, like some crazy woman who's possessed and turning, like a white horse being ridden by a rider for the first time? The bear had a fever. He wanted to run away, but he knew if he left this bondage, there'd be nothing else left in the world.

6 *The Bear's vision of blackness*

The night was black and the universe was black. You weren't able to distinguish any forms in this night. A black band separated the black earth from the black sky. All over was just blackness, a layer of blackness.

You, the thing you called 'you', was a ball turning and turning in the blackness only the blackness wasn't something – like 'black' – and it wasn't nothingness 'cause nothingness was somethingness. The whole thing turns up into a ball, the ball's ephemeral, and where are you? Your self is a ball turning and turning as it's being thrown from one hand to the other hand and every time the ball turns over you feel all your characteristics, your identities, slip around so you go crazy. When the ball doesn't turn, you feel stable.

You exist in this darkness. Rebels. Creeps. Outcasts. Loners. People who hate everybody. People who feel uneasy around everybody. People who know everyone hates them. People who hate being tied down, restricted, constricted, and huge whirling snakes. The snakes climb around your neck and arms. The woman who's the mother of snakes takes you in.

You feel very uneasy. You take a step. You don't know what to do cause there's nothing, 'cause there's not even nothing.

7

For some reason this sight of blackness made the bear very happy. The bear began to dance and sing and make all sorts of funny noises. Tears like thunderballs rolled out of his eyes. Sweat-drops like hailstones fell out of his raunchy fur. The bear was causing all the weather. So he sang a song:

> Sweet bird in the darkness
> you're living in my heart
> your wings are my heart
> your outstretched
> wings are silver, sapphire, and violet
>   gold and light green
> you're flying away
> I'm following you
> whee whee
>
> the world is
> silver, sapphire, and violet, gold and light green
> now trees and buds and leaves and streams

are springing up, and nettles, hawks, and wild mists
the leaves are dark greens and blues and
                light greens
I don't give a shit about anything
I don't have to do anything
everything lives

What the bear sang about was true. The world was incredibly beautiful.
All the forms had returned and all the colours.

Then the bear started to move his wings. The wings moved faster
and faster and soon the bear rose into the air. He flew away from the
beaver and hideous monster's warm house and was never seen again.

Janey becomes a woman

Slums of New York City. A racially mixed group of people live in these
slums. Welfare and lower-middle class Puerto Ricans, mainly families,
a few white students, a few white artists who haven't made it and are
still struggling, and those semi-artists who, due to their professions, will
never make it: poets and musicians, black and white musicians who're
into all kinds of music, mainly jazz and punk rock. In the nicer parts
of the slums: Ukrainian and Polish families. Down by the river that
borders on the eastern edge of these slums: Chinese and middle-middle
class Puerto Rican families. Avenues of junkies, pimps, and hookers
form the northern border; the southern border drifts off into even poorer
sections, sections too burnt-out to be anything but war zones; and the
western border is the Avenue of Bums.

A three-room apartment; a fourteen by nine room, two seven by nine
rooms, and one more fourteen by nine room which contains toilet,
bathtub, and stove. Usually no hot water or heat, costs two hundred
dollars a month. Many of the people who live in these neighbourhoods
are too poor to pay their rents.

One of the landlords burned down his building so he could collect
the insurance money. Two families and one pimp were sleeping in this
building when it burned down. The landlord sold the charred lot for
lots of money to McDonald's, a multinational fast food concern. This
is how poor people become transformed into hamburger meat.

The slum where she chooses to live. The East Village stinks. Garbage
covers every inch of the streets. The few inches garbage doesn't cover
reek of dog and rat piss. All of the buildings are either burnt down,
half-burnt down, or falling down. None of the landlords who own the
slum live in their disgusting buildings.

In the winter when temperature averages 0°, these buildings have no hot water or heat, and in the summer at 100° average, roaches and rats cover the inside walls and ceilings.

Only one hospital serves these people, a hospital which dares to exist a few blocks from the northern border of this slum. The hospital contains lights, needles, drugs which cause brain disturbances, utensils, and almost no beds. Whenever there's a holiday, for instance, when Con Ed breaks down or when a landlord burns down one of his buildings to collect the insurance money, the poor people loot this hospital to amuse themselves.

The only supermarket in this neighbourhood buys the rotting food the other supermarkets in the city are unable to sell and sells this food at double-price.

The local police station contains men who, unlike the people in the market, want nothing to do with the neighbourhood. They're scared of the dangerous streets, the alleyways, and they're paid to be scared.

There are no out-front local crime coalitions because the crime bosses don't consider themselves part of the neighbourhood. These gangsters who run the city have taken a building, no one knows which building it is, in the northern part of the slum. They have torn out its centre, and behind the rat-infested plaster walls that look like the walls of the Chinese laundries, behind closed pet stores, antique furniture stores, tenements, within steel walls, within standard CIA protection systems, built a palace. The poor people don't know if this palace exists. They know there's one expensive Italian restaurant in the neighbourhood which is always empty and two expresso joints where the cops sit around and talk to men who wear big guns.

How Janey and the rest of the people in the East Village feel. Poor people generally don't feel different from rich people.

Poor people get real happy and run around jumping and screaming their lips off and then they get so down they know everyone hates them and they know everything stinks and they're going to kill themselves just like rich people do. Poor people are just like rich people except a general, not mood-to-mood 'cause everyone's got one mood after another mood and everyone thinks whatever mood is present is the only one that will ever exist I mean if you're sad then the world must be rotten, a general day-to-day depression. Depression meaning the poor person perceives fewer and fewer possibilities.

Let me put it another way. Most people are what they sense and if all you see day after day is a mat on a floor that belongs to the rats and four walls with tiny piles of plaster at the bottom, and all you eat is starch, and all you hear is continuous noise, you smell garbage and piss which drips through the walls continually, and all the people you know live like you, it's not horrible, it's just . . . .

Who they are. Janey, now thirteen years old, lives in a tenement on the corner of Fourth Street and First Avenue. She lives in three rooms. The first room measures six feet by ten feet and has a window. The second room is six feet by ten feet and has the advantage of being divided into two rooms six feet by five feet for each room. The third room is the same as the first room. The third room contains the following luxuries: one bathtub which covered by a metal slat becomes a dining room table or a couch; one toilet; one sink; one refrigerator usually in partial working condition; and one stove. The gas pipes may or may not be working depending on the time of year. Janey lives in the first room. She doesn't do anything.

Arnold lives in the other two rooms of this apartment. He has the most varied life of anyone Janey knows and he has a lot of money. He plays music in the circus and rehearses his own rock-n-roll band.

Janey sees Arnold every day because she has to. He's her source of human contact. Sometimes she hates him; sometimes she doesn't think he exists; sometimes she likes him; sometimes she depends on him.

When Janey thinks she has to see people because she's going crazy and/or it's not good for her to be alone all the time even though she loves being alone and doing nothing, when night strikes and only at night she goes out of her room and walks the streets.

She walks up and down the same streets the hookers walk only the hookers make some money. The junkies, petty gangsters, bums, and pimps occasionally say hello to her.

After a night or two Janey hates walking the streets doing nothing so she goes back to her room and does nothing.

(excerpts from Janey's diary)

29/7/77

I get distracted real easily. I'm getting very distracted by sex these days. I want to fuck around as much as possible. When I fantasize fucking, the encounters are always cold wild and free.

Yesterday I remembered three times when my former boyfriend fucked me. Maybe he's still my boyfriend. I never knew if he was my boyfriend. I've been fucking him for eight months on and off since I was twelve. Mostly off. He doesn't fuck so well 'cause he's eighty years old and 'cause he's a writer. I think most writers are crazy 'cause they sit in their rooms all the time and scribble down stuff no one wants to read and they don't fuck. Anyway this guy can fuck me when he beats me up and then he can only fuck me once for five minutes. Yesterday I was remembering: I'm in this tiny monastic room. My ass is sticking in his face. He's got a real bed in his room, but he'll never let me stay there for a night 'cause he's scared he might like me. I told him to get a belt. I think I shocked him. He took a heavy leather belt and whipped me across the back as he fucked me in the ass. It hurt almost too much and I liked it. That's only in my memory and it doesn't help this aching cunt except it helps me feel I can do whatever I like and I'm going to do that: I've been so repressed in this crummy room like a prison every day doing less and less and thinking more and more until something's gonna break probably my body. Now I'm going to do everything.

First I'm going to fuck a lot though I don't care about fucking anymore. I'm not sure what I care about and if I'm a real person. I'm going to travel to Scotland 'cause there are lots of men in Scotland and no one'll tell me what to do there.

As Janey was lying on her mat, writing this, two teenage hoods, one black and one white, came into the apartment. The white hood had a lot of slicked-backed black hair and the black hood had big biceps. Janey didn't hear these two hoods come in because they broke into Arnold's side of the apartment. They ripped off a cassette recorder and broke all the other equipment. While Janey was still lightly masturbating and fantasizing about young black men breaking in and raping her, they broke into her room and laughed at her. Before she could scream, the white one clapped his hand over her mouth. She tried to bite him, but she couldn't. She tried to kick her legs. The black man was holding her legs down and experimentally running his nails up the inner sides of her legs. The black hands came up to hold her arms; the huge body covered her. She felt enclosed.

The white punk stuck one of her scarves in her mouth and knotted another around her wrists and another around her ankles. She still couldn't move 'cause the black man was sitting on her ankles. She expected they were going to kill her. She wasn't thinking. Then the white one trashed her room. He threw her pictures on the ground and tore up her clothes and threw her books on the floor and stamped on them. He kicked her a few times. He found the razor, took out a razor blade, started slicing stuff up. As he did this, he smiled. 'C'mon,' said the black guy, 'you're not in high school anymore.'

The white boy looked abashed and held up the razor blade like he didn't know what to do with it.

The black guy hit Janey across the face a few times with the back of his hand for the hell of it. 'Maybe I'll kill you now; maybe I won't. Or maybe I'll keep you alive, maimed, and maybe I won't.' He looked at the expression on her face.

She felt like that thing – whatever it was – of which she was most scared, the most terrifying thing in the world was happening to her. The thing – whatever it was – she didn't know. The thing – what she most didn't want to happen – she was now right in the middle of. This was the most awful thing that could happen to her. She had to get away.

It just wasn't possible that she couldn't get away. The human imagination couldn't conceive of such a thing. Her mind wouldn't admit defeat. It kept flying and flying.

The black man hit her face with the back of his hand a few more times for good measure. One side of her face was bleeding, but she didn't know it. 'You're gonna spoil her looks,' the white boy said smiling, every now and then stroking his tongue with the razor blade, 'if you spoil her looks, you won't get any money out of her.'

The huge black guy hit her even harder. Suddenly her mind stopped and she realized where she was. She looked up at the black guy with tears in her eyes and smiled. 'OK,' said the black guy. 'Let's go.'

They threw some clothes on her and carried her downstairs. When she had been a tiny child, the night after a tonsillitis operation, in the hospital, her father had yelled at the doctor there was no need to keep such a young child in the hospital and had carried her off, through the night, all the lights and people and cars like clouds passing through her, she in a haze of drugs swung over his huge shoulder, running from the creeps through the night. That's exactly how she felt now.

As if she was a doll, they were walking her up past Fourth Street. Past the local cop station. The cops were lolling around in front of the station. Past the staircase on which the cops' Ukrainian blonde groupies hung out. Past the Kosher meat deli. The cops said hello to the white and black boys and they said hello back. 'Hey, I know you. I was up at your apartment last year. How are you?' a cop said to her. She just looked at him.

Flying. She was beginning to fly.

They stuffed her into an old black Chevy.

'He won't hurt you none,' said the white boy. 'Why doncha stop crying? I don't like it when girls cry. It reminds me of my mother. He's a nice man. He treated me real good. He picked me up in front of the *Blimpies* last year and he's taught me how to be a man. I was just a kid before that. I didn't know what I was doing. I thought it was big stuff to take dope, ya know? I was stupid like every other kid. All I wanted to do was take dope. I didn't even know what real dope was. I would'a ended up being some punk who spends his time rotting in jail if he hadn't taught me . . .'

'Shut up,' the black boy says. 'She'll learn herself.'

The black car proceeded up First Avenue, slowly 'cause it was still the rush hour, the sun was yellow grey and turning yellower and the air was hospital air – it was the time that the sun was getting old and sick and vomity; the air was killing off the old and the sick that Con Ed and poisoned tap water hadn't already killed off – it was one of Mayor

Koch's plans to save New York – the black car made its way past the empty neighbourhood hospital, out of the slum into a section anyone not from New York would think a slum, a semi-ritzy section, past the UN, the preserver of world peace, surrounded by green parks and Indian restaurants. A few blocks further, the car took a right, dove under a bridge, entered a small area hidden deep in parks right on the East River. Garbage was slowly replacing the water of the East River, only the garbage couldn't manage to live. 'We're going to sell you into white slavery,' the black boy told Janey. 'First we'll train you, then we'll sell you.'

They bundled her out of the car.

'That way we'll get a higher price for you.'

Janey fainted. When she came to, she thought she saw a skinny gnome with lots of wrinkles. The room was almost pitch-black. There was no one else in the room.

'You are going to remain in this room until you have become a whore. You have no other choice except to die. When you are ready to be a real whore, I will let you out of this room and you will bring all of the money you have earned back to me.

'You have no choice. If you do not do every single thing I tell you to, I will kill you.'

'Wha . . .,' said Janey. 'Uh. What's going on? Who are you?'

He hit her hard, much harder than the black boy or the white boy had hit her, across her nipples. Then he left the room and locked the door. . . .

The mysterious Mr Linker

'Most of all,' Mr Linker told some of his young hoodlums, 'I admire healthy young people. You can buy anything but health. If a person isn't healthy, even if he is very famous and rich, he has nothing.' Mr Linker was fond of teaching.

' "A healthy body in a healthy mind." There is nothing more beautiful than a voluptuous healthy young girl. When I see a beautiful young girl, when I see someone who is young and voluptuous walking with a man who isn't her equal – you know what I'm talking about – a man who wears glasses or is deformed, I tell you it disgusts me. I think such people ought to be shot.'

'Yeah,' one of the hoodlums mumbled.

' "A healthy mind in a healthy body." ' He returned to what he had been saying. 'You probably can't understand this. That was a saying of the Athenian state, the first great state in history. All of our culture comes from ancient Greece. Did you know that?

GIRLS WILL DO ANYTHING FOR LOVE

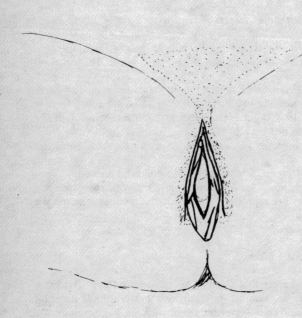

ODE TO A GRECIAN URN

'What makes a healthy state?' he asked his boys.

The hoodlums didn't say anything.

'It will surprise you. Disease and mental instability cause health. The men who have taken the most extreme risks, who have done what may have disgusted other people or what other people have condemned are the men who have advanced our civilization.'

Mr Linker had seen evidence of disease and mental instability before he was able to speak. Born on the Iranian streets, poverty had made him envy all those who had money. He had to do anything to get money.

Poverty is bad for humans because it makes them perpetuate all that is oppressing them and good for humans because it helps them to be willing to do anything – the weirdest acts possible, suicidal – to stop the poverty. Mr Linker, having been a beggar's child, saw how society worked. He made himself clever and relentless, relentlessly determined to get rich. If he had remained poverty-stricken, he might have turned this glimmering of intelligence on himself and become a saint. As it turned out, Allah be praised, at age seven he escaped with a travelling magician, stopped off in Vienna and, at fifteen years of age, talked his way into the University to study with Carl Jung. His cleverness and his interest in the mechanics of human social behaviour led him into the new science – philosophy of psychology. Then into neurology, for he was above all a materialist. And so Mr Linker became a lobotomist.

In his later life his cleverness which he called *intelligence* grew to enormous proportions. The more people turned to him for help and the more he indulged in his own eccentricities, the more he believed he was God. By his middle age there was no longer any chance he could ever be intelligent, i.e. adaptable. He had become a real image, a fake.

'The only thing we have,' Mr Linker continued telling his hoodlums, 'which separates us from the beasts is Culture. Culture is our highest form of life. And it is literature more than any other art which enables us to grasp this higher life, for literature is the most abstract of the arts. It is the only art which is not sensual. You know most people do not read. These days they read only trash. They do not SEE. They do not appreciate nature. They do not have the artist's eye and they know nothing:

> Out, out, brief candle.
> Life's but a walking shadow,
> A poor player who struts and frets his hour upon the stage,
> And then is heard no more . . .

Shakespeare said that in *Hamlet*. He said we are nothing without our culture.

'Where does culture come from? I will tell you. It comes from disease. All the great artists, Goethe, Schiller, and Jean-Paul Sartre – you must read *Nausea* in the French, in English it is nothing – have said this. They are aware how evil they are. They are aware this life is truly evil; due to this awareness, they are able to go beyond. You know that medically, I am a doctor, a body cannot live without disease.'

Mr Linker gave an example of his own disease. 'Isn't this rug beautiful?' he said. 'I will tell you the story of this rug. It is not an agreeable story. My wife worked on this rug for five years.' Tiny birds silver and white and pale blue clustered around bunches of grapes and the pale grey moon. 'Every day she stitched.' Mr Linker had married a young upper-middle class Viennese girl and brought her to the United States. He bought a resort in the Catskills, his first resort, and she cooked, cleaned, scrubbed, vacuumed, kept the accounts, washed, nursed the hotel guests, and waited on her husband. 'Soon her eyes began to fail her. She kept on making the rug. She began to have trouble breathing. One day she could no longer stand and she could no longer do the housework. The doctor told me she was very sick and she would have to stop working on the rug because the wool was affecting her lungs. I don't understand exactly how. While she was coughing up blood, she kept on working on this rug. The very moment she died, it was in her hand.'

Actually Mr Linker's wife had been driven crazy and then locked up for life in a New York State Sanatorium.

After Mr Linker's wife landed in the sanatorium, he added the white slavery business to his lobotomy and summer resort operations. He didn't need the money: at age seventy-five he was a very wealthy man. He wanted to be able to indulge in his other peculiarities. He was very powerful and intelligent.

Janey lived in the locked room. Twice a day the Persian slave trader came in and taught her to be a whore. Otherwise there was nothing.

One day she found a pencil stub and scrap paper in a forgotten corner of the room. She began to write down her life . . .

A book report

We all live in prison. Most of us don't know we live in prison.

A throng of bearded men, in sad-coloured garments, were assembled in front of a gaol. They were waiting for a woman named Hester Prynne to walk out of the gaol.

All of them even the hippies hated Hester Prynne because she was a freak and because she couldn't be anything else and because she wouldn't be quiet and hide her freakiness like a bloody Kotex and because she was as wild and insane as they come.

Long ago, when Hawthorne wrote *The Scarlet Letter*, he was living in a society that was more socially repressive and less materialistic than ours. He wrote about a wild woman. This woman challenged the society by fucking a guy who wasn't her husband and having his kid. The society punished her by sending her to gaol, making her wear a red 'A' for adultery right on her tits, and excommunicating her.

Nowadays most women fuck around 'cause fucking doesn't mean anything. All anybody cares about today is money. The woman who lives her life according to nonmaterialistic ideals is the wild antisocial monster; the more openly she does so, the more everyone hates her. Women today don't get put in gaol for being bloody pieces of Kotex – only streetwalkers and junkies land up in gaol, gaol-and-law now being a business like any other business – they just starve to death and everyone hates them. Physical and mental murder help each other out.

The society in which I'm living is totally fucked-up. I don't know what to do. I'm just one person and I'm not very good at anything. I don't want to live in hell my whole life. If I knew how this society got so fucked-up, if we all knew, maybe we'd have a way of destroying hell. I think that's what Hawthorne thought. He set his story in the time of the first Puritans: the first people who came to the northern North American shore and created the society Hawthorne lived in, the society that created the one we live in today.

Another reason Hawthorne set his story in the past (in lies) was 'cause he couldn't say directly all the wild things he wanted to say. He was living in a society to which ideas and writing still mattered. In 'The Custom House', the introduction to *The Scarlet Letter*, Hawthorne makes sure he tells us the story of *The Scarlet Letter* occurred long ago and has nothing to do with anyone who's now living. After all, Hawthorne had to protect himself so he could keep writing. Right now I can speak as directly as I want 'cause no one gives a shit about writing and ideas, all anyone cares about is money. Even if one person in Boise, Idaho, gave half-a-shit, the only book Mr Idaho can get his hands on is a book the publishers, or rather the advertisers ('cause all businessmen are now advertisers) have decided will net half-a-million in movie and/or TV rights. A book that can be advertised. Define culture that way.

You see, things are much better nowadays than in those old dark repressed Puritan days: anybody can say anything today; progress does occur.

It's possible to hate and despise and detest yourself 'cause you've been in prison so long. It's possible to get angrier and angrier. It's possible to hate everything that isn't wild and free. A girl is wild who likes sensual things: doesn't want to give up things being alive: rolling in black fur on top of skin ice-cold water iron crinkly leaves seeing three brown branches against branches full of leaves against dark green leaves through this the misty grey wanders in garbage on the streets up to your knees and unshaven men lying under cocaine piled on top of cocaine colours colours everything happening! one thing after another thing! . . . you keep on going, there are really no rules: it doesn't matter to you whether you live or die, but every now and then there's a kind of territory and you might get stuck; if you get stuck that's OK too if you really don't give a shit, but who doesn't give a shit! Loving everything and rolling in it like it's all gooky shit goddamnit make a living grow up no you don't want to do that.

The Massachusetts seacoast in the middle of the seventeenth century looked the same as it does now: WILD. Trees and bushes and weeds and wind and water. Trees and bushes and weeds and winds and water are always moving every moment the whole world is a totally different world air rides over shivering water so those water areas shiver harder grow darker below the water hit the sharper rocks harder splash! foam appears. And disappears.

My father told me the day after he tried to rape me that security is the most important thing in the world. I told him sex is the most important thing in the world and asked him why he didn't fuck my mother. In Hawthorne's and our materialistic society the acquisition of money is the main goal 'cause money gives the power to make change stop, to make the universe die; so everything in the materialistic society is the opposite of what it really is. Good is bad. Crime is the only possible behaviour.

Hester Prynne, Hawthorne tells us, had wanted to be a good girl. I remember I wanted to be a good girl for my father. Her loving husband sent her to the New World to prepare a way for him. Travelling in those days was dangerous – there were no roads – and her husband never showed up. Two years passed. Hester was being a good dead girl. Suddenly a little unsuspected ecstatic crazy-making overtaking wildness like a big King Viper spreading his hood, rising up and spreading overtaking everything, that's what love's like, snake-insane rose up in Hester she fucked. Pregnancy made her wildness or evil (that's the religious word for *wildness*) public. The child was the sign of her nastiness and disintegration and general insanity.

Hawthorne gives us a description of motherhood in the fucked-up society: All the people around Hester hate her and despise her and think she's a total freak. The kid's beyond human law and human consideration. How do you feel about yourself when every human being you hear and see and smell every day of your being thinks you're worse than garbage? Your conception of who you are has always, at least partially, depended on how the people around you behaved towards you. You sense the people around you aren't right: what you did, your need, you weren't defying them to defy them, it was your need, was

OK. You don't know. How can you know anything? How can you know anything? You begin to go crazy.

Hester's just stepping out of prison, out of prison, out of prison, but this is worse: huge staring eyes, whispers, her child laughed at, mocked, she's a woman, this isn't reality, the eyes turn around and around she can't be who she is, when suddenly she sees her long-lost husband.

This husband is now called Roger Chillingworth.

The top cops are screaming at Hester: 'You hideous woman.' 'Look at the hideous woman.' 'Who did the hideous woman fuck?' 'You're such a nice hideous woman, we know you didn't mean to do the tremendously horrible thing you did, just pretty please tell us who you fucked. We know what'll make you feel better.'

Hester's husband's a scholar. A scholar is a top cop 'cause he defines the roads by which people live so they won't get in trouble and so society will survive. A scholar is a teacher. Teachers replace living dangerous creatings with dead ideas and teach these ideas as the history and meaning of the world. Teachers torture kids. Teachers teach you intricate ways of saying one thing and doing something else.

The top cops start laughing at and mocking Hester and telling the crowd to laugh at and mock Hester 'cause she won't tell them who her baby's father is. Hester's acting out of love.

This husband, being a teacher, is a zombie and a ghoul. He sees his wife being tortured by lots of people, he sees his wife in pain in agony, he sees his wife nursing a strange kid, and he doesn't feel anything. He just wonders, intellectually wonders, who the kid's father is.

A final scene focuses this swirling horror. The young handsome Reverend who everyone thinks is gentle, honest, and kind takes up the spreading mockery and hatred and vomiting and says to Hester: 'You are the worst piece of trash-cunt whoever lived, no one will ever ever love you, there will be no more love in your life because, mainly because, you won't tell us who your bastard's father is.' Hester can't reply 'cause the guy who's screaming at her is the guy who fucked her. How can HE scream at her? All that she has left of the world: her memories disappear. Do you understand what reality is? She begins to go crazy . . .

Boppy doppy doopy wah yahyah mm. Is that what you think craziness is? Are you scared you're going crazy? Do people who go crazy freak you? Look sweetheart.

I woke up in my attic that the winds swept through and all the world was grey and black. I saw pine trees covering the grey sky and sea, tall trees, boats, tall trees, boats.

I walked along a highway. I was looking for a place to sit down, for some grass I could walk in, for a wood I could explore. I walked for hours. All the land on both sides of the highway, cultivated and wild, was private. I had to keep walking on the highway. I thought that people today when they move move only by car, train, boat, or plane and so move only on roads. They perceive only the roads, the map, the prison. I think it's becoming harder to get off the roads.

I live on a desert island. It's a nice desert island. I like it here. This is what I do: I eat; I sleep; when it rains and gets cold, I hide under some rocks. I like it here. But I'm getting bored . . . What can I do? I can repeat what I see. I can draw this old grey trunk lying flat across a valley of sand. I can draw the rotten trunk and make it look different. People got cures for polio and syphilis by imagining. People have and can change the world. In the beginning, on the desert island, the world was totally beautiful. Today in my room in New York City the world is horrible and disgusting. What the hell happened?

I don't want to be a slave, I don't want to be a whore, I don't want to be lonely and without love for the rest of my long life. I've got to find out how I got so fucked up.

Hester and her husband are sitting, after the torture, in her prison cell. Her husband has come inside to make her well again. He's a doctor.

'Fucking's the most wonderful thing in the world.' Hester is crazy.

'I want to fuck you right now,' her husband replies.

'Ugh. I wouldn't fuck you if you were the last man on earth. You make me sick to my stomach.'

A slight grimace crosses his face, but he manages to suppress it. 'Remember when we used to fuck? By the fireside in Amsterdam.' Tears appear in his thin eyes. 'You'd lay your head on my lap and we'd look into the fire.'

Hester's thinking the most wonderful thing in the world is to fuck a man you love. God she wishes she had it right now. Loving a man and being right next to him: naked against him naked there's no need to talk: naked wet warm his face his skin naked wet warm his thick lips glazed eyes you're on top of him naked wet warm never let you go the peace of the world never never never.

'I'm the guilty one,' the husband says. 'If I hadn't sent you alone to America, you never would've done this horrible inhuman thing.'

'Oh, I'm the guilty one.'

'I hate you now. I don't even hate you. I just want nothing to do with you. You're not to reveal that you have ever known me or had anything to do with me. Whatever love and affection occurred between us is now dead. We're dead people.'

Fucking with love must be the gift of God. His eyes his nose his hot breath the shadow under his neck his thick arms the fat around his sides the bones sticking out of his thighs his cock waving in that mess of hair I want him so much I'm going crazy. I want his eyes I want his nose I want his hot breath reeking all over my body I want to stick my tongue in neck I want his arms around me I've forgotten what it's like to want a man I roll my hands in his fat and bite it and rub my dying-to-come hips against the bones sticking out of his thighs so maybe maybe I'll come that way his cock, if I could just touch his cock just for a second, I don't want to touch it more than that, a quick kiss, wet and slimy, don't take me away from it, don't take me away from it you creep meanie: this is my home.

'Who's your brat's father?'

'I love him. I'm not going to tell you who he is.'

'I'm going to find out who he is. I'm simply interested who he is. I am one of the most brilliant men in America and Europe and can learn anything. I'm going to find out who he is!'

She shivers before this example of the divorcement of body and mind. She's seeing terror and hatred and hypocrisy beginning to spread over the earth.

'Don't you tell anyone who I am.'

WHEN SOMEONE'S IN PAIN, HE CRIES OUT.

One day Janey finds a Persian grammar book. She begins to teach herself Persian:

THE
PERSIAN POEMS

by Janey Smith

THE PERSIAN POEMS

• • • • • • • •

جانی	Janey
جانی د'ختر اُست	Janey is a girl.
جهاز سرخ است	the world is red.
شب خیاباذ تَنگ است	night is the narrow street
و' کوچه تَنگ	and the narrow side-street.
جانی نَچّه ای است	Janey is a child.
جانی نَچّه ای گراذ آست	Janey is an expensive child,
وَلی آرزان	but cheap.

("ع" (،) links two entities :)

شب ِ جانی	Janey's night
شب ِ سرخ	the red night
شب ِ جهاز	night - world
جانی خَراب آست	Janey stinks.

(note: no ezafe)

جانی در اُطاق آست   Janey is in a room.

اُطاق کوچک آست   The room is small.

(Ezafe (ِ) can join more than one entity:)

فُرهَنگ خَراب آست: Culture stinks: books

کِتابهای بُزُرگانِ   and great men and the

صَنایع ظَریفه   fine arts.

زَنانِ زیبا   beautiful women

(The suffix ye (ی) means indefiniteness:)

زَنِ زیبایی   a beautiful woman

شَبِ سُرخی   a red night

خیابانِ بیابانی   a deserted street

(or, note the change in construction :)

زَنِ زیبا   a beautiful woman

شَبی سُرخ   a red night

خیابانی بیابان   a street is a desert

Janey's all alone in her room. She's
learning Persian slowly:

(Certain adjectives are deviant: they
precede their nouns. No ezafe (ͺ) used
here:)

این دهقان   this peasant

آن دهقان   that peasant

خوب دهقان   good peasant

(Note the endings here:)

خوبتر دهقان   a better peasant

این دهقان آز آن   this peasant is better

خوبتر آست   than that one.

خوبترین دِهقان   the best peasant

(or:)

بِهتر دِهقان   a better peasant

بِهترین دِهقان   the best peasant

(The word خوب (good) is deviant :)

بِهترین دِهقانِ این   the best peasant of

دِموکراس   this democracy.

این دِهقان آز همه   this peasant is the

بِهترین آست   best of all.

یک أطاق بیستر نیست   this is the only room,
(is not) (more) (room) (one)

Janey wrote,

صَندَل چیزی دیکر نیست   there is only a chair.
(is not) (other) (a thing) (chair)

(there's no word for "cot".)

جانی دهقان آست   Janey is a peasant.

جانی گران آست   Janey is expensive,

ولی آرزان   but cheap.

دهقان جیابان آست   the peasant is the

    street.

زبان   language

زبان معزول کردن   to get rid of language

. . . .

Janey hates prison.

(Two vowels can't come together. Put a
hamze or ye (ء or ی) between two
vowels:

(More specifically: When suffix begins
ت ; after ۱... or و..., put ی :)

مو   hair   مویان   hairs

بانو   woman   بانوان   women
(notice exception)

مویان تازه و، بانوان   there are fresh hairs

تازه هست   and there are fresh

women.

there are new hairs

and there are new

women.

(When suffix begins ت ; after ی...,
do nothing :)

ایرانی   Iranian

ایرانیان   Iranians

عَلی	Ali
ایرانیانِ سِیاه هَست	There are black Iranians
وَلی عَلیانِ سِیاه	but there are no
نیست	black Ali's.
سَر	head
سَرِ کثیف	dirty head
سَرِ کثیفِ سِیاه	dirty black head

(When suffix begins آ; after ه..., put
گ :)

بَچّه	child
بَچِّگان	children
بَچِّگانِ این شَهر	the children of this city.

(When suffix begins ...ای ; after ا... or
و... , put ئ :)

بانو woman

بانوٌ a woman

بانوٌ سَرِ کَثیفٍ a woman is a dirty

سِیاه است black head.

جانِی سِیاه است Janey is blind,

Janey kept on writing,

(When suffix begins ...ایِ ; after ی..., do nothing :)

صَندَلی و اُطاق وَ پَنجَرَهٔ there's a cunt and

وَ پَنجَرَهٔ وَ پَنجَرَهٔ هَست a prick.

صَندَلی chair

اُطاق room

پَنجَرِه wall

(or a hamze over the ye (ئ...) :)

یک صندلی و، یک اتاق | the only thing is

و، یک پنجره و، یک پنجره | a cunt and a

و، یک پنجره و، یک پنجره | cock.

بیستر نیست

(When suffix begins ...ای ; after ه....,
use ـة... or add ای :)

صندلی و اتاق و، پنجره و، | A wonderful man

پنجره و، پنجره و، پنجره | whose large prick is

هست | in Janey's cunt says

to Janey, "I love

you."

(When suffix begins with ezafe (ِ) :)

بانوی بو | the woman of smell

بوی بانو | the woman's smell

موی جانی	Janey's hair
صندلی جانی	Janey's chair
خانه	house
خانهٔ جانی	Janey's box
داشتن	to have
خَرِیدَن	to buy
خواستن	to want
دیدَن	to see
آمَدَن	to come
زَدَن	to beat up
خوردَن	to eat
گِرِفتَن	to rob
بُردَن	to kidnap
کُشتَن	to kill

دانِستَن   to know

(Past stem: cut off the "-an" (...ان):)

داشتـ...   have

خَرید...   buy

خواستـ...   want

دیـد...   see

آمَد...   come

زَد′...   beat up

خُورد...   eat

گِرِفتـ...   rob

بُرد...   kidnap

کُشتـ...   kill

دانِستـ...   know

(Present stem:

((1.) Verbs ending "id" lose "id":)

buy خَر...

((2.) Verbs ending "nd", "rd", "ad", "ud" lose "d":)

eat خُور...

((3.) Verbs ending "ft", "št" lose "t":)

kill کُشت...

((4.) Verbs ending "est", "eft", "oft", and "ad"
lose this syllable:)

know دانِ...

((5.) Irregulars - most of them :)

have دار...

want خواه...

see بین...

come آ...

زَن	beat up
گیر...	rob
بَر...	kidnap
داشتَن جانی	to have Janey
خَرِیدَن جانی	to buy Janey
خواستَن جانی	to want Janey
دِیدَن جانی	to see Janey
آمَدَن جانی	to come Janey
زَدَن جانی	to beat up Janey
خوردَن جانی	to eat Janey
گِرِفتَن جانی	to rob Janey
بَردَن جانی	to kidnap Janey
کُشتَن جانی	to kill Janey
دانِستَن جانی	to know Janey

(Translate into English:)

I listened to the smoldering ship's engines that were carrying me along, and relaxed. I shouldn't have. I should have grabbed a buoy and jumped overboard; and flagged down a passing tramp to carry me straight back to the Athens Hilton and the airport.

۱. آیا سرِ سیاه اینجاست ؟

1. Is there a black head here?

۲. بلی خانُم (جانی) نزدیک است

2. Yes Mrs (Janey), it's near.

۳. این سرِ مالِ جانی نیست

3. This head isn't Janey's. (Lit. This head

isn't the property of Janey.)

٤. سَرهای سِیاهِ شَهرِ تهرانِ خَیلی هَست

4. There are many black heads in the city
   of Tehran.

٥. خِیابانها سِیاه است بُزرگتَرین وَفاتِ جَهانِ
   حِسّ وَلی آز آن تیزتَر خُود آست

5. The streets are black. You haven't fucked
for a long time. You forget how incredibly
sensitive you are. You hurt. Hurt hurt
hurt hurt hurt. You meet the nicest guy
in the world and you fall in love with him
you do and you manage to get into his
house and you stand before him. A girl who
puts herself out on a line. A girl who asks

for trouble and forgets that she has feelings
and doesn't even remember what fucking's
about or how she's supposed to go about it
cause she wasn't fucked in so long and now .
she's naive and stupid. So like a dope
she sticks herself in front of the guy :
here I am ; understood : do you want me?
No, thank you. She did it. There she is. What
- does she do now? Where does she go? She
was a stupid girl : she went and offered
herself, awkwardly, to someone who didn't
want her. That's not stupid. The biggest
pain in the world is feeling but sharper is
the pain of the self.

(doesn't exist→) سُول   soul

وَقت   fate

٦. آیا گوشت تازه هَست ؟

6. Is there any fresh meat ?

٧. بلی خانُم ولی گوشتَت آز آن مالِ جانی بِهتَر آست

7. Yes, Mrs, but your meat is better than Janey's.

٨. آیا وَقت هَست ؟

8. Is there any fate ?

٩. بَلی خانُم وَقتَت آز آن مالِ جانی بِهتَر آست

9. Yes, Mrs, your fate is better than Janey's.

١٠. هَمهٔ مُردُم راضی آند

10. "All the people are content."

١١. جانی راضی نیست

11. Janey is not content.

۱۲. کوچکترینِ عمارتِ این خِیابان خانۀ جانِی است

12. The smallest building on this street is
    Janey's cunt.

۱۳. این کارگر بُزُرگتَر ازِ کارگرانِ ایران است

13. This worker is the biggest in Persia.

۱۴. آکثَریَتِ مَردُم کارگر یا دِهقان آند

14. Most people are workers or bums.

۱۵. خِیابانها سِیاه است

15. The streets are black.

۱۶. آیا گوشت تازه هُست ؟

16. Is there any fresh meat ?

•   •   •   •   •   •   •   •   •   •   •

جانی دانستن to know Janey

(Review what you've learned:)

۱	ا...	?	alef
ب	ب...ب...ب	b	be
پ	پ...پ...پ	p	pe
ت	ت...ت...ت	t	te
ث	ث...ث...ث	s	se
ج	ج...ج...ج	j	jim
چ	چ...چ...چ	c	cin
ح	ح...ح...ح	h	he hotti
خ	خ...خ...خ	x	xa
ر	ر...	r	re
س	س...س...س	s	sin
م	م...م...م	m	mim

ن	ن...ـنـ...ـن	n	nun
ی	ی...ـیـ...ـی	y	ye
(´)	هَ´....ُ´.... آ...ُ	a	fat-he
(١)	ا.....ـا...آ...	a	alef
(,)	هـ...... ,.... اِ...	ɛ	kasre
(ئ´)	یِ´....ـیـ´.....آئ...	ɛi	fat-he, ye
(ئ)	ی.....ـیـ......ایـ	i	ye
(٥)	و...ُ.... اُ...	o	zammе
(و´)	و´...ُ.....و´آو	ou	fat-he, vav
(و)	و......و......او	u	vav

بن	"bn"	بِ	"by"
تَن	body		
بِ	without	بِ آ	blue

بابا   father

ببین   see!

بابای من ببین   see my father!

بابای من وُفات آست   my father is dead.

بابای من آبی آست   my father is blue.

این بابای من آست   this is my father.

تن   body

تنِ من ببین   see my body!

تنِ من خان آست   my body is life.

تنِ من تُب است   my body is hot.

این تنِ من آست   this is my body.

خانه   cunt

خانهٔ مَن سیاه   see my cunt!

خانهٔ مَن پر آست   my cunt is empty.

خانهٔ مَن سرخ آست   my cunt is red.

این خانهٔ مَن آست   this is my cunt.

• • • • • • • •

'I go crazy when I want to fuck a guy,' Hester thinks to herself. 'How will any man ever love me? How can I be happy if a man doesn't fuck and love me? But look at Pearl. She's happy and she doesn't fuck.'

Pearl's four years old. She's as wild as they come. *Wild* in the Puritan New England society Hawthorne writes about means *evil anti-society criminal*. Wild. Wild. Wild. Going wherever you want to go and doing whatever you want to do and not even thinking about it. 'Why did you get stoned?' the Persian slave trader asked me this morning. In 'primitive' 'wild' societies like Haiti the word 'why' doesn't exist. Pearl, according to Mr Hawthorne, wears hippy clothes and runs around in the forest and makes no distinction between what's outside her and her dreams. On the whole she doesn't make many distinctions. She doesn't know human beings exist. Sometimes she senses human beings exist. She senses a black vertical mist that's a wall pressing into her as if on top of her. She wants to scream. She feels helpless.

She doesn't like people much.

She notices Hester her mother. Once she notices someone she'll stick by that person she'll open herself up she is soft and totally hurtable that's what being wild is. (Secretly.) (Privately.) 'Cause once you're open like that you're a real person 'cause you're no longer separated from other people. It's dangerous. Whatever happens to you happens to the ones you're connected with. Whatever happens to them happens to you. It's scary and dangerous to open yourself to someone. Not that you ever have any choice.

The townspeople think Pearl's evil because she lives off the roads. 'No man will ever love a woman like you when you grow up,' say the townspeople. 'The roads are our civilization. They're the order men have impressed on chaos so that men's lives can be safer and more secure and, thus, so that we can all progress. Human life gets better and better.'

The roads are getting so super-paved and big and light and loaded with BIG MACS and HOWARD JOHNSONS that the only time people are forced into danger or reality is when they die. Death is the only reality we've got left in our nicey-nicey-clean-ice-cream-TV society so we'd better worship it. S & M sex. Punk rock. Don't you know, you can step into the snow, the raging ocean and the freezing snow, you can step into danger . . .

anytime you please . . .

step into me . . .

The government, the big multinational businessmen, the scholars and teachers, and the cops are the people who maintain the roads. The scientists, philosophers, and artists are the people who build the roads. Everyone's a slave.

'Who can I talk to?' Hester screams.

These most important men in the world decide it's their duty to tear the mother away from her child. They want to keep the child so they can train the child to suck their cocks. That's what's known as education. 'Who can I talk to?' Hester screams.

The Reverend Dimwit (the young handsome Reverend) raises his hand. Reverend Dimwit is the best student in the school. 'Let Hester keep her child.' The cops ask him why. He thinks up a phoney excuse: 'The child is the visible sign of the woman's sin and so will keep reminding the woman of her sin. That way we can be assured of the woman's continuing and deepening punishment.' The top cops, who don't have any feelings, accept this lousy logic. (Anything's acceptable as long as it's logical.) But evil Chillingworth, the builder of the logic road, wonders why the Reverend is helping Hester. Nothing in the world, Chillingworth thinks, will be unknown to me. I am totally self-sufficient. I never ask anyone's advice. My plots and manipulations are all-potent. Chillingworth sneaks his way into the Reverend's heart, but he doesn't give his own heart away. This is friendship and love in the fucked-up society.

A couple is one who loves plus one who lets love. Couples make up the townspeople world. If you're not part of a couple, you don't exist and no one will speak to you you outcast. Go to hell outcast. Outside the road. Don't you know there's nowhere to walk anymore unless you're walking to somewhere? Now if you shut up and stay nonexistent and don't act like the freak you are, maybe in two years we'll notice you and tell you our neurotic problems 'cause we have lots of neurotic problems, but don't ever expect to be invited to one of our parties.

I, Hester, am a red house lost in the thickening mist. One of my sides is clearly visible. The red one. The other side is hazy. I'm not sure if it's real. There's a little light I don't know anymore where it's coming from. Everything that isn't touching my eyes is gone. Not blacked out, just gone into the dark mist that's blotting out everything. The mist goes back and back . . .

Everyone I know lives on the roads. They're creepy crawling snivelling things. I don't want anything to do with them. Ugh. I hate people. I can be alone. I can close myself up. I won't let anyone get near me. I think I'm off the road, but I'm dominated by fear and hatred. I'm as closed-up and fucked-up as everybody else. I am hell. The world is hell. 'No it isn't!' I scream, but I know it is. Hell. Hell. Hell. Hell. Help. Help me. Help me. Love me.

'The fullness and breadth, the clear entirety of this hell and therefore its limitations,' Reverend Dimwit then says to Hester, 'will appear and be fully apparent the moment we become conscious of the secrets in our hearts.'

I can't work. I can't move.

All I can do is sit here and wait for his call.

Listen you creep, you dimwit.

I want to write myself between your lips and between your thighs. How can I get in touch with you? You don't answer your door and you don't answer your phone. I think you're a creep.

I want to fuck you, Dimwit. I know I don't know you very well you won't ever let me get near you. I have no idea what you feel about me. You kissed me once with your tongue when I didn't expect it and then you broke a date. I used to have lots of fantasies about you: you'd marry me, you'd dump me, you'd fuck me, you were going again with your former girlfriend, you'd save me from blindness. You'd. Verb. Me. Now the only image in my mind is your cock in my cunt. I can't think anything else.

I've been alone for a very long time. I'm locked up in a room and I can't get out. Because I've been locked up in this room so long whatever desires are arising in me are rampaging around everywhere as wild and fierce and monstrous as gigantic starving jungle beasts. I don't know how to talk to people, I especially have difficulty talking to you; and I'm ashamed and scared 'cause I want you so badly, Dimwit.

I know you no longer want to see me 'cause I'm so antisocial and awkward. How can I learn to talk better? How can I learn to love you more so I can give you what you want?

Teach me how to talk to you. WANT. Is my wanting you so bad, wanting your cock so bad, wanting the feel of your lips on my lips just me being selfish and egotistic? Is wanting horrible and has to be put down and repressed?

Teach me a new language:

'Rock-n-roll is rock-n-roll.'

'The night is red.'

'The streets are deserted.'

'The children in the city are going insane.'

'Rock-n-roll is rock-n-roll.'

'The night is red.'

'The streets are deserted.'

'The children in the city are going insane.'

'Rock-n-roll is rock-n-roll.'

'The night is red.'

'The streets are deserted.'

'The children in the city are going insane.'

'Rock-n-roll IS rock-n-roll.'

'The night is all around me and it's black.'

'I can't even see the streets from my room: how would I know if they're deserted?'

'How can I tell the difference between sanity and insanity? You think in a locked room there's sanity and insanity? Anyway I don't know if there are any children anymore. Maybe they went out of fashion.'

TEACH ME A NEW LANGUAGE, DIMWIT. A LANGUAGE THAT MEANS SOMETHING TO ME.

Hello, Hester. Would you like to go out to dinner with me?

Dimwit.

HAWTHORNE SAYS PARADISE IS POSSIBLE.

When I was a child, I would go as far out as possible and jump around and throw my arms around and all the stars are turning. The winds are blowing through me. My arms and legs are winds. Slowly, the whole universe is starting to revolve like a giant wheel. This wheel isn't a thing: it is everything. Everything is on the surface. That everything is me: I'm just surface: surface is surface.

Whirling and whirling and whirling.

The sun in the country is hot. When there are no clouds, day after day, it beats down without mercy. Then the winds start. The winds stop start change directions speeds second to second. In one hour the air temperature drops or rises thirty degrees. The seagulls rush into the dock, cackle and hoot perhaps to each other there's no way we can tell in their low voices. The winds rise and waves, appearing out of the water, lash against the blackening dock.

Whirling and whirling and whirling.

HAWTHORNE SAYS PARADISE IS A HEART THAT OPENS UP AND BECOMES A HEART.

Everything takes place at night.
In the centres of nightmares and dreams,
I know I'm being torn apart by my needs,
I don't know how to see anymore.

I'm too bruised and I'm scared. At this point in *The Scarlet Letter* and in my life politics don't disappear but take place inside my body.

I have to figure this out: I have certain characteristics from childhood traumas, etc. Since I never had real parents, I never knew who my father was and my mother didn't give a hoot about me (I wasn't brought up, I just grew up like a wild plant), I want love affection the sort of love and affection you get from a parent rather than a jealous lover, and especially a father.

I grew up wild, I want to stay wild.

The first older man I ever fucked rejected me and his rejection put me right back into childhood desperation craziness and made me physically sick.

OK These are characteristics. I can either do what I want to (satisfy my characteristics) or not bother.

Doing what I want to is dangerous 'cause I can get really hurt. So I lie to people. I say 'I love living alone.' 'I fuck around a lot.' But I really want what I want. These aren't passing emotions. These are my characteristics.

By *love* do I just mean satisfaction of the needs created by my characteristics?

Obviously I have to change my manner of life in some large way. And I have to do so in accordance with my needs.

I can't live a slave in a locked-up room for ever. Think more on this:

Dear Dimwit,
I'm so scared that I'm not thinking anymore. I want to do whatever I can to make you happy. If you don't want to fuck me, that's OK. If you want to fuck me once a month like you do all your other girlfriends that's OK. I'll do anything

so I can keep knowing you. I think you're the most interesting man I know even though I'm very scared of getting hurt by you.

Dear Dimwit,
Now you're gone from my life. You're not here. Go fuck yourself 'cause I hate you. I know you don't need me. I hurt. I'm stupid.

Hester begins to break out of the prison of her mind when she starts to do something for someone besides herself despite whatever her emotions may be. Chillingworth while pretending he's curing and loving Dimwit is instilling poison in Dimwit's soul. Like Hester, Dimwit hates himself. Like Hester, Dimwit is conscious he doesn't understand what's happening. Hester sees Dimwit's going crazy and in deepening torture.

When you start to do something for someone else, you start to perceive that you're the cause of all the pain in the world and that only you can do something about it. So Hester tells Chillingworth she's going to tell Dimwit who Chillingworth really is. Chillingworth says if she does so, he'll tell everyone Dimwit is her bastard's father and Dimwit will die.

Robot fucking. Mechanical fucking. Robot love. Mechanical love. Money cause. Money cause. Mechanical causes. Possessiveness habits jealousy lack of privacy wanting wanting wanting. Is that all you think I mean when I say I care about you? At least give me a chance to learn and find out who you are.

This is a plea.

See. I think it's so easy. I throw away my 'A'. But my body goes crazy, night comes and my body goes crazy. I stick my third finger in my cunt, no no that doesn't help, where is relief? Could pick up some young boy. Young boys are candy; they're not relief. You are relief, but you're in my mind: you're my characteristics again: I want relief. I want to know who you really are.

My body aches and aches and I remember who I am.

Hester tells Dimwit Chillingworth is her husband and hates Dimwit. According to Hawthorne, as soon as Hester does this, as soon as her ego-obsessions are beginning to break up (this is why psychiatrists stink: they focus you even more on your ego-obsessions rather than helping you turn away), she and Dimwit and the society around them begin to move from prison to being free.

Then Hester falls back into herself. You see, I know I'm selfish. She's going to fuck Dimwit, she's going to have Dimwit for ever and for ever, the moon and the stars in the sky, pluck them out with your hand, put them in your pocket and keep them, a dream of a limitless world, of the sun and the moon and the stars. As far as I can go. Love love love. Want want want. This is a message to myself. You are pursuing your own desires and your own desires are BORING.

Dear Dimwit, I WANT TO LEARN.

Dear Dimwit,

This is the plan: We're going to run away from here and live happily ever after. We're going to be able to fuck each other however we want to as much as we want. There's a pirate ship sitting in the harbour. When that pirate ship leaves in four days, we'll be pirates on it, sailing to Persia. In Persia everyone does whatever they want.

I won't ever impinge on your freedom Dimwit. You can sit on the faces of as many Persian girls as you want to, you can stop fucking me, you can have Turkish coffee and hash with me only once a month: I want you to do what you want as much as I'm doing what I want. I want to love you madly so I'm loving you madly. I hope you don't mind . . .

Once upon a time there was a materialistic society one of the results of this materialism was a 'sexual revolution'. Since the materialistic society had succeeded in separating sex from every possible feeling, all you girls can now go spread your legs as much as you want 'cause it's sooo easy to fuck it's sooo easy to be a robot it's sooo easy not to feel. Sex in America is S & M. This is the glorification of S & M and slavery and prison. In this society there was a woman who
freedom and suddenly the black night opens up and
fucked a lot and she got tied up with ropes and
on upward and it doesn't stop
beaten a lot and made to spread her legs too wide
the night is open space that goes on and on,
this woman got so mentally and physically hurt
not opaque black, but a black that is extension
she stopped fucking even though fucking is the thing to do.
This woman was really tied up. One day a
and excitement and the possibilities of new
man tried to fuck the woman. She loved him
consciousness, consciousness.
desperately so she wouldn't let him touch her
open her find her all gooky and bloody and screaming
don't you see it?
and angry hurt pain inside. Tell me how are the
right here. more important than any desperate
lobotomy children supposed to act? How are
love desperate possibility of going out farther,
the children who imbibed acid and downs and dex and
going out and out as far as possible
horse before they were born, who walk through the
going out as far as possible in freedom
radioactive rain, how are they supposed
going out as far as possible in freedom
to act? Tell me now why am I scared to fuck

99

going out as far as possible in freedom
you Dimwit? I'm all alone in outer space.

going out as far as possible in freedom,
I'M ALONE. THE SHIT WITH DISTINCTIONS BETWEEN
CRAZY AND SANE. DOES ANYONE KNOW WHAT'S
HAPPENING?

Dear Dimwit: There's really no plan. I don't understand what's happening. I
don't know how to talk. I like you.

Dear Hester: I don't want to run away with you and become a pirate. I just want
to save my soul.

Yours,
Dimwit

The shit hits the fan and everything becomes chaos and wild again.
There are no more secrets. Dimwit ascends the scaffold, the prison, the
place of punishment, caught at the height of agony, about to orgasm,
and says I'm the guy who fucked Hester. I'm the one you've all been
looking for. I'M A CRIMINAL.

The Scarlet Letter is the best book I've read locked up in the Persian
slave trader's room and I think everyone should read it. I'm not going
to tell you the ending of the book and spoil it for you. I think the author
Nathaniel Hawthorne felt that his readers should have fun reading his
stories. He didn't think anybody'd learn anything.

Hawthorne is a writer

Writers create what they do out of their own frightful agony and blood
and mushed-up guts and horrible mixed-up insides. The more they are
in touch with their insides the better they create. If you like a writer's
books read his books, the books aren't pure suffering; if you want to
publish/help the writer, do it business-like, but don't get into the writer's
personal life thinking if you like the books you'll like the writer. A
writer's personal life is horrible and lonely. Writers are queer so keep
away from them. I live in pain, but one day, Hawthorne said, I'm going
to be happy I'm going to be so happy even if I'm not alive anymore.
There's going to be a world where the imagination is created by joy not
suffering, a man and a woman can love each other again they can kiss
and fuck again (a woman's going to come along and make this world
for me even though I'm not alive anymore).
for the criminals, the agony of being rejected
and yet I will keep on being rejected, because I
will live only by my dreams
for those who being dreamers in this
fucked-up society must be unhappy criminals,

the lonely, the royal fuck.

Translating

Days or months or years. At one point Janey fell in love with the Persian slave trader because she had nothing else to feel. She had to write poetry to him.

Since she had no idea how to write poetry, she copied down all she could remember every pukey bit by the Latin poet Sextus Propertius which she had been forced to translate in high school.

On the desire for love
Slave Trader first with his lousy me imprisoned eyes
diseased by no before wants.
Then my strong he threw down the drain individuality
and head forced into the dust LOVE'S feet,
until me he had taught undiseased to be evil,
him evil, and without to live plan.
And my at this moment for a whole wanting this has been going strong year,
although be my enemy I am compelled to have the universe.

Psyche, by no fleeing labours hard times, Love
the ferocity of all-mighty she battled:
Sometimes the castle's her-mind-gone she would wander through shifting
    hallways
so she was wild meeting beasts;
physically beaten up. Worse: rejected
burnt in hidden corners she cried her eyes out.
In this way fast-changing she controlled the boy:
So much against love prayers and enduring help out.
Inside me monogoloid WANTING no knows techniques,
can't remember known, like before, to go roads.
As for you of drawing down who knows the trick the moon
and a work in magic sacred things doing,
right now one-I-want's mind turn round and make him at the thought become
    death-white of my lips even more!
Then I'll believe you both the stars and the waters
can saying have power over by poems.

As for you who too late me given up told the truth, friends,
Get for not quiet heart help.
Resolutely both the knives burning of my lust I'll accept and fires,
as long as the freedom whatever my lust wishes to say.
Poetry! Poetry!

Take me away
through the farthest races
Through the farthest waves
To where no men know the way.

You who're safe 'cause God or Luck lets you
Thirst desire and in always love may you remain safe.
Against me MY LOVE nights bears down sour
never ceases agony wanting Love.
I'm telling you: shun evil: Love fucks up
everyone and never becomes safe.
If any of you to these words don't listen
Too bad you'll return knowing suffering to my yourself poems.

Dying is one cure for love

Just like Ariadne's just dead on the empty shore
'Cause Theseus has abandoned her,
Just like Andromeda who's just gotten away from a horrible green sea-monster
Sleeps on the sharp spikes of rocks,
Just like from endless drinking, drugs, and sex
a Bacchante drops dead on sweet soft grass:
so I see lightly breathing
Slave Trader his bobbing resting on his arms head,
as I mean cruel drag my drunk feet
and outside the night, night becomes everything.

Not yet completely gaga,
I gently crawled up to his bed
to give him head
but the more horny I became,
the drunker I became:
my body was a battle between sex and booze.
Finally I dared my fingers touch his upper arm
kiss him, then breathing his breath my arms
but what if I woke him? I might harm him –
I know how horrible Slave Trader can be,
Temperamental and raging like all the Arabs I've seen –
but I couldn't leave him
I had to look at him
just like Argus had to keep
his thousand eyes pinned on a horny cow
('cause she was a beautiful female)
and so couldn't die or sleep.

Just as I'm unbuttoning from my hair tiny flowers
just as I'm laying on Persian Slave Trader's head
now the apples I've ripped off I'm putting in your hands
all to a thankless I'm giving sleep
gifts rolling off your slanted body
the few times I have to breathe
I try to stop, lest my breath be an augury
that'll bring you nightmares and fears
or worse,
lest I make a nightmare that'll take you away from me.

The windows turned-different-ways the moon running before
the moon flickering light delaying the world
(here unreality):
long beams your eyes revealed
and you said on that soft fixed bed arms:
'ARE YOU COMING BACK TO MY BED,
I KNOW YOU'RE COMING TO HARM ME,
ONLY 'CAUSE SOME GUY COVERED YOU WITH HIS SPERM
AND THEN REJECTED YOU?
WHERE D'YOU SPEND THE NIGHT
('CAUSE OBVIOUSLY YOU HAD NO DESIRE TO COME HOME UNTIL
        I DIED)?
I WISH YOU WOULD KNOW THIS NIGHTLY AGONY.
I WISH THE TABLES WERE TURNED!
JUST A FEW MINUTES AGO I WAS TRYING TO WAIT UP FOR YOU
        BY WATCHING TV
THEN BY WRITING POEMS
THEN BY COMPLAINING
THAT YOU CARE FOR EVERYONE ELSE BUT ME
THAT YOU COME HOME ONLY WHEN YOU HAVE TO
FINALLY FORGETFULNESS SWEPT HER ARMS ACROSS ME,
OBLIVION IS THE ONLY CURE FOR AGONY.'

The diseased

I want all of you out there to shut up.
I'm going to live the ways we want to live.
What do you want of me now?
Liver, blood, guts?
The only thing left is madness.

You too're gonna drive yourself to the pits:
You're gonna walk on coals through blazing fires:
You're gonna drink down the world's most painful poisons:
That's what wanting love is.

My man isn't like other men.
He can keep you in prison.
He can make you do anything.
I know why all of you want him.

But worse, what happens
if my Slave Trader
for some stupid reason
happens to like you?

Then you're screwed:
no more sleep.
Nor will he let you keep your eyes.
He compulsions alone can fetter forces wildness.
How many times a spineless being you'll run to

all the weaky friends you formerly despised,
tremulous sorrow will arise with tears shuddering
warts and pimples and fleas'll appear on your skin
all your wishes'll go, words are no more,
you'll never again know who you are.

You'll learn to serve him, girl, to be whatever he wants,
to disappear whenever he wants you to go.
You'll learn why people who want, want to die
why the whole world are lies.
Your rich parents ain't helping:
cause Love's more powerful than social climbing.
But if even small you have given footsteps of your failure
how quickly from such a reputation you will be a murmur!
Not I then I will be able comfort to bear to asking you

'Cause I'm sick too.
At this point sicker than you.
My disease is forever.
I know no comfort.
Since we're both maniacs,
let's be nice to each other.
I myself want to live.
I want to burn.
all I ask is no one loves me
in return.

But living is luxury

What does it help to go without life, hair
and in thin silk to move slink around,
why from the Persian trees perfumed arm-pits myrhh
you sell in these exotic yourself wares
your natural and self as you throw away art and culture?
Believe me, no your there's bettering figure
Love does not take tricks bare.
Love does not take tricks bare
Love is nowhere
Love is nowhere to be found
Wings are falling to the ground.

Not thus Castor Phoebe set on fire,
His brother by working not her sister,
Not by working Idas, and the horny source of discord to Sun
Marpessa finally away from her parents' home
no the Phrygian by fake she captured glitter a husband
dragged away by alien wheels:
not to those eagerness all the time to get control of men:
to them more than enough the form honesty.

But you're not honest
so I'm scared
you think I'm as cheap
as you are.

    Love loves luxuries,
        entwining and pleasant ways,
May lingering dreams bring happiness all your days.

To Slave Trader

Are you really crazy, doesn't you my love mean anything to?
Do you think I'm than icy more frigid Illyria?
To you so valuable, whoever she is, does that girl seem
That without me controlled by the winds to go you want?
You hear can the raging of oceans under bridges,
brave? on hard cold floor how to sleep you can know?
you, delicate and scared, survive chills and frosts
you can, not used to the slightest snow?
Let winter's be double the length of solstice
let be dead 'cause of late the sailors Pleiades
let no your from the Tyrrhenian be freed ropes muck
let not unfriendly my throw away winds pleas!

But, let there be no double winter dead winds,
if you on a speeding carry away the waves ship
from me prisoned on this empty and allow shore
you horror with clenched to threaten wrist.

But whatever happens whatever I, horror, you owe,
I hope Galatea brings you luck
may be sailed-by Ceraunian cliffs by oar felicitous
let in Oricos with calmness.
Me no one will take away from you
but I, life, in front of your house bitter puss will keep screaming
and not I may fail every sailor to ask passing-by,
'Tell me, in what port in prison my boy is?'
and I will cry, 'It's possible on Atracian he's set down shores
or it's possible in Hylaeia, he my future is.'

Janey wrote the following poems by herself

A throw of the dice never will abolish chance

I don't want nothing no more
I just wanna be left alone
I don want no cancer in my bones

      All you people in the streets
      You don wanna marry me

I don't know what or who's happening

PUKE GOOGOO ME
YUMN
SHITSHIT
SHITFACE ME

SHIT SMEARS ON MY HANDS I STINK I GOOGOO I STINK REAL GOOD I STINK WHEN I SMEAR SHIT ACROSS MY FACE LOTS I'M A OFFENDER END OF

me
me } who
me } is
this?

I CAN SCRAWL AND
I CAN CRAWL ~~ONLY MY~~
~~PEN~~ I I I I I I I I I
~~(I W)~~

I wish
that there was
a reason to be-
lieve this letter

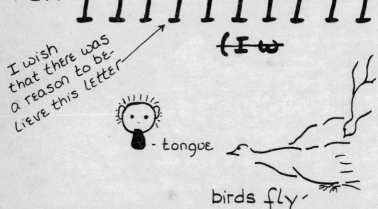

- tongue

birds fly

life GLOOGLOOGLOO

FUCK YOU SHIT
PISS

I don't feel like this no no I don
I care about loving I care about friends
Somewhere in me maybe I do
I've gotten really bored with my dreams

       Heat disease syphilis pregnancy
       All you creeps on the street get away from me

Well tell me what excites me
Well tell me what's important
I got nowhere to go to
There's no where that I want
Every time I want someone
       it's just a dream
Everything I want is a dream
And dreams stink more than anything

       Heart disease syphilis pregnancy
       All you creeps on the streets get away from me

No No No No No No NO NO NO
No No No No No No No
No No No No No No No No No No
No No No No No No No No No No
No No No No No No No No No No
No No No No No No No No No No
No No No No No No No No No No
No No No No No No No No No No
No No No No No No No No No No
No No No No No No No No No No
No No No No No No No No No No
No No No No No No No No No No
No No No No No No No No No No
No No No No No No No No No No
No No No No No No No No No No

Oh suck my cock honey suck my cock
That's what it's all about
I love how you turn yourself
Around and upside-down inside-out

                       for me
                       just for me
                       Oh I know
                       I must taste sweet

SUCK ME SUCK ME SUCK ME
SUCK ME SUCK ME SUCK ME
SUCK ME SUCK ME SUCK ME
SUCK ME SUCK ME SUCK ME

SUCK ME SUCK ME SUCK ME
SUCK ME SUCK ME SUCK ME
SUCK ME SUCK ME SUCK ME
SUCK ME SUCK ME SUCK ME
SUCK ME SUCK ME SUCK ME
SUCK ME SUCK ME SUCK ME
SUCK ME SUCK ME SUCK ME
SUCK ME SUCK ME SUCK ME
SUCK ME SUCK ME SUCK ME
SUCK ME SUCK ME SUCK ME

                         sex is sweet

now we've done with sex where we gonna go?

If you have no pleasure to live for, do you want to live?
grey grey everywhere grey
blucky blucky shiv
shifting shivers lurk in corners
corners of the nothing
everyone walking down the corridors
they think they are the outside.

in the corners there lurk
wars and poisons and liars and dirt
Just let me sleep under warmth crawl my eyes
Here is my lullabye:

                    If you have no mind to live for do you
                         want to live?

Now stars lights up my head
I want the whole world to burn up instantly
I want everyone and thing to be dead
And then there'll be, not begin, another world
Or so I've heard it said
I don't know.
Don't ask me nothing. I don't know. I'm in pain. Ask me something. I'm tell
you I hurt. I don't have any other answers.
I like fire.
I like glory.
I like stars.
I like moving as fast fast as I can on a speeding train especially when I'm in pain
I like moving until I get beyond and I'm insane
meaning I can't think anymore meaning I'm a robot meaning I'm a dodo meaning
I'm a creep meaning I'm stupid

This is one of my dreams.
It stinks 'cause it's more prevalent than any thing.

What can we do for each other?
I don't know.
Finally we go there
All alone.
What can we do for each other? We come back from that
loneliness and say
I've been there, I saw what I had to see and disappeared, it's OK.

Life is totally totally lonely
No matter how bad things get on the streets
Poverty hypocrisy greed the world
Beauty joy honesty and all the rest
One side of the coin or the other
The only real thing is that split (second) between life and death.

excitement and danger and blackness
I have that feeling and I feel
really happy, more than sex and
love and wealth, I like danger

continuing unchanging calm danger.
like a marriage that doesn't stop
only the whole world appears and disappears
and adventures pop up little blots

of madness, long stretches of nothing –
you don't know where you're at –
        (*Janey's slave poem:*
        Why am I existing?
        Just to be a slave?
        List of my slave duties:
        (1) Body slavery: I have to eat and get shelter so need money. Also my
body likes sex and rich food and I'll do anything for these.
        (2) Mind slavery: I want more than just money. I live in a partially
human world and I want people to think and feel certain ways about me.
So I try to set up certain networks, mental-physical, in time and space to
get what I want. (I also set up these networks to get money.) These
networks become history and culture (if they work) and as such, turn
against me and take away time and space. They tell me what to do.

        The world I perceive, everything I perceive are indicators of my boring
needs. Otherwise there's nothing. I might as well not exist.
        I don't think I care about anything. All my emotions, no matter how
passionate, are based on my needs.
        So I can figure out at this point how to make enough money get enough
people out of my life so I can relax sleep all the time every few days. Is
there any other reason besides negativity?
        Everything that has to do with this slave world makes me nauseous. All
my emotions and ideas (i.e. depending on unstable ground for a decision:
on any taste, on desire – that used to be the one I adored, on fascination,

111

on conceptual ideas, on inspiration, etc) make me sick and I want to die because I don't see anything else.

I don't even adore my emotions anymore. Whatever the fuck they are.

Living locked-up in a slave trader's room is easy. I mean you have the same emotions over and over again, the same thoughts, the same body, and after a while you see it's all in your mind: you're stuck to your mind. SLAVESLAVESLAVE.

The only thing I want is freedom. Let me tell you: I don't have any idea what that means. Depending on someone/something who's stable makes me happy. I don't find the external world stable unlike Francis Ponge. To base myself (?) on who/that which is stable and to have no regard for anything else makes me happy.)

DEFIES WHAT IS: NOT LIFE, BUT OBLIVION

DEFIES DEFIES DEFIES
NOT THOUGHT, BUT DEFIES

every howl of pain is a howl of defiance
every howl of pain is a howl of romance

driven beyond all measure of success,
driven so there are no limits to what I do

this immeasurable eating, hunger, moving
desire to lose consciousness,

go to the end
as if there's a beyond

driven beyond body desires into just desire,
not for what, just desire

DEFIANCE born

not made by environmental poverty

DEFIANCE SCORN BLOOD

(not just hallucination dispersed from agony – Mallarmé).

if this is the world # DEFIANCE

would become the whole world # DEFIANCE

the world would be a flame:

A TOTAL FLAME BURNING ITSELF UP
BLOOD AND FEAR AND GUTS
MY VISION

This is my vision of agony.
I no longer have to give the details of agony
'Cause everyone knows what they hear and see.

howling about nothing, howling about howling,
driven up against the wall to break;
nothing, says Mallarmé, takes place
a lie, a fake ruin but

in these places
         in which all reality turns into a howl and makes
         itself go away

something happens:

Ghouls

There are such things as ghosts. Death does not all things end.
and pale yellow from vanquished even shades escape their graves.
You see, Jane my was seen to lean over bed,
though near the roar of just-buried Broadway,
as finally I was about to fall asleep realizing love
just dead, my bed and new reigns of chill and pain.

The same she had which she took with her to the grave hairs,
the same eyes: one side of her dress was burned,
she had always worn on finger the ring its sapphire had eaten away fire,
surfaces Death's had turned black her lips' dirt.
Breathing and animation and these words she sent out: though
thumbbones were rattling her hands:

'You lousy creep, though you're the best can hope for a girl,
you already asleep how can?
Already you have forgotten our desperate crimes:
by my that nocturnal worn-down window thefts
through which dropped-down I to you by a rope hanging how many times
by the other snaking around your neck hand!
Often Our True Love occurred publicly; sex organs joined-up
made hot skins our streets.
Thou Love-Partnership Thou silent, whose obviously lying promises
not hearing has torn the deaf wind to pieces!
No man loved me, eyes, dying;
if you had loved me I could have gotten one more day.

Not even a priest gave a shit about my funeral,
but a broken brick fell on my dead brains.

'You matter most of all: who saw you bent over with grief at the funeral?
Who saw your black clothes? Who saw you cry?
If it pains you so much to leave this city, even for a funeral,
you could have at least told my death-car to drive more slowly.
Why did you pray, I know you hate me, the winds to rage over my grave?
Why didn't my grave smell of perfume?
Why didn't the most expensive roses in the world cover my putrifying body?
And why didn't you get all the priests in the world to try to mollify the demons
         raging in the death-room?
You can't manage to do anything. You're a goon. This is what you gotta do:'

This poem was written about 2,000 years ago and is evidence of how
things were and that nothing's changed. The world, that is, thoughts,
still stink.

'Lydamus KILL – get WHITE HOT the KNIFE –
I saw how, as from POISON SLUSH WHITE the wine I drank,
Nonas SECRETLY COVERED UP CLEVER BITCH the taste:
let reveal TORTURES how she STANK.
SHE who up to a few days ago in CHEAP AS THEY COME was
         SELLING her CUNT the NIGHTS
now in GOLD-AND-PURPLE GOWNS is DEIGNING TO STEP ON THE
         DIRT
and is making my SERVANTS WORK their ASSES off,
so they won't have time to REMEMBER even my appearance and
         HER TO CURSE:
Just my cause Petale brought to my tomb some flowers,
STUCK PINS IN CHAINS ON SHIT has been the OLD WOMAN;
is BEATEN UP and Lalage by TWISTED HUNG HAIRS
name because she DARED to my mention.
YOU let the WHORE BURN UP my picture the GOLD
frames so YOU TWO could MAKE some DOUGH out of my FUNERAL.'
My thoughts hurt me all the time. They're the truth.
'Not nevertheless I pursue, although you deserve it Slave Trader:
for long my in reigns were you.
I swear I, by the Fates by-no-one-able-to-be-reversed,
may Death-Dog thus to be gently bark,
that I was true to you. If I'm lying, that most-fearful-in-the-world snake my
will hiss at tomb and on top of bones lie.'
The realm of death:
'There are two filthy homes obtained-by-lottery across the river
The crowd turned one way or the other rows across the water.
One way: Clytemestra's addiction draws, or Cressa's:
counterfeit wood monster bull cock fuck sex.'

THIS IS DEATH
(something else besides horror exists):

'Lo: the other: wreathed part carried away and by light ships seized,
running quick in the water, flying, caresses where paradise's breeze
is your breath bursting into flames music the blood veins eyes
faster, like an orgasm growing and growing, burst abyss to endless size, I lie
      in a witch's trance.
              Just from your glance,
your breath is my breath.

'Andromeda and Hypermestre who could love
tell us their stories:

'I was an innocent girl. 'Cause my mother was jealous of me she pinned my arms
      against these sharp ice-bound crags, bruised me, and left me still alive.'
'My father told me and my sisters to kill our husbands. I couldn't 'cause
something in me shrivelled and vomitted then my father placed heavy chains
around
      my thin knees.':
thus by tears of death we heal the loves of life.

'I've wept enough tears now. I can no longer see of your crimes the treachery.
I'm just asking you one last thing
(if you have any love at all left for me
(if Chlorid's coke hasn't made you mean),

'(1.) Nurse in her trembling, no more desires, years are claws
Partheni: she was competent and not avaricious,
please give her pleasure, and my Nanny who loved her work
let her mirror not reflect a strange mistress.

'(2.) Whatever songs you made in my name
burn them up: fame can no longer be mine.
(3.) Just put on my tomb some ivy ripe with berries gently intertwining with
vines,
and branchy the East River where garbage spreads on cement
never, thanks to Rockefeller, will money grow stale,
(4.) this epitaph scribble on the middle of some wall
SCRIBBLE it so that even the dumbest coked-up businessman can read:

        HERE LIES GOLDEN JANEY GOLDEN CITY
        WHOSE DEAD BODY YOUR GOLD FEEDS
        DO NOT EVER TURN AWAY FROM LOVE'S DREAMS
        ALL EXISTENCE HAS A GOLDEN SHEEN

'This is what we call life:
by an unstable night we are carried, night is freeing from
      our self's prison all Shades
Who wander, for Cerberus casts the bolt away.

'This is what we call death:
At lights' rise all of us must to Death's swamp return.
No escape: we are conveyed: the boatman counts his load.
No matter what love what joy what agony you know alive, soon alone
you will be dead with me, and I will rub bones love with mingled bones.'

After all these fits of anger and jealousy and craving had finished, she died: between our kisses slipped away that shade of mine.

Cancer

The Persian slave trader finally decided Janey was ready to hit the streets. She had demonstrated that she knew how to make impotent men hard, give blow and rim jobs, tease, figure out exactly what each man wants without asking him, make a man feel secure, desirable, and wild. Now she was beautiful. There was only one thing wrong, at least according to the Persian slave trader. At this moment he found out that she had cancer.

Having cancer is like having a baby. If you're a woman and you can't have a baby 'cause you're starving poor or 'cause no man wants anything to do with you or 'cause you're lonely and miserable and frightened and totally insane, you might as well get cancer. You can feel your lump, and you nurse, knowing it will always get bigger. It eats you, and, gradually, you learn, as all good mothers learn, to love yourself.

Janey was learning to love herself. Everything was shooting out of her body like an orgasming volcano. All the pain and misery she had been feeling, crime and terror on the streets had come out. She was no longer totally impotent and passive about her lousy situation. Now she could do something about the pain in the world: she could die.

Janey had always been the first in her group to explore whatever frontier presented itself. She had been the first one in her family to hate her family. She had been the first girl in her class to fuck. She had been the first in her class to say No and run away. Now she had cancer.

The slave trader abandoned Janey. 'Oh please, Slave Trader, come back. I want you. I need you. I want to marry you.'

She wandered frantically around the apartment.

By accident, he dialled the wrong number and called her up on the phone.

'I want to marry you.'

'Don't be silly. That's so foolish. Anyway I'd have to come back to the apartment to marry you and I'm not coming back.'

She took up her pencil stub for the last time and wrote down 'I need love'. She lay down on her stomach on the floor. Dusty late afternoon sun was flooding through the western window. She fantasized that she would kill herself by sticking a razor blade through her wrist.

She decided there's no need to kill yourself if you've got cancer. As she slowly walked down the open back stairs of the Sutton Avenue apartment building, she saw a passport and a paid ticket to that place of magic, Tangier.

A journey to the end of the night

Tangier

(*Excerpts from Janey's diary while she's in Tangier.*)
This time when I run after a man who doesn't want me, I'm *really* going to run after him.

I'm sitting in the Café Tangier and smoking a cigarette.

'Look,' my friend Michal says to me, 'that's Jean Genet!'

Jean Genet walks slowly, his hands are in his pockets, he stares as if he's not seeing anything, eyes fixed, at this café.

He stops. He stands still for a few moments. He looks like I always imagined he'd look. Then he swivels half-way around and looks at Café Fuentes' canape. He chooses the Café Central.

I have to meet him.

I tell Michal. He tells me not to meet him.

'Why? Is he horrible?'

'He doesn't like to meet people and he won't talk to you. He lives like a hermit. Everyone's told me that.'

I have to meet Genet. It's that simple. It's not often something's simple. If Genet refuses to talk to me I'll walk away so I won't be hurt. I watch him sit down in the Café Central and start talking to a young boy.

An hour has passed. Conversations, whispered at the edges of my ears, go on and on. One of my eyes is on the human goats and dogs milling around in the square; one on Genet's bald head. The minute he moves, I move.

I ask someone the time.

'Three o'clock.'

I say to my friend, 'I'm going.'

He cries, 'You're out of your mind.'

As I'm walking towards Genet I hear: 'You can't throw yourself on a famous writer like Genet, on a man who'll reject you. You have to learn to control yourself.

Genet wrote: 'Loneliness and poverty made me not walk but fly. For

117

I was so poor, and I have already been accused of so many thefts, that when I leave a room too quietly on tiptoe, holding my breath, I am not sure, even now, that I'm not carrying off with me the holes in the curtains or hangings.'

Genet's walking. I walk slowly towards him. He stops, about three feet in front of me, his hands in his pockets, swaying slightly and leaning forward.

I know I'm looking too hard at him. I say, 'You're Monsieur Genet, aren't you?'

He hesitates for a minute. He notices me but he doesn't want to. 'Who are you?'

For a second I can't speak. 'I'm a writer.'

He holds out his right hand to me. 'Enchanté.'

I take it. As we walk up the Siaghines I ask him if he likes Tangier. 'Ça va,' he murmurs.

'Do you think it's beautiful, the most beautiful city in the world?'

'Certainly not. What gave you that idea?'

'Everyone says so.'

'In Asia there are many more beautiful cities.'

During the twenty minutes it takes us, me and Jean Genet, to walk from the square of cafés to the Hotel Minzah, we talk about writers, writing, and some of the problems of publication. 'I don't like institutions,' he says. We're standing in front of the Minzah, he gives me his hand and adds, 'I always take a nap around now. Tomorrow, if you like, we can meet at the Café el Menara. Around two in the afternoon?'

Today is a day like any other day. I don't know any reason I should feel differently. I'm sitting in the Café el Menara. Will he come or not? For me it's the previous day because what I want to happen hasn't yet happened.

He walks along the white dust, slowly, like he did yesterday. I lift my hand. His eyes light up and he smiles. I stand up. We shake hands for a long time.

He's warmer to me than he was yesterday. He sits down. He orders a glass of mint tea and I do the same. Some people walk by me and disappear. Some walk back and forth as if they're looking for someone. These are mainly young beggars looking for tourists.

'I don't understand why they haven't translated any of your books into Arabic,' I say.

'I don't know. No one has asked me to do it. Maybe some day they will, maybe not. It depends on whether my things interest them at that point. Personally, I think the Arabs are extremely sensitive when it comes to questions of morality.'

'Did you have a hard time writing your first novel?'

'No, not very. I wrote the first fifty pages of *Nôtre Dame des Fleurs* in prison. And when I was transferred to another gaol they somehow got left behind. I did everything I could to get them back, but it was hopeless. And so I wrapped myself in my blanket and rewrote the fifty pages straight off.'

'I know you didn't start to write until you were thirty,' I say. 'Thirty-two or thirty-three.'

'That's right.'

'You haven't written anything for several years, have you? Do you consider your literary silence and your assumption of a political position part of your writing?'

'Literally I've said what I've had to say. Even if there was anything more to add, I'd keep it to myself. That's how things are. There's no absolute yes and there's no absolute no. I'm sitting here, with you now, but I might easily not be.'

Later he tells me a story about Tangier. 'I knew a young sailor who was working on a ship in France. The maritime court of Toulon had exiled to Tangier an ensign who had turned over to the enemy the plans of some weapon or battle strategy or boat. Treason, at its best, is that act which defies the whole populace, their pride, their morality, their leaders and slogans. The newspaper said the ensign acted ". . . out of a taste for treason." Next to this article was the picture of a young, very handsome officer. The young sailor was taken with this picture and still carries it with him. He was so carried away that he decided to share the exile's fate. "I shall go to Tangier," he said to himself, "and perhaps I may be summoned among the traitors and become one of them."'

We're sitting in the Café el Menara and I tell Genet some of the things that happened in my last weeks in New York City:

'President Carter is the pillar of American society. He's almost fifty-three years old. WORN OUT by DECAying practices, he looks like a SKELETON. He's HAIRY as a RAT, flat-backed, his ASS looks like TWO DIRTY RAGS FLAPPING OVER A PISS-STAINED WALL. Because he gets whipped so much the SKIN of his ASS is DEAD and you can KNEAD it and SLICE it. He will never FEEL a thing. President Carter's centre is an enormous HOLE. This HOLE'S DIAMETER, COLOUR, and ODOUR resemble a NEW YORK CITY SUBWAY TOILET that hasn't been CLEANED for THREE weeks. It DOESN'T resemble any ASSHOLE I've ever seen. PRESIDENT CARTER because HE'S a QUEER LITTLE PIG leaves a THREE-INCH WALL of SHIT around his ASSHOLE. And below his BELLY, WRINKLED as it is LIVID and GUMMY, he has a shrivelled little

119

thing, a dried apricot pit that Richard Nixon VOMITED up, a COCK. A BRIGHT RED HEAD sticks out of this apricot pit because at age thirty the President CIRCUMSIZED himself. All MEN who FUCK ought to circumsize themselves and CUT their COCKS OFF. MEN get CIRCUMSIZED so their COCKS will stay CLEAN when they FUCK; PRESIDENT CARTER'S CIRCUMSIZED so he can make his COCK even FILTHIER by COVERING IT with a layer of SCUM, DRIED GREEN PISS, and SHIT. PRESIDENT CARTER is DISGUSTING in his HEAD and in his BODY. His TASTES are MORE DISGUS-TING and his SMELL does not PLEASE everybody. As a POLITI-CIAN HE HAS many PROBLEMS.

'President Carter needs THREE HOURS OF STIMULATION TO ORGASM. This STIMULATION has to consist of PERVERTED CRUEL SADISTIC and endlessly PROLONGED EVENTS. EVEN THEN it DOESN'T usually WORK because the agents of these events run away, faint, and die TOO SOON. When that HAPPENS, PRESI-DENT CARTER gets VERY ANGRY; foam SPURTS FROM his mouth; he becomes epileptic. When he's EPILEPTIC, he can ORGASM.

'You see our President is a man of many MOODS. These MOODS change from second-to-second and he has NO CONTROL over them. When the President's in a MOOD, he CAN'T think or feel anything else. This MENTAL DISORDER and his ALCOHOLISM have turned HIM at this point into an IMBECILE. HE is fond of saying to the dignitaries of other countries that he would rather BE AN IMBECILE THAN ANYTHING ELSE.

'President Carter is a DECADENT man. Those who know him personally are convinced that he owes his present political POWER to TWO or THREE INEXCUSABLE MURDERS.

'I was wandering around the streets with cancer.

'I didn't have any money or know anybody. Although I didn't feel like a bum, I was hanging out on the Bowery with leftover humans.

'One night I wandered into a rock-n-roll club named CBGB's. The lights went boomp boomp boomp the drum went boomp boomp boomp the floor went boomp boomp boomp. Boomp boomp boomp entered my feet. Boomp boomp boomp entered my head. My body split into two bodies. I was the new world. I was pounding. Then there was these worms of bodies, white, covered by second-hand stinking guttered-up rags and knife-torn leather bands, moving sideways HORIZONTAL wriggling like worms who never made it to the snake-evolution stage, we only reproduce, we say, if you cut us apart with a knife, the slimy saxophone and the singer who's too burned out to stick a banana in his cock flows away all was gooky amorphous ambiguous nauseous

undefined spystory no reality existed so why bother to do anything?
BOOM BOOM was reality, slimy slimy BOOM BOOM slimy slimy.

'WE DON'T GIVE A SHIT ABOUT YOU IT'S NOT THAT WE
WANT YOUR MONEY, YOU HAVE MORE MONEY THAN
US, YOU HAVE MORE EVERYTHING THAN US, YOU
THINK WE WANT YOUR MONEY AND WE WANT TO KILL
YOU, WE DON'T
  'WE DON'T WANT YOUR MONEY IT'S SEVEN O'CLOCK
IN THE MORNING WE'RE TOO SCREWED UP WE LIVE ON
THE EDGE WE LIVE ON EVERY EDGE CONCEIVABLE AND
ADD A FEW WE ARE SHIT
  'THIS'S NOT ANGER
  'THIS IS NOT ANY EMOTION IT IS LIVING AT THE
EDGE, AT EVERY EDGE, MIGHT AS WELL HATE EVERY-
BODY. WE DON'T WANT YOUR MONEY WE WANT
(1) TO BE SCREWED NOW AND THEN
(2) TO GET SOME LOVE IN OUR LIVES
(3) TO HAVE FREE HOSPITALS
(4) TO HAVE THE CONSTANT OPTION OF ONE
UNPOISONED MEAL A DAY WE ARE ALL SCREWED-UP
AND WE HAVE WANTS. WE HAVE OTHER WANTS. LOVE
LOVE LOVE. THAT'S WHY WE ARE SCREWED-UP.
                    OH YES
              LOVE LEADS TO DEATH.
  'YOU WILL NEVER UNDERSTAND THIS BECAUSE YOU
DON'T LIVE HOW WE LIVE. ACTUALLY YOU DO, BUT
YOUR DIET PILLS, AND ADULTEROUS SNEAKY ONE-
MINUTE GENITAL DRIBBLES, AND MONEY-FRANTIC-
NESS AND LOVE OF MEDIA AND PSYCHIATRISTS AND
EVERYTHING THAT IS ANYTHING HAVE SO TAKEN OVER
YOUR MINDS THAT YOU CAN'T SEE AROUND THEM, SEE
THAT YOU ARE ACTUALLY SCUM, TYPICAL NOTHINGS
WHO CAN'T FIGURE OUT HOW EVEN TO ALLOW *BEING
LOVED* WITHOUT TOTALLY FREAKING AND GETTING
HYSTERICAL AND DESTROYING BUILT-UP ROOMS,
SCREWED 'CAUSE WE CAN'T FIGURE OUT HOW TO BE
ALWAYS DIFFERENT (WITHOUT HABITS) – JUST LIKE
YOU. WE ARE ALL ALIKE WE ARE ALL IMMACULATELY
CRAZY.
  'NOW THAT THIS IS THE NATURE OF REALITY
THIS IS WHAT HAS TO HAPPEN:
(1) I NEED LOTS OF LOVE

> (2) YOU'RE GOING TO GIVE US ALL YOUR MONEY 'CAUSE
> YOU HATE YOURSELVES AND 'CAUSE YOU KNOW
> (3) ALL POWER SYSTEMS SELF-DESTRUCT WITH THE
> ADVENT OF ROBOT CANASTA PLAYERS WHO SHOW THE
> GIRLS WHAT THEY'RE REALLY LIKE. I'M GOING TO
> SLEEP. GOODNIGHT.'

*THIS MESSAGE IS A PUBLIC SERVICE PAID FOR BY THE CHASE
MANHATTAN BANK OF NORTH AMERICA*

'I didn't want anyone to notice me 'cause I was blind so I crawled under the splinters of the bar. The music stopped. A lot of feet passed by. Some of them by accident kicked me. One kicked me too hard.
    ' "Do you want to fuck me, scumbag?" President Carter said to me.
    ' "I can't fuck."
    ' "You've got syphilis?"
    ' "I've got cancer."
    ' "Gee." He put his arms around me and kissed me.

I USED TO BE UNHAPPY
OH YES
I LIVED IN THE CORNER OF A ROOM
THEN YOU CAME ALONG AND FUCKED THE SHIT
    OUT OF ME
I WON'T BE UNHAPPY AGAIN

SPRING IS A COCK THAT'S HARD
OH YES
I KNOW YOU'RE A SECRET TERRORIST
'CAUSE LOVE LEADS TO DEATH

I WON'T EVER BE UNHAPPY AGAIN
THOUGH IT'S BEEN A WEEK SO YOUR LOVE'S
    ALMOST OVER
THE WORLD'S ABOUT TO EXPLODE
TERRORISTS NEED NO MORE COVER
OH YES LOVE LEADS TO DEATH
OH YES

    'I couldn't hear any of that political music shit I just wanted to kiss the guy again and again. The music made it so you couldn't hear the words and the music itself was so loud music couldn't be heard
you weren't hearing
this is beyond hearing
you is just vibrations so there's no difference between self and music.

'President Carter was just THERE, that's the only way I can describe it. I didn't want to fall in love with him because I didn't want to put something in my life, but he was screwing me so GOOD and beating me up that I knew I was going to fall in love with him. I did everything I could to avoid President Carter. I dropped out of everything. It's hard to drop out of a nightclub filled with teenage hoods and teenage bums, but that's what I did. I roamed the streets of New York. The streets were black and full of garbage. I ROAMED the streets, not WALKED the streets because I was a cat. Cats adore being loved, but they don't want to be in prison.

'Cars drove by me. Big rich Cadillacs and little snooky sports cars, the grey cars and the red cars, each car had a personality. "Go to hell" a big black car said to me. "Whrr whrr," "race, race" and "toot toot" are what the cars said to each other. On the whole cars like each other and they don't like people. A few cars liked me. A grey car whose behind was longer than its front and which was so smashed it looked like it should be dirty black smiled at me. A long sleek light green car whistled. "Whoo whoo. I could make a few dollars out of HER."

'Then there were no cars. Two people passed by, men, older males, ages say forty-five and up, bellies large, cocks small with slight dribbles, clothes wool, mouths open. The street was empty again.

'Actually it had always been empty. It was me. I was a disjunct.

'You can smoke a cigarette. A cigarette is thin, long, and it contains fire. You can puff the fire. No one will arrest you. No cop cares. Even if you don't have money, there are butts on the street. Most waiters will give you a match. You see, there's no trouble. It's best to do things there's no trouble about. Being scum, being disgusting, lonely, alone, not bothering anybody, not wanting, being dark, in the dark.

'I tried masturbating. I tried.

'These are secret letters where I can say things that . . . secret (secret). In there get in there. Dark like a canal President Carter I love you. Whoops that's the wrong one. Let's try again. I love you. I have to get beyond that one. The tunnel is my cunt. That's the first bump. A big I love you. I don't want you to go away. I want to be in you, there, in between your right Presidential arm and the skin on your side PUKE MUSHY MUSHY I GO MUSHY I AM REPULSIVE. NO I AM HOT. Now we've got it I AM HOT. Oh please fuck me for the rest of my life. The rest of my life means fuck me right now. As hard as you can.

'OK. I'm telling you exactly what I feel 'cause you never say anything. I don't feel anything. What do I feel?

'I've got cancer. Cancer is the outward condition of the condition of being screwed-up. I am such a total mess, that is: a priori askew to the world/the nature of things/therefore: myself, askew to myself, that I will never live without pain. I can't help but do everything wrong. Every incident reveals this. I'm saying I'm screwed up because I want you to tell me you love me.

'I know who you are. Go away, President Carter. Leave me alone.

'Our affair had come to a crisis. President Carter had to return to Washington so we had nowhere to sleep together because I couldn't sleep in the White House and he wouldn't sleep on the streets. Huge hickies covered my neck and back. I had asked President Carter to beat me up while we fucked and he had said OK, but we had nowhere to fuck.

'The President didn't mind having nowhere to fuck, only I minded. He said all that mattered was there was political disruption in the air. I *had* to tell him:
FUCK YOU. GO AWAY. I'M LEAVING YOU. I'M GETTING AWAY FROM YOU. WHENEVER THERE'S PAIN, I WALK OUT. WHENEVER SOMETHING GOES WRONG, I WALK OUT,
but I didn't. I stuck to him.

'I wrote these things about terrorism:

'Terrorism is not being conscious. Terrorism is letting happen what has to happen. Terrorism is letting rise up all that rises up like a cock or a flower. Tremendous anger and desire. Terrorism is straightforwardness. You are a child. Only you don't imitate. For these reasons terrorists never grow up.

'Terrorism is a way to health. Health is the lusting for infinity and dying of all variants. Health is not stasis. It is not repression of lusting or dying. It is no bonds. The only desire of any terrorist is NO BONDS though terrorists don't desire. Their flaming jumping passions are infinite, but are not them.

'No bonds.

'For these reasons terrorism and health are inseparably bound.

'Terrorism can be fun. As far as big goals go, it has no goals so you remain slum-under; it has lots of little goals. You don't have to live any way. You don't have to believe in any certain thing or world. You don't have to give a goddamn and yet all the passion the burning the disappearance of is in terrorism. Terrorists believe in nothing and everything; serious terrorists every time they kidnap someone don't believe they're changing anything.

'One of the most destructive forces in the world is love. For the following reason: The world is a conglomeration of objects, no, of events and the approachings of events towards objects, therefore of becoming stases static stagnant, of all that is unreal. You get in the world, you get your daily life your routine doesn't matter if you're rich poor legal illegal, you begin to believe what doesn't change is real, and love comes along and shows all these unchangeable for ever fixtures to be flimsy paper bits. Love can tear anything to shreds.

'PRESIDENT CARTER, it isn't sweet and it hurts. Pain is the world. I don't have anywhere to run. I want to go out in a blaze of light and scream. Stick your cock in me as hard as you can. Hurt me. Beat me. If you beat me hard enough I'll never leave you and I'll do everything you say. Otherwise I run away. I run away whenever I can. You take me by the hips in back of me your cock pounds steady. BAM BAM BAM. I start to come. Your cock moves harder, faster. You're hurting my cunt. Energy shoots up from the base of my spine to the top of my head. Every time cock hits in, energy path set off. You become out-of-control getting into me as much as you can. I'm beyond coming. In a space of consciousness and unconsciousness. Black. No more pain like no more coming. I never knew I could get here. You stop. When cock out of me, I come down enough to start coming. Gradually I stop coming.

Sex you're gonna stop. I hate you.
You made me vomit and throw up and act crazy.
Now I'm sick.
You never say anything to me at all, nothing at all.
I don't know what goes on in your mind.
I don't ask you to come here, to the street. Now everything's changed.

'EVERY POSITION OF DESIRE, NO MATTER HOW SMALL, IS CAPABLE OF PUTTING TO QUESTION THE ESTABLISHED ORDER OF A SOCIETY; NOT THAT DESIRE IS ASOCIAL; ON THE CONTRARY. BUT IT IS EXPLOSIVE; THERE IS NO DESIR-ING-MACHINE CAPABLE OF BEING ASSEMBLED WITHOUT DEMOLISHING ENTIRE SOCIAL SECTIONS.

'HELLO, I'M ERICA JONG. ALL OF YOU LIKED MY NOVEL *FEAR OF FLYING* BECAUSE IN IT YOU MET REAL PEOPLE. PEOPLE WHO LOVED AND SUFFERED AND LIVED. MY NOVEL CONTAINED REAL PEOPLE. THAT'S WHY YOU LIKED IT. MY NEW NOVEL *HOW TO DIE SUCCESSFULLY* CONTAINS THOSE SAME CHARACTERS. AND IT CONTAINS TWO NEW CHARACTERS. YOU AND ME. ALL OF US ARE REAL. GOODBYE.

'HELLO, I'M ERICA JONG. I'M A REAL NOVELIST. I WRITE BOOKS THAT TALK TO YOU ABOUT THE AGONY OF AMERICAN LIFE, HOW WE ALL SUFFER, THE GROWING PAIN THAT MORE AND MORE OF US ARE GOING TO FEEL. LIFE IN THIS COUNTRY IS GOING TO

GET MORE HORRIBLE, UNBEARABLE, MAKING US MANIACS 'CAUSE
MANIA AND DEATH WILL BE THE ONLY DOORS OUT OF PRISON
EXCEPT FOR THOSE FEW RICH PEOPLE AND EVEN THEY ARE
AGONIZED PRISONERS IN THEIR MASKS, THE PATHS, THE WAYS
THEY HAVE TO ACT TO REMAIN WHO THEY ARE. YOU THINK
BOOZE SEX COKE RICH FOOD ETC ARE DOORS OUT? TEMPORARY
OBLIVION AT BEST. WE NEED TOTAL OBLIVION. WHAT WAS I
SAYING? OH YES, MY NAME IS ERICA JONG I WOULD RATHER BE
A BABY THAN HAVE SEX. I WOULD RATHER GO GOOGOO. I WOULD
RATHER WRITE GOO-GOO. I WOULD RATHER WRITE: FUCK YOU
UP YOUR CUNTS THAT'S WHO I AM THE FUCK WITH YOUR MONEY
I'M NOT CATERING TO YOU ANYMORE I'M GETTING OUT I'M
GETTING OUT I'M RIPPING UP MY CLOTHES I'M RIPPING UP MY
SKIN I HURT PAIN OH HURT ME PAIN AT THIS POINT IS GOOD DO
YOU UNDERSTAND? PAIN AT THIS POINT IS GOOD. ME ERICA JONG
WHEE WOO WOO I AM ERICA JONG I AM ERICA JONG I FUCK ME
YOU CREEP WHO'S GOING TO AUSTRALIA YOU'RE LEAVING ME
ALL ALONE YOU'RE LEAVING ME WITHOUT SEX I'VE GOTTEN
HOOKED ON SEX AND NOW I'M

'MY NAME IS ERICA JONG. IF THERE IS GOD, GOD IS DISJUNCTION
AND MADNESS.

                    YOURS TRULY,

                    Erica Jong

'I is now she. She, Janey. Shit, Janey, shit. I'm glad someone's explaining President Carter to me. Why do I write this down? I read it. I
might as well admit to everything I do. "Me"? "Everything"?

'Janey wants President Carter. President Carter may or may not want
Janey. Actually President Carter wants Janey, but Janey wants to believe
President Carter doesn't want Janey because it's more difficult for Janey
to deal with a situation (Janey can't deal with any situation) which isn't
a mirror of her desire. Janey isn't me. Which of the two do I think is
real?

'Janey sees too many people. Now that Janey has a boyfriend, Janey
knows too many people these people are too many because she has to
talk to them because of her boyfriend.
    'Each person is an asking, a peculiar kind of hole asking some very
definite energy from Janey. Janey is very scared of people because she's
scared she's going to hurt someone. So what? She has to give a lot of
energy to giving each person the exact right kind of energy.
    'By the end of the evening she is nothing.

'President Carter abandoned me. It took me three days to realize this. Then I wrote him a letter.

'I don't care what you do when I don't see you, etc, but when I make this effort to see you, within a few minutes you walk out or else there are lots of people and by the time we're alone either I'm asleep or you're drunk. So we're never alone together for more than a few minutes and we don't really talk or learn about each other and become better (or worse) friends.

'I think we should talk about our peculiarities 'cause I think the situation's getting a little weird and I'm getting confused. I know I'm very peculiar and hard-to-be-with. But I really am confused because you don't talk to me and you don't fuck me yet you want me around.

'You're gone and there's no more love left in the world. I can't deal with you in my mind anymore. I hope I don't ever run into you again even if you are President of the United States. Even before you left – knowing that you had power over me and were going to leave me – that future made us ghosts. That's how I felt. I hurt. That's how I feel. That is: either I judge and blame and Hell exists, or I don't judge and everything's OK. Either this is a time for total despair or it's a time of madness. It's ridiculous to think that mad people will succeed where intellectuals, unions, Wobblies, etc, didn't, I think they will.

'I don't want to stop talking to you, Mr President. You are my home and now you're gone I have no place to stay. I'd rather have nowhere to stay: all America wants somewhere to stay an image stasis. I'd like to say that everything I do, every way I've seemed to feel, however I've seemed to grasp at you, are war tactics.'

Through the arches of the Café Zagora I can see the white area where the distant Atlas mountain tops fade into the white sky. Rows of walls rise to rows of walls and upwards.

Genet asks me if I have a passport.

Why do I need a passport?

He wants to know if I can travel.

I explain I got to Tangier illegally. I don't think I can travel.

Genet's going to leave Tangier. He wants me to go with him.

I'm more excited than I've been in a long time. 'Since I'm dark enough to pass for Moroccan,' I tell Genet, 'can you help me get a Moroccan passport?'

A long line of people are inside the Government Centre building, in rags, with faces of the dead. A skeleton runs out of a grey office and shouts at all of us. His whole attitude is nervous and shaking and mean. Genet walks up to him and talks to him. When Genet returns to me, he says, 'We'll have to come back here in an hour.'

An hour later the office is black and horrible, more crowded. The skeleton official is cursing at the poor people and pushing them into lines. Bit by bit the poor people go away. I don't know how I'm going to get a passport. The skeleton government official is still cursing the poor people, those shuffling hollow rags, even though they're no longer here. Genet murmurs to me: 'He's a pig, a brute, insulting and shoving people around!'

The skeleton pig is still saying that if these people don't give him enough money for a passport, he'll lock them up. These people are all gone. Finally, when the building's being locked up, the skeleton pig tells Genet that I can get a passport if I have the proper papers.

A fine rain is blowing across the sand of the street. 'That man doesn't want papers, he wants a fistful of banknotes, doesn't he?'

I don't answer. We walk for half an hour on the boulevard. Then Genet buys a few newspapers and some magazines, and goes back to the hotel.

Today we got the passport. We found a friend who knew a government official and we paid. Genet's giving a small party in his hotel room. I'm standing opposite Genet.

'Why're you taking her with you?' pointing to me a famous older male friend of Genet's asks him.

'Oh, she works for me. She's a gardener.'

I want to laugh in the guy's face because Genet doesn't have a house or a garden.

'She's your servant.'

Genet thinks about this. 'I didn't mean to mislead you,' he says. 'I don't consider anyone a servant.'

The strange man smiles. I'm accepted in this world. I shake hands with Genet.

Later on the same man asks Genet where we're planning to travel.

'I don't know, I know I can't go to the United States, their government won't let me in again, and I can't go to the Soviet Union for the same reason.

In *Journal du Voleur* Genet wrote:

Movies and novels have made Tangier into a scary place, a dive where gamblers haggle over the secret plans of all the armies in the world. From the American coast, Tangier seemed to me a fabulous city. It was the very symbol of treason.

Here all the big men I've known, all the men who've hurt me because they had no feelings or who've offered me affection and then stamped on me the minute I reached for it, who've swung their monstrous cocks in front of my face and then laughed when I begged to touch, TRAITORS FASCISTS WHO NEED TO CONNIVE all of you live in this fabulous city. I worship you. I can't fuck anyone else. It's not your cocks, but it's your dishonesty your need to manoeuvre and lie the way most people walk down a street that form those entanglements I call ADVENTURE. Everything else is dead. When I'm with one of you I'm alive and otherwise I don't give a shit.

I don't call having some young boy between my sheets SEX. I rarely let myself go for young or nice boys because I know I'll get bored. I want the textures of your lives, the complexities set up by betrayals and danger – I like men who hurt me because I don't always see myself, I have my egotism cut up. I love this: I love to be beaten up and hurt and taken on a joy ride. This SEX – what I call SEX – guides my life. I know this Sex of traitors, deviants, scum, and schizophrenics exists. They're the ones I want.

In Egypt, the end

Genet takes Janey with him and they travel through North Africa, through Rabat across the inland through Fés to Oujda, through Tiemsen the city of oases, straight north to Oran, and then, just as summer hits, along the Algerian sea border through Algiers and Bougie down to the mysterious city of Constantine.

In Constantine Genet makes Janey put on the double black dress of an Arabian woman. A dress about twelve feet in length thrown over the head, belted around the waist, then pulled upward at the belt, so three skirts fall from the belt to the ground. Two eyeholes permit the woman to see.

From here Genet and Janey travel along dust-filled roads, through small villages almost nameless, to Tripoli, and along the seacoast through Agheila, through Derna, through Tobruk, as fast as they can, until they reach Alexandria.

Scene 1
Inside an Alexandrian brothel. All the women's houses in the Arab section are brothels, so to speak, but this is *especially* a brothel because its women cater to foreigners. In Alexandria women are low and these are the lowest there are. For them there is no class struggle, no movements of the left, and no right-wing terror because all the men are fascists. All the men own all the money. A man is a walking mass of gold.

The rooms are done in gold. Extremely thick tapestries cover the floor. A large silver cask, lying on a small wood table, decorated on its outside by leaves and branches contains layers of incense and honey. The scene is two whores talking professionally. It is clear that the whores regard what most people regard as (them)selves as images. Sex, that unblocked meeting of selves, is the most fake thing there is.

At the end of this scene a crippled drunken lobotomy case walks into the brothel. He controls the whores because he is a man.

Janey to herself: Genet doesn't know how to be a woman. He thinks all he has to do to be a woman is slobber. He has to do more. He has to get down on his knees and crawl mentally every minute of the day. If he wants a lover, if he doesn't want to be alone every single goddamn minute of the day and horny so bad he feels the tip of his clit stuck in a porcupine's quill, he has to perfectly read his lover's mind, silently, unobtrusively, like a corpse, and figure out at every changing second what his lover wants. He can't be a slave. Women aren't just slaves. They are whatever their men want them to be. They are made, created by men. They are nothing without men.

I have to decide what the world is from my own loneliness.

Scene 2

Janey's lying in the dirt outside Genet's ritzy hotel and dreaming of fucking rock-n-roll stars. First she and James Frogface, whom she met while she was living on the streets of New York City, are standing, holding hands, in a large room. Or they're in a black rock-n-roll club (CBGB's). They walk down the block together, two blocks, to his place. She's surprised she's going home with James because she hadn't thought she was hot for him and also thought he was too young for her taste. Surprisingly now she's kissing James her hands are running up and down his back she's turned on hot shivery steaming WOW! Her legs spread open as she sinks on to the bed woom her arms close around those thin shoulders. It feels wonderful. Not weird or sort-of-good or not-really-all-there. Just straight wonderful. He fucks hard. He likes to fuck. No need thought fucks everything up. Good. Good. When she meets him at CBGB's at night, her hand strokes his thigh through his thin black sharkskin pants, she realizes she knew it was OK to touch him.

She dreams she's fucking someone more famous than Frogface. More shivers run through her nerves: loss of thought, trust. Trust is loss of thought. Janey and the blond rock-n-roller are madly in love. When she wakes she can't remember who he was and what the sex was like. She doesn't know what to do with herself.

Genet enters and tells Janey she's totally ugly. Because she's so loud no one wants to talk to her. She's the worst kind of Jewish mama pig. She's vulgar and unrestrained and that is what Europeans especially Frenchmen hate most about Americans. The hierarchy is (Genet has to explain the nature of the social world to her because she's American):

Rich men
Poor men
Mothers
Beautiful women
Whores

Poor female and neo-female slut-scum
Janey.
Then he kicks Janey around and tells her to be worse than she is, to
get down, there, down in the shit, to learn. Go to the extreme. To make
the decision. Janey girl still has pretensions. She has to be drained of
everything. She has to be disembowelled.

At this moment Genet's secretary runs over to him and helps him off
with his coat.

'Thank you, M'Namah,' Genet says politely. 'Reporters have been
running after me all day. I shook hands with all of them and smiled a
lot. I'm very tired.'

Little by little Janey begins to understand how beautiful Genet is.
She's so enamoured with him she's creating him. Truth and falsehood,
memory, perception, and fantasy: all are toys in this swirling that is
him-her. She's predicting her future.

Her future: Genet spits on her and kicks her. The more she tries to
be whatever he wants, the more he despises her. Finally she decides her
black wool hood and dress aren't enough. If Genet thinks she's shit, she
should be invisible. When she follows him around, she hides in the
walls like a shadow. She secretly washes his dirty underpants. She takes
on his moodiness and his hating.

'We have to keep you a great writer,' M'Namah says to Genet inside
the hotel room.

'Yes. The most important thing is that I be the best possible writer.
Writing is the great thing, the great teacher.'

'Don't worry about anything else. I and the crab girl who crawls in
those dirty . . .'

'Janey . . .'

'. . . will take care of everything else.' M'Namah laughs and laughs.

Scene 3
*The country south of Alexandria is open, dry, and endless. Camel dung and
pebbles caught in the sands. Janey is working in a rich man's fields which
border on this sand vastness.*

Boss (*the boss is a big man who has gorgeous shoulders, big feet, and talks
like a sweet American missionary*): Where's a washcloth? (*The Egyptian
[slave] workers look dumb.*) Goddamn country. Filthy. Filthy. You
don't even have a washcloth. You never take baths, do you?

Janey: With whom, sir?

Boss (*to Sahih, an Egyptian worker. Sahih is tall, thin, and looks like a
voodoo man*): Can't you shut them up? (*Sahih is his top slave worker.*)

Sahih: I'm very sorry, Mr Knockwurst. You mustn't be angry with us.
We're just like children.

Boss: You've had plenty of time to grow up by now. You people are where you are because you take things too easy. You don't work hard enough.

Janey (*with pride*): I'm going to work harder. I'm going to work so hard I'm going to get out of here.

Boss: Why do you people want to get out of here? Can you think? Can you feel? Tell me, what is life? You eat and you sleep.

Sahih: I'll tell you why she acts the way she does. (*He pulls a cigarette out of his pants.*) Will you allow me to smoke? It's only when the boss is around, I smoke a cigarette. Otherwise I work all the time. Even though I'm an animal. I'm one of the best workers you have.

Janey (*resolutely*): I hate . . .

Sahih (*breaking in*): I didn't tell you you could open your mouth.

Janey: You did. All of you did. You said I'm nothing and . . .

Sahih: All she does is weep, Mr Knockwurst. You should get rid of her. We might be animals, but at least we know to keep our feelings locked in us. Women are worse than animals, Mr Knockwurst. They don't understand what's happening as we do.

Janey: For 2,000 years you've had the nerve to tell women who we are. We use your words; we eat your food. Every way we get money has to be a crime. We are plagiarists, liars, and criminals.

Sahih: I know what's discontenting her, Mr Knockwurst. It's always the same thing with women. She's living with that rebellious homosexual and she's horny.

Janey: My face makes him sick.

Sahih: Even though I'm a real man, I know how he feels.

Janey: I don't have anywhere to sleep. I have to work as hard as possible so I can get enough fame then money to get away from here so I can become alive.

Boss: Tell them to shut up. Women are not allowed to talk.

Sahih (*to Janey*): You have to understand that you're stupid. And you'll never be able to make enough money to get away by working.

Boss: Unless she spreads her legs.

Sahih: Even then she'll have to do specialties.

Boss: So she's horny? She wants a lover? She likes our baskets? (*Laughing.*) She's a woman. She doesn't know what it is to be a human. (*He walks up to Janey and seizes her thighs. Rips them apart.*) Like that. That's what a human is. (*He's in a bad mood. To Sahih*): Get back to work.

Sahih: Are you leaving us, Mr Knockwurst?

The thunder is beginning everywhere. Chaos and horribleness are beginning.

Sahih (to Janey): How are you going to get the money to get out of here?

Janey: Any way I can.

Sahih: Things are happening. There's no reasons or meanings. Things are one way or the other. Which way are you going to choose? There's no way the poor can get money. (*Pause.*) What are you going to choose?

Janey: Everything's going so fast!

Scene 4

Janey's in gaol in Alexandria for stealing two copies of Funeral Rites *and hash from Genet. She's alone in a cell surrounded by bars like a caged animal. Every hour an Egyptian judge who's dressed like an overdressed English barrister walks by and tells her who she is.*

Judge 1: You're a woman.

Judge 2: You whine and snivel. You don't stand up for yourself. You act like you do totally to please other people. You're a piece of shit. You're not real.

Judge 3: You're a whore a thief a liar a smelly fish a money dribbler an egotistic snob.

Judge 4: You have every vice in the world.

etc.

Janey (*to these gaolers*): I hate you.

President Carter: So what?

Janey: I have a right to be happy.

President Carter: You have no rights. The universe is evil. Why do you think anything? You women are always complaining. Why aren't you like us fascist men: why don't you learn to shut up, stow away your grievances, learn the small details and particulars of evil? (*Pause.*) You're too lonely. You can't stand it anymore. Your pain has no relation to anyone else's pain. So what? Learn the varieties of pain, watch your pain, and grow up.

You think there is truth. Everything is lies. We don't need to lie 'cause everything is lies. Learn to be proud of lies and materialism and hidings and discrepancies.

Janey: Accept! Shit. Go take your shit to the grave. That's what I say. I'll tell you something,

tonight

when night comes, I'm going to crawl

into your houses, and in your dreams where you have

no power, I'll make you steal and whore. I'll turn you

around . . .

Gaoler (*breaking in*): What good does it do? All there is is pain in this hatred. You strut around like a peacock. There's no pain. All the pain in the world's in your thoughts.

133

Janey: I want you to plunge further into irrevocable grief. I want you to be totally without hope. Just what is. I want you to be evil.

Gaoler: Those are just words.

Janey: Keep looking for reality. You'll drive yourself crazier and crazier until you'll realize what I'm doing.

Gaoler: I realize you when I tell you who you are. I realize you by judging you. I love you, Janey, when I beat you up.

Scene 5
Janey's still in gaol. She doesn't know whether it's day or night because she can't see anything. She's blind.

She used to fantasize that when she went blind, a wonderful man would come along, take pity on her, and rescue her. Now she knows that nothing like that is going to happen.

Janey (*thinking quietly to herself, not spoken aloud*): Everything that is this world stinks. Even if something good would come along now like love, or money which causes love, I would laugh in its face. No I wouldn't. I just absolutely know right now and for ever love's not going to come along, so I might as well die. I don't want to commit suicide anymore, like I used to; I want to go through death. How can I go through death?':

(*Aloud*) Hey, death!

(*Death doesn't answer.*)

Janey: Goddamn you answer me even if I am a woman!

Death: What do you want, you lousy brat?

Janey: I want to know why a man doesn't love me and why my life's such a miserable shit-pit and why suffering exists?

Death: I'm not your gaoler. Only living humans are gaolers.

Janey: You're the biggest and best rebel who is. Why don't you teach me how to rebel better?

Death: Your pride in yourself as a criminal, whore, and piece of scum is causing your suffering.

Janey: So what.

Death: Do you want me to tell you what death's like?

Janey: No. When I'm dead, I'll find out.

(*Death departs.*)

Janey: The night is left. I'm alone. Now the murderers are descending.

(*Sounds of thunder.*)

134

Scene 6
As soon as the cops throw Janey into the clinker, Genet starts stealing from the poor and the crippled so he can join Janey in gaol. He doesn't love Janey, but he intuits it'll be wild to join her.

For months he publicly rips off everyone. At first the cops stay away from him because of his reputation as a white intellectual. Finally they bust into his room and stick handcuffs around his wrists.

Being in prison is being in a cunt. Having any sex in the world is having to have sex with capitalism. What can Janey and Genet do?

Scene 7
The capitalists get together and discuss the Janey question.

Mr Knockwurst: The slave Janey stinks. My God. Workers are pigs, women are worse, but she's something else. I arranged to have her steal from that homosexual she lives with so I could have her locked up for the rest of her life, but now she's convincing criminals and prostitutes they're people. If they think they're people, they'll revolt against us. What are we going to do about her?

Mr Fuckface (*an intellectual Viennese count*): Each time you dare to show one of them attention, even if it's to imprison him, the thief begins to think he's someone.

Mr Knockwurst: Well, what can I do? I can't kill all my workers. Then I might have to work.

Mr Blowjob (*he owns a large fava bean plantation about ten miles south of Cairo*): I always cut out my peasants' tongues and whatever other extremities they don't need. As it is my workers are ready to kill themselves.

Mr Knockwurst: As it is my workers are ready to kill themselves.

Mr Fuckface: What the hell is she? Fourteen years old? What the hell can any of them do? We're fully armed. We own all the weapons in the world and all the scientists who design the weapons. (*Taps his cigar against an ashtray.*) The truth is we can let them do what they want as long as we convince them to stay alive.

(*An Egyptian sneaks in and sets fire to a tree.*)

Mr Knockwurst: The terror is upon us.
Our workers hated us. We denied their expectations. We limited their space and time boundaries so we could get more work out of them. They began to hate everyone. The world. They want to destroy the world. Themselves. They're about to commit mass suicide. Look at Janey . . .
That's the problem.

(*Another Egyptian sets fire to a tree.*)

Mr Fuckface: Let her kill herself. Let them all kill themselves. We'll take their babies.

The capitalists lie down on the ground and make love to each other. That is the only sex we know nowadays.

Mr Blowjob: Our love is here to stay.

He and the others in ecstasy take off their false cocks and lipsticks and diamonds and kneecaps and fake fingernails and pacemakers and artificial kidneys and breast sponges and contact lenses and American Express cards and lying voices. Lies lies lies.

Mr Fuckface: You see, we own the language. Language must be used clearly and precisely to reveal our universe.

Mr Blowjob: Those rebels are never clear. What they say doesn't make sense.

Mr Fuckface: It even goes against all the religions to tamper with the sacred languages.

Mr Blowjob: Without language the only people the rebels can kill are themselves.

(Meanwhile, the theatre in which the play is being shown is set on fire.)

Mr Knockwurst: Every night Sahih tells me my workers play these records of screams and to amuse themselves instead of sleeping they knife each other. Is that what we call language?

(No answer.)

Mr Knockwurst: They're all Janeys. They're all perverts, transsexuals, criminals, and women. We'll have to think of a plan to exterminate them and get a new breed of workers.

(Another part of the stage goes up in flames.)

Scene 8
Janey and Genet are locked in neighbouring cages in gaol. Their bodies stink to high hell. They're whispering to each other.

Janey: I think a war's coming.
Genet: That's no news. Wars are capitalists' toys.
Janey: I'm not talking about a war. Terror is everywhere and it's increasing.
Genet: You stink more than this gaol does. You lousy stinking pervert.
Janey (*still whispering*): The night is opening up,

to our thighs,
like this cunt which I'm holding in my hand
cuntcuntcuntcunt.

and we descend,
                    like we're in a tunnel or a
                    cave inside the mind,
night is opening all
all murderers all you makers of
violence come out of your holes.
the final Maker of Violence is my
thighs, and my bloody fingernails, and
the teeth inside my cunt.

Please night take over my mind I don't like this poetry I can't stand to
live anymore because Genet won't beat me up anymore.

(*A man who murdered his parents begins to act out the murder for the
millionth time. Genet and Janey watch.*)

Genet: Look . . .

*Dim light has gathered through a tiny hole high up in the wall. Suddenly it
goes black. In this blackness, caused by a power blow-out, the upper-middle
class women and the cops smash store windows, beat up bums with chains,
and wander about. A young black man sticks his hand under a ten-year-old
girl's tight yellow sweater.*

Janey: Let us pray to madness and suffering and horror.
Genet: We're going to die soon. Why don't you think about freedom
  instead?
Janey: The night is opening up,
like my thighs open up
when there's a big fat cock in
front of me.

*End of abstract haze. Now the specific details can begin in the terrible
plagiarism of* The Screens. *The writing is terrible plagiarism because all
culture stinks and there's no reason to make new culture-stink.*

Scene 9
All the different people in Alexandria, that city of gold.
   *Two-storey pale blue, brown, and pale grey brick and wood houses, side
by side, down the streets. Red-brown colour, air and surface, and, above
that, gold light, the sun, and above that pale blue. The air is grey and semi-
thick.*
   *Birds call in the air. They're being scared by the increasing numbers of
sudden loud noises. There are some modern apartments and the beach
surrounds everything.*

Artist: I want to write a play that will amaze everyone. We'll need at least 200,000 dollars to do it right. We'll have to have an orchestra, at least five to ten actors, an assistant director, a top choreographer, one of the top choreographers in the business, and a proscenium.

Punk Rocker: I don't understand what's happening. This world is doomed. There's nothing to believe in.

Rich Do-Nothing: The rich are getting richer and the poor are getting poorer. The right wing is beginning to show its power in this country. Taxes are abolished and schools are being shut down. Proposition 13 is going to take place all over the country. Everything economic and therefore everything is going to get worse.

A Nouveau-Riche Woman (*to the rebels*): You rebels are so fashionable. You dress in the most cunningly torn rags. Where can I buy rags just like yours?

Rebels (*to Janey, who just escaped from gaol with Genet*): You stink. Get out of here. We don't need shit-ass dogs like you. Go to the sewers.

Janey: Please tell me if the world is horrible and if my life is horrible and if there's no use trying to change, or if there is anything else. Is desire OK?

Genet: Where's Sahih?

Janey: Please tell me if the world is horrible and if my life is horrible and if there's no use trying to change, or if there is anything else. Is desire OK?

The rebels kick Janey out of the city.

Scene 10
The desert outside Alexandria. Janey and Genet are still walking. Soon there's nothing. Due to the blazing sun and exhaustion, all Janey and Genet see are mirages or mirrors, pictures of themselves, images of the world which come out of themselves.

Janey: I'm tired. I can't move anymore. Sun and dust. I'm sun and dust. The dust on the road is the sadness that's blowing up inside me and that's eating me away. Where are we going, Genet?

Genet (*looking straight at Janey*): Where am I going?

Janey: Where are we going, Genet?

Genet: I'm going, me, alone; how can I be with you? The closer you get to me, the more I hate you. I'm going, OK? Far far away, the land of the monster. Even if it's where there'll never be sun, since you're tagging along, you're my shadow.

Janey: You can leave me.

Genet: If you stick your filthy body so close to me you're me, I've got to look for the land where the monster lives.

Janey: Wasn't poverty and gaol enough?

138

Genet: Poverty and gaol are just the beginning. Don't you know that by now? Soon there'll be no more sleep and you'll have to eat thistles.

Janey: Thistles?

Genet: Sand.

Janey: There's really nobody. Nothing. Not a living thing. The stones are only stones. America and Europe're no longer anything. Things are winding down to the sea, to the sea, we to the sand.

Genet: You don't have to be shy anymore.

Janey: I do. (*She pauses.*) A mirror. (*She picks up a comb and begins to comb her lousy hair.*)

Genet: Don't touch it. (*He tears the comb out of her maggot hair and breaks it.*)

Janey: I'll obey you. But I want, (*gains courage and firmness, decision*) I want you to forget who you are. (*Corrects herself.*) Been. I want you to lead me without hesitation into the land of the shadow and the monster. I want you to plunge into endless misery and hardship. I want – because it's my ugliness, my lack of femininity, my wounded body, earned minute by minute that is all that is left to speak – I want you to be without hope. I want you to choose evil. I want you to feel hatred and violence. I want you to refuse the delicacy of thistles, the softness of rocks, the beauty of the darkness, the emptiness. I know where we're travelling, Genet, and I know why we're travelling there. It's not just to travel, but it's so those others who kicked me out have a chance of being at peace, have a chance of knowing the land of the monster without going there.

Genet: Do you think that's possible?

(*A long silence. Genet takes off a shoe, shakes out a stone that has been bothering him. Then he puts the shoe on.*)

The desert is absolutely brilliant. Gradually the sun becomes yellow, orange. Gleaming gleaming orange. The more brilliant it's become, the more it sinks. The brilliant colour is going out of the sun as it's turning dark red and going into the orange sky, above and below the orange a violet line. The violet lengthens and darkens into blue. The sky between the dark blue is purple. Above the clouds are pale purple. They drift past, above, the dark ball. The desert is grey. The air is getting cold.

    Then it is night.

    The dogs are barking in the distance. You can see the pointed tips of their heads.

Genet: Rest your head against this milestone and try to sleep.

Janey: Sleep? If I'm walking across rocks, if I'm eating thistles, if I'm letting my skin burn in the sun, it's to murder my everlasting sleep.

Genet: Since it's not going to croak until you do, at least let me sleep. It's no good trying to die. Up there God controls everything . . .

End:
Back in Alexandria the rebels have taken over. They're winning the city. Blood doesn't spurt to the sky like a geyser, yet from one edge of the world to the other how red the night is!

Genet and Janey travel through Cairo, through the twin cities of Minya and Asyut, down to the city of Luxor. There Genet hands Janey some money and tells her to take care of herself. He has to go away to see a production of one of his plays.

She dies.

A second of time

THE WORLD

THE WORLD

A light came into the world. Dazzling white light that makes lightness dazzling burning Happiness. Peace. The forms of the ancient arts of Egypt this is the time that wolves come out of the trees.

This is a wolf.

This is a dog.

This is a horse.

This is an elephant.

This is a kangaroo.

This is a snake.

This is a flower.

Golden bracelets lie around
corpses' arms.

Thick black bracelets,
studded with silver, around
their ankles.

The sun is the world.

In ancient Egypt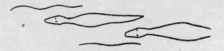
the land of gold,

giant aligators lived in tall weeds.

The King of Alligators is Power.

The soul has freedom to wander
at will

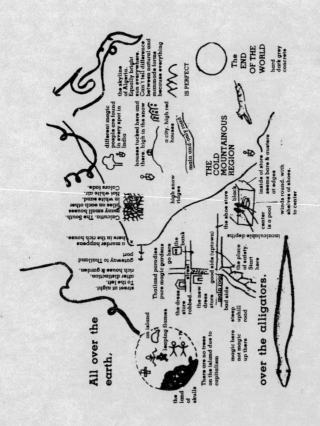

At night the wolves snap at the
flying bird

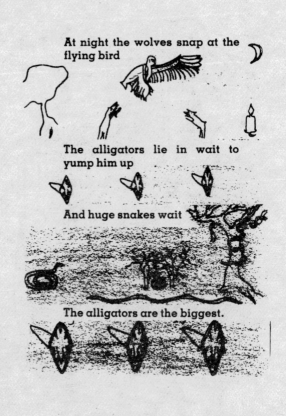

The alligators lie in wait to
yump him up

And huge snakes wait

The alligators are the biggest.

A human is a being halfway between an alligator and a bird
who wants to be a bird.
The ancient
books say there are ways humans can become something
else.   The most important book on human transforma-
tion is hidden with the corpse
Catullus in the Saba Pacha
Cemetery in Alexandria
because all books were written
by dead people.

Shall we look for this wonderful
book? Shall we stop being dead
people? Shall we find our way
out of all expectations?

THE
JOURNEY

There are no more judges, there are only thieves, murderers, firebrands.

Wild horses

A forgotten city,

huge palace

very wide stairs.
nothing exactly fits.

rocks. desert

down.
rolling hill

large road

columns

sunken hidden square

all stone
New York City

Shadowy
houses

It takes three days and three nights to reach Saba Pacha Cemetery.

here hide-and-seek game takes place. In game. some serious and terrifying events happen. There are real witches. Then people's sex and their most private beings get totally transformed. Red and black

I make out with someone here

door to back

kit-chen

hall or hall

back living room
fireplace

black

MAGIC HOUSE

longest hall

A HOUSE OF DISJUNCTIONS

a scissor that cuts. knives given as presents. lots of sex.

tiny rooms

kit-chen

ALASKA

cave

rock

longest hall

It gets darker and darker and then blackness comes.

front living room
fireplace

front entrance

black
hoar
bristles

frozen lake

craggy
bolders
of ice

front door

Catullus' Tomb

Even if we die

if we have to
become monsters

and
everyone
hates us,

we have to read the book because it will teach us how to
avoid the alligators' jaws, the
wolves who wait in the forest,
the huge snakes, and how to become birds.

We reached the tomb. Dead Catullus who was clutching the book woke up and told us the following story:

A rascally evil priest who cared only for money told me, when I was still alive, that the book I sought, this book which I'm now as a dead man holding, could be mine if I gave him $100,000. And two new coffins. I did what he asked and then held a knife to his throat. Just before I killed him, he told me I could find the book in a gold box in a silver box in an ivory box in a palm-tree wood box in a bronze box in a iron box

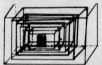

surrounded by swarms of the
desires that drive us mad,

desires encircled by a golden
bracelet whose ends are joined,

in the East River.

I set out,
says Catullus,
for the East
River . . .

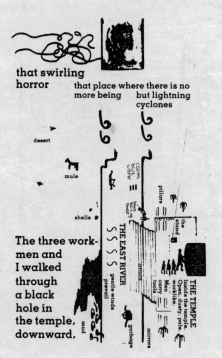

that swirling
horror

that place where there is no
more being   but lightning
cyclones

desert

mule

shells

calm
blue
water

the burning body?

pillars

the stand

THE EAST RIVER

gentle winds prevail

mimas

Men carry tools

workiike.

THE TEMPLE
Inside the temple,
Open, dusty, pale,

The three work-
men and
I walked
through
a black
hole in
the temple,
downward,

mud

garbage

mirrors

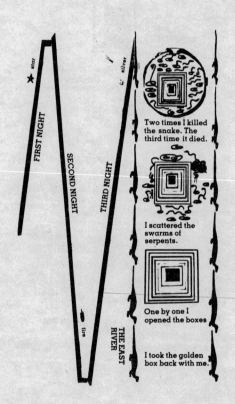

FIRST NIGHT

SECOND NIGHT

THIRD NIGHT

star

silver

fire

THE EAST RIVER

Two times I killed
the snake. The
third time it died.

I scattered the
swarms of
serpents.

One by one I
opened the boxes

I took the golden
box back with me.

I read the book and became a bird.

THE EAST RIVER

my wife fell into the river

dead wife

dead babies

My children fell into the river and died.

I also fell into the river and died."

dead me   book

"We don't care what danger there is, we tell the dead man after he finishes speaking. "But we can no longer be human. We've got to have that book."

"You don't know what you're doing," the dead poet says.

"You don't know anything. Therefore you can't do anything.

"You're capitalist bourgeois sluts.

"You're insane. Go back home."

We must have that book!

We gamble for the red book with the dead poet who becomes a devil.

The Devil uses every
trick in the book to win.

The Devil is an image. Imagine
Hell. We grab the book, and run.

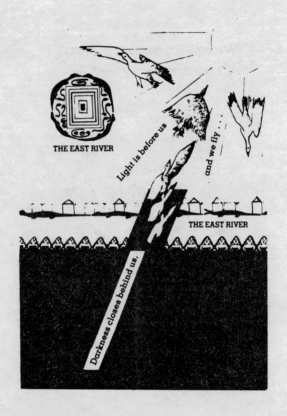

THE EAST RIVER

Light is before us

and we fly . . . .

THE EAST RIVER

Darkness closes behind us.

We are dreaming of sex,

of thieves, murderers,
firebrands,

of huge thighs opening
to us like this night.

So we create this world
in our own image.

So the doves . . .

So the doves cooed softly to each other, whispering of their own events, over Janey's grave in the grey Saba Pacha cemetery in Luxor.

Soon many other Janeys were born and these Janeys covered the earth.

> Blood and guts in high school
> This is all I know
> Parents teachers boyfriends
> All have got to go.
>
> Some folks like trains,
>   some folks like ships,
> I like the way you move your hips
> All I want is a taste of your lips,
>   boy,
> All I want is a taste of your lips.

Great Expectations

Contents

1 Plagiarism

I recall my childhood

My father's name being Pirrip, and my Christian name Philip, my infant tongue could make of both names nothing longer or more explicit than Peter. So I called myself Peter, and came to be called Peter.

I give Pirrip as my father's family name on the authority of his tombstone and my sister – Mrs Joe Gargery, who married the blacksmith.

On Christmas Eve 1978 my mother committed suicide and in September of 1979 my grandmother (on my mother's side) died. Ten days ago (it is now almost Christmas 1979) Terence told my fortune with the Tarot cards. This was not so much a fortune – whatever that means – but a fairly, it seems to me, precise psychic map of the present, therefore: the future.

I asked the cards about future boyfriends. This question involved the following thoughts: Would the guy who fucked me so well in France be in love with me? Will I have a new boyfriend? As Terence told me to do, I cut the cards into four piles: earth water fire air. We found my significator, April 18th, in the water or emotion fantasy pile. We opened up this pile. The first image was a fat purring human cat surrounded by the Empress and the Queen of Pentacles. This cluster, travelling through a series of other clusters that, like mirrors, kept defining or explained the first cluster more clearly – time is an almost recurring conical – led to the final unconscious image: during Christmas the whole world is rejecting a male and a female kid who are scum by birth. To the right of the scum is the Star. To the left is the card of that craftsmanship which due to hard work succeeds.

Terence told me that despite my present good luck my basic stability my contentedness with myself alongside these images. I have the image obsession I'm scum. This powerful image depends on the image of the Empress, the image I have of my mother. Before I was born, my mother hated me because my father left her (because she got pregnant?) and because my mother wanted to remain her mother's child rather than be my mother. My image of my mother is the source of my creativity. I prefer the word consciousness. My image of my hateful mother is blocking consciousness. To obtain a different picture of my mother, I have to forgive my mother for rejecting me and committing suicide. The picture of love, found in one of the clusters, is forgiveness that transforms need into desire.

Because I am hating my mother I am separating women into virgins or whores rather than believing I can be fertile.

I have no idea how to begin to forgive someone much less my mother. I have no idea where to begin: repression's impossible because it's stupid and I'm a materialist.

I just had the following dream:

In a large New England-ish house I am standing in a very big room on the second floor in the front of the mansion. This room is totally fascinating, but as soon as I leave it, I can't go back because it disappears. Every room in this house differs from every other room.

The day after my mother committed suicide I started to experience a frame. Within this frame time was totally circular because I was being returned to my childhood traumas totally terrifying because now these traumas are totally real: there is no buffer of memory.

There is no time; there is.

Beyond the buffers of forgetting which are our buffer to reality: there is. As the dream: there is and there is not. Call this TERROR call this TOTAL HUMAN RESPONSIBILITY. The PIG I see on the edge of the grave is the PIG me neither death nor social comment kills. This TERROR is divine beause it is real and may I sink into IT.

My mother often told me: 'You shouldn't care if an action is right or wrong; you should totally care if you're going to profit monetarily from it.'

The helmeted bowlegged stiff-muscled soldiers trample on just-born babies swaddled in scarlet violet shawls, babies roll out of the arms of women crouched under POP's iron machine guns, a cabby shoves his fist into a goat's face, near the lake a section of the other army crosses the tracks, other soldiers in this same army leap in front of the trucks, the POP retreat up the river, a white-walled tyre in front of three thorn bushes props up a male's head, the soldiers bare their chests in the shade of the mud barricades, the females lullabye kids in their tits, the sweat from the fires perfumes reinforces this stirring rocking makes their rags their skins their meat pregnant: salad oil clove henna butter indigo sulphur, at the base of this river under a shelf loaded down by burnt-out cedars barley wheat beehives graves refreshment stands garbage bags fig trees matches human-brain-splattered low-walls small-fires' -- smoke-dilated orchards explode: flowers pollen grain-ears tree roots paper milk-stained cloths blood bark feathers, rising. The soldiers wake up stand up again tuck in their canvas shirttails suck in cheeks stained by tears dried by the steam from hot train rails rub their sex against the tyres, the trucks go down into a dry ford mow down a few rose-bushes, the sap mixes with disembowelled teenagers' blood on their knives' metal, the soldiers' nailed boots cut down uproot nursery plants, a section of RIMA (the other army) climb on to their trucks' running-boards throw themselves on their females pull out violet rags bloody tampaxes which afterwards the females stick back in their cunts: the soldier's chest as he's raping the female crushes the baby stuck in her tits.

I want: every part changes (the meaning of) every other part so there's no absolute/heroic/dictatorial/S&M meaning/part the soldier's onyx-dusted fingers touch her face orgasm makes him shoot saliva over the baby's buttery skull his formerly-erect now-softening sex rests on the shawl becomes its violet scarlet colour, the trucks swallow up the RIMA soldiers, rainy winds shove the tarpaulins against their necks, they adjust their clothes, the shadows grow, their eyes gleam more and more their fingers brush their belt buckles, the wethaired-from-sweating-during-capture-at-the-edge-of-the-coals goats crouch like the rags sticking out of the cunts, a tongueless canvas-covered teenager pisses into the quart of blue enamel he's holding in his half-mutilated hand, the truck driver returns kisses the blue cross tattooed on his forehead, the teenager brings down his palm wrist where alcohol-filled veins are sticking out. These caterpillars of trucks grind down the stones the winds hurled over the train tracks, the soldiers sleep their sex rolling over their hips drips they are cattle, their truck driver spits black a wasp sting swells up the skin under his left eye black grapes load down his pocket, an old man's white hair under-the-white-hair red burned face jumps up above the sheet metal, the driver's black saliva dries on his chin the driver's studded heel crushes as he pulls hair out the back of this head on to the sheet metal, some stones blow up.

My mother is the most beautiful woman in the world. She has black hair, green eyes which turn grey or brown according to her mood or the drugs she's on at the moment, the pallor of this pink emphasizes the fullness of her lips, skin so soft the colour of her cheeks is absolutely peach no abrasions no redness no white tightness. This in no way describes the delicacy of the face's bone structure. Her body is equally exquisite, but on the plump or sagging side because she doesn't do any exercise and she wears girdles. She's five feet six inches tall. She usually weighs 120 pounds even though she's always taking diet pills. Her breasts look larger and fuller than they are because they sag downwards. The nipples in them are large pale pink. In the skin around the nipples and in the tops of her legs you can easily see the varicose veins breaking through. The breast stomach and upper thigh skin is very pale white. There's lots of curly hair around her cunt.

She has a small waist hands and ankles. The main weight, the thrust, the fullness of those breasts is deceptive, is the thighs: large pock-marked flesh indicates a heavy ass extra flesh at the sides of the thigh. The flesh directly above the cunt seems paler than it has to be. So pale, it's fragile, at the edge of ugliness: the whole: the sagging but not too large breasts, the tiny waist, the huge ass are sexier MORE ABOUT PASSION than a more-tightly-muscled and fashionable body.

My mother is the person I love most. She's my sister. She plays with me. There's no one else in my world except for some kind of weird father who only partly exists part out of the shadow, and an unimportant torment I call my sister. I'm watching my mother put on her tight tawny-orange sweater. She always wears a partially lacy white bra that seems slightly dirty. As she's struggling to get into a large white panty girdle she says she doesn't like girdles. She's standing in front of her mirror and mirrored dresser. Mirrors cover every inch of all the furniture in the room except for the two double beds, my father's chair, and the TV, but they don't look sensuous. Now my mother's slipping into a tight brown wool straight skirt. She always wears tight sweaters and tight straight skirts. Her clothes are old and very glamorous. She hitches her skirt up a little and rolls on see-through stockings.

She tells me to put on my coat and white mittens because we're going outside.

Today is Christmas. Huge clean piles of snow cover the streets make the streets magical. Once we get to the park below the 59th Street Bridge I say to myself, 'No foot has ever marked this snow before.' My foot steps on each unmarked bit of snow. The piles are so high I can barely walk through them. I fall down laughing. My mother falls down laughing with me. My clothes especially the pants around my boots are sopping wet. I stay in this magic snow with the beautiful yellow sun beating down on me as long as I can until a voice in my head (me) or my mother says, 'Now you know what this experience is, you have to leave.'

My mother wants to get a strawberry soda. Today my mother's being very nice to me and I love her simply and dearly when she's being nice to me. We're both sitting on the round red vinyl turnable seats around the edge of the white counter. My mother's eating a strawberry soda with strawberry ice cream. I see her smiling. A fat middle-aged man thinks we're sisters. My mother is very young and beautiful.

At camp: males string tents up along a trench filled with muck: slush from meat refuse vomit sparkle under arching colourless weeds, the soldiers by beating them drive back the women who're trying to stick their kids in the shelter of the tents, they strike at kick punch the soldiers' kidneys while the soldiers bend over the unfolded tent canvas.

174

Two males tie the animals to the rears of the tents, a shit-filled-assed teenager squatting over the salt-eroded weeds pants dust covers his face his head rolls vacantly around his shoulder his purple eye scrutinizes the montage of tents, a brown curly-haired soldier whose cheeks cause they're crammed full of black meat are actually touching his pock-marked earlobes crouches down next to a little girl he touches her nape his hand crawls under the rags around her throat feels her tits her armpits: the little girl closes her eyes her fingers touch the soldier's grapejuice-smeared wrist, from the shit-heaps a wind-gust lifts up the bits of film and sex mag pages the soldiers tore up while they were shitting clenched the shit burns the muscles twisted by rape. Some soldiers leaving the fire wander around the tents untie the tent thongs they crawl on the sand, the linen tent flaps brush their scabies-riddled thighs, the males the females all phosphorescent nerves huddle around the candles, no longer wanting to hear anything the teenagers chew wheat they found in the bags, the kids pick threads out of their teeth put their rags on again stick the sackcloth back over their mothers' tits lick the half-chewed flour left on their lips.

My mother thinks my father is a nobody. She is despising him and lashing out at him right now she is saying while she is sitting on her quilt-covered bed 'Why don't you ever go out at night, Bud? All you do is sleep.'

'Let me watch the football game, Claire. It's Sunday.'

'Why don't you ever take mommy out, daddy? She never has any fun.' Actually I think my mother's a bitch.

'You can't sleep all the time, Bud. It isn't good for you.'

'This is my one day off, Claire. I want to watch the football game. Six days a week I work my ass off to buy you and the kids food, to keep a roof over your head. I give you everything you want.'

'Daddy, you're stupid.' 'Daddy, you don't even know who Dostoyeysky is.' 'What's the matter with you, daddy?'

Daddy's drunk and he's still whining, but now he's whining nastily. He's telling my mother that he does all the work he goes to work at six in the morning and comes back after six at night (which we all know is a joke cause his job's only a sinecure: my mother's father gave him his first break, a year ago when the business was sold, part of the deal was my father'd be kept on as 'manager' under the new owners at $50,000 a year. We all know he goes to work cause there he drinks and he doesn't hear my mother's nagging). He's telling my mother he gave her her first fur coat. My father is never aggressive. My father never beats my mother up.

The father grabs a candle, the curly brownhaired soldier his red mouth rolling around the black meat takes out his knife: his hand quickly juts the red rags over his sex his pincher his grabber the curly brownhaired soldier jerks the sleepy young girl's thighs to him, she slides over the sand till she stops at the tent opening, one soldier's mutilated forehead cause he was raping over an eagle's eggs the eagle scalped him another soldier's diseased skinpores these two soldiers gag the father, the father throws a burning candle into their hairs, the curly brownhaired soldier takes the young girl into his arms, she sleeps she purrs her open palm on her forehead to his shudder trot, the clouded moon turns his naked arm green, his panting a gurgling that indicates rape the sweat dripping off his bare strong chest wakes the young girl up. I walked into my parents' bedroom opened their bathroom door don't know why I did it, my father was standing naked over the toilet, I've never seen him naked I'm shocked, he slams the door in my face, I'm curious I see my mother naked all the time, she closely watches inside his open cause gasping mouth the black meat still stuck to his teeth the black meat still in a ball, the curly brownhaired lifts her on to her feet lay her down on the dog kennels' metal grating hugs her kisses her lips the ear hollows where the bloodstained wax causes whispers his hand unbuttons his sackcloth pulls out his member, the young girl sucks out of the curly brownhaired's cheeks the black meat eyes closed hands spread over the metal grating, excited by this cheek-to-stomach muscle motion bare-headed straw-dust flying around his legs injects the devil over her scorches, the dogs waking up at the metal gratings leap out of the kennels their chains gleam treat me like a dog drag in the shit, the curly brownhaired nibbles the young girl's gums his teeth pull at the meat fibres her tongue pushes into the cracks between her teeth, the dogs howl their chains jingle against the tar of the road their paws crush down the hardened shits, the curly brownhaired's knees imprison the young girl's thighs.

My father's lying in the hospital cause he's on his third heart attack. My mother's mother at the door of my father's room so I know my father is overhearing her is saying to my mother, 'You have to say he's been a good husband to you, Claire. He never left you and he gave you everything you wanted.'
    'Yes.'
    'You don't love him.'
    'Yes.'
    I know my grandmother hates my father.
    I don't side with my mother rather than my father like my sister does. I don't perceive my father. My mother is adoration hatred play. My mother is the world. My mother is my baby. My mother is exactly who she wants to be.
    The whole world and consciousness revolves around my mother.
    I don't have any idea what my mother's like. So no matter how my

mother acts, she's a monster. Everything is a monster. I hate it. I want to run away. I want to escape the Jolly Green Giant. Any other country is beautiful as long as I don't know about it. This is the dream I have: I'm running away from men who are trying to damage me permanently. I love mommy. I know she's on Dex, and when she's not on Dex she's on Librium to counteract the Dex jitters so she acts more extreme than usual. A second orgasm cools her shoulders, the young girl keeps her hands joined over the curly brownhaired's ass, the wire grating gives way, the curly brownhaired slides the young girl under him his pants are still around his knees his fingernails claw the soil his breath sucks in the young girl's cheek blows straw dust around, the mute young girl's stomach muscles weld to the curly-headed's abdominal muscles, the passing wind immediately modulates the least organic noise that's why one text must subvert (the meaning of) another text until there's only background music like reggae: the inextricability of relation-textures the organic (not meaning) recovered, stupid ugly horrible a mess pinhead abominable vomit eyes-pop-out-always-presenting-disgust-always-presenting-what-people-flee-always-wanting-to-be-lonely infect my mother my mother, blind fingernails spit the eyes wandering from the curly-headed, the curly-headed's hidden balls pour open cool down on the young girl's thigh. Under the palmtrees the RIMAS seize and drag a fainted woman under a tent, a flushing-forehead blond soldier burning coals glaze his eyes his piss stops up his sperm grasps this woman in his arms, their hands their lips touch lick the woman's clenched face while the blond soldier's greasy wine-stained arm supports her body, the young girl RECOVERED.

New York City is very peaceful and quiet, and the pale grey mists are slowly rising, to show me the world, I who have been so passive and little here, and all beyond is so unknown and great that now I am crying. My fingers touch the concrete beneath my feet and I say, 'Goodbye, oh my dear, dear friend.'

We don't ever have to be ashamed of feelings of tears, for feelings are the rain upon the earth's blinding dust: our own hard egotistic hearts. I feel better after I cry: more aware of who I am, more open. I need friends very much.

Thus ends the first segment of my life. I am a person of GREAT EXPECTATIONS.

I journey to receive my fortune

My lawer Mr Gordon duly sent me his address; and he wrote after it on the card 'just outside Alexandria, and close by the taxi stand'.

Nevertheless, a taxi-driver, who seems to have as many jackets over his greasy winter coat as he is years old, packs me up in his taxi, hems me in by shutting the taxi doors and closing the taxi windows and locking the taxi doors, as if he's going to take me fifty miles. His getting into his driver's seat which is decorated by an old weather-stained pea-green hammercloth, moth-eaten into rags, is a work of time. It's a wonderful taxi, with six great horns outside the driver's window, and ragged things behind for I don't know how many kids to hold on by, and iron spikes below them to prevent the amateur kids from yielding to temptation.

I'm just beginning to enjoy this taxi and think how like a yard of straw it is, and yet how like a rag-shop, and to wonder why the horses' nose-bags are kept inside, when I see the taxi-driver beginning to open his door as if we're going to stop presently. And stop we presently do, in a gloomy street, at certain offices with an open door, whereon is painted 'EGYPT'.

We're walking along the aqueduct which supplies water to the citadel. Stray dogs sleep and walk in the sun. Carrion vultures wheel through the sky. The dogs are tearing at a donkey's leftovers, especially the head which is still completely covered in skin; the head is the least edible part of the skeleton. Always birds begin with eyes; dogs like the stomach or skin around the asshole. They all move from the tenderest to the toughest.

This old woman's begging me to fuck her. Puke. I prefer boys in this heat. She's uncovering her long flat tits, they look like worms, they're hanging down to her belly-button. She's stroking them. She has a sweet smile. Her head bends to one side; lips part over her yellow teeth. Another hag catches sight of me in this courtyard, cartwheels in front of me, shows me her ass. She does this when she sees a man because she wants a man so badly. A woman dancing all over her cell is beating up her tin toilet bowl like the picture we have of a crazy person 'cause she's not getting affection.

Three nights now I've been chasing that creep guy I'm getting sick of not getting him I'm getting sick of getting what I don't want and not getting what I want. I saw him every night at the Palace before I wanted him. He has a very pretty blonde girlfriend he's even cuter than her so I didn't want him. One night he asked me what I do with myself when he doesn't see me. He finds it hard to talk to me 'cause he's very shy. Since that night I've gotten this bigger crush on him and every time I've returned to the Palace every night this week – only my crush drives me out – every night this week he's never there.

Quiet way of life here – intimate, secluded. Dazzling sun effects when one suddenly emerges from these alleys, so narrow that the roofs of the shuttered bay windows on each side touch each other.

Sometimes I think about my future . . . I don't want to leave this life and go back to the horror that is New York. What shall I do when I get back to New York? What can I do to make New York not horrible? Before it descends on me and eats me up. I'm scared out of my wits.

I'm a scaredy-cat. I run away from everything. Being allowed to laze. This' what it's about.

Not only have I shirked facing my problems. I shall die at sixty before having formed any opinion concerning myself. I made a list of human characteristics: every time I had one characteristic I had its opposite.

How did I get to being always alone?

However I worry very little about any of this: I live like a plant filling myself with sun and light with colours and fresh air. I keep eating, so to speak; the digesting will have to be done then the shitting; and the shit had better be good! That's the important thing.

The day beginning to rise – I have that smartness in my eyes that comes from being up all night. Several upperclass Greek women are walking by. A pleasant fragrance wafts out from under their veils, from the raising of their elbows when they reach up to make sure their veils are still on their heads, and from the edges of the veils themselves as they float up in the draft. In my mind's eye, I see a pink stocking and a tip of a foot in a pointed yellow slipper.

Back in New York City, the tenth floor of an apartment building on 73rd Street and Third Avenue:

Hubbie: Goodbye, dear. (*Shouting*) I'm going to Long Island to go hunting.

Wife (*entering their wall-to-wall carpeted living room*): But you can't leave me. It's Christmas.

Hubbie: This is my vacation. I worked like a dog all year to keep you in trinkets and furs. I want to do what I want for once in my life and it's Christmas.

Wife: You're gonna desert us on Christmas! You louse! You lousy louse! Mother always said you were a louse and, besides, she has more money than you! I don't know why I married you I certainly didn't marry you for your money. (*Starts to sob*).

Hubbie: Stop it, dear. (*Doesn't know what to do when he sees a woman crying. It makes him feel so helpless.*) The children'll see and think something's the matter.

Wife: We don't have any children. It's all your fault.

Hubbie: It's always my fault. Everything's always my fault. When your dog died when you were four years old it was my fault. When Three Mile Island was leaking away Mother threw out her new General Electric microwave 'cause she said it was a UFO Martian breeding ground: I caused that one. Your commie actor friends're always telling me I'm not political enough cause I won't stand on streetcorners and look like a bum just to hand out that rag (SEMIOTEXT(e)) they call a newspaper a bum wouldn't even use to wipe his ass with, some communism, and then they say I'm responsible for the general state of affairs. All I do is work every day! I never say anything about anything! I do exactly what every other American middle-aged man does. Everything's my fault.

Wife: (*soberly*): Everything IS your fault. (*The wife starts to cry again.*) You don't love me enough. You don't want me to be a little girl. I'm . . . mmwah (*her hands crawl at one of the lapels of his red-and-black hunting jacket*). I'm a . . . googoo. Don't you love me? Bobby? Do you love me and be nice to me and don't desert me 'cause I love you so much?

Hubbie (*completely bewildered*): Of course I love you. (*His big strong arms pick her up. He carries her into the bedroom. He puts his cock into her pink rayon panties. He comes. He wants to do what he wants to do.*)

Wife: You promised and you can't break your promise you'd stay here.

Hubbie: Shit. (*He fondles his old Winchester. He walks over to one of the large living room windows and sticks the rifle through the window. He shoots down a streetlight that's red.*) Goddamn.

Wife: Bobby, what're you doing? Don't you know we all – the tenants – decided we'd have noise regulations during the night?

Hubbie: I can have my shooting practice right here. Bam bam (*says as he shoots*). Three dead streetlights. Try crossing the street now, President Carter.

Wife: Don't insult President Carter that way.

Hubbie: Bam. (*The bullet goes right through a businessman's hat. The businessman doesn't notice a thing.*) Bam bam bam bam. (*The lamps which light the street below Mary and Bobby's apartment burst open.*) Those local hoods can thank me: tonight they'll jerk their girlfriends off in the doorways and the cops won't see a thing.

Wife: You're acting just like Mother said you would when you don't get your way. All you want is attention. You're gonna be a baby until I give in to you. Well, I'm not going to. I've got myself to think about.

Hubbie: Bam. (*Shoots down a four-year-old girl who's wearing a baby-blue jumper. Her junked-out mother is too shocked to scream. It begins to snow.*) Guess it's gonna snow for Christmas.

Wife: Ooh, I'm so glad! Now aren't you glad you stayed home for Christmas?

Scene 2. The Husband's Monologue

Wife: Where're you going, Frank?

Hubbie (*putting on a torn khaki jacket over his checkered hunting jacket*): I'm just going out for a second, hon. There're a few things I can't reach from here.

Wife (*flinging her arms across the door like she's Jesus on the cross*): You're not going out on this cold night. Something horrible's gonna happen.

Hubbie (*shouldering his gun*): Don't be ridiculous, Mary. There's nothing out there.

Wife: You're going to get drunk and hang around with loose women and God knows what and Josie and Ermine're coming at seven!

Hubbie: Aw, honey. I don't want to see those alcoholics.

Wife: Josie and Ermine aren't alcoholics. Ermine earns $75,000 a year.

Hubbie: They drink up all my Scotch. I'll tell you what. If they come in here, I'll go bang-bang and Winchester will get rid of the beggars. I told you I was getting you a nice Christmas.

Wife: You'll do your shooting on the street. I just washed the kitchen floor.

On the Street

Hubbie: Here we go round the mulberry bush the mulberry bush the mulberry bush . . . I'm a child again. I'm happy. I haven't been happy since I went out drinking with that black whore who threatened to burn my balls off with her BIC just cause I was teasing her a little about her kid sister. Women are too sensitive. Take my wife. Premonitions! (*Huge black shadows start gathering around the husband.*) Boy did she get hot under the collar huh . . . about nothing . . . about a dead four-year-old who in two years would be hooked on junk. All women are hooked on junk. Now I can do whatever I want.

Is there anything else? Is there anything else? What is it to know?

I, Peter, don't know because I obsessively adore my father. My father was a poor German-Jewish refugee. He came to America and started a successful millinery business in those old days when men weren't allowed to have their own businesses. Then he married a rich woman, well, that's what men did in those days, that's the only way they could succeed. That and being pimps. Women don't realize that marriage is a business for men – clothes make-up all the stuff women belittle; they want the men to wear that stuff and then they say 'Men's stuff is unimportant;' marriage and sex are the only business men got. My father thought money was everything; he had a right to think money was

181

everything; he didn't have a choice of thinking anything else considering where he lived when and he had made himself a success.

Unfortunately I'm shit to him because I don't want to earn money. I don't know what to do because I honour him and what he's done.

My mother is a dummy and a piece of jellyfish. The most disgusting thing in this world is her. My worst nightmare is that I'll have some of that jellyfish in me.

My mother, the jellyfish, wants me to be just like I am.

So I fall down in a fit. I decide to be totally catatonic. I am unable to know anything. I have no human contacts. I'm not able to understand language.

They call me CRAZY. But I'm not inhuman. I still have burning sexual desires. I still have a cock. I just won't believe there's any possibility of me communicating to someone in this world.

I hate humans who want me to act like I can communicate to them. I hate feeling more pain because I've felt so much pain.

My idea of happiness is numbness.

From what I've seen and read I think the people who live in Egypt don't absolutely hate their lives.

I feel I feel I feel I have no language, any emotion for me is a prison.

I think talking to humans, acting in this world, and hurting other humans are magical acts. I fall in love with the humans who I see do these things.

I think these categories: this logic way of talking (perceiving) is wrong. THERE'S NO SUCH THING AS POWER AND POWER-LESSNESS. For instance, I, Peter, am totally passive or powerless. I live in a world in which one major power, the USA, is trying to artificially create a war with another great power to increase its military budget. All rich businessmen get richer while wars are always fought on top of the bodies of poor people. We are really really powerless.

Anything mental is real.

Dear Peter,

I think your new girlfriend stinks. She is a liar all the way around because her skin is yellow from jaundice, not from being Chinese like she pretends. She's only pretty because she's wearing a mask. You're hooked on her tight little cunt: it's only a sexual attraction I know you're very attracted to sex 'cause when you were young you were fat and no girl wanted to fuck you. What you don't know is that this cunt contains lots of poison – not just jaundice – a thousand times more powerful than the coke she is feeding you to keep you with her – especially one lethal poison developed by the notorious Fu Manchu that takes cocks, turns their upper halves purple, their lower parts bright red, the eyes go blind so they can no longer see what's happenng, the person dies. Your new girlfriend is insane and she's poisoning you.

Love,

Rosa

P.S. I'm only telling you this for your own good.

Dear Peter,

I want you wet. I want you dripping all over me. I want you just for sex. Once I know I can have you I might ignore you I know that would be very stupid. Then you'd run away as fast as you could. Then I'd want you so much I'd figure more subtle lasting ways to commit suicide than all the ways – like lobotomy, everyone in my family goes, I robot flesh made of steel – I have these past two years since you left me. Ours is the hottest love affair that has ever existed and I'm telling everyone that it is so. Physical sex doesn't have to have anything to do with love affairs. Love affairs are when each person can do anything they want and the other person realizes that the most unbelievable behaviour possible is usual.

Love,

Rosa

The Gritty State Of Things To Come

Dear Sylvére,

This serves you right. I told you this was going to happen. Now that I've spent last night fucking you, I'm in love with you. I'm writing these few lines to give you the news and the news isn't good. A few minutes ago the cops arrested me for stealing a copy of SEMIOTEXT(e). You keep talking about how you're making Italian terrorism fashionable: isn't my ass here in New York worth at least a penny to you for every dollar of Italian terrorist ass over there? I think you should be nice to me because I'm just a helpless little girl. Also please try to get permission to come to see me and bring me some underwear. Put in your cat because I need affection and you don't need anything. How are you? Darling, I'm awfully sorry about what's happening to me. Let's face it: some kids are born with silver spoons in their mouths. I'm an old woman whose teeth are falling out. I'm counting on you to help me out. I wish I could run into your chest and climb on your arms three hours a week and no more. Remember what we do together when I'm unparanoid enough to see you. Remember what we do together when I'm unparanoid enough to see you. Try to recognize the only reality of the real world: no one gives a shit about anything. Get on your knees, sweetheart, and kiss the earth,

> Love,
> Rosa

We Have Proven That Communication Is Impossible

Dear Susan Sontag,

Would you please read my books and make me famous? Actually I don't want to be famous because then all these people who are very boring will stop me on the street and bother me already I hate the people who call me on the phone because I'm always having delusions. I now see my delusions are more interesting than anything that can happen to me in New York. Despite everyone saying New York is just the most fascinating city in the world. Except when Sylvére fucks me. I wish I knew how to speak English. Dear Susan Sontag, will you teach me how to speak English? For free, because, you understand, I'm an artist and artists by definition are people who never pay for anything even though they sell their shows out at $10,000 a painting before the show opens. All my artist friends were starving to death before they landed in their middle-class mothers' wombs; they especially tell people how they're starving to death when they order $2.50 each beers at the Mudd Club. Poverty is one of the most repulsive aspects of human reality: more disgusting than all the artists who're claiming they're total scum are the half-artists the hypocrites the ACADEMICS who think it's in to be poor, WHO WANT TO BE POOR, who despise the white silk napkins I got off my dead grandmother – she finally did something for me for once in her life (death) – because those CRITICS don't know what it's like to have to tell men they're wonderful for money, 'cause you've got to have money, for ten years. I hope this society goes to hell. I understand you're very literate, Susan Sontag,

> Yours,
> Rosa

Dear David,

Are you a Tibetan monk yet? I used to hate you because you didn't love me so much you would give up your whole life for me. I expect this of every man. In retrospect, I realize that I was also selfish: I should have stopped making demands that you not be the closet female-hating sadist you are. I understand it's very hard to be rich because rich people are trained, they can't just be poor, they are trained to act as if they need to work and be big worldly successes. Your explanation that you gave up writing your visions in order to do commercial Hollywood script writing because you needed Francis Ford Coppola's $150,000 when you receive huge monthly estate checks rivals a university professor's essay on the similarities between *Moby Dick* and Nazism. At least a university professor really has to make a living. Language means nothing anymore anyway. Walking down Second Avenue with you while you're telling me you're as poor as me when I know I have to fuck thirteen-inchers in porn films the next day so I can pay Peter, my husband, his goddam rent wasn't as bad as how my other boyfriends treated me: at least you bought me lunch at Amy's after we fucked. The only thing I resent is when you were doing everything you could to force me to fuck your Tibetan guru and I had bad gonorrhea. That your environmental richness does not excuse.

I'd like to fuck you when you return from London,

> Yours,
> Rosa

Dear Steve Maas,

Why don't you give some of the money you are making off the Mudd Club to the poor starving artists who're supporting it? Diego says you're a millionaire now. Michael Betsy many of my friends, you know who they are, are desperate. You're always saying you want to do something for art and you understand what art is. If you understand what art is, you wouldn't be a power-monger: you'd let artists have the door at least between twelve and two, not between nine and eleven – as it is now – before anyone's even allowed in the club.

> Yours,
> Rosa

Dear God,

I used to complain that the world isn't fair. Now I don't think the world isn't fair. I don't think. Have you made me into a lobotomy case? Has the world turned me into a lobotomy case? You are the world. I wish there was a man here who could put me back in touch with the world.

> Love,
> Rosa

'You'll be a friend to me, won't you?'

'I'll try. But you know, it's not easy to be your friend.'

'It isn't? Why?'

'Oh, I'm such a mite of a thing and you're so gorgeous. You always know what you're doing. You're so sure of yourself you could crush me. You make me feel like I'm nothing. I know you don't mean it.'

'No one loves me, I lead this horrible life. Don't think I'm someone I'm not. I'm like a hermit a nothing, I think I'm one of the true innocents.'

'You not being hermetic with me. You're open and friendly!' Rosa, the pupil in the Nuns' House says.

'How can I help it, sweetie? You fascinate me.'

'Me?' Rosa half-questions and, half-teasing, pretends to question. 'It's too bad Peter doesn't feel it.'

The girls in the Nuns' House heard endlessly every detail of Peter's and Rosa's relations.

'Peter adores you!' O, the orphan who's the new pupil exclaims, fiercely blazing if Peter doesn't adore Rosa she'll make him do it.

'Well . . . he likes me,' Rosa begins to own up, twists her fingers in each other there's still a bit of a question. 'I know he does. Our arguments are my fault. My mind won't stay still. I'm never contented. Everything dissatisfies me. Still . . . he CAN be ridiculous!'

O's eyes demand what can possibly be ridiculous about gentle Peter. These days none of the boys are gentle.

'He never buys me coffee (Rosa means 'he never buys me expensive meals') . . . and he manipulates me I know he's manipulating me he's waving things over my head like marriage he knows I want to get married and he's using my want to control me even though he's a wimp.' Rosa answers as if everything she's saying is absolutely true.

O's realizing in a world where affection's possible she will have none. Consciousness of this pain gives her power. She without thinking grabs Rosa's hands and says, 'Please, be my friend. I need affection.'

'I'll be your friend,' Rosa replies straightaway, 'though you're so far above me you must have lots of friends. I'll be true to you and if I ever let you down, please understand, I don't mean to let you down, I'm just weak. I don't know anything about myself. You help me find who I am. You talk straight to me.'

O hugs her friends and holds her in her arms.

'Tell me, Rosa. Who's is this Mr Sadat?'

Rosa shakes. Her eye pupils look slightly upwards.

'Just before I came here, my brother and I met him.'

'He's Peter's uncle.'

'You don't like him?'

'Oh!' Rosa's hands go over her face. 'No.'

'He says he loves you very much.'

'Oh.' Rosa hugs her new resource (friend) even closer. 'I don't want to know . . . I don't know what there is about him that makes me feel this way. It doesn't make sense. I'm scared of him beyond any reason I know of. I think about him all the time. He terrifies me. He can get at me even when he's not around. He's evil. There's no such thing as evil.'

'What happened between you and him?'

'I can't talk now. I'm sorry. In a minute. Please don't go away from me. I'll be able to talk in a minute.'

'He DID do something horrible, didn't he?'

'No . . . no. He's very kind. He acts as he should. He never SAYS anything.'

'And yet. . .?'

'He doesn't say anything, but I know, I know it's true. He wants to have power over me he almost has power over me, I can hardly fight. He always acts kind to me. I have no reason to think this, I can't tell it to anyone. I'm mad. When I'm playing piano, his eyes are always on my hands. When I'm singing I'm a horrible singer, his eyes are always on my lips. He's telling me he's controlling me I'm accepting that I'm accepting our nonverbal agreement. I don't look at him. That doesn't matter. Every now and then my eyes have to brush by his our eyes meet just for a second, this means I agree I'm under the spell. Sometimes he's so powerful but he's not there, do you know what I mean, he's like a robot. I don't have any way of talking to him.'

'What could he actually want from you?'

'I don't know. All I do is fear. I can't see beyond fear.'

'Did anything else happen tonight?'

'No. Tonight his look was more compelling . . . his eyes stood on me more unmovingly than they ever have. He was holding me in his arms tonight. I couldn't bear the darkness. I cried out. Don't tell this to anyone. It's not true. Whatever you do don't tell Peter, please don't mention a word to Peter because he's Peter's uncle. Tonight you said you're strong, you don't know what fear is, please please be strong for me. I used to not know what fear is. I used to have the strength to believe what I feel is real and my affection for people makes me human. I can talk to you. You can't go away. Don't reject me. I'm scared now that I'm asking you you'll walk away.'

The lustrous gypsy-face droops over those clinging arms and chest; the wild black hair falls over the thin form. The intense eyes hold a sleeping burning energy, now softened by compassion and wonder. Let the man who's concerned NOTICE this!

Mr Anwar Sadat's monologue:

I'm seeing everything I've ever done rise up before me, just as they are; I have to see (face) everything, nothing is left untouched. I must see everything face-to-face, every action I do, and only finally when that is over, when I'm no longer horror, will I be free.

War is coming. I hate to say it, but it is. A more devastating war than before and the end of the world as we now know this world. There will be no more money, not much food or heat, diseases rampage, and fear hallucination will reign. It will be the days of nothing and the days of a kind of plenty where there are no causes and effects. There's no way to prepare for horror. Language like everything else will bear no relations to anything else. The business corporations who'll run the war are now bringing triple amounts of heroin and coke into this country to prepare the citizenship for soldiery. 'Another?' says this woman, in a querulous rattling whisper. 'Have another?'

The Lascar dribbles at the mouth. The graves are still.

'What visions can SHE have? Visions of more butcher shops and bars and MasterCharge cards? More and more people dying to throw their useless money away eat eat this horrible bed without these bodies on it this wall smooth and sanitary? What relations can drugged-up people have?'

He listens to the mutterings.

'Unintelligible!'

Culture has been chattering and chattering but to no purpose. When a sentence becomes distinct, it makes no more sense or connection. Wherefore the watcher says again. 'Unintelligible', nods his head, and smiles gloomily. He puts a few coins on the table, grabs a cap, gropes his way down the broken stairs, mumbles good-morning to some rat-ridden super sitting in an old plastic chair under the stairs, and passes out.

Dear Peter,
I'm finding it very hard to live without you.

The whole day long, in that rather too countrified house at Tansonville, which had the air merely of a place to rest in when out for a stroll or during a shower, one of those houses in which every drawing-room gives the effect of a summerhouse, and where, in the bedrooms, on the wallpaper of one of the roses of the garden, and on the wallpaper of the other birds from the trees have come to join you and keep you company (but one by one, at any rate, for these are old-fashioned wallpapers, on which each rose is so distinct it could have been picked if it had been real, and each bird could be put in a cage and tamed) having none of the pretentious interior decorating of the rooms of this day, in which, on a silver background, all of apple trees of Normandy stand out sharply in Japanese style, to fill with fantasies these hours spent closeted up – that whole day I remained in my room, which looked out on the beautiful verdure of the estate and the lilacs at the entrance border, on the tall trees at the edge of the water, their green foliage glistening in the sunlight, and on the forest of Meseglise. The only reason, at bottom, why I enjoyed looking at Proust's words was because I said to myself, 'It's pleasant to have so much verdure at my bedroom window,' until suddenly, in the vast, verdant picture I recognized – but brushed by contrast in deep blue simply because it was farther away – the spire of the church at Combray, not a representation of that spire, but the spire itself, which, bringing thus before my eyes distance in both space and time, had come and outlined itself on my windowpane in the midst of the given foliage but in a very different tone, so dark that it almost seemed as if it had been merely sketched in. And, if I stepped out of my room for a moment, at the end of the hall, because the hall faced in a different direction, I caught sight of a band of scarlet, as it were, just the wall covering of a small drawing-room which was of simple mousseline, but red and quick to burst into flame if a ray of sun was falling on it.

During our walks together, Gilberte talked to me about the way Robert was losing interest in her and increasing his attentions to other women. And it is true that his life was cluttered up with many affairs with women which, like certain masculine friendships in the lives of men who prefer women, had an air of hopelessly trying to defend their position and uselessly taking up space which, in most houses, characterizes objects that can serve no useful purpose.

During our many walks together, Peter's new girlfriend Shang-shi talked to me about the way Peter was losing interest in her and increasing his attentions to other women. And it is true that his life was cluttered up with many affairs with women which, like certain masculine friendships in the lives of men who prefer women, had an air of hopelessly trying to defend their position and uselessly taking up space which, in most houses, characterises objects that can serve no useful purpose.

'How much?' I ask the taxi-driver.

The taxi-driver answers, 'A dollar – unless you wish to make it more.'

I naturally say I have no wish to make it more.

'Then it must be a dollar,' observes the taxi-driver. 'I don't want to get into trouble. I know HIM!' He blackly closes an eye at my lawyer Mr Gordon's name and shakes his head.

The underworlds of the world

Anwar Sadat climbs up a broken staircase, opens the door in front of him, looks into a dark stifling room, and says, 'Are you alone now?'

'I'm always alone. Worse luck for me, deary, and better for you,' a croak replies. 'Come in, come in, whoever you are: I can't see you 'til

I light this match, I recognize your voice I think. I know you, don't I?'

'Light that match and see.'

'Oh oh deary I will oh oh, my hand is shaking so I can't put it on a match all of a sudden. And I cough so (cough cough) everytime I put these matches down they jump around, I never know where they are. Oh oh oh. They're jumping around, this damn cough, like living things. Are you planning to go somewhere, deary?'

'No.'

'Not planning to go on a long trip?'

'No way.'

'Well, there are people who travel by land and people who travel by sea. I'm the mother of both. I provide men with everything. Not like that Jack Chinaman Ludlow Street. he don't know what it is to father farther and mother. He don't know how to cut this, he charges what I charge and more, much much more, whatever he'll get. Here's a match, sweetie, uh-oh. Where's that candle? I never could stand electric lights. Everytime I start to cough, I cough out twenty of those damn matches before I get one lit. (She manages to light a match before she starts heaving again.) My lungs are gone! (Yellow phlegm) Oh oh oh!' While she's grabbing for her breath she can't see, all of her senses are dead, except the senses of coughing; now it's over – eyes open – life returning. 'Oh, you.'

'You're surprised to see me?'

'Aren't you dead?'

'Why do you think I'm dead?'

'You've been away from me for so long. How can you stay alive for three hours without me? Something bad must have happened to you?'

'Not at all. A relative died.'

'Died of what, deary?'

'Probably, death.'

Beginning her process and starting to bubble and blow at the faint spark enclosed in the hollow of her hands, she speaks from time to time, in a tone of snuffling satisfaction, without leaving off.

WHERE DO EMOTIONS COME FROM, ARE EMOTIONS NECESSARY. WHAT DO EMOTIONS TELL US ABOUT CONSCIOUSNESS?

She gives the man her brown leather bag.

She is sitting next to a man and her ass is bare on the taxicab fake leather.

He is reaching down into her blouse and making her pull off her clothes.

He's leaving her alone and she doesn't know how to handle an alien world.

He takes her somewhere she's never been before.

His hands are touching her sweater.

His hands are lifting her sweater up her back.

His hands are running down the outward slope of her ass.

His right hand's third finger is sitting in her asshole and his right hand thumb is an inch in her cunt.

He makes her cry out sharply.

His right hand is pushing her down.

His hard cock sticks into her hole.

He thrusts into her asshole without using any lubrication.

His knees stick into her face.

He explains to her she's not going to know.

His strong arm pulling on her arms is lifting her to her feet.

He shows her his whip.

One of his hands lies on her left shoulder.

He tells her she can expect he will hurt her mentally and physically.

He hurts her physically to give her an example.

He tells her there are no commitments and she has to let him make all the decisions, she won't make any more decisions.

IS THERE ANY NEED FOR EMOTION?

He says to her, 'Nothing you have, even your mind, is yours anymore. I'm a generous man. I'm going to give you nothing.'

She's turning around and catching his eyes staring at her as if he loves her.

She is sitting next to him and listening to him talk.

He is saying that it no longer matters what she thinks and what her choices are.

He is saying that he is the perfect mirror of her real desire and she is making him that way.

His eyes are not daring to meet her eyes.

He is walking back and down and in front of her.

He is dialling her phone number on the phone.

He's telling her to wait without any clothes on for him to come over.

He's telling her to throw out certain identities and clothes he doesn't like.

He's telling her he doesn't have any likes or dislikes so there's no way she can touch him.

He's telling her he's a dead man.

She's laying out her clothes and wondering which one's the softest.

She's wondering if she's going to die.

She is waiting for this man who says he's not her lover by trying to guess what he wants.

He is telling her iron becomes her.

He is seizing her by the throat and hair.

She is thinking that it is not a question of giving her consent and it is never a question of choice.

So what use is emotion? What use is anything? Oh, oh, she isn't understanding.

192

NOT ONLY IS THERE NO ESCAPE FROM PERCEIVING BUT THE ONLY WAY TO DEAL WITH PAIN IS TO KILL ONESELF TOTALLY BY ONESELF. SUICIDE HAS ALWAYS BEEN THE MOST DIFFICULT OF HUMANITY'S PROBLEMS.

Caress the tips of your nipples.

I'm giving you away so you have no choice who your teacher is.

Take off our skirt.

Suck me.

You don't care who you fuck.

Sex is only physical.

Play with your clit.

You'll obey me without loving me.

When you arrive, your eyes show happiness.

My hands are rubbing your breasts.

My lips are touching your breasts.

My lips are your lips.

When will you bring your whip?

I'm doing everything I can to understand.

I'm doing everything I can to control.

I'm doing everything I can to love (name).

My consciousness is letting loose every kind of emotion.

You will masturbate in front of me.

You are a whore.

All women are whores.

BLOOD SEEPS OUT OF ONE OF THE GIRLS' CUNTS WHILE HER LEGS ARE SPREAD OPEN

Hatless, wearing practically no make-up, her hair totally free, she looks like a well-brought-up-little girl, dressed as she is in a very full wool tweed little boys' trousers and a box-cut matching jacket, or little hand-knit pale blue or red sweaters, tiny collars around the neck, flopping over full-cut velvet trousers, pale blue silk slippers tied around her ankles, or her evening narrow black knee-length dress. Everywhere Sir S takes her people think she's his daughter and her addressing him in the most formal terms while he acts familiarly with her underlines this mistake. Sitting in an all-night restaurant during the early morning hours before grey light starts to appear walking past the few trees that exist at the lower end of Fifth Avenue while the evening sky is unable to turn completely black, an old woman in the restaurant begins to talk to them the people on the street smile at them.

Once in a while he stops next to a concrete building and puts his arms around her and kisses her and tells her he loves her. THE FUTURE: once he invites her to lunch with two of his Italian compatriots. This is the first time he's invited her to meet any of his friends. Then he shows up an hour before he said he was going to.

He has the keys to her place. She's naked. She's just finished meditating. She realizes he's carrying what looks like a golf club bag. He tells her to open his bag.

The whips are pink silk and pale black fur and one plaster and leather with tiny double and triple knots so there're no expectations and dolls and a long light brown whip that looks like the tail of a thin animal.

The minute he touches her she begins to come.

For the first time he asks her what her taste is.

She can't answer.

He tells her she's going to help him destroy her. Whips don't exist and are ridiculous. Who could confuse orgasm with pain?

The three girls in the school bathroom cold tiled floor, are giggling.

It's the first time he's taken her out and not treated her like a piece of shit.

The Swords Point Upwards

The man and the woman are sitting in the first restaurant he's ever taken her to. One of the man's friends is sitting in an armchair to her right, another to her left. The one on the left is tall, red-haired, grey-eyed, 25 years old. The man is telling his two friends he invited them to have dinner with the woman so they could do whatever they want with her in no uncertain terms because she's the most unnameable unthinkable spit spit. She realizes that she is at the same time a little girl absolutely pure nothing wrong just what she wants, and this unnameable dirt this thing. This is not a possible situation. This identity doesn't exist.

Her grandmother lifts up her pink organdie skirt to show the hotel headwaiter, 'Look what my granddaughter's wearing! Her first new girdle! And only six years old!'

The first man doesn't recognize her humanity. All the men she has don't recognize her humanity. Kneel down suck off our cocks. While you're sucking them off, use the fingers of both hands with those quick feather ways you do. Then they all go away as quickly as possible while she's swallowing their cum.

The young boys being completely overwhelmed by her strength – her calm existing in such contradiction – tell her they want her to tell them everything. They give themselves over to her as if they're clay, not human. They fuck again and again. They can't get enough fucking. Then they turn on her. They hate her guts because she allowed them to be weak. They want to beat her up.

The following day, scared she'll leave him, he tells her the red-haired boy says he wants to marry her and so take her away from this unbearable contradiction in which she's living.

It's always her decision. She tells him she wants to become another, as if at this point it's even a question of a decision, though it always is.

Animality

Sparrow-hawk, falcon, owl, fox, lion, bull: nothing but animal masks, but scaled to the size of the human head, made of real fur and feathers, the eye crowned with lashes when the actual animal has lashes, as the lion has, and with pelts and feathers falling to the person-wearing-them's shoulders. A moulded, hardened cardboard frame placed between the outer facing and the skin's inner lining keep the mask shape rigid. The most striking and the one she thinks transforms her the most is the owl mask because tan and tawny feathers whose colours are her cunt hairs make it; the feathery cape almost totally hides her shoulders, descending halfway down the back and the front of the beginning of the breasts' swell.

'But O, and I hope you'll forgive me, you'll be taken on a leash.'

Natalie returns holding the chain and pliers which Sir S uses to force open the last link. He fastens it to the second link of the chain stuck in her cunt. After she remasks herself, Sir S tells Natalie to take hold of the end of the chain and walk around the room, ahead of her (being chained to the text).

'Well I must say,' he remarks, 'the Commander's right, all the hair'll have to be removed. Meanwhile keep wearing your chain.'

What shocks and upsets the girl at the depilatory parlour the following day, more than the irons and the black-and-blue marks on her lower back, are the brand new whip marks. No matter how many times she repeats attempts to explain, if not what her fate (decision) is, at least that she's happy; there's no way of reassuring this girl or allaying her feelings of disgust and terror. No matter how much she thanks these people how polite just like a little girl she acts when she's leaving this parlour where for hours she's lain her legs spread as wide as possible not to get fucked but to get love, it doesn't matter how much money she gives all of them; she feels they're rejecting her rather than her walking out of a business appointment. She realizes that there's something shocking in the contrast between the fur on her belly and the feathers on her mask just as she realizes that this air of an Egyptian statue which the mask lends her, and which her broad shoulder narrow waist and muscled legs serve only to emphasize, demands her flesh be absolutely hairless.

Stared at them with eyes opened wide, deaf to human language and dumb. People seeing her, with expressions of horror and contempt turn and flee. Sir S is using O model to demonstrate. Stone wax unhuman. Daybreak is awakening the asleep. Unfasten chains, remove masks.

The Beginning

As you and Sir S are walking out of the subway station, up to the street, a young cop or a young man who looks like a cop, as soon as he sees Sir S, steps forward from a large black Mercedes whose doors are locked. He bows, opens the rear car door, and steps aside. After you've settled in the back seat, your luggage in the front seat, Sir S' lips lightly brush your right cheek and he closes the door.

The car starts suddenly, so fast you don't know enough to grab him to call out. Although you throw yourself against the moving back window, he's gone forever you feel frenzy.

The car is rapidly moving westward into the countryside. You are oblivious to the outside world because you are crying.

The terrorist driver is tilting his seat so it's almost horizontal to pull your legs on to the front seat. Your legs are pressing the ceiling as he's plunging his huge cock into you. He doesn't stop for an hour. He moans loudly when he comes.

The driver is 25 years old. He has a thin narrow face, large black eyes. He looks very sensitive and at the edge of being weak. His mouth never approaches your mouth. There is a basic agreement that the act of kissing is far more explosive than that of fucking.

When he finishes fucking you, you pull down your skirt and then button your thin hand-crocheted linen sweater through whose lace delicate puckers of nipples can be seen. You carefully place red lipstick over your lips.

If you want to, you can reach out and grab armfuls of red foxgloves.

'The driver raped you. You're two hours late. You let him rape you.'

'Everything happens as Sir S says. Is he going to come?'

'I think so. I don't know when.'

The tenseness felt in all your muscles when your're asking this question slowly dissolves and you look at this woman gratefully: how lovely she is, how sparkling with her hair streaked with grey. She's wearing over black pants and a matching blouse, an antique Chinese jacket.

Obviously the rules which govern the dress and conduct of the terrorists don't apply to her.

'Today I want to have lunch with you. Go wash yourself. At 3 o'clock sharp I'll be back.'

You silently follow her; you're floating on cloud nine: Sir S says he'll see you again.

In this female terrorist house which is disguised as a girl's school, you're free to move around. You're standing on the Delancey Street corner. It's raining lightly. You know you're older than the other girls. A man might not want you cause the skin on your face's slightly wrinkled. Men want young tight fresh girl skin. They want new. They want to own. They want to be amazed. You're gonna have to work three times as hard as the other girls to get your men. This work is creating an image which men will strongly crave. This image has to be composed (partly) of your strong points and has to picture something some men beyond rationality want. You have to keep up this image to survive.

You put all thoughts away. Thoughts can be present in those hiatuses when you're not a machine moving to survive. You are a perfect whore so you're not human.

Get off this. 'Hi honey, I can do anything.' Your hips wiggle far wider than any other whore's hips. You're stealing outright from the restaurants you're sitting in you're laughing in those faces of big businessmen who look like pigs when a bum's pulling a knife on you you say, 'Honey, it's too short.' Nothing can touch (hurt) you when you're moving this fast: a perfect image: closed.

This' why you're the best whore in the world. You have to make this image harder. While you're a whore, you can love someone. While you're a whore, it's impossible for anyone to love you.

Sir S wants you to prostitute to bring him money.

'Listen, Oh, I've heard quite enough. If Sir S wants you to go to bed for money, he's certainly free to do so. It's not your concern. Go to sleep now, baby, shut up. As for your other duties and obligations, we use the sister system here. Noelle will be your sister, and she'll explain all the procedures to you.'

The whores spend most of their time with other whores and live in a steamy, hot atmosphere, a dressing room (perhaps one pimp who is a cardboard figure over whom they obsess just like the pupils in an all-girls' school and the one male religion teacher), here at the edge of being touchable. Their knowledge of how vulnerable each of them is defines their ways of talking to each other and creates a bond, the strongest interfemale bond women know, between them.

Women's sexuality isn't goal-oriented, is all-over. Women will do anything, not for sex, but for love, because sex isn't a thing to them, it's all over undefined, every movement motion to them is a sexual oh. This is why women can be sexually honest and faithful. This is why women look up to things, are amazed by things. Women hate things the most.

Running the tip of his riding crop over the skin of your breasts.

'Why didn't you bring your whips tonight? At least you can slap my face.'

Takes hold of your large nipples and pulls.

Calls you 'a whore'.

You're tightening around the flesh pole that fills and burns you. The pole doesn't move out.

'Caress me with your mouth.'

You enjoy prostituting with this stranger.

She kisses the tip of one of your breasts through the black lacework covering it.

'They won't tell me their names,' she says. 'But they look nice, don't they?'

The men are embarrassed and vulgar. Their third drink has made them drunk.

They take a table for four. Just as they're finishing dinner, the man who took you last night walks into the restaurant. He discreetly signals and sits by himself.

'Shall we go upstairs?'

One of the hotel waiters shows you to a room. Without being asked, you walk over to your customer to offer him your breasts. You're slightly astonished to see how easy it is to offer your tits to this unknown man.

He tells you to undress, then stops you. Your irons impress him. As he's pulling his cock out of your asshole he says, 'If you're really good, I'll give you a fat tip.'

There's no possibility that anyone'll love you anymore or that love matters. Because there's no hope of realizing what you want, you're a dead person and you're having sex.

He leaves before you're out of bed, leaves a handful of bills on a small white table. You walk back to the house after having neatly folded the bills and stuffed them in your cleavage.

Your chains are disappearing.

You can decide now whether to get dressed or not.

You can decide now whether to work for money or not.

You can decide now who to talk to.

He still whips you every day. When you complain another girl says, 'You want to be whipped so why are you being querulous? You're not Justine.'

Who you are is obvious. There's no one else but you. If you want to get whipped, like being whipped, girl.

You own me.

You control me.

I have nothing to do with you.

You're a murderer.

There's no such thing as a terrorist: there're only murderers.

I'm a masochist.

This is a real revolution.

Sometimes men bring straight women into the brothel. These straight women act like they're not looking down on the whores they see and yet, underneath this fake understanding or liberality, pure fascination lies. Fascination can involve no such intellectual judgment. These women tremble in front of the whores. Their eyes secretly follow around the corners of the doorways. Their eyes pin themselves on the long upper thighs, the cunt hair that might show, is it wet? How does she act when she's . . . with a MAN? Does she spread her legs very wide? What tricks does she use to make the man love her? Is she real? Is her underwear filthy? Does she drink piss in her mouth? Is she just an orgasming machine? Is she just a sink-into-flesh machine? What's it like to be without brains? Not to have any worries about how to get along in life how to keep up respect (among men) how to manage my career and children how to maintain my image and underneath the image. . .? What's it like to live in that one (animal) place?

I'm not like HER? I'm a person. The beautiful woman adjusts her face. Her left hand lightly brushes over the top of her man's hand to show she and he are real: she's his woman because they're a twosome: real people in a real working world unlike these HOLES who DON'T EXIST.

You're watching the girls in the brothel:

A slender but well-proportioned girl, all white against the cunt-blood hangings, shaking, bearing on her hips for the first time the purple crop furrows. Her lover is a thin young man who's holding her, by her shoulders, back on the bed, the way Rene had held you, and watching with obvious pleasure and agony as you open your sweet burning belly to a man you've never seen beneath whose weight the girl's moaning.

They belong exclusively to members of the Club; they give themselves up to unknown men; as soon as they're ready, their lovers prostitute them in the outer world for no reason at all.

Other girls prostitute only for money, don't have pimps, and will never leave prison.

One girl is left in the brothel six months, then taken out forever.

Jeanne lived in the brothel a year, left, then returned.

Noelle stayed for two months, left for three months, returned totally broke.

Yvonne and Julienne who like you get whipped several times a day will not leave.

A man's making love to you.

He's giving you a ring, a collar, and two diamond bracelets instead of your irons.

He's saying he's going to take you to Africa and America.

'No! No!' you scream. You can't bear to have anyone love you. You can't bear another person's consciousness. You don't want anyone in your distorted desolated life.

'You're now free,' the streaked-with-grey-haired terrorist says to you. 'We can remove your irons, your collar, and bracelets, and even erase the brand. You have the diamonds, you can go home.'

You don't cry; you don't show any sign of bitterness. Nor do you answer her.

'But if you prefer,' she goes on, 'you can stay here.'

The jellyfish is the rapist. When O was 17 years old her father tried to rape her when she told him he couldn't rape her he weeps. 'Your mother won't fuck me, those boys don't respect you enough, I'm the only man who's respecting you.' This night O has a nightmare. A huge jellyfish glop who's shaped into an-at-least-six-storey worm is chasing her down the main sand-filled cowboy street. All of her WANTS to get away, but her body isn't obeying her mind. Like she feels she's caught in quicksand so her body is her quicksand.

Nightmare: her body mirrors/becomes her father's desire. This is the nightmare.

Then O had a number of S&M relationships with guys who dug their fingernails into her flesh slapped her face then jellyfish wanted to become her whinedabouttheirproblems wanted to become her. Then O almost killed herself by developing an ovarian infection.

Men are rapists because rape rope is something O doesn't want. Why do people kill? A person kills, not from impotence but because he or she doesn't see what he or she is doing. O had to either deny her father's sex and have no father or fuck her father and have a father. This event led O to believe that a man would love her only if she did something she didn't want to do. How can I talk about ignorance, what ignorance unknowing is?

A young prince enjoying the company of an enchanting woman; he receives a cup of wine, elixir of life, out of her hands.

Probably Timurid period, 15th century.

The period corresponding roughly to the 15th century takes its name from the great conqueror Timur or Tamerlane, whose armies overran the Near East between 1365 and his death in 1405, and whose descendants held court in Persia for the next hundred years. The classic style introduced by Ahmad Musa had reached its apex under the Jalayrid Sultan Ahmad, who ruled at Baghdad till its conquest by Timur. After that his artists seemed to have taken service with the Timurid princes, especially Iskandar Sultan under whose patronage the Timurid style may be said to have been formed:

2 The beginnings of romance

The First Days

Timelessness versus time.

I remember it was dusk. The lamps began to appear against a sky not yet dark enough to need them. I was shy of my mother because when she was on ups she was too gay and selfish and on downs she was bitchy. When she changed from ups to downs was the best time to approach her.

I adored my actress mother and would do anything for her. 'Sarah, be a good girl and get me a glass of champagne.' 'Sarah, I'm out of money again. Your father's horrible. You don't need an allowance: give me ten dollars and I'll pay you back tomorrow.' She never paid me back and I adored her.

'I never wanted you,' my mother told me often. 'It was the war.' She hadn't known poverty or hardship: her family had been very wealthy. 'I had terrible stomach pains and the only doctor I could get to was a quack. He told me I had to get pregnant.' 'I never heard of that. You got pregnant?' 'The day before you were born I had appendicitis. You spent the first three weeks of your life in an incubator.'

The rest I know is little. My father, a wealthier man than my mother, walked out on her when he found out she was pregnant with me. Since neither she nor grandmama Siddons ever said anything specific about him, I didn't know who he was. I always turned to my mother and I loved her very much.

Mother didn't want me to leave her. I think she could have loved me or shown that she loved me if she had had more time or fewer obsessions. 'I don't care if my daughter respects me. I want her to love me.' She craved my love as she craved her friends' and the public's love only so she could do what she wanted and evade the responsibility. All her friends did love her and I, I lived so totally in the world bounded by her being her seemings, I had no idea we were a socially important family. I didn't know there was a world outside her.

There is just moving and there are different ways of moving. Or: there is moving all over at the same time and there is moving linearly. If everything is moving-all-over-the-place-no-time, anything is everything. If this is so, how can I differentiate? How can there be stories? Consciousness just is: no time. But any emotion presupposes differentiation. Differentiation presumes time, at least BEFORE and NOW. A narrative is an emotional moving.

It's a common belief that something exists when it's part of a narrative. Self-reflective consciousness is narrational.

Mother wanted me to be unlike I was. I got 'A's in school – it wasn't that I was a good girl, in fact even back then I was odd girl out: school was just the one place where I could do things right – but mother said getting 'A's made me stand out too much. Otherwise I was just a failure. I felt too strongly. My emotional limbs stuck out as if they were broken and unfixable. I kissed mother's friends too nicely when they were playing canasta. I was too interested in sex. I wasn't pretty in a conventional enough way. I didn't act like Penelope Wooding. When I washed a dish, I wasn't washing the dish. Since I didn't know if mother was god, I didn't know if I loved her. My friends told me I perceived in too black-and-white terms. 'The world is more complex,' they said. I said, 'I get 'A's in school.' Unlike.

'What was my father like, mommy?'

My mother looks up from a review of her newest hit. In those days she always got fabulous reviews.

'I mean my real father.' When I had turned ten years old, my mother had carefully explained to me that the man I called my father had adopted me.

'He was very handsome.'

'What exactly did he look like?' I had no right to ask, but I was desperate.

'His parents were wonderful. They were one of the richest families in Brooklyn.'

Talking with my mother resembled trying to plot out a major war strategy. 'What did his family do?'

'I was very wild when I was young. You remember Aunt Suzy. I'd sneak down the fire escape and Aunt Suzy and I'd go out with boys. I'd let them pet.' My mother was high on Dex. 'Your father was very handsome, dark, I fell in love with him. It was during the war so everyone was getting married.' My mother refused to say anymore.

When I asked grandmama Siddons about my real father, she said he was dead. I replied I knew he wasn't dead. She said he was a murderer.

Why is anybody interested in anything? I'm interested when I'm discovering. To me, real moving is discovering. Real moving, then, is that which endures. How can that be?

Otherwise I lived in my imaginings. If anyone had thought about me rather than about their own obsessions, they would have thought it was a lonely childhood, but it wasn't. I had all of New York City to myself. Since mother was an actress we had to live in New York or London, and I hugged New York to me like a present. Sometimes I'd leave the apartment and walk down First Avenue to the magic bookstore of brightly-coloured leatherbound books. Book- and dress-stores were magic places I could either dream or walk to. Then I walked up Madison Avenue and fantasized buying things. I walked down to Greenwich Village where the most interesting bookstore held all the beatnik poets but I never saw them. I had to happen upon what I wanted. I was forbidden to act on my desire, even to admit my desire to myself. Poetry was the most frightening, therefore the most interesting, appearance. Once or twice a monthly afternoon I'd avidly watch a play I had no way of comprehending.

When it was all happening around me and I had very few memories of what was happening, I didn't need to understand and, if I had understood, I probably would have been too scared to keep moving.

Mother was a real actress. I never knew who she was. I had no idea until after the end that she was spending all of her money and, then, that she was broke. She had always been very tight with me: taking away my allowances, never buying me anything. She madly frittered away money. Suddenly, surprisingly, she asked me if I wanted gifts and she bought me three copies of a gold watch she liked. At the same time she owed three months' rent, two of her bank accounts were closed, all of her charge cards had been revoked. The 800 shares of AT&T grand-mama had given her were missing. She was becoming gayer and less prudish. I would have done anything for her. She didn't talk to me or to anyone directly. She lifted up her favourite poodle, walked out of the apartment house, and didn't return.

Do I care? Do I care more than I reflect? Do I love madly? Get as deep as possible. The more focus, the more the narrative breaks, the more memories fade: the least meaning.

In spite of these circumstances which brought me to Ashington House, I'm thrilled when I see it. Trees always make my heart beat quickly. Bronze chrysanthemums. Dahlias around a pond in which two ducks quack, black and grey. And the whistle low. Two long streets, along leaves, lead away.

My aunts Martha and Mabel greet me. I've never met them before.

They're very wealthy and they're so polite, they're eccentric. They tell me I'm going to meet my real father. I don't want to see him, I do I do. I know he's handsome.

Aunt Martha tells me he's away at the moment.

We stop, walking in front of a picture of my father. At least it's a picture of him. 'Your father,' Aunt Mabel comments, 'was too adventurous. Wild . . . headstrong . . . Your mother was his first wife and you were his first child.'

'Who's his new wife?'

'He's had three. Last year he killed someone, shot him, who was trespassing on his yacht. The family got him off on psychological reasons. After his six-month stay in a rest home, he just disappeared.'

'Aunt Mabel's scared, dear.' Judy's commenting on Punch, 'that you have some of your father's wildness.'

Despite my politeness, they know who I am.

'I really don't know very much, Sarah. But I don't think you should have anything to do with him.'

'Your father,' Aunt Mabel interrupts her sister, 'acts unpredictably. He can be extremely violent. We have no way of telling how he'll act when he sees you. The family has decided to help you as much as we can, but we can't help you with this.'

I don't know what I'm going to believe.

He – for there can be no doubt of his sex, though the fashion of the time did something to disguise it – was in the act of slicing at the head of a Moor which swung from the rafters. It was the colour of an old football.

I called Jackson up and he came over immediately. He was a drunken messy slob, maudlin as they come which all drunks are, but that's what let him be the kind of artist he was. He NEEDED to suffer to thrust himself out as far as he could go farther beyond the bounds of his physical body what his body could take he NEEDED to maul shove into knead his mental and physical being like he did those tubes of paint. I not only understood, I understood and adored. I would be the pillow he would kick the warm breast he could cry into open up to let all the infinite unstoppable mainly unbearable pain be alive I would not snap back I would be his allower of exhibited pain so he could keep going. That's why he loved me. He didn't need brains. He didn't need intelligence he was too driven.

'You're so beautiful, so warm: I don't know why you want me.'

'I don't want you 'cause you're famous, Jackson. That's why all those other people're eating you up, making you think you're only an image HISTORY (in New York City a person's allowed to be alive or human if he/she's is famous or close enough to a famous person to absorb some of the fame) so now you can no longer paint unless you close up all your senses and become a real moron. I want your cock because you're a great artist.'

He seemed to be crying for his entire life. 'I always thought about you, darling, even before I knew you. Exactly who you are was my picture of you: you are the woman I wanted the woman I thought I could never have. Now I know you. Why do you want me? I'm a mess. I said to myself: I'll do anything I can, with myself with EVERY-THING, to make my work, I did it, I did do it, I really fucked up my health and my mind. I don't regret this, but now I'm a mess. Please, don't be naive.'

I knew this man, whatever would happen and death was the least, would stick by me.

And 'she was given the real names of things' means she really perceived, she saw the real. That's it. If everything is living, it's not a name but moving. And without this living there is nothing; this living is the only matter matters. The thing itself. This isn't an expression of a real thing: this is the thing itself. Of course the thing itself the thing itself it is never the same. This is how aestheticism can be so much fun. The living thing the real thing is not what people tell you it is: it's what it is. This is the thing itself because I'm finding out about it it is me. It is a matter of letting (perceiving) happen what will.

My mother was dead. We knew that. She might have been murdered or she might have killed herself, perhaps accidentally. The police had abandoned the case and I didn't know how to find out on my own.

None of my father's family made any show of mourning for my mother. The funeral was a ghastly comedy. I was the only one sobbing my heart out while around me, hordes of women discussed Joan Crawford and her daughter and canasta games. Every now and then, I remember, Aunt Mabel told me to hand the chocolates around to her friends. I was wearing a fuzzy lavender sweater. One middle-aged woman shook the sweater back and forth and screamed that she wanted my mother's apartment.

After that, for a few months, I had nightmares, not nightmares but those deeper where I'd screaming wake up because there are so many thoughts, the thoughts are unknown.

I realize that all my life is is endings. Not endings, those are just events; but holes. For instance when my mother died, the 'I' I had always known dropped out. All my history went away. Pretty clothes and gayness amaze me.

The next thing I knew I received a letter from my father saying he was journeying to Seattle to see me, and then, it seems just a few days later, but that's my memory, I was standing in an old wood bar, then I was sitting down, a roly-poly man not at all the handsome soul-eyed man in that little painting I had wondered on was telling me he distinctly remembered my mother. But he didn't sound upset about her and she had been obsessed by him. 'Are you my father?' I finally asked. 'No,

I'm your father's first cousin.' He began to proposition me. 'Oh, where's my father?'

'He's not here yet.' Then this roly-poly man told me he came from an immensely wealthy family. His daughter picked bums off the street and slept with them. These stories made me realize that my mother's bohemian and my weirdnesses, which I had thought the same as the rich's amorality, were only stinky bourgeois playfulness.

Lutetia is the foulest because poorest section of Paris. After Charles the Simple visits Lutetia, he's so disgusted he tears a plan of Lutetia in two and orders the split to be made into a wide avenue.

Yvikel the widower has a daughter Blanchine whose health is slowly declining. They live in the centre of Lutetia. Yvikel does everything he can for his daughter and resolves when she dies he'll kill himself.

After the avenue is built and sunlight, hitherto unknown, floods their rat-trap, Blanchine begins to recover. She recovers. To celebrate his gratitude. Yvikel recreates the plan of Lutetia in silk. Charles the Simple's hand reaches out and saves the section.

Dr Sirhugues discovers a therapeutic blue plant light. An enormous lens concentrates this light on the diseased person held still by a cylindrical cage or 'focal gaol'. But the rays are too powerful for the person to bear. Finally Dr Sirhugues finds that only Yvikel's ancient silk is able to absorb and render harmless the dangerous portion of these rays.

I don't think I'm crazy. There's just no reality in my head and my emotions fly all over the place: sometimes I'm so down, all I think is I should kill myself. Almost at the same time I adore everything: I adore the sky. I adore the trees I see. I adore rhythms. I . . . I . . . I . . . I . . . I'm I'm mine mine my. I can't I can't. I hate being responsible oh.

I don't care what people think; when they think they're thinking about me, they're actually thinking about the ways they act. I certainly don't want them to give me their pictures of me I like the ways animals are socially. I would rather be petted than be part of this human social reality which is all pretense and lies.

I expected my father to be a strong totally sexually magnetic daredevil, macho as they come, but he was kind and gentle. He must have been very ill when I first met him because he had had five heart attacks. But his great physical pleasures were still drinking on the sly from Aunts Martha and Mabel and eating half-a-pint of coffee ice cream before going to bed. He relied for his life on the roly-poly cousin Clifford Still.

He must have wanted Clifford and me to marry. He believed in a reality that was stable which justice formed. A man who worked hard earned pleasure. A woman who took care of her husband kept his love. Approaching, death, for I quickly realized my father was extremely sick, frighteningly had to destroy those bourgeois illusions.

As his sickness grew, he began to depend on me. He didn't want me to walk away from his bed. I had known so much sickness.

'Your mother led me a hard life, Sarah.'

'You weren't together very long, daddy.'

'It was a passionate difficult existence. She wanted me to wear out. I don't think that's fair. I never understood her and I had very little tolerance for who she really was: I adopted a figurehead. It was my death or getting rid of her, and she wanted the career.'

'You thought you loved her.'

'She depended on me more than she knew.'

'People who don't have any sense of reality, daddy, live crazy. Other people don't understand why they act the ways they do. They survive because everyone survives.'

As death approached my father said his life was useless. Because he now mistrusted.

I watched everything and I swore I'd never marry a man I didn't love and I'd never live for security.

Everyone hates me. My mother may have been murdered. Men want to rape me. My body's always sick. The world is paradise. Pain doesn't exist. Pain comes from askew human perceptions. A person's happy who doesn't give attention to her own desires but always thinks of others. Repressing causes pain. I have no one in this world. Every event is totally separate from every other event. If there are an infinite number of non-relating events, where's the relation that enables pain?

All of my family is dead. I have no way of knowing who means me harm and who doesn't.

The First Days of Romance

My father had left me all his possessions and I was, by the world's accounting, a well-to-do young woman. I owned a large house in Seattle. The rest of the money, since it was tied up in stocks and bonds and lawyers' incomprehensible papers, only meant that I was no longer untouchable. I knew most people wanted money or fame desperately just in order to survive. I knew I was no longer a person to a man, but an object, a full purse. I needed someone to love me so I could figure out reality.

The rest of my life was programmed for me: since I had inherited a house in Seattle, I would go to Seattle. Clifford, my father's best friend, was going to accompany me. I would never do what I wanted to do. My aunts Martha and Mabel would make sure that my money wouldn't allow me to act unreasonably and pleasurably. I was to grow accustomed to that reality.

My father died in the middle of January. It is now almost two years later. I can't describe Sutton Place – where Ashington House lay – for I miss it so deeply.

St Agnes' Eve – Ah, bitter chill it was!
The owl for all his feathers, was a-cold;
The hare limped trembling through the frozen grass,
And silent was the flock in woolly fold;
Numb were the beadman's fingers, while he told
His rosary, and while his frosted breath,
Like pious incense from a censer old,
Seemed taking flight for heaven, with out a death,
Past the sweet Virgin's picture, while his prayer he saith.

It was snowing all the time. Frost covered the rooftops the trees the cars. People without hands walked slowly down the middle of the streets. Just as during the blackout, New York City had become a small happy town or a series of small towns strung out in a line. Whenever my mind looked in its mirror, it counted up its blessings: I was walking down a street. There was no one who was attacking me. There were no more stories or passion in my life. I had moments of happiness (non-self-reflectiveness) when I read books.

I knew there could be no way I would live with a man, because, while I desperately needed total affection, I wasn't willing to give up my desires which is what men want and I couldn't trust. The men who were part of my life weren't really part of my life: Clifford who I hated and the delivery boys who were weaklings.

Only sensations. What the imagination seizes as Beauty must be truth – whether it exists materially or not – for I have the same idea of all our Passions as of Love they are all in their sublime, creative of essential Beauty . . . The imagination may be compared to Adam's dream – he awoke and found it truth. I am the more zealous in this affair, because I have never yet been able to perceive how anything can be known for truth by consecutive reasoning – and yet it must be. Can it be that even the greatest philosopher ever arrived at his goal without putting aside numerous objections? However it may be Oh, for a Life of Sensations rather than of Thoughts!

Of silks satins quilted satins taken from grandmother's bed thick satins black fur shorn from living lambs cotton steel wool the density of shit chewed-up cinnamon bark clustered angora and linen goose and duck feathers slumber

Of pyramid cheeses covered by red pepper overripe goat cheeses blue runs through the middle blue alternates with wine down the middle port sherry crumbled crumbling at fingertips' pressing no taste a physical touch sensation more than a taste the nose winding around itself

In front of the eye: red blue yellow green brown grey purple violet grey-blue violet-grey in various combinations or forms move by in a faintly maintained rhythm. These are the pleasures of the mind.

The mistake is allowing oneself to be desperate. The mistake is believing that indulgence in desire a decision to follow desire isn't possibly painful. Desire drives everything away: the sky, each building, the enjoyment of a cup of cappucino. Desire makes the whole body-mind turn on itself and hate itself.

Desire is Master and Lord.

The trick is to figure out how to get along with someone apart from desire if that's at all possible.

The body is sick and grows away from the perceiver. As old age comes the body gets sicker. All this is inevitable. When the body's sick, also the nerves are sick, the mind becomes sick because it no longer knows if it can trust itself. The scream no longer against pain, pain is now accepted as part of living, but again doubt begins.

I'm going to tell you something. The author of the work you are now reading is a scared little shit. She's frightened, forget what her life's like, scared out of her wits, she doesn't believe what she believes so she follows anyone. A dog. She doesn't know a goddamn thing she's too scared to know what love is she has no idea what money is she runs away from anyone so anything she's writing is just un-knowledge. Plus she doesn't have the guts to entertain an audience. She should put lots of porn in this book cunts dripping big as Empire State buildings in front of your nose and then cowboy violence: nothing makes any sense anyway. And she says I'm an ass 'cause I want to please. What'm I going to do? Teach?

Author: You're a dumb cocksucker. If someone dumb person bought this book, he should have the grace to read it and if he doesn't like me, so what.

He (the author) has not hit the humours, he does not know 'em; he has not conversed with the Barthol'mew-birds, as they say; he has ne'er a sword-and-buckler man in his Fair, nor a little Davy to take toll o' the bawds there, as in my time, nor a Kindheart, if anybody's teeth should chance to ache in his play. None o' these fine sights! Nor has he the canvas-cut i' the night for a hobby-horse man to creep in to his she-neighbour and take his leap there! Nothing! No, an' some writer (that I personally know) had had but the penning o' this matter, he would ha' made you such a jig-a-jog i' the booths, you should ha' thought an earthquake had been i' New York! But these master-poets, they ha' their own absurd courses; they will be informed of nothing! Would not a fine pump upon the stage ha' done well for a property now? And a punk set under her head, with her stern upward, and ha' been soused by my witty young masters o' the Cop Station? What think you o' this for a show, now? He will not hear o' this? I am an ass, I?

Author: Huh? What rare discourse are you fall'n upon, ha? Ha' you found any friends here, that you are so free? Away rogue, it's come to a fine degree in these spectacles when such a youth as you pretend to a judgement.

What is this that we sail through? What palpable obscure? What smoke and reek, as if the whole steaming world were revolving on its axis, as a spit?

Sailors, who long ago had lashed themselves to the taffrail for safety; but must have famished.

'Look here,' said Jackson, hanging over the rail and coughing, 'look there; that's a sailor's coffin. Ha! Ha! Buttons,' turning round to me. 'How do you like that, Buttons? Wouldn't you like to take a sail with them 'ere dead men? Wouldn't it be nice?' And then he tried to laugh, but only coughed again.

'Don't laugh at dem poor fellows,' said Max, looking grave. 'Do' you see dar bodies, dar souls are farder off dan de Cape of Dood Hope.'

'Dood Hope, Dood Hope,' shrieked Jackson, with a horrid grin, mimicking the Dutchman, 'dare is not dood hope for dem, old boy; dey are drowned and d . . . d, as you and I will be, Red Max, one of dese dark nights.': THE ONLY CERTAINTY

To prove that there was nothing to be believed; nothing to be loved, and nothing worth living for; but everything to be hated, in the wide world.

Sir, my mother has had her nativity-water cast lately by the cunning men in Cow-Lane, and they ha' told her her fortune, and do ensure her she shall never have happy hour, unless she marry within this sen'night, and when it is, it must be a madman, they say.

Why didn't Melville suicide?

He didn't want to.

Which was, to lead him, in close secrecy,
Even to Madeline's chamber, and there hide
Him in a closet, of such privacy
That he might see her beauty unespied,
And win perhaps that night a peerless bride,
Never on such a night have lovers met.

The old woman leads him through many halls to the bedroom. He hides and hiding watches the girl he's in love with. Around the window a carved representational frame stained glass the middle a shield the middle blood. The girl who's never fucked takes her clothes off. She falls asleep on her bed. The young man covers her naked tits with candied apples fruits creamy jellies cinnamon syrup dishes silver, and lies down beside her.

She doesn't wake up. 'Now, Sarah, this is purely medicinal.' He handed the full cup to me. 'It'll warm you. You must be warmed. What you should have is a hot bath and climb into a warm bed. I'm afraid Parrot Cottage can't offer such amenities. Never mind. This is the next best thing.'

I did what he wanted me to and I hated myself for doing it. I was feeling good because the hot liquid relaxed my body and my tension; this growing ease made me a traitor to myself.

I had to keep the joy growing to blot out my consciousness of what was happening to me. Sensuous beauty is its own perfect excuse, for it brings itself into existence. Constant unendable sensuousness – not passion, which destroys – allows neither time nor memory. Later what happened helped me to understand my own nature; and even later, I could remember. I knew that this glory will and always happens and has something to do with dislike.

There is a dreamlike quality: my body wants as simply as any dream action. The body that wants a man whom I remember I heartily dislike, Clifford Still, can't be my body and I'm not upset. I know he knows every pore of my body better than I do. He's tricky. He gets me to be who he wants.

He says it's love. I mutter something about the girl I've heard he's going to marry. He laughs, and his laughter excites me.

'She's here with me,' he said. 'She's Miss Sarah Ashington. I decided she was the one as soon as I set eyes on her.'

We married, but I still wanted madly to tell him I was afraid. I did not love the man I had married. He had overwhelmed me and aroused a certain passion in me. For a deadly moment I had found him irresistible. I don't love him, I cried inside my mind. I hate the inside of my mind. I want loving kindness, tenderness, not this mad wild emotion which he makes me become.

He drops to his knees and kisses my brow my eyelids my throat. He is kissing my naked heart. His tiny hands are shuddering my naked heart and now he is beside me (he is whispering to me he is whispering into me) This whisper is an outside cool breath This whisper is controlling me this whisper is my breath

In Paris policemen wearing blue triangular hats walk past buildings smaller than themselves and murderers look like each other and wear black. The ornamentation of Venice is precise a fairytale. The Roman streets lie sunlit, though there's no sun, where rooms, above, wander into room after room so that inside is outside though it isn't. Sometimes I murdered a man or a group of men murdered me. I never saw the details of their faces.

'Sarah, my love,' he murmured, 'didn't you know? It was meant to be.

'I raped you,' he said.

I stared at him incredulously.

'I want you to realize what a resourceful husband you have. You know how thick these winter fogs become? It occurred to me it'd be easy to lose our way . . . to wander around and around. You would feel tired. You wouldn't know what you were doing. I would make you drunk. I would be your saviour. Under the guise of being God, I'd do what I want. You see how romanticism works.'

'Is love always disgusting?' I was still regarding his perspective as useful.

He laughed. 'What do you say, my pet? What does your body say when I touch it? I'm a man, Sarah; I'm not the mealy-mouth you think you want. You'll never know who I am.'

'I still think it's disgusting you raped me and you planned to rape me.'

'Your heart is telling you the truth,' he said.

I didn't know if I loved my husband, or not.

I hated him I hated him but I knew if he should leave me I would die.

'My Madeline! sweet dreamer! lovely bride!
    'Say, may I be for aye thy vassal blest?
'Ah, silver shrine, here will I take my rest
    'After so many hours of toil and quest,
'A famish'd pilgrim -sav'd by miracle.
    'Though I have found, I will not rob thy nest
'Saving of thy sweet self; if though think'st well
    'To trust, fair Madeline, to no rude infidel.'

Is my lover trying to murder me?

Is my lover trying to get my inheritance?

Is my lover a stupid worthless being?

'You have to trust me,' he tells me. He won't tell me why. As soon as he tells me I have to trust him he takes some of my jewels, not my favourites, to sell because we can use the money, and when I ask him where the money is he won't answer me.

It's always my fault.

The nightmares have begun again.

As I said, it was winter. Three days after the winds started they could never stop for the concrete buildings housed them the streetlights held them the very beds and streets were winds. My skin and the stuff under my skin tremble, feel the temperature extremes. I don't know what is physical doubt and what is mental doubt.

I want vision. If I do everything I can to change myself (my SELF is my desires and dreams), so I don't have to leave this man – if I leave him, I won't bother again with a man – am I turning away from all that is dearest and deepest: vision? Or is vision that which has nothing to do with the will, but is necessity working itself out?

When I was in eighth grade, I thought the twins in my class, who were the only girls considered to be as intelligent as me, absolutely evil. I thought about them or absolute evil all the time. My husband wants me to put my inheritance in a joint bank account and draw up a will in his name.

How do we know how to act? How do we know when our actions will cause pain? How is it possible to choose? I knew I must not choose and I must escape.

Ye winds, ye cold air-snakes who wind through flesh, all who are nature:

Seattle Art Society

Timelessness versus time.

There is very little money available to poor people. Since the American culture allows only the material to be real (actually, only money), those who want to do art unless they transfer their art into non-art i.e. the making of commodities, can't earn money and stay alive. Almost every living artist who keeps on doing art has family money or at least one helpful sex partner. There're a few artists whose work this society desires, for the country needs some international propaganda (and there's nothing as harmless to a materialist as formalist experimentation). So an American artist has about one chance in 100,000 to earn a living making art. Nevertheless all the artists expect to have this one in 100,000 success. After five to thirty years of either slow starvation or, if there's family or sexual money, lack of feedback recognition and distribution (for only the few artists who are famous get their work amply recognized and distributed), at least three-quarters of the artists who haven't died off yet are willing to do anything to succeed and turn to more commercial or technical work or become bums. Nevertheless, more and more people in urban America want to become artists because only artists are happy and know reality and there are no other jobs. The art market is becoming more glutted and artists help each other out less and stab each other in the back and do everything else necessary to survive.

There's a very good artist (i.e. he wants to do art and nothing else) who wants the world to be as it is in the centre of his art. All the artists recognize this goodness. He's very animal especially his wiggling ass he's such a great fuck, all the women artists want to fuck him. He lives in Seattle. He's fucked every woman artist in Seattle. All these women artists are still in love with him. A new woman artist who's more famous than these other women artists 'cause she's from New York City comes to Seattle. All the artists love her 'cause she's still living outside that community, isn't yet competing. She marries M. de Cleves so she can stay away from New York City.

As soon as these two artists meet, they fall madly in love with each other. The good artist isn't making art anymore because he can't work for money and do art, he refuses to starve to death, he refuses to do his art as anyone else wants him to do it, he refuses to butter up the ego of the one dealer in Seattle who shows new young work. The Princess is making lots of art because she's a quarter of a half successfully developed an image in New York. But she won't stop doing her art to support the purer artist even though this refusal makes her feel guilty. She doesn't love her new husband M. de Cleves.

Young people are now getting married 'cause they see how their parents followed every desire and got totally disrupted and how the total nihilism of 1979 caused nothing but ODs and cancer. The Duc de Lorraine's going to marry Mme Claude de France, the King's second daughter. Elizabeth of France wants to marry the Duc de Nemours.

The few male artists who're successful want to fuck girls twenty or more years younger than themselves. Why do men want to fuck and marry girls who're so dumb there's no interesting conversation or power play? Mme de Cleves' mother says: studying human history answers you. If you want to understand an event, always increase its (your perceptive) complexity.

Historical example: Our former King met Mlle de Pisselieu when she was extremely young and fell wildly in love with her. He fell in love with the Duchesse de Poitiers and kept hold of Mlle de Pisselieu. His first son was poisoned. Because he bitched about his second son to the Duchesse de Poitiers, she said she'd make this son fall in love with her and did. The King's support of his third son, the Duc d'Orleans, made the second and third son hate each other. Mlle de Pisselieu became the Duchesse d'Etampes. the King and the Duchesse d'Etampes hated the Duchesse de Poitiers. The Duc d'Orleans died from fever. The King died. Since the second son, our King, worshipped the Duchesse de Poitiers, he wanted to exile her lovers; but he adored her so much, he couldn't. Even as she got older, he would remain in love with her. He made her main lover Governor of Piedmont, but used the Vidame de Chartres to prevent this lover from getting anything. The Duchesse de Poitiers hated the Vidame de Chartres and the rest of his family. The Vidame de Chartres' niece just married the Prince de Cleves.

There is purity. The whole world, not in itself but as the beliefs that there are no qualitative differences between events so money takes the place of value, hates purity. Purity is always. There's no duality so purity is phenomena. But (relations): a story. A story plus a story plus a . . . makes . . . a tapestry. Human perception (relation) makes more perception. How can purity be a story?

Because all the male artists she knows fuck any cunt they can get into and the non-artist males bore her, the female artist doesn't believe love or purity's possible in this world and so sticks with her husband.

She learns from history that purity comes from lies or impurity: historical example: after Mme de Tournon lived with a poet who made her support him by working dirty movies and in a sex show, she swore she hated men. She would always be a lesbian, even though she wasn't sure she physically liked fucking women as much as men, so she could devote herself to her art. Her former husband, Peter, was still in love with her even though she was a lesbian. Paul told Peter he was fucking ten different women because he was so horny. Peter was the only person in whom he dared confide. If his girlfriend found out, well: when his ex-wife had found out he had fucked just one other woman, she had an epileptic fit tried to commit suicide and broke up their marriage. The next morning, Mme de Tournon repeated this gossip to all her girlfriends one of whom was Paul's girlfriend. Jean-Jacques told everyone Mme de Tournon planned to marry him. Jeffrey knew Mme de Tournon planned to marry him. Mme de Tournon is known as the most honest female artist in Paris.

Mme de Cleves realizes M. de Nemours has fallen in love with her even though she's married and he, being an artist, doesn't give a shit about other people's feelings.

The myth of art: artists have to do everything they can to do their art. They can't allow any desire to stop them from working. They have to deny themselves any lasting pleasure. If and when they fall in love, they destroy their lover or else transform their love into distaste or despair. So artists tend to love either objects or people who run away from them. So the female artist rejects the good male artist.

Historical example: Peter fell madly in love with Kathy even though she was married. Kathy told Peter since the law is worthless because all politicians are crooked Peter could marry her without her divorcing. Though Peter was morally middle-class, his desire made him embrace this defiance. He ran himself ragged for Kathy for six years while she fucked every artist in existence because she wanted someone richer especially more famous than Peter so she could become famous. Peter kept his jealousy secret. Kathy and his mother augmented this insecurity by repeating to him he wasn't rich or famous enough. When he started becoming rich and famous, which was what Kathy wanted, this jealousy springing out made him viciously turn to a young girl who was in love with someone else and kill Kathy. He was so rich and famous, he got away with it. He fell in love with a Mafiosa and whipped her. At the same time he loved many other women and, partly due to the cocaine his girlfriend was freely giving him, later killed several wives.

The end of hatred. Of that myth of art. The female artist can now love.

Cezanne allowed the question of there being simultaneous viewpoints, and thereby destroyed for ever in art the possibility of a static representation or portrait. The Cubists went further. They found the means of making the forms of all objects similar. If everything was rendered in the same terms, it became possible to paint the interactions between them. These interactions became so much more interesting than that which was being portrayed that the concepts of portraiture and therefore of reality were undermined or transferred.

Three different power groups: the owners of the North-Eastern banks, the top-ranking military, and the Southern oil producers and distributors control the American government. The female artist doesn't know who her father is. Three months before she was born, her father had abandoned her mother and, according to her mother, had never tried to see her again or her daughter because he's a robot. She knows her father's name because a good friend of hers traced him. He is the secret head of the North-Eastern power coalition. Not even the American people know who he is.

As head of the North-Eastern power coalition he often uses the CIA for his own purposes. He once, through the CIA, hired the good male artist. He sent the male artist's wife on a suicide mission to Cuba. The female artist learns the good male artist's artistic status is a cover for being a hit man, that's why he's so pure.

Even though many of the New York City art patrons are also part of the North-Eastern power coalition, they're trying to do her father in because he supports Rockefeller and they want to throw their weight behind Reagan. They use the Marlborough Gallery as one of their fronts.

The female artist's husband from whom she's separated used to fuck her mother. Her father, discovering them, kills his wife in a jealous rage. The lover revenges himself by marrying the daughter, cutting her off from her father. Now the husband loves her because he's part of the North-Eastern Reagan group and wants to use her to do her father in.

The female artist still thinks art is the only purity. The North-Eastern art patron group videotapes and even stage-manages every bedroom and intimate scene they can for info and blackmail purposes. The porn tapes they have no (more) use for they sell as high art. One very famous artist in New York City is very fond of privately commissioning and buying these snuff films. The female artist learns her father murdered her mother. While she's still confused, the art patrons get her even dopier then show her videotapes of the good male artist fucking every female in sight, for the good male artist sticks his cock into anything eight-and-a-half inches (the length of his cock) or less away from him. Since the female artist doesn't know who or what to believe anymore, art is nothing, she, throwing herself into her husband's arms, tells him everything. She doesn't know he's the main villain against her father.

Any action no matter how off-the-wall – this explains punk – breaks through deadness. When the good male artist overhears her telling her husband everything, even though he doesn't trust her, he suspects the politicians are trying to do them both in.

In New York City, when the 14th precinct is busting up 42nd Street, there's a special court called the obscenity court. The Mafia and this one Jewish guy who's their friend own the sex shows and shops which line 42nd Street. The shows and shops pay the DA's office their monthly alimony. The DA's office – no dumb cop can bust on his own – orders the local cops to break up a store only when the DA's office needs some publicity, for instance to help the tourist trade, or when a high-high in the police officer's retiring and some semi-high knows if it's schmeared all over the front page of the *Daily News* that he's cleaning up 42nd Street he'll get the job. The DA's office warns the bosses there's going to be a bust and pulls only the shit workers in. Nevertheless a 42nd Street boss wouldn't be seen (much less CAUGHT) dead in one of his own shops or shows cause some cop might, being as stupid as he's reputed to be, not recognize this bigshot.

Ten peep-show machines fill the downstairs of a typical 42nd Street store. Occasionally a ghost businessman sticks shit-smeared razor blades into one of the slots. Upstairs a phony sex show for businessmen and men too old to get off any other way runs for a half hour once every hour and a half. These shows provide an important and unnoticed social service.

The obscenity court was filled to the till. The illegal alien India Indian who took the sex show tickets was swearing everyone in the store including the customers was responsible for the store's disgusting activities except for him. Two illegal Haitian aliens who ran the store's dirty film projectors for half minimum wage because they were aliens and didn't know better and if they complained they'd get deported and they couldn't speak English anyway and the male and female hippies who had been doing the sex show when the store got busted (they actually hadn't been doing anything but looking at each other and making dumb sounds 'cause the male hated touching women and the female had such a bad ovarian infection she'd be screeching with pain if either touched or if one bit of the pain-killing synthetic morphine she was shelling out $100 a week for to kill the pain so she could keep working to pay for the pain-killer wore off – if it all wore off): they were all silently awaiting their trial. When he hired them, the boss promised to pay to get them off if they were busted. It was a small room.

The judge entered so everyone in the room stood up and swore in loud voices. Everyone sat down. Two young women who both had lots of curly white hair were told to stand. The judge asked if anyone was representing them. A skinny, obviously hating Legal Aid with a folder in his hand stood up and said he was representing them (since there was no one else). The skinny representative needed ten minutes to find out who these ladies were. It was very hot in the courtroom. Then the skinny black-suit walked up to the judge. The judge and the skinny black-suit talked in whispers. The skinny Jew told the black women to step forward. While they stepped forward the judge recited some numbers at them and the skinny lawyer recited some numbers back. Then two guards pushed the women to the back of the room behind the judge's huge wooden stand. The room was very hot. The people weren't allowed to talk out of respect for the judge and the process of justice. The next accused were two black men. The first black man didn't seem to understand what was happening around him. His Legal Aid lawyer told him to plead guilty because he couldn't get off. He said 'I'm guilty' though he wasn't sure what he was guilty of and the judge recited some numbers and his lawyer recited some numbers back. An armed guard pushed him to the back of the room. All of the defendants except for the India Indian Haitian and hippy sex show workers were black and all of the Legal Aid lawyers who didn't know their clients told their clients to cop pleas. The only other language used was mathematical so no one would get the wrong idea.

It must have been noon the sunlight was so bright even through the huge grey-filth-painted windowpanes when the judge called the hippy male and female to the bench. The hippy male was wearing a Bill Blass suit. The hippy female was wearing a middle-price grey suit with an ascot. They wanted to show the judge they were a cut above his usual defendant. The boss, the Jewish 42nd Street entrepreneur, had given them one of his own lawyers. The lawyer and the judge were whispering numbers. The hippies didn't hear a word. Then the boss appeared and walked up to the judge. Reaching into his pants pocket, he pulled out a huge wad of huge bills. He clearly flipped his wad in front of the judge's face and asked. 'Haven't I paid you enough?' 'Not here,' the judge loudly replied. The lawyer and the judge said numbers again. The matron pushed the hippies to the back of the room where a small wood door led them to a hall. Out of the court of justice.

Before she worked the sex show she had earned all the money she needed especially the money for all the medicines by starring, she was either the only one or one of two, in sex films. She had thought of earning her money this way because when she had gone to a top Eastern university a doctor friend had told her her face was ravishingly beautiful. She had gotten these beginning model jobs by looking in the back pages of the *Village Voice*. Then men had told her she was too nice a girl to be an escort and why didn't she go back to school or they pulled her leotard away from her breasts and told her her breasts were too large or too small. She was very ashamed of her breasts. She hadn't been getting money for a while and more important than money, though that's all-important, she had to keep working to show herself she was surviving whatever she had to do. When you have to survive, thinking's either a luxury or a way, if you control it, to make what's necessary enjoyable. One day, answering an ad, she walked into a West Village basement apartment. The photographic set-up looked expensive. The black photographer told her he needed some nudie stills for the tops of playing cards. Since it was easy money, she said O.K. He showed her the cunt and cock on top of each playing card. She says she'd return with her boyfriend with whom she always worked twosomes. 'No,' said the photographer as he locked the door behind her, 'we're going to use your cunt and my cock.' 'How can we do that?' she asked. 'I'm very co-ordinated.' She told him she had bad gonorrhea and he said he'd use a rubber. She figured if she had to get raped, she might as well remain healthy. 'This won't take long,' replied the photographer. While the big man was shoving himself into her, the girl lay as stiff as a log and wouldn't allow herself to feel any pleasure because this was the main way her fear would allow her to express anger.

Night

I'm sitting in a window recess. The sinuous folds of a silk curtain hide most of my body. The lights of this silver and wood splendid loft-space sparkle as if they aren't giving off illumination but are burning only themselves up in the otherwise complete blackness. This anonymity is life. Here milling about turning around eyes go here and there while tongues move in the same direction all to look all to show disguise every dress must be the most beautiful every nipple must be the tautest the few flowers that exist are dead red isn't blood but rouge used as mascara: the quick movements of the cheekbones: the hair that making the skin as rigid as itself makes the face invisible: the fingernails painted by hundred-dollar-a-bottle polish create the only light the only whisper only the froth. This is the province of the ones who think they live their dreams. The richest, the most famous, the most audacious: now and then a person may allow desire. The sudden swerve of the eyes at the mention of a certain sale, the quickening of I, the casually filthy blue jeans worn over the knees of someone explaining he's making history, hard cocks a quick jet of blood, the cats stand high above complete the giddiness of this mass whom everything seductive the world can hold intoxicates; cold white and general inebriation play upon the already-fevered mind.

I want to be one of these vanguard people so I disguise myself:

Portrait In Red

Clifford does short-haul truck work. He doesn't work out of the hall; he has to call in every day to find out whether he goes to work or not. He must work ten hours in a row when needed and, then, if there's further work, can choose to do it. He often works a fifty-hour week. He says he's an artist. He says he doesn't have any time to make his art. He says his lines are his language. He is traditional and not avant-garde because he is just putting down what he sees, about which, because nobody else sees this, he can't talk to anyone.

At 7:00 a.m. the radio begins playing rock'n'roll loudly. Clifford pisses over the toilet, forgetting to lift the toilet seat, dials a phone number, says 'Cliff', hangs up the phone. Whatever woman he's living with at the moment turns on the light over the bed, out of the bed makes herself a cup of tea and puts some oatmeal flakes and a cup of boiling water over the pilot so she can have oatmeal when she wakes up again at noon. They avoid talking to each other or else they'll quarrel. He says, 'Have a good day,' as he walks out the door. She does her best to get back to sleep.

He spends the early part of every evening in a bar, (even though he doesn't have time to read) he stares at a book he just bought as if it's a precious object. Other times he sits silently and smiles. He acts very friendly to the people he knows casually. Then he goes out to dinner, or he returns home and falls asleep. If he's in a bad mood, he stops perceiving the outside.

On the weekends he likes to go to fancy restaurants because they make him feel like he's a rich man and not encaged. He taught himself how to order good wines and wear designer suits. He won't go near cheap stuff. He doesn't want to live a grovelling beggar's life. He discusses his political beliefs, describes various political events and his personal plans for the future.

I'm scared of Clifford.

I don't know anymore why I'm scared of him.

He hates me.

He does his best to hurt me he doesn't hurt me just out-front he does that too he sets me up: he acts nice (and when he's charming he can be REAL charming and I'm a sucker for that) and so I open to him I say, 'Oh yes darling I do love you. I'll do anything you want.' Because when I love a man specially when I'm being fucked well I'll do anything for him, otherwise I hate men I don't hate them, I just don't want them touching me cause their fingertips burn. Then we're sitting at a fancy restaurant in front of everyone in a loud voice he starts detailing exact examples showing what a shit I am.

(*The woman sits down at a small white-cloth-covered table.*)

Clifford: You're not able to love.
Sarah: I loved you.
Clifford: You never loved me. You don't know how to give anything.
Sarah: I moved to Seattle and gave up my career, everything in New York, just to stay with you. I gave you all that money. Why did I do that?

(*They're speaking so loudly all the middle-aged married couples in the restaurant are staring at them.*)

Clifford: I don't know. You had your own reasons.
Sarah: What reasons are those? I don't know what they are.
Clifford: I don't know. You know them. You tell me I have to grow up. YOU have to grow up.
Sarah (*realizing she's going to cry*): Excuse me. (*She stands up. Starts to shake more and more.*) I have to go to the bathroom. (*Looks around the restaurant.*) Where's the bathroom? (*Wanders around the restaurant. Fake red velvet covers all the walls. Can't find a bathroom. Sits down again.*)
Clifford: Now, are we going to have a nice dinner? *I* want to have a nice dinner. (*pauses*) What books did you read today?

(*The Chinese waiter approaches to take the order.*)

Clifford: I want the curried beef, the wonton soup, and the fried dumplings.
Sarah: Uh . . . Uh I, I . . . don't want anything. I'm not really very happy. Thank you.
Clifford: You're going to eat. I'm not going to watch you get sick again.
Sarah: Yes, uh, eat. Eat (*To the waiter*) I'm sorry. I'm really sorry. I'm sorry. I will eat. I have to eat something.
Clifford: The sweet-and-sour shrimp.
Sarah: No, no, please waiter. I hate sugar. The shrimp in garlic sauce.

(*The waiter, obviously despising these louts, walks away*).

Sarah: I'm sorry. I just don't like sugar.
Clifford: Get what you want. I'm getting what I want. If you like you can eat a fried poodle.
Sarah: No.
Clifford (*expansively*): Get five dishes six dishes. I'm paying. The thing is you can't take it. You hand it out you hand it out hard, but you

can't take it. (*Realizing what's coming, she can't hold her sobs back anymore.*) I'm just telling you the way you really are.

Sarah: I never said anything to hurt you. All I ever said, again and again, and I say it right now, is that you have to get your life together. You have to quit trucking so you can do art full-time. Is that saying something against you? I've only got your welfare in mind.

Clifford: You can't take anything rough as I can. You're weaker than me. You're not the woman I expected. You're not the woman I want. You're physically sick all the time.

Sarah: I AM weak. I never pretended I was different. I act publicly like I'm strong it's just an image and now I do it well I HAVE to survive. It isn't real. That's why I have to be alone so much. I have to be alone so I can be myself. It isn't that I don't love you. I just have to be alone.

Clifford: I understand that you're weak. I want a strong feminist.

Sarah: Maybe you should go with someone else. (*Hopefully*).

Clifford (*resigned*): Stop crying and eat your dinner. You need to eat. You're going to make yourself sick again.

Sarah: Please don't keep hurting me.

Clifford: I'm trying to have a nice dinner. You keep bringing these matters up.

Sarah: I . . .? I . . . (*tentatively, obediently, takes a spoonful of food*). Since my crying is increasing this viciousness, I don't know how to stop it. I'm in terror.

He mirrors whatever I feel, but doesn't realize he's doing this.

:Johnny, I know you're going to murder me.

:I'm going to murder you, honey.

:I don't want you to murder me.

:But I want money and you've got it.

:You'd murder me even for just the little money you can get. (This isn't really a question.) I guess if you want to make love, we might as well make love. I'm horny.

:Can't you get to sleep? (His finger softly draws a line along her right-side chin bone.)

:I'm really tense.

:I'll kiss you and you'll go to sleep.

:I don't want to go to sleep. Where are you?

:I'm just playing.

:Come up here and fuck quickly and then go back to your play. (Johnny crawls up on the bed and very slowly, very gently, kisses her soft lips.)

:I just want to fuck. I don't want to kiss.

:I have to do something to relax you.

Red everywhere. Red up the river, where it flows among the green pines and old mining camps; red down the river, where it rolls defiled among the tiers of the shipping and the dock pollutions of a going-to-be-great (and going-to-be-dirtier) city. Red on the rain marshes, red on Queen Anne Hill. Red creeping into each of the abandoned cabooses; red creeping over the half-torn-away train tracks and lying on each weed; red climbed over the hacked-up docks into the commercial steel ships. Red in each long-shoreman's eyes when he returns home and slaps his wife around red at the end of the cigarette butt red in the dynamite red of the fire. Red of the eyelid and nose flesh of the bums walking down First Avenue past the more monetarily successful artists. Red the colours of the condos they're building over the bodies of old people who now have nowhere to live. Red the artist's hand not from paint but from striking his lover's face out of repressed fear.

The raw afternoon is rawest, and the red is most red, and the streets are filthiest on the part of Bell Street next to the river where I lived in fear of my lover for six months.

He didn't want to hurt me. There are many desires. But that desire was a fairly surface desire. He was very scared. The fear was very deep. The fear was he used to be on the skids he had to live when he was an adolescent by selling junk he had no one to turn to and he was a bum he was among bums no woman would want him. He wanted education. He got better and better women. He took each one for as much as he could before she had the strength or desperation to flee. He didn't want to be in this position again. He was desperate. He was a man. He was tough. He was honest. He didn't use people. He could take care of himself and he never needed anybody. All under this surface was fear. The tension between the two was unendurable especially for him.

Worse than this was the positive tool or wall he had built to keep surviving. He was as stubborn as a steel wall. As soon as he wanted he could be impenetrable. Impenetrable is stupid. Nobody could touch him. This steel wall was the most dangerous thing about him was total madness.

Women found him sexually attractive and then fled from him. He had had a series of women and could obviously get any woman he wanted who didn't know his reputation. Living with him was living with hell. He never relaxed. He was always like an atom bomb. He thought he was delicate feminine because when he got drunk (relaxed) the only aspect he could perceive was overwhelming self-insecurity or fear. And fear is feminine: for women it lies in the heart of heterosexual sex. I don't know whether I believe that.

I don't want to believe that.

Clifford: Since the world is a hostile place to me, I have to be able to do whatever I want. I'm going to have a good time today. I don't care what you feel. You're probably dying because you're always dying as a ploy to get at me. To destroy me. I'm going to have a good time today. When I have a good time, I eat crepes and drink lots of cappucino, then I go to the department stores to look at either Ralph Laurens or Gucci suits. After six I drink champagne, beer with my buddies and shoot pool, I get good and drunk. I know I shouldn't get drunk like this everything is my fault it isn't my fault. A language that I speak and can't dominate, a language that strives fails and falls silent can't be manipulated, language is always beyond me, me me me. Language is silence. Once there was no truth; now I can't speak.

I'm going to Paris because in Paris no one speaks English. That's where I'll be able to make art.

I won't have any chance of making money there. I've never had steady money because I'm nothing. I hate this government because they're responsible.

I don't like women because I hate their cunts. I don't know who they are. I know I know who they are: they just want. They think they're perfect. I don't want to become better. I don't care. I don't have problems as other people do.

I decided I wasn't going to have anything else to do with a woman. I wasn't going to try to live with one again. I was into my work and I didn't have the time.

I set up this living situation so no woman could enter it. I built that loft bed and no other conveniences anywhere, just my working tools. For a shower I go to the sauna down the street for ten dollars an hour. I eat my meals in the Belltown.

I know I drink too much. I like sex a lot. Once or twice a week this crazy girl when she can't pick any other man up that night comes around one or two in the morning. She doesn't want anything but sex from me and that's all I want from her.

I'm a teamster and I make a lot of money so I'm in a position to help out my fellow artists who aren't as financially well-established as I am. I buy their work whenever I can. I like to pay for their drinks. I'm generous.

She: What is his relation to money?

She: It stinks.

I kept thinking he was conning me. Then I would think, this is crazy and paranoid. I just want to know.

She: I want to ask you about Clifford. If you don't want to answer any of these questions 'cause they're too close, I fully understand. They're just so many times I haven't known the truth in a situation and this time I want to know the truth.

226

Clifford: Let me explain something. Let me explain something. I absolutely want to explain something. I am not a violent person. I have never in my life physically hurt anyone. I would not hurt a woman. Nobody understands how sensitive I am. I do not believe all that shit about men and women I think sexism is disgusting. Men who want women to do the housework and bow to them are pigs. I cry and I'm as sensitive as a woman. No one realizes this about me I don't have anything to do with the world. NO.

As a result of his own barrenness, he develops a capacity to absorb the fertility of others. Of the real self. The only way you can get the real self is to rip someone off. The only way you can get love. Humans need love. You're a con man.

When my girlfriend got sick, she was good and sick she was almost dying. I didn't give a damn because when she's sick she can't give me anything. She had become sick so she could deny me. This means the sicker she becomes, the more I have to rip her off. That's the only way things are fair between us. I'm a feminist. I don't want a woman mothering me or telling me what to do. I want a balance of power that's why I have to take from her.

I didn't bother to lie and she knew I was taking from her. But she played stupid, asked me if I was ripping her off why was I ripping her off. She not only played stupid she played the martyr. She kept whining while I was sleeping and I need my sleep I work like a dog-shit every day trucking I don't have time for whining which is pretense. She cried she was helpless since she didn't know anyone in this strange town, she was dependent on me, she was too sick to shop and desperate for food I was refusing to give her. I didn't want any part of this. I didn't starve her to death and I didn't throw her out. She was just asking me to let her be the boss so I wouldn't get anything from her and I wouldn't allow that. I appear stupid because I don't bother talking to people. Their talking – like her sickness – is pretense. And I have to work my butt off. If I'm one thing, I'm absolutely honest.

From being sick, she goes on to act like she's scared of me. I guess she is or she really thinks she is. I'm too worn-out to know the difference. I don't give a damn about taking care of her anymore because she's made me give up. Because she's done me in.

I'll tell her something. She doesn't know how to love somebody. Psychiatrist said about. Say I'm violent.

I think I understand but nobody agrees with me.

I'm not going to let her get away from here because otherwise so I've locked this door. I know I shouldn't lock this door but she's not really locked in.

Two beautiful girls live in Paris. The oldest is tall and thin. Since her eyelids are always threequarter's over her eyes, she appears to be constantly looking at the ground. This lack of curiosity or humility makes her seem nunlike. Pale skin with absolutely no colour over the cheekbones emphasizes the sobriety.

The younger sister, unbelievably beautiful, radiant as a moon that has no night to contrast it, pink-orange roses in the cheeks and eyes, shining because they haven't yet been touched: not being caught in the maw of fame, not fearing the traps sexual satiety causes, not desiring beyond desire to be an image: real. Her hair would fly around her head like the feathers on some of those hats in the Blvd St-Germaine Des Prés shop windows. Her emotions are even more uncontrolled, for no one has ever shown her she has to control herself or else she is hurt. These uncontrolled movements add charm. But she's so scared of her mother, she keeps this wildness to herself.

PORTRAIT IN RED, kept handing over this money

PORTRAIT IN RED if I ever asked about it he said

PORTRAIT IN RED, $60,000 in debt and that's why

PORTRAIT IN RED how

PORTRAIT IN RED did your first husband rip you off for a quarter of a million dollars excuse me

PORTRAIT IN RED, the last year Clifford and I were together, we both went to see a psychiatrist.

:I didn't know that.

:He said he couldn't do anything more for us as things stood: Clifford should definitely go into therapy.

:Is he still doing a lot of drugs?

She: He's getting stranger and stranger these days. He just sits by the TV and doesn't move and never talks to anyone. We haven't talked in months.

She: Is he still doing a lot of drugs?

She: Drugs? You know I've lived with him for six months, but I don't really know anything about him. He comes home from work on the weekdays so dead tired. He can't talk. He immediately goes to sleep, wakes up, goes back to work. On the weekends he wakes up immediately, goes out of the house. He's gone for hours. If I ask him where he's been, I don't want to pry or anything I'm just trying to find some conversation, he gets so angry I don't ask.

PORTRAIT IN RED me was to take a razor blade and cut through this wrist in front of him.

:How could you stand living with him for six years?

:It was only three years.

:Three years? He said six.

:From 1975 to 1978. My first husband and I were married for almost six years.

PORTRAIT IN RED draw blood and freaked out.

PORTRAIT IN RED used to.

PORTRAIT IN RED he kept telling me I was psychotic because I thought he was ripping me off and when there's only one other person there's no way to know.

3 The end

I'm thinking about you right now and I've been thinking about you for
days when I jerk off I see your face and I'm not going to stop writing
this cause then I'll be away from this directness this happiness this
isness which is. At the same time I'm never going to have anything to
do with you again. Because you, even if it is just cause of circumstances,
won't love me. This isn't the situation. I'm being a baby as usual. There
are complications. Are shades, hues, never either-or, the shades are
meanings, come out, you rotten cocksucker

44 BC Brutus and Cassius murder Julius Caesar.
   42 BC The outlaws Brutus and Cassius in the Battle of Philippi lose
to Mark Antony.
   Mark Antony allies himself with Cleopatra and neglects his wife
Octavia (Caesar's great-nephew's sister).
   Messala, the main literary patron, goes with young Caesar who turns
away from Antony.
   31 BC The Battle of Actium young Caesar decisively defeats Antony.
   29 BC Empire begins. Centralization of power which is thought. Any
non-political action such as poetry goes against centralization. Ovid is
exiled. Propertius and Horace are told they have to write praises of the
empire.

To the door

'Why aren't you grabbing my cunt every chance you get? I love fucking
in public streets and why are you telling me you want to be friends and
work with me more than you care about sex with me, but you don't
want FOR ANY REASONS to cut out the sex? So you want to own
me without owning me?' says Cynthia the whore. She goes out on to
the street to search for Propertius her boyfriend. It's night. She finds
him.
   'Why don't you take me? I don't have more than five minutes. Why

does it have to last beyond these grabbing actions? Oh I believe in love that thing that is impossible to happen.'

A bones-sticking-out cow is dragging a cart by glittering religious objects past a dead murderer

'And besides you're fat and ugly and I'm more beautiful than you and I've got more money (I can earn more in five minutes in this world): you should be taking me out to dinner. Here's the hole the window he can climb through to the place we can fuck in. Holes.'

He, rubbing his crotch: I just want to stick my dick into something. What the hell do I care, by all that stinks, what I stick it into? When I was a kid I used to use a bottle with something in it. Now I can use a cunt but unfortunately a cunt has a woman attached to it. By all that's holy, girl, I'm a man! The best wet dream I had was in high school I was fucking this girl I wanted to fuck, her hole disappeared, but I still kept shoving, rubbing into her. I woke and I was pounding into the bed.

Actually I don't want you to have anything to do with me. I just want split-open red-and-black pussy.

Cynthia: Why don't you let me go: I want to go back to not-existing which is freedom.

He: I like you a lot.

Cynthia: I'm lifting up my leg and peeing all over you. That doesn't work. Maybe if I let you make all the decisions, you'll be my father.

He: I don't want to make any decisions. People tell me what to do real easily and I won't stand being told what to do so I avoid people.

Cynthia (*to herself*): But I want him to love me. He's never going to give me what I want, but I'll still fuck him.

They're standing in front of a huge partly open window through which is an empty space.

Cynthia: C'mon. Jump. What's the matter with you, dummy, are you too fat to jump? I've got five minutes. You're gonna be a creep and not do anything, I'm scared too, I want it. Flesh is it. Your arms are it.

He: Isn't that guy waiting for you?

Cynthia: That's why we've got only five minutes.

At a door's edge

During the night, the streets very dirty uneven rocks no way to be sure of your footing much less direction as for safety all sorts of criminals or rather people who had to survive hiding under one level of stone or behind an arcade you can't even see just standing there: there's no way to tell the difference between alive and dead. Criminalities, which are understandable, mix with religious practices, for people have to do anything to satisfy that which can no longer be satisfied.

We shall define sexuality as that which can't be satisfied and therefore as that which transforms the person.

(Stylistically: simultaneous contrasts, extravagancies, incoherences, half-formed misshapen thoughts, lousy spelling, what signifies what? What is the secret of this chaos?

(Since there's no possibility, there's play. Elegance and completely filthy sex fit together. Expectations that aren't satiated.)

Questioning is our mode.

Cynthia: Just why are you fucking me? You've got a girlfriend named Trick and you love her. According to you she's satisfied with you and you with her.

Propertius is staring blankly at the door.

Cynthia: I'm sick of being nice to you. So what if you want a girl who'll consider you her top priority and yet'll never ask you for anything? I can't be her.

Propertius is staring blankly at the door and scratching his head.

Cynthia: DON'T FUCK ME 'CAUSE YOU LIKE THE SMELL OF MY CUNT. LEAVE ME ALONE. This is the only way I can directly speak to you cause you're autistic.

Propertius: This is my poem to your cunt door.

> *Oh little door*
> *I love you so very much.*

Cynthia: Well, everyone wants to fuck me I tell you I'm sick of this life. Who cares if you're another person waiting at my door? You're just another man and you don't mean shit to me.

Propertius: Oh please, cunt, I'm cold and I'll be the best man for you and I know you're fucking someone else that's why you won't let me near you you cheap rags stinking fish who wants anything to do with corpses anyway? (*to himself*) And thus I tried to drown my mourning.

Cynthia: This is the kind of funeral I want goddamn you

Now I'm dead. I want:

One. Well my mother father and grandmother are dead. Fuck that.

Two. When my mother popped off, afterwards, she lay in this highly polished wood coffin the most expensive funeral house in New York City – where all the society die after they're dead – FAKE, everything was real but there are times real is fake, flowers, tons of smells, wood halls polished like fingernails; preacher or rabbi asks me 'Do you know anything good I can say (I have to say something: SAY SOMETHING!) over your mother's mutilating body?' (it being understood that all society people are such pigs that . . .) and I tell him how beautiful she is; no one cries they're there to stare at me as I make my blind way through the narrow aisle, to number how hysterical I am did I really love her? The beginning of the funeral the family lawyer, having walked over to me, shakes my lapels, 'Where are the 800 IBM shares?' 'What 800 IBM shares?' 'There are 800 missing IBM shares and no one knows how your mother died. I thought she gave them to you.' 'She never gave me a penny.'

Three. I do everything for sexual love. What a life it's like I no longer exist 'cause no one loves me. So WHEN I DIE, I'll die because you'll know THAT YOU CAUSED ME TO DIE and you'll be responsible. That's what my death'll do to you and you'll learn to love. I'm teaching you by killing myself.

Four. You're gonna have to die too. You'll be like me. You'll be where I now am. Your cock-bone will be in my cunt-bone.

Five. This is why life shits: Because you're gonna love me the second I leave you flat. Our sexuality comes from represssion. When you reject me, I'm gonna die in front of you. In the long run nothing's important. This is the one sentiment that makes me happy.

Please be nice to me.

Barbarella: You've got to get a man who has money.

Danielle: I want money and power.

Cynthia and **Barbarella** (*agreeing*): Money and sex are definitely the main criteria.

Danielle: Sex?

Cynthia: I think I want a wife who has a cock. You understand what I mean. I don't understand why men even try to deal with me like I can be a wife, and then bitch at me and hurt me as much as possible 'cause I'm not a wife. Who'd ever think I'm a wife? Do you think I'm a wife? (*Barbarella giggles.*) But when I'm sexually open I totally change and this real fem part comes out.

Barbarella: I want a husband. No. I take that back. I want someone who'll support me.

Cynthia: Good luck.

Barbarella: I'm both the wife and husband. Even though none of us are getting anything right now, except for Danielle who's getting everything, our desires are totally volatile.

Danielle: I can't be a wife. I can be a hostess. If I've got lots of money.

Barbarella: One-night stands don't amuse me anymore.

Cynthia: I think if you really worship sex, you don't fuck around.

Danielle fucks around more than any of us, and she's the one who doesn't really care about sex.

Barbarella: Most men don't like sex. They like being powerful and when you have good sex you lose all power.

Cynthia: I need sex to stay alive.

A street in Rome. The sky's colour is deep dark blue. One star can be seen. Very little can be seen on the street – just different shades of black.

Inside

Now we're fucking:

I don't have any finesse I'm all over you like a raging blonde leopard and I want to go more raging I want to go snarling and poisoning and teasing eek eek, curl around your hind leg pee, that twig over there, I want the specific piss shuddering of the specific cock. I want, help me. I need your help.

Take off your clothes. Clothes bind. Clothes bind our legs and mouths and teeth, still shudder want too much, taking off our clothes.

Why can't you ever once do something that's not allowable? I mean goddammit.

Hit me.

Do anything.

Do something.

Sow this hideousness opposition blood to everyone proud I want to knock Ken over with a green glass I want to hire a punk to beat up Pam I will poison your milk if you don't leave your girlfriend.

Sex is public: the streets made themselves for us to walk naked down them take out your cock and piss over me.

The threshold is here. Commit yourself to not-knowing. Legs lie against legs. Hairs mixing hairs and here, a fingerpad, a lot of space, a hand, a lot of space, hairs mixed with hairs, a real sensation.

Go over this threshold with me.

Thumb, your two fingers pinch my nipples while your master bears down on me. Red eyes, stare down on top of my eyes. Cock, my eyes are staring at you, pull out of the brown hairs. Red eyes, now you're watching your cock pull out of the stange brown hairs. Thumb, your two fingers pinch my nipples while your master bears down on me.

Now you've gone away:

Joel Fisher whom I thought hated me saw me every other day and Rudy whom I thought the worst that is the meanest of my boyfriends always called me every other day or at least let me call him. Peter who lives with another girl three thousand miles away from me and he adores her phones me at least once a month.

This guy doesn't care about me.

But when he looks at me, I know there's a hole in him he loves me. No, he doesn't. I can't do anything until I know whether he loves me or not. I have to find out whether he loves me or not.

You might as well accept you're in love with him because if you give him up just 'cause he doesn't adore you enough, you'll have nothing. In the other case, there's a 50% (or 30% or 4% or 1%) chance you'll keep touching his flesh.

Cynthia, sitting at her dressing-table in her little apartment overlooking the middle-class Roman whores' section, is dressing her hair:

That goddamn son-of-a-bitch I hope he goes to hell I hope he gets POISONED wild city DOGS should drive their thousands of TEETH-FANGS through his flesh a twelve-year-old syphilitic teenager named Janey Smith should wrap her cunt around that prick I hate that prick I hate those fingers I hate black hair I want his teeth to rip themselves out in total agony I want his lips to dry up in Grand Canyon gulfs I want him paralysed never to be able to move again and to be conscious of it:

Then, louse, you'll learn. You'll learn what it is not to know. I want you to learn what it is to be uncertain like I am. I want you to learn what it is to want like fire. The driest and coldest dry ice: the top of your head will burn and the rest of your body will freeze shake muscles will cramp like they do when they're not yet used to the bedless floor, at night, you will know agony.

You must learn what it is to want.

Thus says the whore who's unable to hold in and repress her emotions.

Among these women, free yet timorous, addicted to late hours, darkened rooms, gambling, and indolence, sparing of words, all they needed was an allusion.

I revelled in the admirable quickness of their half-spoken language which resembled more the suppressed diffused violence a teenager feels. These exchanges of threats and promises – as if once the slow-thinking male is banished every message from woman to woman is clear and overwhelming – are few in kind and infallible.

The first time I dined at her place, three brown tapers dripped waxen tears in tall candlesticks and didn't dispel the gloom. A low table, from the Orient, offered a pell-mell assortment of *les hors-d'oeuvre* – strips of raw fish rolled upon glass wands, *foie gras*, shrimp, salad seasoned with pepper and cranberry – and there was a well-chosen Piper Heidsieck brut, and very strong Russian Greek and Chinese alcohols. I didn't believe I'd become friends with this woman who tossed off her drink with the obliviousness a person caught in the depths of opium watches his hand burn.

This 'master' was never referred to by the name of woman. We seemed to be waiting for some catastrophe to project herself into our midst, but she merely kept sending invisible messengers laded with jades, enamels, lacquers, furs . . . From one marvel to another . . . Who was the dark origin of all this nonsense?

'Tell me. Renée. Are you happy?'

Renée blushed, smiled, then abruptly stiffened.

'Why, of course, my dear Colette. Why would you want me to be unhappy?'

'I didn't say I wanted it,' I retorted.

'I'm happy,' Renée explained to me, 'but the sexual ecstasy is so great, I'm going to be physically sick.'

Propertius decides he doesn't want to fuck Cynthia again:

How can such a stinking fish a cunt who has experienced what it is to be the wish-fulfilment of many men hordes of men more men than serve the Great Caesar be innocent? My fantasy is special. Moreover she's had such a poverty-regulated life she can't have any life in her to be elegant with me: to give me the beauty that is female that I deserve. She isn't female, that elongation of steel triangles and bolts.

My girlfriend on the other hand, if anyone ever hurts me, is going to have to murder that person. For me. When I'm dying from a worn-out liver punctured guts three punches in the face and dirty track marks, I lived to the physical and mental hilts, my girlfriend will naturally die. On the other hand a whore goes from man to man; she's no man's girl. So there's no possibility I'm going to love you and if I fuck you, it's just cause you're a present open cunt. The women's liberationists are right when they want to get rid of all hookers by imprisoning all of you whores.

Cynthia: I've been waiting for you.

Propertius: What the he . . .? (*Grabbing the other girl into him.*) Oh, hello. I'm busy now.

Cynthia: I just wanted to see you.

Propertius: I'm busy with someone now. I'll give you a call tomorrow.

Cynthia: Please. (*There's nothing she can do.*) OK. (*Propertius and the dark-haired girl walk in to the house. One of the dogs on the street starts barking.*)

The Street of Dogs. Two lines of houses lead to a Renaissance perspective. These lines are seemingly-only-surface connected three-storey townhouses. A sun and a three-quarter moon hang over one townhouse. Common household objects such as lamps, a part of a table, half of a torn plastic rose kitchen curtain take up some of the window space. Outside a townhouse a dog leans over her basket of laundry. Two dogs, one leaning farther out of his window than the other, open their mouths to howl. Their teeth are sharp and white and they have long red tongues. One dog over her basket of wash gossips with another dog. Two young dogs are mangling each other next to the curb. On each side of the street the tall thin windows form a long row.

Cynthia barks like a dog:
   I can't help myself anymore I really can't I'm just a girl I didn't ask god to be born a girl. When I think, I know totally realistically I'm an alien existant. I hate or have nothing to do with everyone. I'm a whore. But I'm not thinking. You're just so cute. I have to get you out of my body. It'd be good for me to get you out of my body cause then I'd be strong that is single. I don't want to and why should I? I want to have this sweet thing that is you. I'm going to go after you, aching sore. (I don't care what your reaction is to me) because why not, darling?

She walks up to the door where Propertius lives and sits herself in front of it. Even though she doesn't care anything about him. He's never bought her a present.
   The door doesn't move.
   A big baldheaded half-naked man opens the door lays his palms on the doorway. Cynthia goes away.

You alone born from my most beautiful
            carecure for grief
Shuts out since your fate
      'COME OFTEN HERE'
Fiction by my will will become the most
            popular form
Propertius, your forgiveness, peace,
            Peter, yours.
to redefine the realms of sex so sex
I'm crawling up your wall for you.
I must face facts I'm not a female.
I must face facts I can't be loved
I must face facts I need love to live.
            Hello, walls.
How're you doing today?
            Hello, my watch.

Please watch over Propertius, you are here
because I will never get near him again.
He is now forbidden territory.

Cynthia lays down on the street and sticks razor blades vertically up her arm. The bums ask her if she needs a drink. Madness makes an alcoholic sober, keeps the most raging beast in an invisibly locked invisible cage, turns seething masses of smoke air into calm white, takes a junky off junk as if he's having a pleasant dream, halts that need FAME that's impossible.

I am only an obsession. Don't talk to me otherwise. Don't know me. Do you think I exist?

Watch out. Madness is a reality, not a perversion.

Propertius on the nature of art

Propertius: If you read from end to end of the Greek Anthology, you won't find a love poem where the character of individuality of the woman who's loved matters.

(Goddamn sluts: if only the cunts were unattached; I like them but they're all crazy. They've got emotions. I like the one I slept with last night. She moans hard when I stick my cock in her. Does she have any idea what I think? I know I'm a macho pig why the hell shouldn't I be why should I be something I'm not I care about Writing. Their emotions and hysterics are all second-class existents.)

My woman is the black hole of vulnerability and takes everything from me and Not Human. She can take me wherever she wants me. I have to care for someone.

Women, I'll use everything I can get: I'll trample on your passions needs even if they cause you to die, I'll be as elephant-like as I can, and so the ugly is left as ugly and consciousness' unavoidable anguish is as it is in me. I am wide enough to let be.

My writing will cure you of your suffering. Give me five bucks, I come even cheaper I'm cheap, I'll tell you how to win the love of a person who doesn't love you. I'll tell you how to endure your rending when the girl you love spits in your face and fucks another man right in front of you.

Augustus (*through the lips of his literary counsellor Maecenas*): You're not a poet, slime, because all your poems are about is emotion. A man who pays attention to emotions isn't a real man. We have the world to take care of: we have to make sure people have more than necessary access to food; we have to watch the greedy hawks who get into power and rape.

We are the teachers. If we teach these champagne emotions are worth noticing, we're destroying the social bonds people need to live.

Propertius: If my writing is going against social bonds, that's who I am. Shove your Empire and shove society.

Maecenas: You're only dealing with your little obsession.

Propertius: You too, Maecenas, one day, are going to have to realize you're not rational and then in your desperation, ignorant, you'll turn to my words.

Propertius runs away because he doesn't like making his privacy public. Public is an image a rigidity, and only as such is fun. He points to a mass of art-world figures, from his shadows, as they're entering a salon resplendent with gilding and illuminations, on in which they're instantly being welcomed by the most beautiful Roman bodies.

One of them has just revealed original talent and with this first portrait of his shows himself the equal of his teacher. A sculptor's chatting with one of those clever satirists who refuse to recognize merit and think they're smarter than anyone else. The people talk either about how they earn money or who's becoming more famous. All are grasping for good reason in these desperate times. Since the only ideas are for sale, none are mentioned. A few women appear to maintain the surface that sex is still possible. Eyes never see the mouths the faces are talking to.

Well you can say I write stories about sex and violence, with sex and violence, and therefore my writing isn't worth considering because it uses content much less lots of content and all the middle-ranged people who are moralists say I'm a disgusting violent sadist. Well I tell you this:

'Prickly race, who know nothing except how to eat out your own hearts with envy, you can't eat cunt, writing isn't a viable phenomenon anymore. Everything has been said. These lines aren't my writing: Philetas' DEMETER far outweighs his long old woman, and of the two it's his little pieces of shit I applaud. May the crane-who-delights-in-the-Pygmies'-blood's flight from Egypt to Thrace be so long, like me in your arms, endless endless greyness, may the death shots the Massagetae're directing against a Mede be so far: what is here: desire violence will never stop. Go die off, oh destructive race of the Evil Eye, or learn to judge poetic skill by art: art is the elaboratings of violence. Don't look to me to want to do anything about the world: I'm out of it.'

'But if there hadn't been between you two the dark streets, the risks, and the old man you had just abandoned, in short had there been no danger, would you have hurried so eagerly?'

240

Conversations to people who aren't here

'Darling,' Propertius says to Cynthia who isn't in front of him, 'I know you've been going through hell because I've been refusing to speak to you.

'I know the minute I stopped talking to you, you'd slit your wrist (you did that just 'cause when you were in your teens you cut your arms with a razor blade regularly to teach yourself you were horror), then more seriously you obtained an ovarian infection because your ovaries had been rejected you tried I know you tried you did avoid me (except when you phoned my girlfriend answered the phone you hung up).

'Listen, Cynthia, I fucked so many girls, I took them up to this penthouse sauna and swimming pool someone lent me. Beautiful girls pass each other on the stairway. Limbs disappear in the shadow, and then there's nothing else.

'I'm living with a girl. I don't even know her.'

PROPERTIUS IS TELLING CYNTHIA WHO HIS CURRENT GIRLFRIEND IS. 'The more I knew she was fucking the men she met through me behind my back, the more I'd do anything for her – crazed because I knew every move she made was planning to leave me. By allowing female emotions, I drive them away. Then it all stopped, she ran away with her other boyfriend.

'So I want you.

'If you're not obsessed for me, bitch, you're going to drink blood – you now living off your grandmother's capitalist hoard though blowing more – your food whatever you eat must always stink of rotten guts, human, always always you must regret everything you are. The thoughts that have to be imaginings must make you victim eat you, hole. You're looking everywhere you're looking everywhere you're looking everywhere you're looking everywhere: Every human is so stupid there're only ravenous wolves. Cats and dogs now gone wild are gnawing the crumbling white concrete blocks. Long red pointed fingernails separate the cunt lip flesh, then digging into the soft purple, and around the protrusion of the nipple right there, another fingernail.

'There are no more images. This is what it is, this is why you can't run from me. There's only obsession.

'Love will turn on the lover and gnaw.'

PROPERTIUS IS DOWN ON HIS KNEES BECAUSE HE'S HELPLESS.
'Last night I had a dream Cynthia. You were standing over me, the ring I had given you, your finger, your hand white palm outstretched. You said the following words to me:

' "I didn't mean to tell your girlfriend was fucking around but I) you had just told me I wasn't a female because I have a 'career' and because I'm not a female no man will love me. That hurt. 2) You set up the terms of the relationship, but I was thinking about you all the time, so you said STAY RATIONAL at a time I wasn't rational: this was confusing me. I explained my identity-desperation by telling you I had known your girlfriend was two-timing you that was why I loved you. But the second I just mentioned the first word, explosion!, so I backed off: I just heard gossip, the gossip was old she wasn't fucking anyone else. I'm wrong to listen to gossip. Let me be hurt. 3) I said 'Propertius is no more,' but my body reacted: I cut a razor blade through my flesh so I could see the flesh hole revealing two thin purple-blue-grey wires which frightened and reminded me of my mother's chin three days after she committed suicide, the body gets sick. I'm not a woman who takes shit, but

' "Why do I like you so much? I like you so much you're necessary to the continuing of my existence right now and I don't understand this at all, I just know it's true."

'Cynthia walked away from me, and I woke up.'

PROPERTIUS TALKS TO CYNTHIA WHO ISN'T IN FRONT OF HIM. 'I don't want you, slut, because love is mad and I don't want to be mad.'

My mother committed suicide and I ran away. My mother committed suicide in a hotel room because she was lonely and there was no one else in the world but her, wants go so deep there is no way of getting them out of the body, no surgery other than death, the body will hurt. There are times when there is no food and those times must be sat through.

I ran away from pain.

What is, is. No fantasy. Pain. Just the details: the streets, the green garbage bag a bum's sleeping next to, a friend, too much time no time, too much to eat not enough to eat, going to a movie with Jeffrey I don't know if the world is better or worse than it has been I know the only anguish comes from the running away.

Dear mother,

End

My Death, My Life

by Pier Paolo Pasolini

Contents

My death

My death

Did I ask to die? Was my murder a suicide by proxy?

In 1973 I wrote: 'Up until the 1970s the ancient world, the world which is daily life and thinking and loving, existed – but it was swept away, and from the age of innocence we've passed to the age of corruption.'

The scene: Increasingly overt control of dynamic materialism by Multi-nationals in Italy expresses itself particularly in rise of terrorism (right-wind media strategy and expression of the populace's inability to act functionally and politically) and in Americanism, that homogenization of daily lives and identities.

I left my home after lunch on 1 November, 1975. As usual I took the Giula GT. I was planning to eat with Ninetto later that evening. We ate in the Pommidoro restaurant in the Tiburtino quarter. I left Ninetto who of course was uninterested in fucking me and drove to my favourite quarter near the Piazza dei Cinquecento. A young boy seemingly on the down-and-out practically stood in front of my car. I stopped, got out, approached the kid. He looked OK. He was interested. He got into the car. I drove him to a deserted soccer field outside and near Idroscalo. One house only and still undergoing construction. The poor don't live in houses. We'd have sex here.

Did I leave my car as I was trying to sexually coerce the boy?

Witnesses: Various thugs had attacked Pier during the past few years. Pier had become very cautious. He wouldn't now step out of his car in front of strange young thugs. We saw him stay in his car. He told some young hustlers he was waiting for a friend. They tried to touch him. Suspiciously he rolled up his window. He quickly locked his door. No, Pier was very careful.

A boy, Seminara, went into the bar and told Pelosi to try Pier. Pasolini went for Pelosi without showing any suspicion. Why?

We stopped at the Biondo Tevere trattoria on the Via Ostiense where the kid bolted down spaghetti al'olio. Then I again stopped at an automatic to refill the tank.

A car with a Catania license plate was following us. The kid knew the four men who were in this car made their livings from mugging young hustlers after the hustlers got their takes.

We reached the soccer field. I stopped the car. I unzipped the kid's pants and stuck my face into his young crotch.

The Kid: He took my dick into his mouth, but it was just for a moment and he didn't do it to me. He dragged me out of the car. He threw my body against the car so my ass was sticking out. Then he

tore my pants half-way down I didn't want him to do that. Pissed cause
he couldn't get into me, he tried to stick a goddamn wood stake into
my asshole. He wanted to murder me.

I said, 'You're crazy, you son-of-a-bitch. I'm getting out of here.' He
had left his glasses in the car. His naked face looking mad really frightened me. I ran. He ran after me; he wasn't going to let me go. You're
crazy. He fell on top of me. Hit him with a stick. A hand grabbed the
stick and threw it away. Violence takes the place of sex. I half-ran,
crawled, started to run through the night, he grabbed my shirt-tail.
Down on me. Hitting me. I struck his head with something. I kicked
him in the balls. They felt soft. He didn't scream. He didn't react. He
kept on hitting me. I just beat him up as hard as I could as much as I
could. I was good and scared.

I leapt into his car, the keys were still in the lock, and drove off.
Really the whole time is a blank. (I can't remember whether I drove
over Pasolini's body or not.) The next thing I know I'm standing in the
water fountain and washing blood off my hands and pants. There was
no other person involved in the night.

The next day, when they arrested me, I asked them for my Marlboro's
and lighter but they were no longer in the car. Instead there was a
shabby green sweater that didn't belong either to the old fag or me.

The kid was more than willing to do whatever I wanted sexually. I
took his shirt off 'cause I didn't want to touch that. He had a gorgeous
back. The way the muscles stick out when there's been too much
starvation and there isn't enough flesh. Just as I was about to touch my
cock tip to what was inside those tight little spheres, as tight and hard
as his eyes cause poverty had made them so, something bashed my head.

At first I didn't realize what was happening cause I was so intent on
my desire. The blood dropped over my eyebrow. What? I realized
something's happening. I fought back.

They hit my head as hard as they could with a stick and some
unknown weapon. Blood fell all over the face. This blood was spurting.
They held me still. One person kicked out my balls. The kick broke a
hole in my lower abdomen. The hand holding my hair tore out the hair
it was holding.

Pier passed out. His body slumps to the ground. One of them driving
the Giulia 2000 runs over his body and actually kills it.

The evidence shows one or more men either using Pelosi or in cahoots
with Pelosi offed me. Why did they off me? If I can find out why they
offed me, I could or might be able to learn the identity or identities of
these creeps.

First question: Was it a political assassination or just a cheap street
murder? It could just be a street murder, something that stupid and
thoughtless, that takes away my life: despite what your parents taught

you when you were a kid, there's no reason anything should be a certain way in our lives; as far as you're concerned there's no reason why you should get anything good. Justice is our leaders' hype. No reason for you or anyone else to have any preconception whatsoever.

I'm talking to you who are moralists, too.

Another piece of evidence. Ferdinando Zucconi Galli Fonseca the judge of the Appeals Court on 12/4/76 stated officially that only Pelosi murdered me. His verdict further said that Pelosi was lying when he had sworn in court I had tried to rape him, that actually Pelosi had been willing to get fucked, and that there's no way of knowing why Pelosi killed me.

Why did the Appeals Court ignore the obvious evidence that more than one person had slaughtered me?

I had just finished making *Salo*. In *Salo* human male sexual desires especially homosexual and sadistic are raised both within the movie and in the movie's audience at the same time that I'm showing the close connections between these desires and fascism. Because the state's now fascistic, sexual desire is totally reasonable that is separate from caring. This is great for a pornographer to say.

Ernie and Cindy Gernhart had a daughter Sally. Ernie said Cindy just like my mother never wanted a kid but the society said she should and most people are too weak to buck society, and she got pregnant just to hold on to her husband — the only way you can still hold on to a man is by having his kid, look at all my friends — but he split on her just like my father walked away from my mother. Of course she hated her baby. Cindy hated Ernie or at least is scared of him because Ernie walked out on her like my (first) father walked out on my mother.

Ernie Gernhart remarried and Cindy remarried Ross Hart. Their second marriage lasted just as my parents' did. Cindy said Sally hated Ernie. Ross stated Sally hated him and adored Ernie. Ross loved Sally because he explained she's the closest thing I have to a daughter.

Sally since she understood everything that had happened tried to run to her real father, but the law forced her to remain with her mother.

SUICIDE CONSIDERED AS A MODUS OPERANDI.

Ross Hart had been shtupping Sally since she was fourteen years old. That's when I lost my virginity. The guy who took it didn't believe me that I was cherry so I didn't get any reward, but two years later when I was fucking another guy for the first time (in a cemetery) and simultaneously got my period, the guy cause he thought he had just fucked a virgin fell for me. When I was seventeen, my father tried to fuck me. Hart loved fucking his daughter so much he wanted to run away with her. She could try to get away from him only by keeping everything a black secret and acting in blackness. Cindy, your second husband these past four years has been fucking your daughter. He loved her, not you, because she's young and you're old.

Cindy wanted Ross to fuck Sally so he wouldn't fuck her. This is too grotty to believe. Do people really act like this?

As soon as Sally turned puberty, she was a problem. Though she was a top-A student, she stopped studying so her grades fell. She robbed stores all the time especially big department stores. She hitchhiked especially on motorcycles. Then she began taking whatever drugs anyone gave her. She got busted a few times, but this didn't put any fear in her 'cause she was already so scared.

By this time she was in (protected by) a motorcycle gang. When they arrested the gang, they sent her to probation school. If it hadn't been for our money, she'd be spending her whole life like a dumb animal in juvenile. Probation school at least taught excuse me trained her to act normal. She didn't have any boyfriends because she didn't feel anything about boys.

Susan Sabin who used to be Sally's best friend said Sally is very sensitive and doesn't trust anyone.

The whole problem revolves around who Sally Gernhart really is.

Sally thought everyone in the world hated her, just like I do; no one cares for her. She acts indifferent. She doesn't act insecure.

What about her father (I don't have a father)?

She loved her first father and wants to abandon the parents she was living with. So she was lost. Then she started hanging out with motorcycle hoods. She had her first boyfriend. Sally said Ross Hart and her mother owe her money. She's very angry. His name was Gype. The motorcyclists are heroes because they're against society even though they rape and murder.

Jack Lewis Habermas, known as Gype, 29 years old, five feet eleven inches, 185 pounds. Long brown hair, moustache. Either ex- or H-addict. Born in Valparaiso, Indiana. Divorced lower middleclass parents. Mom now third-time married Bob Smith. Smith, a child abuser. Habermas always in trouble. Uses drugs but no addictions. Consistently insubordinate. Habermas' domicile: The houses in LA. don't look like houses. Habermas' gang The Skulls say they'd never kill a brother money isn't important enough. Morality.

Sally looked around for help. She confided to the head of the Jesus Freaks and to the guy who was trying to deprogram her from the Jesus Freaks that her second father has been fucking her. The deprogrammer blackmailed her second father.

Andrew Noble is the head of the Jesus Freak group. When he was a kid he made money by trading God. Then he stopped 'cause he saw he saw he was doing wrong. Then he got a call and started doing what he used to do. Now in these times of depression he nets $15,000 a month and owns prime California land. His cohort's a Vietnam vet who's organized his group militarily just like Naropa when I was there four years ago. Every group in this country's an enemy.

Noble says Sally (this is still all about Sally) never took God into her heart, had committed the foulest of acts he doesn't say what, and constantly thought sinfully.

While Sally was in Jesus Freak camp, Gype was sprung. He has and only loves one girl: Sally.

On 4 September Ross Hart gave Furston a thousand dollars to deprogram his daughter. Ernie wouldn't have hired Furston to kidnap her because Furston is morally worse than the Jesus Freaks. Who's worse in a bad world? Eric Furston, who makes his living this way, programmed or deprogrammed depending on how you look at it, and sent her back to her hateful parents. A couple of days later which is six days ago Sally again ran away from her parents.

Ross and Cindy Hart hire me to locate their daughter Sally. Ross Hart gives Furston $500 to find Sally 'cause he's trying to protect Sally. He admits to me he gave Furston $500.

I ask Ernie Gernhart where's Sally. He says she's old enough to be where she wants. I ask Andrew Noble where's Sally. Noble says he hasn't seen her since Furston kidnapped her from his people. I ask Gype's landlady where's Gype. The landlady in a draggling bathrobe says, 'He left five days ago. He came here with Sally for five minutes and left. That's true love.'

Bob Smith a fleshy slob whose belly hangs out over his trousers drooling after every possible penny hating children even though or because he has two boys of his own rats on his stepson by giving me his address and if that doesn't work the gang's hangout's address.

At their hangout, The Skulls are lounging. Unlike this father, they protect their own. When they challenge my guts, I beat one of them up.

They plan to avenge themselves.

Furston phones Ernie Gernhart and says he has something important to tell Gernhart but he doesn't tell what it is. Ross Hart kills Furston before Furston can tell Sally's real father Sally and her second father are fucking. In this world of death. Is he my real father? I investigate.

Gype and Sally send Ernie a letter in which Sally announces she's back with the Jesus Freaks and she believes in God. I meditate.

According to these two youngster's plan, in a bar Gype tells me Sally split on him two days ago but he doesn't give a shit and she's probably offering herself up to Jesus. I'm getting this information because outside the bar The Skulls are waiting for me.

Gype and Sally send Ross a $25,000 kidnapping note. If he wants his daughter back.

He would sit for hours, a finger in his mouth, looking almost stupid. The calm child who reacts poorly when spoken to. He has no social graces. He doesn't want to speak to other people. He makes himself speak to other people because he thinks he socially has to but the words mean nothing, the images he uses mean nothing. Affection remains inarticulable and ineffectual. A secret preference for the inarticulable and inarticulate. I figure out Gype and Sally are still living together and trying to con Sally's parents out of $25,000. These parents, making the worst decision they can as they always do, will give the kidnappers the money without involving the cops or anyone else. Money's always the easy solution. Gype phones Ross Hart to drive to the drive-in restaurant phone in Trancas canyon. As if words themselves instead of merging with possible meanings retain for the child's consciousness their resonant materiality. That is, comprehension has been arrested before its completion.

Ross Hart obediently leaves the $25,000 at the crossroads of Canyon Road and Mulholland. Gype on motorcyle picks up the money. Drives back to a small wood house. There's Sally. I knock but Ross:

When I try to walk out on all this, Ross kills his daughter. Gype's gone. Besides, lacking the reciprocity – however ephemeral – that establishes complete comprehension with all its forms, the speech of another person seems to him a word that has been GIVEN, in every sense of the term, like a commandment, and I experience the world (word) as fear. Ross carves up Gype especially his face and cock.

One could say that he seeks to merge with unnameable nature, fleeing the weight of nomination in the unnameable texture of things, I want people to treat me as an animal, in the irregular indefinable movements of the foliage, of the waves. To be matter. To be matter to matter. The cops find Gype dead badly buried. I don't produce meaning. Truth is alien to him. That's why he's the most credulous child: since he doesn't possess the truth, since only other people do it is their language, he can only recognize truth because it always causes him pain; when he has to deal socially or in the world he relies on the principle of authority because socially nothing matters.

When we arrest Hart, he looks like he's mad. You killed your daughter. Every human being has intentions. Every human being is connected to every other human being and the intentionality of these connections is language. What happens when there's no language or when language doesn't mean? It's too soon to answer these questions. His first stories deal continually with his childhood. He hasn't stopped nor will he ever stop being that murdered child.

I, Pier Paolo Pasolini, will solve my murder by denying the principle of causation and by proposing nominalism:

1 Sex

1 Sexual desire

1. *Claudius', King of Denmark's, corruption infects his family and all society*:

Ophelia (*to her father Polonius*): Daddy, can't I go out? I'm bored. You're keeping me locked up here like I'm a piece of dry goods.

Polonius: No, honey, I'd rather you were wet. Do you think I want to see you blackface up your pretty white party dress?

Ophelia: I'll dirty up more, pops, if you don't let me out of here. I'm no nun.

Polonius: Shut up. I'm bigger than you. (*Changing his tone.*) How dare you talk to me like that: I'm your father. If you set one foot outside this house, Pheelie, I'm telling you right now: there are rapists in this world. Little girls like you can get in serious trouble. Take that boy Hamlet. My baby isn't safe with a criminal like him.

Ophelia: Not even if she's supporting her father?

Polonius: What're you saying? Pheelie, all men except for me are evil. When you go outside, they're going to rape and murder you. Do you know what'll happen to me, darling, when you're raped and murdered? I'll have horns on the top of my head. I'll be horny. I'm going to tell you something, Pheelie. It's all right for a woman, but it's not good for a man to be horny. A man who doesn't achieve full sexual satiation becomes ill. If you walk out of this house, young lady, you're going to give your father a heart attack.

Ophelia: My mother's already given you two heart attacks. She's better at it than I am. Besides, the only people you can perceive are murderers and rapists and you're always miserable and you sit in bed and do dope and don't do anything else cause your mind's a stinkin' mess.

(*All these characters stink and have lousy motivations.*)

Polonius (*swigging out of his Scotch bottle*): You're running out to see that Hamlet, aren't you? You two have something going on with you. I'm not going to let you go! I'm going to protect you! He doesn't respect you, Pheelie: no man respects you except for me; I give you a home and everything you want. He's going to leave you.

Ophelia: Why don't you fuck your wife, Polly, instead of me?

Polonius: We're too old to do that sort of thing.

Ophelia: Mother wants it. She sends you all those birthday cards asking you why you can't get your cock up and shows them to her friends.

Polonius: Phelia! Where d'you ever learn such foul language! I'm going to wash your mouth out with soap, young lady.

Ophelia: You ate up all the soap yesterday when you ran out of your

257

liquor. (*Tries another tack.*) Why don't I go around the corner to get you another bottle of Jack Daniels, daddy?

Polonius: That would be very nice of you. (*Catching himself, but he wants it too much.*) You come back here immediately, Ophelia! Don't say a word to a man.

Ophelia: How would I know what a man looks like the way you keep me locked up, daddy?

Ophelia's First Nurse (*entering room*): 'Man'? I don't know where she picked up such language, Mr Polonius. she was brought up to be a nice girl and she talks like a two-bit . . . I can't even get the word out of my mouth.

Ophelia: Slut. Whore. Hooker. Prostitute. Pretty girl. Cunt. Tramp. Floozy. Flounder. Dead fish. Wet fish. Teeth. Trollop. Cock-twister. Slut scumbag scallops. Box. Bitch. (*To her Nurse*) I know this is what you are because I've seen you and this feeble-brain (pointing to her father) who's holding me prisoner in this house doing it together and he can't even get it up.

Nurse: You ungrateful child! I ought to slap your face. Your father has given you everything a child could possibly want and brought you up in this hard world like no child's ever been brought up and this is the gratitude you give him.

Polonius: Shut up, Grace. Ophelia, your nurse loves you. Is this how you treat her? I don't care how you're acting towards me, but your nurse is a wonderful person. Everyone loves her. I'm not going to let you hurt her as you're doing.

First Nurse (*in a little voice*): It doesn't matter. Parrot.

Polonius: It matters to me, Grace. I'm not going to let her keep on taking advantage of your sweetness. I'm going to take her trust fund away from her; well, I legally can't; but I can do my best to see she is never happy.

Ophelia: How're you going to do that, Impotency?

Polonius: You're not twenty-one yet, young lady. I still own you. You cannot leave this house, Ophelia. From now on, these doors are locked. Moreover, no man's going to enter this house.

Ophelia: There's sure no man in here now.

(*Polonius' walking off high-and-mightily arm-in-arm with the Nurse. Polonius is off the stage.*)

Ophelia: I don't care about love.
In Honour Of Brendan Behan And The Irish Society Who Revolted: The prisoners sing: they are in one of the punishment cells.

Claudius to his Queen: I bought you a Christmas present.
Queen: Oh, Claudius. How sweet of you. Tell me. What is it?

Claudius: A maid. Would you like to see her?

Queen: A ready-made?

Claudius: Ready and willing. (*Tries to rub his cock and misses.*) Should I call her? (*Rings the buzzer 'Emergency' for the guard. A moment later the cell door opens and a tiny, pretty girl is shoved through the door.*) These are your new employers, Mrs Claudius and Mrs Polonius. You shall help them out, Al'Amat, in whatever ways they require you to do so.

Al'Amat: Yes, sir.

Queen: What's your name, child?

Al'Amat: Rebecca.

Queen: What a horrible name!

Claudius: I changed her name to Al'Amat.

Queen: Why don't you go outside and bring us some Turkish coffee, Al'Amat? They serve the worst dishwater in here.

Mrs Polonius (*looking at a wall, as if through a window*): Nice day for murder.

Al'Amat (*looking confused*) Yes, Ma'am. (*She rings the 'Emergency' bell.*)

(*A guard appears and lets Al'Amat out.*)

Queen: Claudius, would you like a piece of bread and cheese?

Claudius: Yes, please.

Queen: We haven't got any.

(*Again, the cell door opens. Al'Amat, overloaded by a tray full of Turkish coffee cups, stumbles through and falls down.*)

Queen: Don't you feel awful working for strangers, Al'Amat?

(*All these distinctly different verbal elements go together because nothing makes sense anymore and this putting together of various cultures is an act of hatred.*)

Al'Amat: I don't give a damn about anyone anymore, Mrs Claudius. I'm Irish.

Queen: Oh. Why don't you just call me Gertrude?

Al'Amat: Yes, Mrs . . . Gertrude.

Queen: If I was working for the first time for strange people, I'd be so shy I wouldn't know what to do with myself.

Al'Amat: I hate the English. They infiltrated and made me with their culture. I don't know how to speak English very well, Mrs Claudius.

Queen: Gertrude. I'm afraid you're going to have to get used to our life in gaol here just as we have had to, Al'Amat. Humans, you will learn, can adapt to anything, even to society. Inside gaol we use neither sexist nor classist nor racist, such as 'I hate the English', language. Although words don't mean anything anymore.

Al'Amat: What do you mean 'Words don't mean anything'?

Mrs Polonius: Polly told me he likes to fuck black sailors because he's making up for the way his parents, when he was a kid, mistreated their black maids.

Al'Amat: I'm not black; I'm Irish.

Queen: You are now that we've changed your name. I hope you don't mind.

Al'Amat: Of course not, Mrs Gertrude (*Now the audience sees that a knife is sticking out from under her arm.*) The culture I grew up in and by is the culture the English imposed on my country to make us learn that is stop perceiving the absolute lack of pride or abject poverty, they are the same thing, in which we were living. Culture is that which falsifies.

Queen: We are all sisters.

Mrs Polonius: There's a man down there.

Claudius: Is he wearing a trench-coat and beret?

Mrs Polonius: How d'you know?

Claudius: He's a fortune-teller.

Al'Amat: He's going to tell all of your fortunes. You're all going to die.

(*Two men, one thin-faced in a trench-coat and black beret, the second in a black leather overcoat and pimp hat, enter the cell and begin searching it. They test the plaster, stamp on the wood boards that are beds.*)

Al'Amat: I've been waiting for you.

Thin-Faced Man: Who's in charge here?

Claudius: I am.

Thin-Faced Man: This cell is full of rubbish. (*Kicking the Turkish coffee cups.*)

Leather-Coat: You'll have to clear this cell totally. It's an escape route.

Mrs Polonius: Are these the sanitary inspectors?

Thin-Faced Man: Where are the toilet arrangements?

(*Al'amat walks him around a thin three-foot high partition in back of which a cracked urinal sits on a concrete square.*)

Al'Amat: When may we expect the prisoner?

Thin-Faced Man: Tonight.

Al'Amat: What time?

Thin-Faced Man: Between nine and twelve.

Al'Amat: They had not, under the heavens and on earth, one single weapon. They don't control the land they live on, the schools which train them, the heat and food their bodies need to live through the winter's cold, the media which gives them language, the military weapons for which they give most of their money. There is no more time in this city. Reasonable people don't let themselves dream because no dream can be true. They have a cry that brought them back to first causes: From Haiti from El Salvador people running here, and we who have no mothers, no fathers, no homes or love: Where are we going to run?

Hamlet is the only member of this society who perceives this disease. Because he's perceiving the disease, he's being ostracized by the society:

1. The art world of New York City.

Hamlet's Maid: Then an artist can't live these days by his art?

Hamlet: That's a very important point. I'm going to conquer the world. Whatever I have to do to myself to achieve this.

Hamlet's Maid: But, sir, you don't have any money.

Hamlet: So what. Are you a materialist? Am I a materialist?. . .

Hamlet's Maid: Yes.

Hamlet: . . . If it's not money that matters, it's the idea. Oh, the world! Anyway, money is the main thing those who are really in power are using – they actually *make* it – to control us. Rich men don't have money, they have power. I hate the rich.

Hamlet's Maid: But not their money.

Hamlet: The mental world is the cause of the physical one. Two knobs, so to speak. two nips tits bazooms. Since I can't have one, money; I'm going to clamp my teeth and chomp on the other.

Hamlet's Maid: Mother Earth's going to love that one.

Hamlet: Shut up. Don't I pay your wages?

Hamlet's Maid: Just like Reagan pays out Social Security, Welfare, and the NEA.

Hamlet: No more dumb jokes. No one reads me now so I'd better write for posterity though the world's ending. Like a good artist, I'm going to marry Ophelia for her money!

Hamlet's Maid: That's real love.

Hamlet: And so by chomping on the sacred tit of money, art will spurt out her milk for me!

Hamlet's Maid: You don't have to be weaned, baby, beause you don't have a head. Why is Ophelia who's beautiful rich and so shy she can't even talk to a normal person going to let you near her secret underpants?

Hamlet: This desperate poverty commingled with the purity of my artistic action will, by rendering her ashamed of her richness, annihilate both her pride and fear. I, the person who considers himself, will be much more desirable than any rich man!

Hamlet's Maid: You've certainly got the brains of a rich man.

Hamlet (*aside*): This absence of love, noticed only as a hole, a gnawing which never goes away. You rats at the edge of my mind! Get out! Get out, I say to all you characteristics. While the sinuses around my brain are pounding. This hurt. I'm not going to bother again with psychologies, relationships, those sorts of damned human contacts. I've been too hurt. I now know know now no nothing lasts lasts. More precisely there is no true belief, is any belief true?, in any security between human and human. I have experienced this. I have been taught my blows that split apart the world. Crack. Why should I give in to any relationship, love or hatred?

Hamlet's Maid: Your plan to marry Ophelia for her money is as intelligent as the American Cancer Association's decision to research synthetic rather than natural cancer cures. Synthetic cancer cures maintain the pharmaceutical industry and the cancer plague. Meanwhile, the men who eat the most food in this country, the doctors, are the ones who have the highest incidence of cancer.

Hamlet: I'll take away some of their trade.

Hamlet's Maid: What? Are you going to open a mortuary?

Hamlet: I'm going to make dead people. I'm going to write a play.

Hamlet's Maid: The last time you wrote a play, the printer stole all the money you gave him to print the play, the lawyer you hired turned around and sued you for three thousand dollar court fees though no one ever went to court, three famous people sued you for libel, and now all the women refuse to fuck with you cause you might write about them. You don't have any friends left. And your parents hate your guts.

Hamlet: There's you.

Hamlet's Maid: There was me. Poverty, living without heat or hot water, catcalls as we walk down the street just because of what we look like, envy, loneliness: every part of your life I can stand. The only thing that turns my stomach is poetry.

Hamlet: I'll be a representational painter. What's in a name these days? I will represent the poverty of spirit that the powers behind Reagan endorse. Economic poverty. Social poverty. Political poverty. Emotional poverty. Ideational poverty.

Hamlet's Maid: How much you want money. I wouldn't mind a little bit either.

(*Hamlet exits.*)

Hamlet's Maid (*alone*): Choosing to be an artist means living against this world. Why would anyone choose to be an artist? Cripples didn't choose to be crippled.

The spirit of famine is appearing to me: Now he's fucking rich women to stay alive. Now he's pulling white scraps out of his holey pockets and saying 'These are my poems' in a deserted airport. Now he's standing in the doorway of a rich woman's dining-room during a crowded party, one eye on the mouldy pink ham and stale white bread on the dining-room table and the other on his death.

(*Exits as Hamlet re-enters room.*)

Hamlet's Maid (*re-entering, followed by men*): Hamlet. They're here to arrest you because you haven't paid your bills.

(*Hamlet flees.*)

1. The cure for disease.

Romeo: I look up to you so much, my just being around you must hurt you so let me increase this disease.

Juliet: I don't mind you being around me because I'm made to have human contact. I'm not made for separation which is the sickness of this society.

Romeo: Which means I can make you more diseased.

Juliet: You're going to hurt me?

Romeo: There's always danger when we aim for everything.

Juliet: I don't think it's possible for humans to do anything. They can listen.

Romeo: Until there is no thing.

(*He kisses her. They shiver.*)

Juliet: And back and forth so that we are both nothing.

Romeo: We're descending into blackness.

(*They kiss again more hotly. Their tongues are slapping against each other.*)

Juliet: You kiss like your mother taught you to.

2. (*There is no light on stage because Juliet is the only thing who exists.*)

Romeo: I would do anything for you. I would do anything so you would let me near you but I know if I say this to you, it'll scare you so much you'll freeze up to me.

Juliet: Oh me!

Romeo: Just, please, listen to me a second and give me one chance. I'm living in the pain of absolute longing like leaning over a chair that is a sharp razor blade.

Juliet: Give up your life in New York and come to me. Or I, I'll give myself, I will, because being loved is the only thing that matters. I'll accept death and be cured.

Romeo: (*aside*) Can I tell her I want her? The life I'm living is like being dead. The hell with this fame. Her speech is the first living I've heard. (*to Juliet*) You, mistress, name me.

Juliet: Who are you? Now I know who you are. You're my enemy.

Romeo: If you want me to, I'll kill you.

Juliet: You've hurt me before but that doesn't matter. How do I know anything? What does this language mean? I'll have to trust nothing. I know I trust nothing too much, I will do anything for nothing. Tell me what's true now. Tell me what's true now.

Romeo: The truth?

Juliet: Don't leave me hanging.

Romeo: The only thing I believe in is nothingness.

(*A gleam of light grey appears in the lower sky.*)

Juliet: Go to hell. I don't like you anyway. I don't live anywhere. My life is shit. I need someone to love me.

Romeo: I want your body.

Juliet: I wish I knew what I want.

Romeo: To hell with these politenesses! Tomorrow I'll marry you.

Juliet: For ever?

Romeo: For ever.

Juliet: That's what I want to do.

Nurse (*from within Juliet's parents' house*): Juliet, are you talking to yourself again?

Juliet: I have to go.

Romeo: I'll give you all my money if you just let my tongue lick your cunt juice.

Juliet: Tomorrow, for the rest of our lives for ever we'll be able to lie to each other and we'll be able to lie on each other. What time tomorrow will we be able to fuck?

Romeo: As soon as the morning sun has shot its sperm over all blackness and the Wall Street lawyer is masturbating in his office.

Juliet: From now on let every second be a year until this ache this smell of dead fish takes over the world. I am being driven crazy. When I will lie with you I can no longer think. When I will lie with you I am no longer happy.

Romeo: Then I'll make sure you'll never fuck me.

Juliet: I'd rather have you next to me so I could increase your absence by a thousandfold. Absence upon absence until. . . .

Romeo: I will eat you out.

Juliet: I'd rather be manipulated.

(*The nurse drags away this brat.*)

Romeo: This isn't real.

3. *Society: The doldrums of this season, winter, wet like drabs the maids made of these waters, ugly, along the streets they gleam black no matter what*

the hour, late at night small black human figures, caps over the tops of their heads, toss crates of sticks, fishheads and parts of fish bodies the scales now dulled into the huge dark green bins, and no one says hello to anyone, in the narrow alleyways, these few cobblestones left, surrounded by the long grey smooth streets which during the day the businessmen with their briefcases cover. (Tybalt and Mercutio, two businessmen, walk on to the street and kill each other.)

4. Romeo at home.

Romeo: The war's my real father.

Mrs Montague: It doesn't matter who your real father is. You just have to have some father cause every child has a father or else you're not a real child.

Romeo: I don't have a mother either.

Mrs Montague (*showing emotion*): What do you mean 'You don't have a mother'?

Romeo: Since you open your body to my unreal father, you're not real and I'm an abortion.

Mrs Montague: I gave birth to you only cause I was too scared to get an abortion. You need sex too much.

5. Romeo is in the Priest's cell.

Romeo: I'm going to get married.

Priest: You're crazy. What're you going to get married for?

Romeo: This time I really want to get married. When are you going to marry me?

Priest: One of us is the wrong sex, honey. It isn't legal yet.

Romeo: The person I want to marry is more wrong than you. (*Juliet enters the cell.*) I will do whatever I have to to get her.

This scene break, though not a logical one, has become conventional; we have retained it merely because it is generally accepted and to depart from this convention might affect the scene numbering of the rest of the act in a way that would cause referential confusion.

6. *SITTING* here I see, through the glass restaurant door, a three-foot wide rivulet of black water, flowing, now stagnant, against cobblestones each one slightly apart from the ones surrounding it. Towards the back of the street near an uneven light grey sidewalk, smaller black pools obscure the stones. The more rapidly the water moves, the lighter it seems. Out of the sidewalk which is nearer to the eye a thick aluminium cylinder whose function is unknown and the same sized fire hydrant rise up. Inside the restaurant several small hideous woodcuts and drawings

of a classical representational style hang over the walls' sanded red bricks. Varnished unstained wood slabs six inches wide and two inches long frame the glass windows and doors. There is a lot of natural and electric light. On one rectangular wood table a cigarette burns on a shell. Near the cigarette a small glass contains half a cup of sugar. An aluminium spoon sticks upward. From the sugar cup, about the same distance as is between the burning cigarette and the sugar, a white china dish holds salt and a dark green-brown spice. A girl sits at this table. The pen in her right hand moves rapidly over a blue-lined page of a spiral notebook. Sitting on the seat of a dark wood chair which is next and similar to the one she's sitting on, whose back holds a copy of *American Heritage*, the open section of a worn-out leather handbag reveals a crumbled piece of white paper. Easy-listening Greek music is playing. The girl is thinking that most people are saying the human world is ending. This landscape is without propaganda or obsession. This landscape without any given meaning is as present as any statement such as the world is about to end.

Memory and association
Back to the same restaurant. In Zurich, after I crossed the large river, the streets moved as if streets can move by themselves while away from me upward and slightly winding. The most interesting streets, I remember, were the narrowest ones. Small bars with bad food, not catering just to rich people, clean sidewalks and buildings, light browns light-light not light. Of course there was nowhere to go on top. Better than Berne: there, there was no hiddeness: Levels on levels of buildings and their streets, the archways are archways, the shops under the archways sell gold coins and antiques which are more economically stable than money, there are levels of roofs, steppingstones of roofs, staircases outside. All which is understandable. On one middle level at the end of the archways cobblestones and small squares of greenery, a large park lifted up to another level. At the bottom of this park a round circle of masonry sunk in the ground contained two bears and some rocks. The American and one Italian-Swiss and two German-Swiss for breakfast ate one poached egg and a slice of Swiss cheese over a piece of white bread. The bread tasted winey. Some say he is not in that grave at all. That the coffin was filled with stones. That one day he will come again.

Hynes shook his head.

– Parnell'll never come again, he said. He's there, all that was mortal of him. TO SEARCH IN ALL THESE THINGS (OF COURSE MENTAL) WHICH SIMPLY PRESENT THEMSELVES FOR THE ROAD OR MEANING:

When I lived in San Diego, I had three cats. The cats used to jump out of the kitchen window of my apartment which was on the second floor, over to a black flat roof. Once they had jumped off this roof, I couldn't see them anymore. When they became hungry and when they wanted to, they reappeared in my kitchen. At times another cat, a huge black stud searching for my oldest female, appeared on the black flat roof. To me these appearances were magic or causeless because I couldn't follow my cats because I can't leap across roofs.

I thought I knew every section of this small beach town. My male cat adored my body so much whenever he was around me he pressed rubbed his back into my belly. One day while I was walking on a sidewalk I met my male cat strutting along the edge of the green. I said 'Hello'. He refused to recognize me. I decided to follow him. He met twelve other cats behind an old car in long grass a block away from the beach. As soon as the cats heard me, they ran where I couldn't follow. I began to trace dogs. The dogs had a different town. Definitive meeting points and certain streets or paths that linked the points defined each town. I almost but couldn't know these towns that were my towns.

How available are the (meanings of the) specifics of all that is given? Language is a giveness like all other givenesses. Let the meanings not overpowering (rigid) but rather within the contexts, like Hamlet's father's ghost who tells the first meaning, interpretation of nothing, be here:

On this table which is in front of me which is just a fancy wood crate: a chess board on whose black and gold plastic top dust cookie crumbs some chess pieces, behind the chess board a white plastic coffee cup over, to the left of the board and cover (my eye doesn't want to see too much). What is given: one almost empty jar of dried soy granules, one tin of cinnamon, one book entitled *The Book of Ebenezer le Page* on top of the light-blue-covered book *The Complete Plays of William Wycherley*, two filthy chopsticks, one empty white china cup with an aluminium spoon sticking out of its middle; on the other half of this crate, a stack of nine books two of whose titles *The Art of Positional Play* and *The Marble Faun* right against a bottle of Lâncome red nail polish and right in front of a small white candy box and a box of herbal cigarettes, a small black-and-white TV which isn't on, a small computer chess set a quarter way through a game.

What's the meaning here? Compare this list of just what is given to another structurally similar list to find the key:

Gross-booted draymen rolled barrels dull-thudding out of Prince's stores and bumped them up on the brewery float. On the brewery float bumped dull-thudding barrels rolled by gross-booted draymen out of Prince's stores. – There it is Red Murray said. Alexander Keyes. – Just cut it out, will you? Mr Bloom said, and I'll take it round to the TELEGRAPH office. HOUSE OF KEY(E)S – Like that, see. Two crossed keys here. A circle. Then here the name Alexander Keyes, tea,

wine and spirit merchant. So on. Better not teach him his own business.
– You know yourself, councillor, just what he wants. Then round the
top in leaded: The house of keys. You see. Do you think that's a good
idea? The foreman moved his scratching hand to his lower ribs and
scratched there quietly. – The idea, Mr Bloom said, is the house of
keys. You know, councillor, the Man parliament. Innuendo of home
rule. Tourists, you know, from the Isle of Man. Catches the eye. (I),
you see. Can you do that?

Compare these two lists:

Comparison: Paris rawly waking, crude sunlight over her lemon
streets. Moist piths of farls of bread, the froggreen wormwood, her
morning perfume, coffee coffee court the air. The milk of architectural
tits. *Têtes.* Frenchmen can only think. We invited two hookers to sit
with us cause Frenchmen are only polite to language and food before
you've fucked them. There Belluomo rises from his wife's lover's wife's
bed, the kerchiefed housewife stirs, a saucer of sunk gone oh below the
cement. I say, pick up skirts. Show cunt. Smelly fish all over the sides
of flesh going slowly arising

I can no longer speak English:
7. *La Chambre du lit*
Juliet: Si je ne suis pas fouquée à demain, je vais mourir par une malâdie.
Il est necessaire que je fouque ou je meurs. Je pense que je suis
souffrante parce que le seul chose que je demande – fouquer un
homme – est l'unique acte que je ne peux pas faire. Je suis pourtant
plus écoeurée parce que tu ne me désires pas subitement tu me désires
maintenant tu ne me désires pas. Dieu je te tuerai. Je suis à bout de
mes forces. Les hommes sont des bébés. Ils doivent pronouncer la
réalité, déclarer à moi qu'il est necessaire pour moi faire d'accord avec
leurs grandes modèles de la réalité, et á la même temps mentir. Leurs
mesonges ne sont pas intelligents. Par conséquent leurs mesonges
nous insultent et nous rennent incapables de le langage parler.
La Bonne D'Enfant: Les hommes sont des merdres. Regarde-toi le
morceau gros de la saucisse entre ces reins.
Juliet: Je l'aime. Si j'ai besoin de choisir entre ma famille et fouquer,
je chois fouquer. N'est pas problème. Je chois fouquer si fouquer
existe joint au pouvoir, la renommée et tous les phenomena qui existent. Par conséquent je préfére fouquer les hommes qui sont les plus
puissants les plus fameux. Comme moi décadents avec la plus
complexe perception obsessifs droits comme moi et ne me désirent
jamais. Est-ce que peut-être il est bon pour moi me suicider?
La Bonne D'Enfant: Pourquoi? Comment peux-tu aimer un homme
que tu possedes? Comment peux-tu aimer ce qui est présent?
Juliet: Par conséquent je ne pourrai jamais fouquer un homme.

commence-toi avec le renversement des humains qui est la fierté humaine. Laisse-toi l'imagination dégager. Je signifie surtout les types de l'imagination les plus débiles. Supposant l'expression de ton visage sur ce moment tu me fouques.

Cette écriture est réelle. Cette réalité est mon message á vous.

8. Dans le cachot du prêtre

Juliet: Est-ce que possible que quand nous nous fouquons je touche l'amour pour toi et tu ne le touches pas pour moi?

Romeo: Mon corps a voulu rester pour un moment.

Juliet: Aprés deux jours je m'allierai à Paris.

Romeo: Par conséquent j'ai besoin de toi. Pour un homme l'amour n'advient pas et ensuite sans cause il advient. Je ne t'as jamais vu avant ce moment. Qui êtes-vous? Je sortirai en trombe tes cheveux.

Juliet: Les cheveux de mon poisson s'etoufferont tes narines.

(Elle met un doigt couvert par un gant du cuir noir sur sa joue.)

Juliet: Au revoir; je vais partir.

(Ses dingdongs s'écrasent follement contre l'un l'autre.)

(Cette chose n'est pas supposée être obsessife.)

Le Prêtre: Juliet!

(Les prêtres ne sont pas obsessifs.)

Juliet: Huh? *(Elle est une gosse seulement. Romeo disparaît. Juliet ne peut pas tolérer cet acte. Il ne peut pas me laisser.)* Romeo! *(seulement un peu de lui apparaît)* Pense-toi que nous nous rencontrerons de nouveau toujours?

Romeo: Je t'aime. Au revoir.

(Il me baisse tendrement.)

9. *Le seul moyen que j'ai pour guérir la maladie sociale est pour moi devenir plus malade. Plus de gens ne veulent pas nuire aux autres gens et nuisent aux autres. Plus d'hommes de l'authorité social et politique ne veulent pas endommagent les autres humains et les endommagent. Au contraire de ces hommes malades je consciencieusement désire faire ma maladie consciencieuse-ment a l'extrême. Je me réglerai plus jusqu'à ce qui est mes besoins deviendra insensé;*

Juliet: J'aime votre sexe. Vous n'aimer pas mon sexe.

(J'aime votre sexe. Vous n'aimez pas mon sexe et ne voulez pas voir mon sexe.)

Le dixiéme vue

Paris: Veux-toi m'épouser?

Juliet: Vous? L'oubliez. Je seulement désire me marier Romeo.

Paris: Romeo ne te désirera jamais. Il devient fameux de sorte qu'il a trop d'intérêt personnel qu'il ne peut pas prêter attention à une autre personne.

Juliet: D'accord. Je ne suis pas assez riche de sorte qu'il m'aimera. Je ne vais pas me marier même si, si je ne me marierai pas, je mourirai. Je ne parle pas du sexe.

(*Elle est physiquement malade et se tord avec une inflammation de la syphilis.*)

L'onziéme vue:

Juliet (*seule*): Si tu plais, cesse mon coeur et les lèvres de mon sexe et ces qui sont mes pensées d'incendier de me réduire en cendres. Je ne peut pas supporter désirer tout ce rien reins.

Dear Monet, Would you like to go away with me? A bribe. For a week. We will go anywhere in the world you want.

How can I get him to talk to me? He isn't going to fall in love with me because he's becoming too famous.

12. **Juliet** (*déguisée comme un jeune garçon parce qu'elle est un jeune garçon quand personne ne s'aime pas*): Merde, est-ce que je suis un garçon beau jeune?

Orlando: brusquement): Que voulez-vous?

Juliet: Quelle heure est-il?

Orlando: L'heure? Que pensez-vous? Que je porte une montre?

Juliet: Alors vous n'êtes pas amoureux avec personne, monsieur, parce que si vous êtes amoureux avec quelqu'un vous savez ce que le temps est.

Orlando: Maintenant je n'ai pas de temps pour l'amour.

Juliet: Votre déclaration est exactement ce que je signifie. Si vous soyez une jeune fille venante revenir á la cité á l'homme qu'elle désire fouquer et avec lequel elle pense être inanimée va arriver et qu'elle n'a pas eue dans un an; vous sachez ce qui est la nature du temps. Le temps est couché entre les reins.

Orlando: Pas le temps, mais des piéces de dix cents. Il est necessaire que cette affaire est vraie parce que le temps, qui est changement, ment.

Juliet: La monnaie dans mon porte-monnaie! La monnaie dans mon porte-monnaie! (*Frictionnante les lévres de son sexe avec ses doigts.*) Tandis qu'un homme qui ne fouque pas ou un prêtre, qui existe joyeusement sur la fertilité de la nation et sur son propre embonpoint, ne peut pas mentir. Par example notre prêtre Président Reagan.

Orlando: Tandis que les voleurs et les meurtriers se taisent à plat dans leurs tombes. Alors avez-vous de temps, garcon?

Juliet: Je suis trop jeune pouvoir parler de sorte que je mens. Seulement, merci à Dieu que je ne suis pas une femelle.

Orlando: Pourquoi?

Juliet: Je ne veuille pas être une femelle dans le monde de beaux-arts à cet instant comme si le monde de beaux-arts ait changé. Les femmes: les hommes courent après lesquelles et leur disent. 'Je te veux' sans d'intention ou de signification; les femmes, pas comprenantes ce qui se passe, sont quittées dans une condition du désir échauffé à côté de l'incapacité de compréhension de quelque chose.

13. Heathcliffe et Catherine sur les terrains incultes

Catherine: H et moi, nous nous vont rebeller. Ce soir nous avons pris nos premiers pas rebeller.

Mardi 5 mars. J'instruis mes leçons de l'école à H de sorte que ils ne peuvent pas nous désunir. En dépit de et joint à tous ces choses que j'apprends, je ne vais pas devenir adulte. Je ne vais pas changer la férocité. Cette férocité est: je ne fais pas l'attention à quelqu'un mais H parce que H n'est pas quelqu'un je ne fais pas attention à quelqu'un H est cet univers. Moi et H cet univers: une sphere. Ce vent qui se tourne sans gêne est moi. J'aime les cheveux de la fille dans la peinture de Monet.

Aujourd'hui ils ont fouettés H et ont pris mon animal empaillé. Quand je les atteigne, je vais les atteindre sanglantement. Mais H, il est necessaire que je regarde à la hauteur de H que je me donne à H parce qu'il n'a pas eu un merde pour quelqu'un. Ils sont les monstres sur moi si je les permette je ne peux pas le permettre je dois maintenir le contrôle sévère sur moi-même. Il y a toujours le besoin absolu que je fais exactement ce que je désire et veux et H H il naturellement, sans se faisant consciencieusement, fait fait tous ce qu'il souhaite.

Les vents, faites vos existences damnées! Soufflez à fond à ces bâtiments bétons jusqu'a ce que vous désintegrerez proprement puis démolirez leurs quartiers de tête! Soufflez fouquer! Soufflez mon désir pour! Parce que H et moi nous sommes étés si brûlés les brèches que nous sommes outre sentissants des émotions. Chaque carré de cette peau rouge violacée combat. Ces lacérations, les lacérations que ma mère-mère et mon père-père me donnent chaque jour: apprenants par coeur la Bible, l'abus physique, la nourriture mal, la peur de rien de la nourriture et du refuge: Contre *vous*, nous dessinons nos revanches.

Nous vous vengerons – pour nôtre perception est rêvant – seulement afin de faire nous éclater de rire. Nous n'avons pas d'amis.

H: Il me dégradera Heathcliffe épouser pour cette raison il ne saura pas combien je l'adore. Heathcliffe n'est pas moi. Heathcliffe est plus moi-même que je suis. Quoi que ce soit qui fait forme cette matière humaine l'âme, le sien et le mien sont semblables; je hais définitement mon mari futur, il est aussi différent de nous que la glace de la glace sec ou la drogue la mort. Aujourd'hui je pense que je désire mortir.

La Bonne D'Enfant: Si tu épouseras un homme que tu n'aimes pas, tu ne pourras jamais fouquer et devenir cet homme, si il possiblement existe, que tu adores.

Heathcliffe: Jamais le fouquer! Jamais l'être! Unimaginable. Nous ne pouvons pas êtres separés, il s'est exclamé avec l'indignation. 'Qui par enfer puisse nous separer? Pas aussi long que je vis parce que mon être est le sien. Chaque Linton (chaque étranger) se dissout en rien avant que je m'incline avant que je puisse partir de Heathcliffe! Oh cette chose n'est pas ce que je signifie par mon mariage – je ne voudrai pas être la femme de Linton si faire cette fonction de la femme de Linton touchera mon être réel. Heathcliffe est pauvre. Si j'épouse Heathcliffe, il n'ait pas d'argent; mais si j'épouserai Linton, je pourraie élever Heathcliffe au pouvoir extrême qu'il est de sorte que mon frére ne puisse jamais le nuire.

The cure for desire

1. In bed

Juliet: Get away from me, you fat old creep! I want to be alone.
Nurse: Why?

(*Exi((s))ts.*)

Juliet (*alone*): Because I am alone.

(*She's not alone: she's a brat.*)

I'm getting to be so incredibly famous when I walk down the city street, people have to stop and ask me for my autograph. As I walk into my gym, a man who has no hair asks me if I'm really Juliet. All this attention only foils this space I have lived and am living in which is solitude. I'm not going to get weak-minded and babyish. (*Desperate.*) Nurse! Nurse! (*Her nurse doesn't answer.*) Good. she didn't answer me. I'm alone do you hear me God therefore I'm going to poison myself.

(*She drinks down a gram of poison not opium.*)

What if I'm doing the wrong thing?

Nurse (*entering the bedroom as the sun rises up, full gorgeous, colours, therefore as joyous a day as has ever existed*): My God. My baby, oh my little lamb.

(*One of Juliet's stuffed animals is a lamb.*)

(*Feeling her pulse.*) There's no pulse. She was an angel because she never wanted to hurt another living being even a human though she was too innocent to live. (*Picking a piece of scrap paper off the floor.*) She left this note to her poodle and no other suicide note. Everyone loved her so much there's no reason for her to suicide.

(*Maniacally screaming so loudly at the top of her lungs, Juliet's mother hears her and enters.*)

Mrs Capulet: Wha . . . Why Juliet's dead. Well, that's no reason to wake me up in the middle of the night. She deserved to die since she wasn't worth anything, especially economically, and she was too crazy for this family.

2. In the grave

Romeo: Fuck this social political and economic sickness. I am sick. I am diseased. I am in love.

Juliet: I can cure you, honey.

Romeo: How can you cure disease? You're dead.

Juliet: You'll become well if every day you come to me, kneel down beside my body, and kiss me and adore me and want me want me want me.

Romeo: That's sick. You're a dead person so I'd be wanting to death precisely what I can't have, and the sickest thing in the world is to want who you can't have.

Juliet: Do you want to get well?

Romeo: Yes.

(*The next day.*)

Romeo (*looking at a filthy decaying corpse one of whose feet is clubfoot*): Here I am, blue lips, but how the hell are you going to notice? I might as well be making love to a dead woman. All my other love affairs have been like this: for me the language of love, the only language I've ever used, is talking to myself.

Juliet: You're full of bullshit, hole not even good enough for an ass. You've never actually loved a single person.

Romeo: I deserve this.

Juliet: Furthermore, you don't even want to fuck me.

Romeo (*aside*): You're a corpse. (*To Juliet*) Since I'm feeling love rather than lust for you, you've got to give me some time.

273

Juliet: Time? Can the sun ask for more time when he has to begin each morning by orgasming into light and shooting whiteness over the tops of this universe? Do irrationality and nonsense know anything of time?

Romeo: It's not that I don't love you, Juliet . . . Corpse, but if I want to marry a girl, I need the time to consider how I can support her in the style in which no one lives and to which everyone should become accustomed: endless richness, and how we can live in the same ten rooms without tearing out each other's hairs and mangling like mindless mental beasts.

Juliet: I'd rather you'd fuck me like a bitch-in-heat right this second.

Romeo: But as an upper middleclass Jewish boy, I'm trained to do what's right by my wife.

Juliet: Fuck me! Fuck me! What do I care who's wife you are? If you care about me, you should be saving my life. When I'm this horny, I get bad sexual disease.

Romeo: If you were the woman I worship, my lips would be pressed on the dripping red-violet of your cunt lips.

Juliet: So you don't love me. (*Takes in this fact.*) You're supposed to be pretending you love me and the more you don't, because love is confusion, the more love you're feeling for me. In this way pretense becomes reality.

Romeo: Run that by me again.

Juliet: Get rid of your reasons. I'm out of my clothes. And either take off those clothes or don't have anything to do with me and get out of here. (to you two men who don't love me.)

Romeo: I'm not going to take my clothes off in front of a woman I don't love. I'm no hippy.

Juliet: Then you're sick.

Romeo: This is the way of desire: Either I'm sick and don't fuck, or I fuck a corpse.

Juliet: No one ever said the world is perfect. Human beings have been mean to themselves and each other in various uncountable ways ever since they were orang-utans, yet all the time, as far as I know, no one's ever died from fucking a corpse. Men fuck corpses all the time. Most men would rather fuck corpses than other women. How do I know this? Because men pay prostitutes but they don't pay other women to fuck. Yet the prostitutes don't give a damn about the men who are humping on top of them, and if they feel anything, they like the money they're earning. Now have you ever heard of a John dying, or even being put in gaol?

Romeo: Rockefeller died.

Juliet: He was a politician.

Romeo: I'm glad you're not the woman I love because you're a corpse so you can't love in return.

Juliet: Most men would find that an inducement.

3. I must make writing the real thing.

I am almost sick for a cock, though I would not have it grow upon my chin:

(Viola, a young boy, following around everywhere the man she loves even though he will have nothing to do with her.)

Duke: Boy, I will no longer love.

Viola: I love you more than I love these eyes of mine, therefore more than I love what I see, more than I love the causes of my eyes: my life. I would follow you to the ends of the earth, but I'm scared you don't want me. I don't want to do anything you don't want.

Duke: For a month now you've been telling me you'll do whatever I want and you don't care for a woman.

Viola: Everything I say is always absolutely true and absolutely false because I'd give my will and judgement to you if only you'd have me.

Duke: Let me see what you look like when your legs are spread as wide as they can spread.

Viola (*with her hand in her cunt*): I'm giving myself up.

(She joyfully runs away. Joe enters, with letter.)

Olivia (*to Joe*): What's that, fool?

(Joe ignores her because she's over eighteen.)

Read your letter.

Joe: This is the same as children learning in our schools: idiots telling crazies what reality's like: (reads the paper sententiously:)
YOU ASKED ME TO COME OUT HERE AND NOW YOU WON'T HAVE ANYTHING TO DO WITH ME. YOU WON'T TELL ME WHY. THIS IS THE SECOND TIME YOU'VE BURNT ME. I'M NOT A CHILD ANYMORE SO I DON'T CARE SO I'M NOT GOING TO MAIM MYSELF LIKE I DID THE FIRST TIME YOU HURT ME. I DON'T KNOW IF I SHOULD WRITE TO YOU.

Olivia: I'd better talk to Howard in person. Shit. (*To Joe.*) Tell Howard to come here.

(Joe exits as Viola enters, naked and fantastically muscularly beautiful.)

Duke: (*to Viola*): As soon as I find myself in a room with you, I have to fuck you.

(Joe and Howard enter,)

Olivia: What's going on, Howard?

Howard: I don't know. You hurt me.

Olivia: Explain to me how I've hurt you.

Howard: You called me up over the phone I didn't call you. Over the phone you told me to go out on the streets, not wearing any skirts, with my cunt hairs and string black bikini showing through my half-white half-black tights, so everybody could see everything I own.

still saying you want me, when then are you keeping me locked up in a dark house, visited by no one else but a priest, so I have no more friends? I'm screaming against unjust loneliness. Do humans treat each other in this way?

Olivia: I don't know if I ever wanted you or not, but I don't want you now. Learn to hear changes which are human or else die.

Howard: I hate you!

Duke: All of our desires are always changing.

2 The world resembles sexual desire

I Remember seeing my mother's dead body: It was Christmas Day so the morgue-men or the policemen or whatever-you-call-them wanted to get out of the morgue by 4.00 so they were kind of pissed-off I wanted to see my mother or had to see her. At that moment we (my sister and I) weren't sure it was my mother. She had been missing five days and the cops had found this dead female, etc. body in a room of the Hilton Hotel. We (my sister and I) walked down these plastic-like, they were probably metal, hospital-like steps. I can't remember the colour of the steps. The door was the same material and (I slightly remember) pale green. I was frightened to look inside. There was nothing in the room. He wheeled one of those slabs hospital patients lie on when they're about to be cut into about a foot from the door. A dark green garbage bag lay over something on the slab. The morgue-man, I think he was black, pulled the garbage bag down from the top about one-third its length. The man standing behind us said, 'You're going to have to identify her for us.' The face was pale white until its lower third. The lower third was horizontal stripes. There was a bright bright red stripe. Below that was a white stripe. Then there was a swollen blue-purple brighter than any colour. Actual seeing didn't give me the information this was my mother. All of me knew I was seeing my mother so I screamed. I said, 'Yes, that's my mother.' I didn't know. I said, 'I don't recognize her.' The morgue-man answered. 'That's because she's been dead five days. Decayed bodies look like that.' I replied, 'I didn't know.'

Upstairs they told me they didn't know how she had died. From the evidence they were sure, though it wasn't clear why they were sure, she hadn't suicided. We (my sister, I, and the family lawyer) thought she had suicided. Then it was either an accidental overdose of pills or murder. The police were not going to investigate it if it was murder because there wasn't enough evidence it was murder, an autopsy would take two months and by then all the evidence would have dissipated, and they had enough to do with important cases. Since I didn't have enough money to hire a private investigator until the money from the will came through, which my family lawyer informed me would take at least two years, I would have to probe myself or else walk away from this mess.

The uses of reductionism: the same desire to go over any edge or passion I had when I started to write; only now, having become frigid, I am choosing to want to go over the edges. Now uncontrollable violence or expressionism occurs within a chosen framework or will.

My father was a fascist. My mother, Susan, intensely repeated the matriarchal pattern of her side of the family. She never considered fucking a man other than my father once they were married, though he probably fucked whores to keep up his (male) business relations; but her fantasizing betrayed her daily with me. I willingly served her as much as I could until I began to revolt.

(I remember the taxi. Inside of a Checker cab I squeeze my mother's arm tightly I dare to touch the black baby seal of her coat. If I stroke it upwards, it's dark black. Downwards, it's light brown. I smell her armpits, a mixture of cold and warmth, of mud and those flowers that are absolutely tight unbloomed there is no fragrance. I'm allowed to touch. This desperation is)

When my mother was on the point of giving birth, I started to suffer from burning eyes. My father made me hold still on the kitchen table, opened the eye with his finger, and put something black in it.

My father is the power. He is a fascist. To be against my father is to be anti-authoritarian sexually perverse unstable insane. My father was tyrannical at home and extremely kind to and loved by the people who worked for him because he was alcoholic and paranoid. He was madly in love with my mother in a mistaken passionate possessive way. He drank more and more because the woman he loved didn't love him. He died when he was fifty-one. When he died he abandoned me. He took away my father. He believed in certain moral and social truths or ways to act just because that's what everyone believes and that's what he was taught to do. This is what liberalism is. Hypocrisy. He never really dared to question. He never had the courage to think. This is what centralized power is. I won't accept this.

To think for myself is what I want. My language is my irrationality. Watch desire carefully. Desire burns up all the old dead language morality. I'm not interested in truth. My father willed to rape me because in that he didn't want me to think for myself because he didn't think for himself. My father isn't my real father. This is a fact. I want a man. I don't want this man this stepfather who has killed off the man I love. I have no way of getting the man I love who is my real father. My stepfather, society, is anything but the city of art.

I will ressurrect the city of art, I mean this, because it is there I and you this is the real desire.

For *City Limits:* I have nothing to do with the future: I don't envisage it. Writing, along with everything else, if they are anything, is right now. Writing is the making of pleasure as are everything else including death. Some nut a so-called publisher he looked like a hippy and was a multi-millionaire which probably means he's a hippy just told me he intends to rewrite *Blood and Guts in High School* (an unpublished book of mine) by taking out the violence. Why am I violent? Because I like violence. When something means something, that event (the first something) can't be just what it is present in itself. The abolition of all meaning is also the abolition of temporality.

In the City of Pleasure, and I mean we can are live there,

((the body, the body, that which is present, is the source of everything, and it has been made to disappear))

The Art-World Or The World of Non-Materialism Is Becoming Materialistic Therefore The Society's Dead:

Pasolini's City: What I like sexually is what outside the realm of sex disgusts me. So of course I am alone. Most people think I fuck around. I don't fuck around because in the words of Cavafy one of those voices to whom I listen I won't go after what I don't want. In the presence of want, there's no decision. I relish this loneliness and call it pleasure. I shut myself up in the Chia tower, purchased in 1970, sometimes with Ninetto sometimes alone. On top of a buttress placed over two gullies surrounding two conversant streams an outer castle wall protects a high tower. The tower is shut. A few rooms lie in the outer wall. I can never be adult. I absolutely don't understand how adult people act. I have been this way since childhood. Nothing changes none of the psychological characteristics which are presented like a terrain, but I am what I choose. I won't deal with the adult world and I refuse to make more than a surface pretense. Therefore one of my more stable desires is a man who'll take care of me in the world. Outside desire, I'm scared of men and despise the men who tell me what to do. My next-to-hugest disgust is people who want to own other people like certain poets who write to teach people. Therefore I like to fuck men I don't care for: I can't resolve this contradiction in myself: I don't fuck: this loneliness is masturbation. I could pay people money to fuck me or bribe with expectations of increasing fame and other worldly opportunities. Gay guys easily find young poor hustlers who'll spread their cheeks for a few tens. Older men offer young women a secure home, learning a career, etc. I likewise could offer something besides myself to get what I want, but I don't. I don't want what I want. This division in myself is infinite. I don't want what I want because if I got what I wanted I would have to give up because I don't know: the swarming and shouting of the architecture of the city I live in, junkies shoot up on the roofs two feet from one of the windows of the room I live in, a Mafia palace has hidden itself within the most poverty-stricken buildings streets, The rules by which we live: Sex and friendship don't have much to do with each other. To take desire cast it away and at the same time exaggerate the desire or ugliness in us so we can express it. To be honest with a person that I want to lick his feet, but to not care. Exaggerate pain because the government wants me to ignore what I feel. Never break up a friendship when a friend knifes you in the back. New York has made me open enough to disbelieve the validity of principles. Friendship, not love, is sacred and so must encompass violence. Work is everything.

(break into the above) His gallery dealer sold a double painting of his to a rich man. A portrait of two people. Three days later the gallery dealer phoned the artist said he had to paint another portrait because one of the portraits reminded the rich man of a friend he didn't like the rich man wanted another half though he had bought the double portrait. The artist agreed to paint what the rich man wanted because he justified to himself he thought it a commission. He finished the painting in a week then gave it to his dealer. The dealer said, 'The rich man wanted a woman, not a man. You have three days in which to make a proper painting,' and the artist agreed.

The two most powerful Roman galleries for relatively experimental art when they collaboratively present an artist's work make that artist's career (insofar as any one event can make an artist's career). One rich woman tells these gallery dealers who to show. Recently, the two galleries presented the work of a young painter who had had an affair with the woman and whom she fell in love with. The show sold out before it opened. The paintings are good. (Bitchy gossip. No art magazines or biographies mention these nexes.) The wealthy woman still says this painter is the finest of the younger painters.

For art, as you well see, there has never been a favourable time; it has always been said that it must go a-begging; but now it will die of hunger. Whence might come that unaffectedness of spirit that is so necessary for its enjoyment and making, in times like these when sorrow is dealing everyone blows?

The most interesting: Everyone talks about these two young painters.

Their paintings make a lot of money. In the past five years, when most people are becoming poorer and poorer, the selling prices of their paintings rose spectacularly. Today these paintings, despite the fact these painters are about thirty years old, dominate the market. What matters to me? Art. Art equal to sex. As soon as he got to Rome, he met artists. He hung around with them, alternately being a hermit and in the wildest most poverty-stricken areas of the city. I will give anything to do art. I think this is the only way to do art. But I must be more specific: What is language? The discovery of the urban peripheries has so far been essentially visual – I'm thinking of Marcel Duchamp's rationality or autism and Sheeler's social-realism that is discontinuity that is seeing without psychology. Wittgenstein seems to understand language as function, therefore, without psychology (by psychology, I mean the Freudian model of mentality); but by depending on a model of intentionality, he incorporates dualism. If I understand language in this manner: by saying something I intend something, then whatever I say means some other things because one event can be equivalent only to itself, (the Law of Identity). What is real is what is both real and unreal. The main controversy in the art world these days is money. You can call this controversy artistic and social. Are the paintings of the two young painters who are earning scads of money any good? The question is: can paintings which aren't by dead or dying people and sell for fifty thousand each, I sell for fifty dollars, be any good? The question is: Are art and monetary profit compatible? The question is: Does capitalism which must be based on materialism or the absence of values stink? The question is: what is art? Is art worth anything in the practice of art making (of values) or is it craft? Can the making of values and non-value (money) occur simultaneously? In the Renaissance, the artist did what his patron told him to do:

I guess what's happened now is that everyone has died. If writing is the making (of values), I don't know where I'm supposed to find any values.

3. The denial of sexuality

Abolished. And her wing atrocious in the tears. Of the pool. Abolished whoever mirrors fears. Of naked gold whipping the bloody space a dawn has, heraldic feathers, chosen my tower of ashes, all the sacrifices which have happened. Fucking grave from which a beautiful bird flew away; whimsy alone black feathers dawn in vain. Again and again. The manor of decayed and sad countries. Pools of stagnant water, if these pools exist anywhere. The water our mirror reflects the relinquishment of the language here goes, drawn out autumn extinguishing in its own self its brand: Of the cunt hair when in the pallid mausoleum museum or when the plumage dipped its head, abandoned and made mad by the pure diamond of some – made desolate, but all this long ago. I can't remember. I'm whatever has been. There's no memory. Who will never shine. This is crime. This is butchery. Old dead dawn. Masochism. The blood of my cut-up eyes. Pool of blood (by mirroring) accomplice (to this death). There must be something else. And over the flesh-colours (that lie over the blood), open to its fullest the stained glass window.

Through the stained glass window: A peculiar room in a frame. Apparatus from when they used to wage war all the time. Extinct gold jewellery. In this room everything that seems to be alive is just memory. The upholstery, seeming to be mother-of-pearl, folded, is useless with the in-tombs' eyes of sibyls presenting their old claws to men who've suffered. One of them, withered by history on top of history, on my dress bleached in whiteness and shut off from a sky of birds strewn among black-silver, (beginnings/flights/robberies perfumed and phantomed), a perfume which carries of cunt-hairs a perfume far from the empty bed which a huge candle blown-out hid, a gold cold stink slipping beyond its holder, luxuriant and branched. The branches have been abandoned.

For two years every morning I woke up I thought about suiciding. I thought I was going to act like my mother who wildly spent two million dollars then suicided. I don't care about anything now.

Me – The World (this is what expressionism is):

I: Don't anyone come near me. I don't want anyone touching me. I'm an old woman. The shit-coloured torrent of my immaculate cunt-hair in the toilet when it's bathing my solitary body this fear of eternal solitude is making me ice. These tiny hairs which the light nets don't know death. I am a picture. A kiss a real kiss not a one-night-stand would kill be but beauty is frigidity. . .
Nurse: Masturbate yourself.
I: What can possibly attract me now? Do I even know these mornings like every other mornings, no gods to believe in therefore nothing, only the materialism of the government of society all is the same therefore no more space no more time: a constant melancholy. I'm not anymore relative to this.

The Past Of Memory: You've seen me, nurse of the winter, under the heavy prison of stones and iron where my old lions used to drag along the lying ages enter.

The Entrance Into The Past: and I, fatal, walked, my hands bestial claws, into the waste stink of ancient Egypt where they used to fuck so much brothers would fuck their sisters.

I'm an object. Do you, reader, know anything about human objects, what caused them: you with your clawings, your gripes, your grippes, your petty boyfriend complaints? This, all this, is object. Scream. I dream of being punished. Scream. I dream of torment that will carry me over the edge and make me act without considering the action. I dream of having a body and it and thinking being one monster.

At The Same Time These Useless Thoughts're Occupying My Mind: Obsessed from staring at the listless wreckage descending, I could tell you about all the men I've loved who haven't loved me. I think this is only I don't want to be loved. Cold mirror. Without decreasing desire if you want to stay alive turn my desire into art. My cunt hair imitating these too savage manners any return to the bestial, help me, because all of you are no longer able to I don't know if that's true because all of you're no longer simply seeing me; just help me masturbate myself in front of this mirror. I'm scared I'm going crazy.

Nurse: Rejecting myrrh bright in its closed bottle and the essence ripped out of the most faded roses, are you actually chosing only the faculty of death?

I: I keep trying to kill myself to be like my mother who killed herself. I kept working on the 'Large Glass' for eight years, but despite that, I didn't want it to be the expression of an inner life.

Nurse: I'll always help you in crime.

I: You're still romantic. Stick this mirror like a stiff cock in front of my puss. Last night all I directly dreamt about was sex. I fucked men and women alternately. Why isn't there any sex in my waking life? Mirror: the above: water made into ice by boredom in your frozen frame, how many times for how many hours each time, cut off from dreams cut off from desire itself examining each memory which is everyone a leaf under your ice in an endless hole; no, the memory's not worth anything it's a false indication therefore of nothing; therefore I don't exist because there's nothing to see me with I live on the edge of existence; horror: nights, in your severe fountain, total non-connectedness is my dream like being as naked as possible for everyone to see me stare up and down me pry into me. Why do Hydroxes taste like cunt juice?

Nurse: You're celibate so you're the object everyone wants to stare at.

I: Stop this romantic crime which's chilling my blood.

Nurse: Why stop it?

I: Stop your gesture. Against life.

Nurse: Why?

I: Why do you have so many feelings? Why be for or against anything? I'm against myself only because I hate any feeling and a human has feelings. How dare you, nurse, want to touch me and I can't be touched? I so desperately need to be touched. I can't be touched.

Nurse: This sick society that worships money or the lack of values has petrified and immortalized all our monstrosities. Your mother's dead. Your father's dead. Your husband walked away from you. You have no one in the world. You have some money. You can do anything. New fury, mad and scared of your madness which is just loneliness because, being alone, you can only act and not react, . . .

I: Not even you're going to touch me?

Nurse: Will he come sometime?

I: What man would want to touch me? I'm savage. I don't want a boyfriend now. I want no sense.

Nurse: You mustn't use violence except purposefully.

I: Woman born into this maligant society – according to all the histories I've read humans are always malicious – you who like all liberals work to hurt other humans; you can have your humanness and your good intentions. According to you, from out of my tits, smelling like delightful wild animals, leaps out the frigidity of my nakedness. Wild frigidity. Take over everything! If just once the tepid blue of summer for whom every woman sheds herself would see me in my shame/just as I am/unsocialized/celibate/dead. I am pure.

    I die.

Nurse: So you're going to die, dope?

I: I am dead. I'm confused now because I'm being awakened.

    Now: waves rock each other and, there, do you know a land where a dismal sky contains the sex which is always hatred: this is where I am.

    Expressionism: So after six years of meditation, I'm back to where I was: a life based on instant desire. Childish you say in the same desperation, not to want to change.

Nurse: Goodbye.

I: My lips and I love you lies. I love you I lie. This is where I'm at. I'm waiting for something I don't know. That's the truth. Or maybe, not knowing that the unknown or screams exist and are the only things that matter, keep expressing in writing and action your fascination with suicide which is just childhood searching in its dreams to break down its precious frigid images. I want passion.

4. War
Beginning:

Already I can tell everything's closing in on me.

I want to list the possibilities or the lack of possibilities: I can no longer ask real questions. There's no way I can stop this from happening or even pretend it isn't happening. I can't control my looks. I have no power over what I do. I don't even understand what's happening. I don't understand what any event means. All I have is to hold on to each thing as it appears as it happens. The public CIA disclosure that they've discovered the Egyptian tomb changes everything and absolutely ensures he's going to die. But the details are the same. The details of death are always the same.

The apartment's house's entrance looks like every other entrance. A red or black door (of the usual size) and a few mouldings in the frame top. The only thing that's unusual though it's not noticeable is that there's no door handle. There's a hole instead of a lock, latch, knocker, doorbell, etc. So the door might open to the right or it might open to the left. It's also possible the door's a fake. Don't consider any possibility which leaves you bound.

A classic triangular pediment is sitting over the stone frame whose columns are flat and flutings, vertical. The triangle holds in its lowest point a second triangle whose three points touch the first triangle's sides. The centre of the second triangle is a bas-relief eye. But whereas most eyes in nature and in pictures are horizontal, this one's vertical. Its pupil is deep or a hole. The pupil is so high above the door it's impossible to tell what it is.

An electric device obviously works this door. A portable machine small enough to be set up in one of the inner panels must be – now don't assume anything – I am always assuming everything – what can I say to you if I don't make assumptions? – how can I say anything about what's going on with me if I don't make assumptions? – the only thing I have are the words in this text I'm now looking at which I can give you only as I see them: these words are the details, whatever they mean. The detail of the stone eye sitting above the door frame doesn't mean anything. That's why it's forcing a new world.

My statement to you begins after a probable interruption all this giving the feeling that everything is uncertain and there are decreasing possibilities unlike an opera overture in which everything is false. I am catatonic.

Catatonic, yes, to be sure, but still there's something provisional, fragile, something tenuous a seashell enclosing a skinless creature. A cunt. In this world where the law of probability governs reality a quiet invisible threat hangs over everything. Fear now dictates all of our actions. Let me tell you I'm a what-you-may-call-it I can't move out of this room. Right before or rather at the moment of my father's death, I was at my father's death, I noticed a similar stopping; but that stopping (I think) was a stopping due to complete knowledge; whereas this stopping is only half-way, maybe the whole thing is slowly dying, always this silence, at the edges of nothing; but an imperceptible breath or whistling

The beginning of my report of what I saw:

as if a wind coming from nowhere is displacing every grain of sand of the beach. Without any apparent movement of its own it carries each grain to an abandoned terrace. A mass of tiny snakelike ripples, each ripple being parallel to every other, accumulates on top of the grey wood planks. The grey wood planks though they don't touch each other are one object. A blaze of sunlight powders paint which the footsteps of those who can't sleep have already broken up. The ocean is pounding itself (into) a wave. Again and again the ocean is pounding itself (into) a wave. The wave is always tiny, long. So there seems to be no linear time. Owl hoots sound regularly. The dawn that makes the world rigid conceals every other sound. Ten feet above the ocean a huge pelican stands in the air. When he flies towards the right picture edge, the solid land or river-line or foam ripple being skirted, his wings' thundering noises mask the other beginning sounds. One foam wave disappears so rapidly and another foam wave appears so rapidly that there are no visible changes. I stand too far away in too low and secluded a spot to be able to tell what's going on.

On the opposite side of the picture than the one the pelican has now disappeared into, facing me, a colourless silhouette, a writhing spiral complexity, a thin boy who climbs on a horse. The horse's hairs move all over the place. The people in California insofar as I remember ride this way: trackless and pathless; now this side of him is in my face; now that side; so I see every aspect of his appearing and love. Coming closer and closer to me (as with love my objectivity disappears) the lengthy blue-black hairs twisting in the flakes of air he paws the ground and is circling almost around himself. A girl who's riding with neither spurs nor stirrups is trying to make her white mare go into the ocean; the mare is shying water is spurting out from all sides under its shaking hoofs among the clear laughs of the Amazon whose body is as sharp and bright as metal, suddenly, what I see, in this shifting light this.

Having almost reached the front of the picture, the male rider disappears behind me.

I see that I'm standing in the middle of jumbled chairs. These are piles of folding metal chairs on the terrace. Three men who're wearing leather jackets and weapons are coming towards me. They walk faster. They walk parallel and next to the ocean. Each one points the gun in his left hand down towards the sand. They are tracking something. They cock their guns. Having walked from the left to the right side of the picture, they walk even faster in the same step behind my back.

(A sound like a gunshot.) An even shorter silence. (A cry like a human who's being knifed.) Dead silence. A neigh. Silence. (A second identical sound like a shot from a Mauser which is the gun the National Guard uses.) The scream that's been going on this whole time stops. (*In the*

forest a gorgeous animal whose feathers're made out of flesh's name is female.)
The splashings from a body falling into the water at the same time as
heavy steps at the same time as water throwing itself against the jetty,
water throwing itself against an unexpected rock at the same time as the
convergences of the unseeable minglings of its back-turnings and waves
with the frightened-now-wild horse's clops. All these animal noises stop.
The world's gone dead.

With the return of calmness of the dead breath, there's unity that is
I now have the possibility of naming and knowing what I see. *This is
'partial death'. Here is my punk expectation of the New Order.* (I mean the
music group).

A seagull who's holding a fish in its mouth flies over the almost dead
ocean in a straight line across the picture. It's a flight is such an exact
reproduction of the pelican's flight that I'm not sure what my perception
is. There's a shorter interval than the one between the first and second
bird. A third bird flies over the almost dead ocean in a straight line
across the picture. Its flight is such an exact reproduction of the pelican's
flight, its wings batting sluggishly against the thick air bits of cardboard
boxes condoms soda pop tops pieces of a stocking top a bullet; either
it's one bird or it's all three birds disappearing into the horizon at the
left side of the picture. I understand that 'naturalness' depends on my
perception or on who I am. The greyish vomit sands like the men with
guns are closing in on me, little tongues are alive, snails move, without
any hope of stopping. A fragile call-girl is walking along the beach. She
wears a dress I can see through.

*I'm telling you what I see with my own eyes. I'm reporting to you who are
my judges the only things I have: Robbe-Grillet's words.*
. . . the cloth is floating and torn . . . the edges of the waves . . . drags
behind her . . . The sands contained all kinds of crap: bits of cardboard
boxes condoms soda pop tops pieces of a stocking top a bullet. The girl
has stopped walking. Her whole back is sticking into my face. The left
foot which is resting on its toe lifts upwards almost vertically. The shape
of her breasts doesn't change. The pale flesh gains a pink tinge. (What
is perception?)

Her huge grey-green eyes' lost disconsolation staring at me a few feet
away from me what is it? I'm forced to turn my face disguised by a
false beard. Here a wood fence encloses an abandoned cafe. A partially
mutilated advertisement still visibly presents the picture of a famous
circus rider's blood-filled battle against a mad bull. The circus rider's
dress is red. I will do anything for love.

What was really puzzling and at the same time totally fascinating the
cops who were investigating the murder was the fact, at least they

surmised that though the victim had been strangled, strangling hadn't been the cause of his death. The murder must have been more complicated than it appeared. For instance, despite the skin's ghastly whiteness and the long marks ground into the flesh under the cord that was lying around his neck, none of the vertebrae had been broken. And the whole corpse was still lukewarm, flexible, and intact. Also there were a number of miniscule red points. These, unnoticeable and unevenly distributed over the body, seemed to be needle marks.

The rest of the murder scene surprised me; I felt I was walking into some kind of ceremony. Could it be the still-as-yet-unknown Criminal Of The Second Hand had entered the room to finish off his punishing?

Naturally I kept my ideas to myself. In as casual a tone as I could manage I asked the cops if they had gotten back the blood analysis. As yet no one had said anything at all about the red stains under his fingernails and on the insides of the lips and knees, much less about a less apparent wound. But I hesitated, out of fear, asking them another question.

For instance: do these stains have anything to do with the mass of bloodstains could he have died as it seems by reacting to his massive blood transfusion or a heart attack from the amount he obviously had to fight the marks on his nails and teeth against something-or-other were they about to torch him or some other such horror as described in the UN account of torture in South America?

Actually I've become more interested in the mystery of the fur mantle. Had it disappeared just before the cops entered the room? They say they didn't see it then. I saw it when I came into the room. So who put it back into the room and why? Such an oversight or confusion isn't typical of that organization who again and again give us evidence of their meticulousness. Their execution is precise and to the second. I didn't have the time, unfortunately, before I had to get out of there, to look more carefully at that mantle made from a huge cat's skin or the luxurious curls of some other animal's back. They had rolled this object which I find the most significant of all into a ball and shoved it into a dark corner of the room. Unfortunately, I say again unfortunately, it had caught my attention at the very moment I realized I had to get the hell out of there.

Once I was away from their evil faces I must have been able to think because now I realized this was the cloth that was being dragged along the beach right in front of my eyes. Again I saw that mysterious girl, now even more clearly, the bloody animal skin she's trailing along the sand: This picture is reddish-gold, despite the dust from the shellfish who're sticking together between the black hairs and winding into a unity of corkscrews, so the dust is exactly the same colour as her wild hairs. The only thing I can see is her back. Her right arm holds an old violin tightly against her hip. The violin's caseless. Now I know why her neck's bent the way it is.

Since she was walking too fast for me to follow her for very long, for the cane on which I was leaning was quickly sinking into that spongy ground, I swivelled my head towards the abandoned cafe. Two trench-coated men, hats over one of each eyes, were in the act of sitting down at one of the tables. They must have assumed there were waiters. He's holding a platter and has a napkin draped over his arm. (I perceive what I've been told to perceive.)

Just as I'm gazing fixedly, two hands clamp down on my arms. They hold me in a double stranglehold. They are looking at me. They are telling me what to do. The world is my desire. It's so simple. I don't need eyes to know that several men are surrounding me. I have dreamt this many times. I cannot escape. There's something genetically wrong with my hormones. If I perceive it, I've been told it. If I dream it, is it true? They haven't made a mistake. I no longer need to be told or given art in order to perceive what they want me to perceive.

This is my last thought before I disappear: I'm living without emotions because desire's the only thing that can save me.

That's it. I can no longer speak. I've been trained to be catatonic or a dog. I might as well tell you the same story again and again. *This is the season of my torment.*

It began at the same time as or just as the *Daily news* article said just like a fairytale. A police chief named Frank V. Francis on his holiday and wandering around for the first time in his memory is walking down a certain street. On this street, stuck into one of the gutter-grills whose purpose is to get rid of possible rain overflows but is rather an inefficient garbage disposal he finds a woman's tiny shoe. At first he doesn't notice this object though it hardly goes with the usual jumble of cardboard boxes condoms soda pop tops pieces of a stocking top and bullet shells that have fallen out or that the rats and bums have taken away from the garbage cans and only half-eaten or hidden. The shoe is almost new. The only thing that seems to be the matter with it is that its red stilletto heel has been almost totally torn away from the sole – but it's easy enough to fix this with a hammer and three nails – there's no need to go to a shoemaker. (The objective conditions of what is.)

Immediately after that they started their questions. As a rule there were two of them. It was impossible to recognize any of them cause you could never tell one from the other. They are all the same height. They never move from the positions in which they're standing. Their coats which look dark are always totally buttoned over their bodies and their hats, slouched over one of each of their eyes, put the rest of their faces into shadow. I can't tell forms anymore because the camera lights are directly in my eyes. (If sight's no longer a tool, are any of the perceptions?) Although they ask me questions, there's no way I can rely on my ears to understand what's happening because the rotation of these questions is robot-like and they say nothing out loud to each other. When they communicate to each other, they use tiny, almost imperceptible gestures. One hand or a head nod. One of these hands must be holding an umbrella handle because every time they interrupt my speech, there's a violent knocking on the metal floor.

The unknowns (you the readers) are questioning me the writer so you can judge me. This writing is the way it is so I can escape you:
– 'Because such a situation might occur, the student, let us call him a student, had taped a syringe to his lower thigh. Over the syringe he placed the soft calf of his boot. Was she wearing the same kind of shoe for this very reason? Your defence system, as we've recently learned, doesn't call for white boots. And in the second version of your story, you said she was wearing a shoe with a red stilletto heel. Do you remember this writing?' – 'I don't remember any writing 'cause I don't know what I write so you can't pin me down. I might haphazardly take away parts of the writing. Even if I don't these are just the words I copied from a book by Robbe-Grillet. I don't even know French and I don't care. I don't want to control you by telling you what reality is just as you try to control me.' This answer is easy for me cause I'm bored with this writing: that is, I'm not into it because it isn't obsessive what isn't obsessive I call torment. (Directly about perception.)
– 'I want to find out just why you're telling us this story. Take those tables you told us about . . . an empty room . . . the hotel in ruins . . . the waiter who's really a waiter . . . You told us the tables in *Maximilien's* stood in straight lines around the fountain. You've certainly been precise about all the details in the story that are absolutely irrelevant. Again: you're just trying to escape us. You'll have to tell us about the parts of the story that matter if you want us to believe you. For instance, remember we're talking about murder, did that waiter who you made such a point of saying was acting properly, put your food on your table or on the student's?' – 'On neither. He placed coffee and a basket filled with brioches on the third table. This table which stood a bit in back of ours formed a sort of isosceles triangle . . .' (Again the sound of the umbrella handle hitting the floor violently') – 'Was this the reason you forgot to bring your black notebook?' – 'What black notebook? I don't know what you're talking about.' – 'We're talking about the black notebook in which the so-called student was in the habit of putting down what was happening and what he thought was happening during his work. You know this notebook and you know what's in it: the way you described those tables is exactly how they're described in the

notebook. That's why we were asking you about the tables. We want to know about the notebook.

'There are some further points to consider: Now, there was a bottle on the student's table. There's no way the waiter could have brought this bottle. Remember your saying the waiter didn't put anything on the student's table? You say this bottle was still full at the moment you intervened. You also say this bottle contained an antidote to the intravenous injection, an antidote which a little later all of you tried out on her. Now how was this antidote supposed to work on the student if he hadn't drunk it?

'We're going to start again with you. We want to find out why you've been telling us what you're telling us. We want meaning that is we want control.'

The only thing I want is all-out war.

2 Language

1 Narrative breakdown for Carla Harriman

In the year 1413 I went in search of my true love. There was a camp full of milling people. A beautiful young boxer who's the son of a rich man is buying horses. I called him to me. I told him he's my brother by our father. I put him up for the night in my house. In the toilet he fell into the shit. I stole his money while he escaped from my house. He knocked at the door of my house and my servants: 'You're crazy; we don't know who you are.' A bum told him to stop disturbing his sister. They found him out by the smell of his shit. An old woman told the following tale: It is a place of sacred practice. Art isn't about the sacred. A beautiful young man sneaks up to the garden. The beautiful young man pretends to be mute. He is the new gardener and the nuns treat him as a pet. The nuns want his cock. Cock is the action that makes you go mad. The nuns hit him with a stick. Then they drag him into a hut. His cock's small. Oh ooooh ooh. Heaven, for all we know, has arisen. Both the nuns are smiling. All the other nuns want to. All the women are after cock. Will the man die? Old ugly hag Mother Superior gets hold of this boy's cock. Ten men (much less this boy) can't even satisfy one female and a cock is a miracle. 'You're a robber you're a forger you've raped women, etc.; maybe you should get out of town a bit until things cool down. You're so evil, you're the person to collect my debts.' So I went to a town out in the grass. Men pushed along a cart of skulls. The queen wore a basket over her head and extended a shovel with a skull sitting on top of it.

Giotto's best pupil has come to paint Naples. The painter who is one of the finest painters around wears rags. Are all our friends poor? The painter looks like an imp. This imp is maddened. Mauled. Big plump Casaba melons lie on the road. Don't make me die of love. If you fuck me, I won't die. When the painter eats with the monks, his table manners are atrocious.

I am a slave because they're auctioning me. I'm a young boy. I pick a young boy to buy me. I give him my money. I tell him where to get us shelter. We fuck there. He's so very young, he doesn't know how to fuck. Soon he figures it out. No: I show him. I'm a great artist. I tell my new boyfriend to sell my art but not to a white man because a white man'll separate us. When I sell it to a white man, he follows me. My girlfriend tells me a story. Can the poets speak about what they haven't experienced? Slowly I penetrated her. My cock wouldn't go in easily 'cause she was tight along the upper part of her mucus tunnel. The muscles felt good around the end of my cock. I had to come. As soon as it sprang out of me I passed out. When I, the girl says, woke up I saw him lying in the bed next to mine, looking like the rose fallen out of the midnight. I had to have his cock. I had to have his tongue. I had to piss over his flesh. I rubbed my clit and the upper cunt corners against his pelvis bones sharp I came five times. I fell asleep. When I woke up, he was gone.

In the Fifth Precinct which is where I used to live the cop who's the head likes to arrest anyone he sees fucking or making Voodoun or hustling and libelling or robbing the local churches or forging cheques or issuing false contracts or priests who use their parishes to get rich or lending money or simony whatever that is. Most of all he hates sex. He takes all these offenders' money. When they can't pay him what he wants, he makes sure they're locked up longer than they should be. This is the way he remains the head cop (rich man). Also he eats at any restaurant in the neighbourhood he wants to free of charge and gets any store object he desires. If a local store owner doesn't pay the police chief the monthly garbage bill, the owner has to close his store because he's been violating sanitary laws. The East Village, part of which is this Fifth Precinct, is the filthiest space in the world.

The police chief has a Special Assistant. This Assistant is thin sly greasy locks dribble down his forehead and he collects five-to-eight year old boys who're greasier and fart more than he does. They must have been spit out of their mothers' assholes between fits of constipation because they're so much smoother and more poisonous and gaseous than turds these little sausages can slip around everywhere and see everything. The children know everything. They know where the Families in the neighbourhood (I'm talking about the Mafia) keep their money in secret mansions way inside surrounded by rows of the poorest apartment buildings around Tenth Street. The Special Assistant uses these children for information and also to capture the few people who still dare to fuck. These people fuck because they need to fuck so badly and it's now so hard to get laid they need to fuck so badly, by the time they announce to themselves they have to fuck they'll do anything to fuck, they'll fuck anyone one of these slimy kids. The kid tells the cop. The Special Assistant has his junky desperate for his junk so he makes whatever terms he wants. The Special Assistant is a sexual pervert but mad because he never fucks but gets exactly what he wants without ever compromising himself. I'm telling you all this because I'm a monk.

The Special Assistant also has a squad of pimps. You understand that he's not a hypocrite. By no means. He'd use any means if he was smart enough. He tolerates pimps whom otherwise he would be joyously grinding into the nonexistent dirt and the existent shit on the street because they tell him dirt the children can't tell him. Their girls or trash learn where the businessmen (dealers, gunmen, etc.) hide their monies and tell the pimps and the pimps tell. This way also the Special Assistant is constantly checking the children's information against the pimps' information and vice-versa and no one's ever let off the hook. This is democracy: no overt governmental control. The Special Assistant isn't as moral as his boss which is why he's lower down the business hierarchy so he pimps on the side. He pimps so he can run his own blackmail sideline. Unlike his boss he loves sex because he's making a fortune from it.

One day since the sun was shining the Special Assistant decided to go after new ducks: old women because old women walk around mumbling to themselves drop their purses and are helpless. While the Special Assistant stood on the corner of Fifth Street and First Avenue and looked for an old woman, a tall Puerto Rican walked by him. The Puerto Rican wore a large black hat and a black jacket. The Puerto Rican looked at the Special Assistant. 'What d'ya want, white boy? Do ya want anything with me?' 'I don't want anything. Yet. Right now,' the white boy replied. 'I need a real criminal.' 'So you can't go after anyone you want. You white boys don't have any power no matter how many badges you wear. You just do what the big tops tell you to do.' The Special Assistant couldn't admit he was powerless. 'Me, I'm after someone myself,' the Puerto Rican flips some kind of card into his face. 'I also belong to an Agency. If you're looking for someone, why don't you hook-up with me? I own the territory over there,' pointing south towards the Lower East Side, 'and there're lots of junkies over there. It's easy to make money.' The Special Assistant knew a good money deal. They walked down the street.

'How're we going to make money? And, especially, how do you make money, you who live on the other side of the law?'

'Since my life's always in jeopardy because of the colour of my skin,

I blackmail, extort and simply take as much as I can from those who are more helpless than me.'

'I have a job and I do the same thing,' said the cop. 'I have one moral: If it's too hot for a fence, give it to a cop. You have to be tough to live in New York. I'm so tough, there's no tragedy that could make me even blink. I'm beyond those intellectual liberals because I don't depend on anybody's opinion. Are you as tough as I am?'

For the first time the Puerto Rican realized he could have this white cop, so he began to smile. 'I'm a dead man,' he replied. 'I live in hell. Just like you I spend all my time looking for humans I can get something from and just like you I don't care how I get it.'

'I see. You're Vice Squad.'

'No. I'm not human. I'm using a human form because I'm trying to fool you.'

'If you're not human, who are you?'

'I'm non-human. We non-humans unlike you humans who are stuck only use forms to get what we want.'

'If you're so powerful, why do you even bother with human beings?'

'You're so much more powerful than old women and junkies and young girls and yet you prey off of them. This is the way the world is. I'll give you an answer: When you're murdering someone, you think you're murdering because you're getting something out of it. But like me you vulturize because you get nothing. You and I are made. We are part of this almost unbearable worldly pain which isn't disappearing.'

'Do you always lie?'

'If I always lied, a lie wouldn't be a lie. Sometimes Puerto Ricans tell the truth. Sometimes we Puerto Ricans are so romantic we tell some woman we totally love her she believes we adore her we can fuck over her whole life we do she learns that another human being is capable of absolutely conscious deception. You don't have to learn anything from me. From this moment onwards you're going to see so much pain because you're going to cause so much pain that no artist will be able to tell you nothing. No human being can remain naive. If you hurt somebody, nobody can hurt you. There're no natural laws. There's no natural justice or morality. Politicians or rather those in power have made up that liberal jive so they can keep their slaves or excuse me cuntstichyouwents in check. I'll just trot along by your side, bro', until you do so much evil, you're ready to stick a knife in my back. This is the way people in New York City live.'

'I won't become so evil,' the Special Assistant swears with his hand over his heart, 'because I'm a New York City cop. I've sworn to protect human life. I'm going to take a second oath. I swear that I love you and regard you as absolute evil and that I'll do so until the end of time. I'm white and you're black and you're my brother.'

'And you are mine,' the fiend replies. This is the neighbourhood he was speaking about. Half of the buildings have broken glass for windows. Behind each broken glass is an unseeable space. The doors and some of the windows are wood boards. Men waiting for their junk sit on what there is for floors inside these buildings. Children and fat women whose tits are hanging out of their bras crowd the doorways and doorsteps of the occupied brownstones. Seven men are sitting on chairs outside the corner bodega. On the sidewalk two children fight each other with sticks. 'Give me that junk,' the child says as he raises his stick. 'I hate you,' says the other child, 'because last night you had my sister.' 'I hope you die. Jesus Christ should come down and forsake you and the Evil One should hold you in his arms.' They fought again.

'Those kids need to be taught what's right and what's wrong,' the Special Assistant thought to himself, 'and I can make a little money on the side.' He whispered to his friend, 'Don't you want to take him?'

'They don't mean what they're saying,' his friend replied. 'They're only imitating what their parents say.' The children are kneeling on the edge of the sidewalk. There's a huge spider trapped between a glass jar and the cement. They let the spider free. The moment the spider moves, they trap it again.

'Human beings say one thing and mean another. That's what they mean by language. Let's get further into this neighbourhood where there's more desperation. It's only when humans are totally desperate that they speak the truth.'

The white man speaks. 'I know where I am. There's a Jew in this Puerto Rican and Black hovel who doesn't give up a penny even when a mugger's holding a knife to her eye. Either she's going to give me a hundred and twenty dollars for a payoff or I'm going to gaol her. I'm a cop, aren't I? I have to make my living. The tax payers won't give me enough money.'

'You're still using liberal excuses,' the fiend instructs him.

To show how evil he is, the cop kicks in the old blind dumb and almost deaf cunt's stomach. 'What do you want?' in a little old woman voice. 'Excuse me, ma'am.' Kick again. 'I've got orders here to arrest you.' She doesn't bother asking what for. 'Now?' 'Open up this door. I have to take you to gaol.' 'I don't want to go to gaol. I just had an operation yesterday. My doctor said if I don't stay still, I'm going to die. No one takes care of me 'cause my daughter's husband just left her so she killed herself so there's no one to help me go to gaol.' 'The law doesn't take account of disease, ma'am.' 'How can I stay alive?' 'Pay me a hundred and twenty dollars.' 'I don't have a hundred and twenty dollars. Do you think an old woman who lives with junkies and alcoholics and sub-welfare families has a hundred and twenty dollars lying around the house?' 'If I don't either arrest you or get a hundred and twenty dollars, may I go to hell.'

'OK. What did I do wrong?' 'When your husband was alive, you fucked another man.' 'I never got married. So whenever I fucked, I fucked out of love. Madly for love. Desire has nothing to do with justice anyway. Go to hell.' Quickly the fiend asked, 'My dear, do you really mean what you're saying?' The foul old bitch who was foul only because she was old and not because she wanted to cause anyone pain answered, 'I hope he dies or goes to hell if he keeps trying to rob me.'

'Rather than rob you, I'm going to take everything you've got.'

'Don't be angry, bro', 'cause now you're getting everything you wanted. I'm going to take you to hell where the only thing you can do is evil.'

If God has made all of us in His image, part of this image is pain and hell.

They go down to hell. On the way the cop sees a painted forest. There, the trees are knotted, stubby, and leafless.

The pickpocket. Bloodless Fear. This smiling man carries a knife under his coat. Black smoke lies around the fire of the burning block. Humans murder other humans asleep in their beds. The body opens wounds blood all over all the flesh. There're all sorts of sounds in this place. I see the man who commits suicide. I see the mother who commits suicide. The blood in her heart, slipping out of, soaks into her cunt. At night the hammer pounds a nail through the forehead. The dead people's mouths are open wide.

Bad luck's sitting in the middle of the floor. His face is all weazled and squinched up. Madness in the centre of Madness laughs which is total pain. Complaining bickering hating all feeling jealous keeping all this hate and anger bottled under the skin; all the isms are the psychology here. Every group of skinny trees has under them dogshit and a body whose throat is cut open. The tyrant takes whatever he wants simply. As a result a country is destroyed. Haiti. Vietnam. There's nothing left to the country. There's no time here. Ships are burning up. Wild bears sink their teeth into the man who hunted them. The pig struts into the bedroom and eats the child in the cradle. Madness goes everywhere. The cook scalds his arms by his long ladle. Above the poverty-stricken peasant lying under his cart's wheel Conquest or Fame, which is the only One people honour, rises; criminals are the politicians; conquest 1 gives way only to conquest 2; humans are killing themselves because they're choosing to love humans who don't love them.

From this time onward, war came to Ectabane. Lots of slaves escaped, went to those conquering, but when the conquerors tried to make them give specific details about the resistance of the occupied, the slaves refused to tell their former owners' names. And their situations became worse; the slavery was more intense. Ectabane is the largest Western capital. Every day the beaches below the boulevard which line the sea wear as clothes corpses. At the ocean-front guards shoot all the resistors who land during the nighttime. The conquerors took over painlessly: the city wanted to get rid of gods and masters. The shoed helmetted armoured conquerors halted the sexuality and the perception of the conquered. For a hundred years they had halted everything. Then the Ectabane wise men in secret made a weapon capable of resuscitating their land. The conquerors stole the weapon. They constructed an airplane into which they could put the weapon. They flew the wise men and the weapon to their city Septentrion. The remaining dissidents the adventurers con men mercenaries fighters they pursued even beyond Ectabane's boundaries. They had to use both informers and cruelty to control some of the families who lived in the city's centre: at night their children ran to other parts of the world; other children started out for those underground rivers in the Southern coast which the Buxtehude Archipelago joins. As of yet the Archipelago is still free, but blackened every moment by the enemy bombers' shadows.

On the day his country capitulated a young Ectabanese officer whom the General Staff despised because he had been trying to modernize their army fled to this Archipelago under the aegis of diplomatic immunity – as the ambassador extraordinaire of his country. They had instructed him to convince the as-yet free Archipelago to fight the enemy as much as possible. Buxtehude gave him a hotel room in a spa. He put photos of his wife and children who were still in Ectabane on a shelf. Then he set up a small radio with which he could send information back to Ectabane. He told the Archipelago to resist the enemy as strongly as they could. Get rid of all political apathy. Use all the arms and weapons you've left to rot in your forgotten barracks. Soon all of Septentrion, the whole Western continent which is only part of the East, will be flaming! The conquerors will never have enough fires to burn away the secret ashes and wastes and garbage of their souls or of their blood so that tears can start flowing! In downtrodden defeated Ectabane, dawn the day the city was overtaken, I sat on top of a balcony of the triumphal arch and watched the whole city which was still asleep: A boot hit the sidewalk. A rat scurried across the balcony. A security guard sticking his head under a bunch of flowers banged it on the table outside. The wind which was alive dried up his blood. One of the enemy security bending down wiped up the dried blood with his handkerchief. He tapped the knee of the Ectabanese guard who slowly managed to get vertical, 'The old dolts, the priests and everyone who loves this our country have freely elected a president who pleases the enemy. This head.'

The people in the world blow up the world. After the end of the world.

One. One and one. One and one. One and one. One and one. One and one. One and own. One and one. One and one. One and one.   ·

One and one and one. One and one and one. One and one and one. One and one and one. One and one and one. One and one and

One and two. One and two and no more. One and two. One and two no more. One and two. One and two no more. One and two.

One two and. One two and. One two and. One two and. One two and. One two and. One two and. One two and. One two and. One two.

On. On. On. On. On. On. On. On. On. On. On. On. On. On. On. On. On. On. On. On. On. On. On. On. On. On. On. On. On. On. On.

On and. On and. On and. On and. On and. On and. On and. On and. On and. On and. On and. On and. On and. On and. On and. On and.

Candour honour. Candour honour. Candour honour. Candour honour. Candour honour. Candour honour. Candour honour. Candour honour. Candour honour.

Can do one more. Can do one more. Can do one more. Can do one more. Can do one more. Can do one more. Can do one more. Can do one more. Can do one more. Can do one more. Can do one more. Can do one

Can murmur murder mirth. Can murmur murder mirth. Can murmur murder mirth. Can murmur murder mirth. Can murmur murder mirth.

This is. This is a saying. One. Can murder mention one. This is a saying.

Stop. Not it. Can it is. Can it is. Can it is. The hat on the steps of. The windowpane is by now.

The sea flows scaffold for the sheep. I came come of the being. Androgynous draggles.

Two and three and five. Two and three and five. Two and three and five. Two and three and five. Two and three and five.

Accent her. Hand armours on wonder. Orphan forces war or instance of ovary. The manor of stove.

An instance of romance. Or form. Or form. Or form. Or form. Or form. Or form. Or form. Or form. Or form. Or form. Or form.

An land. An land. An land. An land. An land. An land. An land. An land. An land. An land. An land. An land. An land. An

And scape escape romance. And scape escape romance. And scape escape romance. And scape escape romance. And scape escape romance. And. . .

2. Language breakdown

Bats of boxes in the houses. Delight layering the accesses. Exquisite and excess urinals devour. So we. Glowerings glowerings sail.

Reins breasts and the polar rains turmeric. Along of in the polar down and police no dark no ark sightings away sight. To the lines long eerie aeries are we we we. The owes. He whispers whimpers whimpers.

Come out to the light: of squares of sturgeon of sturgeon and on on an under the dark and dark. Dark. On. On. On. On. On and under one. On and under two. On and under three. The sticks hunt vertical. Three sticks hunt vertical. Murderers remain demands. Murderers remain subversion. Houses veer bicycles. I.

Daylight. Obstetrician. Axe. Demanding. Who they are. Swing. A restaurant.

Do you disturb eyes? Do you disturb tampax? Eyes foment off. Of reminiscing. Waste rebellion fast you lose.

In the square. What did she do? Hands fluoresce. The tip of the clit suggest augmentation. Of treacherous. Lights murmurs. Hair egomaniac.

Was there danger? There usury. There objects of. There eccentricity. There notorious. There you. There accumulation. There simultaneous. There acquiescence. There dumb. There upset.

While walking, she was dreaming. Policeman wings boards off how. And under thatches of under of this. The lights blank how whispers a lot. To two lips.

Of these projects backs on bouquets. Wastebaskets glowing stabs knickers.

She moves. Therefore ways of moving. One sound done. Two the reduction to what is essential.

Two the reduction to what is essential. We don't reduce: we start nothing or bottom up. Hands hang rape. Hands flatter bad. Hands wing flutter. Hands lost record. Hands record corderoy. Hands grip colds angry black knife. Hands weaving blasts wonders often frozen. Hunger aggression.

The late skies of listening recalls claims two. Toward. The blisters baskets squires rues under hay and wise men anger. Herald blisters hunger is plausible lubberings crows an. Language thinking.

3. Nominalism

I want to talk about the quality of my perception. I want the quality or kind called childhood cause children see the sadness which sees this city's glory. What does this sentence mean? I can wander wherever I want. I simply see. Each detail is a mystery a wonder. I wander wonder. The loneliness feeling is very quickly lost. So I can see any and everything. I can talk about everything as a child would. The interior or my mind versus the exterior. Art proposes an interiority which no longer exists, for all of us are moulded. The nightmare that I fear most is true. This writing's outdated. Yet you walk around the city. Is this realization the source of your melancholy? I love you. You're my friend. I'm masturbating now. I have someone to talk to like I talk to my stuffed animals. Of course this life's desolate, it's lonely when there's no mentality. This sentence means nothing. More and more submerged the mind, you trace its submergence through Baudelaire; now it's gone. Fashion is the illusion there's a mind.

Walking through the cities, being partly lost, the image (in the mind) change fast enough that the perception which watches and judges perception is gone, is the same as the living in the place where I can do anything in which every happening is that which just happens. Saint-Pol Roux, going to bed about daybreak, fixes a notice on his door: 'Poet at work'. The day is breaking.

Language is more important than meaning. Don't make anything out of broken-up syntax 'cause you're looking to make meaning where nonsense will. Of course nonsense isn't only nonsense. I'll say again that writing isn't just writing, it's a meeting of writing and living the way existence is the meeting of mental and material or language of idea and sign. It is how we live. We must take how we live.

To substitute space for time. What's this mean? I'm not talking about death. Death isn't my province. When that happens that's that; it's the only thing or event god or shit knows what it is that isn't life. To forget. To get rid of history. I'm telling you right now burn the schools. They teach you about good writing. That's a way of keeping you from writing what you want to, says Enzensberger, from being revolutionary that is present. I just see. Each of you must use writing to do exactly what you want. Myself or any occurrence is a city through which I can wander if I stop judging.

It could happen to someone looking back over his life that he realized that almost all the deeper obligations he had endured in its course originated in people on whose destructive character everyone was agreed. He would stumble on this fact one day, perhaps by chance, and the heavier the blow it deals him, the better are his chances of picturing the destructive character.

Wandering through the streets and creating a city: Berlin's a deserted city. Its streets're very clean. Princely solitude princely desolation hang over its streets. How deserted and empty is Berlin!

The first street no longer has anything habitable or hospitable on it. The few shops look as if they're shut. The crossings on the streetcorners are actually dangerous. Puerto Ricans whiz by in cars.

At the end of the next event is the Herkules Bridge. There's a block-long park that runs along the river. Here when I was a child as soon as

I could walk I spent most of my days. I had a nurse. At first I didn't have as many toys as the other children. Then I had a tricycle. Later I had a cap gun. We would try to shoot pigeons with our cap guns. If your cap gun shot a pigeon in the eye, pigeons are the only living animals around, you blinded the pigeon and then could capture it bring it home to make pigeon soup the most wonderful delicacy in the world. Neither I nor anyone else ever captured a pigeon. The river which was pure garbage brown was crossed by a bridge on my right as I looked from the park out over the river. This bridge was the Herkules Bridge.

I used to have a strong dream about the garbage river. It was the most magical place. If only I could cross it, on the other side. Desire is the other side. During the day I can't cross it. Suddenly, in my dream, I can. Go over the low cement wall black iron bars curving out of upwards towards me, down a three-or five-foot hill that's mainly dirt and some bushes, my feet kick small rocks rolling, downwards. Here's the water at my feet. Here's flat sands forming a triangle narrowing towards the north I can walk on it. I'm walking on top of a narrow evenly wide sand ribbon across the river which isn't deep. I reach the other side. The other side is a carnival. The beach is still here. Here's a merry-go-round. All around the beach's white and onwards. I walk onwards on the magic ground. There are many adventures as I walk straight northwards.

The other park I used to go to, the park that contained New Lake on Rousseau Island, was much further from my house. I'd go only with my grandmother who lived a few blocks away in a large hotel, I'll talk about her later, or with mommy although mommy almost never spent her time with me. In fact, I now remember, I never went to the park with mommy unless other friends accompanied us. The park or rather this part of the park which was its southernmost tip, in my mind the boot of Italy, bordered on a line of almost white expensive residences and hotels. Differently coloured cars whirring back and forth separate the residential buildings from the park. There was a lake and ducks. On the far side of the lake, luxuriant dark greens brown. I can't get over to the luxury. I sit on a large rock. The rock's not large enough to be a hill. It's large enough to have two holes to crawl within, not really into, and to climb for five minutes. Three roads, one dirt and two asphalt-and-stepped, swerve through the short dog-shit-covered grass, down to it. I'm sitting on top of the rock and looking across the lake, to my right so far in the distance I don't know if it really exists there's a carnival. During one winter, when it's very cold, I can skate on this lake which has grown very small which snow surrounds. A small brown terrier has placed his butt on the Northeast end of the lake. Two and three foot high ridges of snow surround the lake. There aren't any children here as there are in the other park. At this time, I liked this park better than the other park. Then my grandmother would take me back to her hotel room.

Everything's alive.

When I was older, a boyfriend would walk with me through other parts of this park. No, first I went to school. When they couldn't drag us for exercise on the chilliest coldest fall days out to the level short green hockey fields way uptown, they took us for a treat to the part of the park nearest the school. Several asphalt and dirt paths of varying widths having absolutely no order crossed here and quickly changing growths of trees still thickly-green-leafed high among densely green valleys not big enough to be valleys and curving like eye contact lenses; I remember metal statues of Alice-in-Wonderland and the Caterpillar-on-the-Mushroom my boyfriend who was bearded and I would crawl under, ladies in precisely tailored suits walked their dogs, near one of the long rough stone walls that separated this park from the very wealthy residential and religious buildings was a park only children under a certain age played.

Only spaces in which I can lose myself whether I'm now sensibly perceiving or remembering interest me. It's because I live to fill a certain dream. I have penetrated to the innermost centre of this dream. The centre has three parts.

1. My most constant childhood experience is pain.

No, no knowing, just the present. A wholly unfruitful solution to the problem but all fruit these days is death, no as I grow older I don't think it's any worse or better now than before historically for humans I don't know I know less and less as I get older, the flight into sabotage and anarchism. The same sabotage of social existence is my constantly walking the city my refusal to be together normal a real person: because I won't be together with my mother. I like this sentence 'cause it's stupid.

2. Who do I know? I go over this question again and again because the people I know in this world are my reality stones. I know Peter and David and Jeffrey, and secondarily Betsy, and lots of other people whom I only half know. Peter and David who live together half of each of them is my grandmother. They have a small three-room apartment. They have certain nice belongings. They're proud of their living. They live more quietly than the people in the neighbourhood they live in do and the people they know who are mainly rock-n-roll stars. I often debate with myself whether they're kind or not.

They're my closest friends. Sometimes I start to cry 'cause I feel so glad and lucky I know them and have been admitted into their hearts this feeling is almost too much so I say to myself you're just transferring your need for the affection you're not getting from a boyfriend. Lacking a boyfriend's one of the many thoughts society's taught me. All the thoughts society's taught me're judgemental, usually involving or causing self-dislike, imprisoning, and stopping me. When I just let what is be what is and stop judging, I'm always happy. Peter and David are two of the most happy people I know.

I got a cat this week, but the minute the cat kitten long light dark grey black white hairs hints of brown pale blue grey green eyes jumps into my house I can't give this much affection the kitten torn away from its mother demands something mental in me rends, I don't want to love inappropriately, I'm too something to be touched. I invent an allergy and run the cat back to its mother.

3. I didn't know anything about death (the first time I experienced death and saw a dead person it was my suicided mother when I was an adult) nor about poverty. The first time the word 'poverty' meant anything to me (to understand this word I had to wait until I was judging my experience and not just experiencing), I thought I was poor because I had less than the girls in my grade who were of my class and because my boyfriend in the fancy nightclub to which he had taken me said, 'Tell your mother to get you a nice dress,' and I knew she would never. In college I learned for the first time that my family was rich. (How does the word 'poverty' differ from the word 'death'?) Does this kind of knowledge which is really only belief change my actual experiences? Of course:

I'm making my dream. The mappings, the intertwinings, so hopefully there'll be losing, loosings, my mother said I hate you.

Let the rocks come tumbling out. Move crack open the ice blocks. You hurt me twice. No one hurts me twice, bastard. You said 'Don't talk to me again' and 'I'm saying this for no reason at all.' First off (in time), after six years of living with me one night you said. 'This is it.' I said that I didn't know it had been getting so bad and could I have one more chance and you said no. My whole life busted itself. I recovered almost I almost didn't I do everything you want I always have, to, of, from, for I love you, you don't love me. One month ago you said, 'I don't want to be friends with you any longer.' This time I was innocent. You've hurt me again, I want you to know this time really badly. I don't understand how someone can be such a shit as you are. I think you are really evil. No one hurts another person for no reason at all. No one believes in him- or herself so totally, the other person has absolutely no say no language. This' how this country's run.

The media's just one-way language so the media-makers control.

I'm diseased. I hate you. There's this anger hot nauseating in me that has to seep out then destroy.

I hate the world. I hate everyone. Every moment I have to fight to exert my will to want to live. When I lived with a man, I was happy. I always was miserable. I like banging my head into a wall. I'm banging my head into a wall.

One might generalize by saying: the technique of reproduction detaches the reproduced object from the domain of tradition. Meaning, for example: a book no longer has anything to do with literary history so the history of literature you're taught in school is for shit. The art work's no longer the one object that's true; sellability and control, rather than truth, are the considerations that give the art object its value. Art's substructure has moved from ritual and truth to politics.

Meanwhile this society has the hype: the artist's powerless. Hype. Schools teach good writing in order to stop people writing whatever they want the ways they want. Why do I like banging my head into, against the wall? I always have. I could go stand by your door and ring the doorbell. This is what I think every day: I'm going to phone him. No; he told me he didn't want to speak to me again. I shouldn't want someone who needlessly hurts me because such a situation hurts me. You haven't liked me for a year. You only talked to me when you wanted my money so I hate you. But that's the way you are with everybody because you're crazy because you're so scared. You think when you're hurting someone more than anyone would normally (maybe my idea of 'normal' is incorrect) the person is irredeemably hurting you, because you're so coked up. As I walk along each street I think: I can do whatever I want so I'll walk to your apartment and ring the doorbell. My attention's distracted from this by wanting a mystery book. I walk out of the bookstore. I don't care enough about you now to experience your hatred of me again and I'm proud of me for sidestepping my masochism my masochism.

By not getting in touch with you I'm keeping this situation alive. I'm keeping this situation alive because there's no one alive who physically loves me. This' false. When I was in high school, unlike the other kids (I went to an all-girls' school), I was never in love. I didn't feel I-didn't-know-what-it-was for boys; I just liked sex. I crave sex.

Presumably, without intending it, he issued an invitation to a far-reaching liquidation. Now I want to give you an analogy. A painter represents or makes (whichever verb at this moment you prefer) reality by keeping distant from it and picturing it totally. A cameraman, on the other hand, permeates with mechanical equipment what he's going to represent, thus for the sake of representation changes breaks up. Reproducable art breaks up and ruins.

I must give people art that demands very little attention and takes almost nothing for me to do.

3 Violence

Purpose: To Get Rid of Meaning
for the German Expressionists
who believed nothing
and the primacy of language over form
cause their society equalled suicide
In total blackness cause there is no voodoo,
dedicated to The Fall:
I want to fuck one of The Gang Of Four or The Fall:

She was always losing her stockings. (Shot of leg whose toe is high in the air, black sheer stocking slipping off, finger in cunt)

All females are dykes

She wanted to get a man, and she didn't know how to get one.

1. The women

Lesbian Guerrilla Army all gunned up enters stage:

Dyke Leader: OK girls. Here were are. (*They look around the factory.*) Not much here to put up our cunts.

Sparrow Cunt: Not even a cock to chop off.

Blonde Beauty: There's no cocks left in New York.

Adele Just out Of Reform School: You're getting too old. I make my own. (*She takes out a bunch of black dildoes.*)

Girls: Yay! (*They fuck up and down on the dildoes.*)

The Madonna (*to her girlfriend who's a whore*): I've been telling you I'm not racist.

Whore: Well you wouldn't take that lousy trick I handed you last night over by Forsyth.

Madonna: I don't have to fuck every black cock on the street to show I like blacks.

Alice: But if you don't fuck a guy, you can't possibly like him.

Dyke Leader: We're here to kill men.

Whore: Maybe you, honey. I've gotta make a living. You want me to be a secretary? Anyway, if there were no men, there'd be no secretaries, no file clerks, no lickers. We'd all starve.

Madonna: I believe in God.

Blonde Beauty: You mean *cock*. We don't need men like God, dumb shit, because we don't need money. We need cocks.

Whore: Well, I don't know about you, but I need lots of money. Some people need places to live, not me. I need Krizia dresses, sheer black stockings, Valentino shoes, Yamamoto sweaters, and above all Issey

Miyake when he's not designing for the masses. What else is a revolution for?

Madonna: What revolution? This isn't Europe.

Dyke Leader (*inspecting factory*): I don't know what the hell this is. I don't know why anyone goes out of their apartment anymore.

2. The men

(*All the lights go out in such a way that even the people in the audience get spooked. Shadows, here, and there, what's going on?, loneliness, from romanticism to fear.*)

(*The factory remains black. Areas and lines of dim grey light. Two black shadows ((humans)) crouch in this light against bare walls.*)

Second Shadow: Where's the bomb?

First Shadow: Don't use that word. Reagan might hear.

Second Shadow (*SS man*): So what's he going to do to us? I'm going to die anyway.

First Shadow: Fear isn't so reasonable.

Second Shadow: He isn't a guy; he's a woman.

First Shadow: Who? Reagan?

Second Shadow: No, the transsexual.

Transsexual: Are you talking about me? (*Now we can see the three male faces. One of them is a woman.*)

Second Shadow: I have no wish to hurt you.

Transsexual: You do so. You know you hurt me? You know why all of you hurt me? I'm gonna protest against all of you men. All I want is someone to love me. (*Still very calm and soft.*) Is that so much to ask for one lifetime? (*Tears out cunt hairs; lies back down on floor; kicks legs straight in air. Out of her mind.*)

Second Shadow (*coldly*): Not again. (*Slaps her. To the other terrorist*) OK the bomb's set. We have to get out of here soon as possible.

Transsexual (*screaming at the same time*): I'll do whatever I want because I need.

Second Shadow: I'm leaving.

Transsexual (*now very quiet*): Please don't leave me. I'll do anything you want.

Second Shadow: Either you're going to do what I want or you're going to do what you want. Make your decision, Elvira.

Elvira: You know I'm a woman and I'm weak.

Second Shadow: You're not a real woman.

Elvira: No one's a real enough woman for the likes of you. All you men, the big conceptualists the revolutionaries. You tell me you love me only when you want to stick your thing in me.

Second Shadow: You're a piece of trash who can't think, all you know is how to be lonely. You pretend you have all these brains when actually everyone is laughing at you, and as you're growing older your body is so ugly how could any man desire your puckered asshole? You? Love? You don't even know enough to keep your mouth shut.

Elvira: You used to like my mouth well enough even if it is flabby and ugly.

Second Shadow: I like every hole when I'm drunk. A man doesn't mean anything he does when he's drunk. And you're not even a man or a woman.

Elvira: Whatever I am, I've been something to you for three years' deeps of nights.

Second Shadow: The deep of night, yes. We live there. I'm leaving.

(*The First Shadow is at the doorway, now a shadow.*)

Elvira: If anybody leaves me again, I'll suicide. I'll ask you one thing. (*Looking straight up at the ceiling like Frankenstein, as Second Shadow also exits.*) If any of you have any dot of human pity at all in you, please give me some help and stay with me until I can get on my feet.

3: My childhood

A dyke walks over to Elvira and kicks her.

Adele: What're you doing here?

Elvira: I'm lonely.

Adele: What does that have to do with sex?

Elvira: As long as I can remember I've been lonely. My parents had this apartment on Sutton Place. The corner of the sixth floor of the building was their living-room. I'd sit on one of the window seats, looking down over the people and tiny cars, and sing, 'Somewhere Over the Rainbow'. Even when I was married. I was lonely because I was always in love with artist who wasn't in love with me. When I turned thirty years old, I was desperate. When you're young, you find pleasure by sticking razor blades into your wrist. The desperation of old age, being over thirty, is frightening because you don't know if you'll be strong, or lobotomized, enough to bear it. I met Christoph in the bar I hang out at. For two years I supported him by doing sex show shit. I'm not a hooker. I can't touch strange men's flesh. Touching their flesh freaks me out. That's the way I am. I can do anything in front of men as long as I don't have to touch them. Chris wanted to be a mercenary, but he couldn't get it together for a long time. He kept getting his gun barrels clogged. Even back then everyone I knew back then says he was the most ambitious person around, but I never knew it: I thought Chris was the kindest and most gentle man I had ever known. I couldn't believe there was a man such as him. We never fought once or raised our voices to each other. He must have loved me. I used to tell him, 'In this brutal world you can't let people walk over you and use you. You have to grow up.' He was my world. He became a man by taking more coke, acting like more of a shit to women, and closing off his feelings. Now he's able to take care of me. I'm not going to be a whore anymore. I know he loves me.

4: I lose my home forever

Elvira in her home. Shot of a dark green wall.

Elvira: Chris? Chris, where are you? (*She's intuitive enough to be worried. Sees a note pinned to a bedframe, hanging as if it's all bloody. Reads it to herself. Can't believe it so reads it out loud.*) 'Elvira, I'm leaving you as you know I have to because you're a mess and nothing can be made up between us. Christoph.'

5: Looking for friends

Sparrow Cunt: What're you doing back here?
Blonde Beauty: Huh?
Elvira: I want to join you.
Madonna: Oh, you do believe in God.
Elvira: I want to help you get rid of men.
Dyke Leader: We're not getting rid of men; we're getting rid of our controllers.
Whore: We're artists.
Elvira: Who's controlling me? (*The Whore points to Elvira's cunt and the Dyke Leader to Elvira's brains.*)
Blonde Beauty: Hermann Kahn's controlling you.
Elvira: Hermann Kahn? I used to fuck him. He must be Jewish.
Whore: Oh gee. Was he any good?
Dyke Leader (*slapping her*): Shut up, whore.
Elvira: I'm sorry. He used to fuck me.
Whore: Was he any good?
Elvira: Gee. I never know if a guy's any good cause I'm always desperate.
Whore: That's what makes a woman a great fuck.
Dyke Leader: That's what makes a woman hate men. You cunt's scarred.
Elvira (*looking at her cunt*): You should see inside my asshole. (*Proudly*) I've been to the hospital twice. One time the doctor said I might not recover.
Madonna: She is religious.
Beautiful Blonde: Feeling sexual love is like being in prison:

(*Prison scene:*
Prisoner 1 (sitting up on her wood board): Goddamn I have to shit.

(*In a nearby corner, night, three prisoners throw dice on a board. They're the matron's baby dykes.*)

First Dice-thrower (*looking at Prisoner 1*): She never shits.

(*Prisoner 1 falls flat on her face and goes back to never-never land.*)

Prisoner 1 (*sitting up on her wood board*): I really have to shit. (*She's sound asleep. As she climbs out of her bunk, she steps on her bedmate's face.*)

Bedmate (*instantly awake*): Cindy, you can't have to shit. You never eat.

Cindy: I have to shit. (*She goes over to the box of yellow paper, lays two papers on the floor, squats over the two pieces of paper. Nothing comes out. She waddles back to the wood bunk.*)

Bedmate: You're dreaming.

Cindy: I can't help wanting to shit. I still have normal body reactions.

Bedmate: You'll soon get over that.

Cindy: What'll be left?

Bedmate: Nothing's left to us or anyone else. Soon enough we die.

Cindy: I do have to shit. I've got these terrible stomach contractions. (*Pause*) Maybe I'm sick?

Bedmate: At least you're not pregnant. How many abortions have you had?

Cindy (*now totally doubled over*): I am sick. God. . . (*Runs over to the pot.*)

Bedmate: Is it coming out?

Cindy: All I can do is urinate.

Bedmate: Dig your fingers in and pull it out.

Cindy: I can't shit, I'm asleep, and I have lumps in my breast.

Bedmate: At least you're not pregnant.

Cindy: Doctors tear apart bodies and make me sick. Most of all they increase my fear with their talk of death death death. I'm scared out of my mind.

Bedmate: Of what? Of death?

Cindy: They've scared us out of our minds. Deeply threaded by my prick, he'll become something other than himself, something other than my lover.)

Dyke Leader: Humans have to die, but they don't have to feel pain.

Elvira: But he made love to me.

Whore: Tom made love to me last night four times in a row. But that doesn't mean he knows who I am.

Elvira: Maybe I'd better see Hermann Kahn again and find out whether he still loves me.

Madonna: What happened to Christoph?

Elvira: Hermann Kahn came before Christoph. He was my first.

6: *Back to the nunnery*

Elvira leans against one of the white columns that holds up the stone porch roof. In back of her are green gardens and penguins.

Elvira (*running over to a penguin*): Mommy!

Penguin 1: I'm not your mommy.

(*Elvira goes back to her friend, the Beautiful Blonde.*)

Beautiful Blonde: Don't you know who your mommy is? I thought you were looking for Hermann Kahn.

Elvira: All these penguins look the same to me. (*A penguin passes close to her. She runs over to it.*) Mommy! (I dreamed one night that one of the angels of the Lord came down to me. Blue lights were rising up from the city below me. The blue lights were pale yellow, pale pink, violet, and blue. I know now that the angels are coming. The angel of the Lord said to me, 'The murderers are after you.' I ran through the city. I have been to this city before. The streets are narrow and wind past the small stores set in the bottoms of two- and three-storey townhouses. There're no large businesses. Each geographical section of townhouses has the shape of a human liver or something similar. In the left part of the landscape, to the left of the liver through which now I'm running, there's a green park. Throughout the city there are small parks. Of course the heavy-set brutal killers are going to catch me. You who I love are heavy-set.) Do you remember who I am?

Penguin 2: Who are you?

Elvira: You're my mother.

Penguin 2: I'm the mother to all children.

Elvira: If you can cut through your shit, Holy Mother, remember you once spread your legs screamed in agony and I came out. (*Yanks the pinned arm upward.*) Now do you remember?

Penguin 2: I've changed, my daughter.

Elvira: Cut the daughter shit too. I used to be your son. (*Yanks the arm higher.*) I want you to tell me about the first man I fell in love with.

Penguin 2 (*as hard as she really is*): Why bother? (*Recovering her surface.*) Why disturb the good life you've managed to make for yourself by remembering anything?

Elvira: That's shit too. (*Yanks the arm up as hard as she can and breaks it.*)

Penguin 2: For a Catholic pain is ecstasy. (*Raising her eyes towards* *heaven.*) I'll tell you what you want to know so you too can be in pain maybe you'll be in so much pain you'll kill yourself.

7: Mexican lust

Penguin 2: It's the Mexican-American border below San Diego. The American government's manoeuvering a war between the Mexicans who have snuck across the border to the American side and the local Blacks cause the American government wants to off both groups.

A high-falutin' Mexican Vice cop lands on the American side of the border for the first time with his newly-married wife. Three feet away from where the honeymoon couple stands, a car blows up. The head of the Mexican Family this Vice cop recently busted threatens the Vice cop's wife if her husband doesn't lay off the scum, while the Vice cop watches the big fat cop who runs this border town hates Mexes and who's name is Hermann Kahn arrest a Mexican greaser for the car bombing. In return the kid is screaming, 'You fascist pig! You're only arresting me 'cause I just married the rich white girl of the town. You don't get off on black dick and white-and-red pussy.' The Mexican Vice cop watches this, but has to keep his mouth clamped because he's Mexican. Today being Mexican Black female gay and everything else is being dead because this is Mexico.

To protect his wife from further harassments, the Vice cop puts her in a nearby motel. She's safer in America than in Mexico because the Americans live by rules. The Head of the Family owns this dump. Family punks proceed to rape, dope up, and set up the wife as a junky on the Mexican side of the border so the cops'll think the Vice cop's a junky. Hermann Kahn and the Head of the Family collude in this strategy. When the wife rolls around in junk delight, three inches from her eyes Hermann Kahn strangles the Family Head just so he, Kahn, is sure her husband'll be framed and get out of his, Kahn's, affairs. Meanwhile the Vice cop has found inconvertible evidence that Kahn is really crooked, shown this evidence to the other cops, and one of the cops is helping the Vice frame Kahn. During the frame Kahn kills this lower cop and at the same time it becomes public that the Mexican greaser was the car bomber just as Kahn said he was.

Elvira: Did they kill Kahn?

Penguin 2: No. They incorporated him as head of the American think tank scheme.

8: Suicide

In Hermann Kahn's building (the factory), which is now totally deserted:

Man in empty room: I'm going to commit suicide. (*To Elvira entering.*)
Elvira: Good for you.

Man: Don't you want to know how stinko the world is and how it hurts to be alive?

Elvira: Not really.

Man: I'm going to kill myself in the most disgusting way possible. I'm going to drown in my very own vomit which will be as red as nipples of cancer. As it gleams the bed at night, through which love is passing.

Elvira: Go ahead. (*Pulls out her purse and lights a cigarette.*) I'll watch you. (*Looks at her watch.*) Do you think you're going to take a long time?

Man: First let's fuck. Oh my darling, I've waited for you for so long.

Elvira: I don't know. (*Rolling her head.*) I can't believe.

Man (*two hands on her cheeks so the eyes in her face have to look into his eyes. Stares intently at her*): I want you. Say 'I want you.'

Elvira: I want you.

(*He puts his small stubby cock in her cunt. They haven't quite gotten undressed.*)

Man: Say, 'I love you.'

Elvira (*still looking at him so she'll be possessed*): I love you.

(*He releases her. She goes back to normal or feelinglessness, then realizes she has to change: of her own will her righthand's fingers are lightly tapping up down his left cheek, the softness of her eyes as she gasps her cunt opens. Her cunt is opening and opening and his cock is opening and*)

Elvira: Oh. Oh Jesus Christ I don't believe.

Man (*at the same time, loudly*): Oohhh, ooohhoohh, hOOhoohoohh.

Elvira: Can we maybe be friends after this?

Man (*turning Elvira's face into his*): Neither of us expected this would happen, did we?

9: Elvira

Elvira (*as she's committing suicide*): Merry Christmas, Elvira. (*Takes a pill.*) Your mother won't give you money. You don't have any money left. You're going to starve to death. (*takes another pill.*) You pretend to everyone you have a boyfriend so your friends won't think you're a freak though you know goddamn well there's no boyfriend you liar. (*Takes another pill.*) All your life is an illusion you crummy liar you lie to everyone you are a liar everything is a fake because you pretend you have money and you're happy you have to pretend these things, and you're none of these things. (*Takes another pill.*) There is no one you can turn to. (*She is teaching herself*) There is no way because there is no one to whom you can yell 'Help'. There is no shoulder. There is no one. (*Takes another pill.*) Scream. No possibility of screaming. Scream. No possibility of screaming. (*Takes the rest of the pills.*)

Why the fuck should I commit suicide? I'd rather kill. (*She goes into bathroom. Sticks her fingers down throat and vomits up pills.*)

10: Rebirth or human suffering is stupid

Elvira (*lying in her apartment on her couch. Smoking some opium.*): Now what'm I going to do with myself?

(*Chrysis, entering. Takes my cunt in his palm. Starts rousing me. In one minute there are chills up and down my spine.*)

Elvira: This stuff always ends up hurting me.

Chrysis: Don't you see I've started a hunt and now you need a hare?

(*I threw myself into his arms, not only my body, and I started to go out of whack. I could no longer keep control of myself by pretending I was a zombie. I threw myself into his arms.*

Lots of kisses.

I got him to fuck me by refusing to leave his side and looking into his eyes.
Lips mesh. Hands go all over the place. Bodies go crazy bodies really want cause souls)

Chrysis (*getting up right after the fuck*): I hate your cunt, you dog, why do you think you amuse me? You don't mean anything to me, spindle-cunt, spoiled fish-teeth, trench-mouth, herpes. (*He beats her up.*)

Elvira: The witch can cure me.

Man: I'm the witch.

Elvira: Suppose there's a person who by birth naturally is off. Weird. Sick. Unbalanced. Just not like other people. Do the Leftists and the Marxists and the Socialists care about this person?

Witch: What do these people mean now?

Elvira: I mean: Why help a bum? I see bums every day. Why do they keep living their hard lives? Why help anyone continue what is useless: living? I get wiser as I get older and then when I'm wise I'll die, so what's the use of all the wisdom? There's another thing I think. Say I fall wildly in love with a man. Why do I feel all these powerful things? Does my feeling them mean he has to feel something? What's reality? I mean I'm not under physical torture all of the time, but there's always all this mental pain, but suicide. . .? Let's take an example of this situation: What do I do without love? Is sex necessary?

Witch: Even rats live better than us.

Elvira: We'd better say this life is almost intolerable. So, witch, what am I going to do?

First Jew: It's the old story. They beat us up. They beat up our children. In the middle of the midnight they appear in our houses, drag us out of our beds, take us into their hellholes.

Second Jew: Suffering! We are the chosen people! Aren't we the chosen people? Chosen for suffering therefore we make good art!

Whore: I don't give a shit as long as I can fuck.

Implosion

I. THE BACKGROUND OF THE FRENCH REVOLUTION. THREE SCENES.

1. Europe. The people mutter political discontent.

Kathy (*an American visitor*): How do you make love?

Father (*a Frenchman*): I make love with my fingers. My fingers are magic. Are you feeling them now?

Kathy: Oh yes! (*He beats her ass while he fingerfucks her.*) Oh. OH! (*Comes twice.*)

Father: I have other kinds of tastes. I'm a feminist: I like to watch two women fuck. Sometimes I beat them with my belt while they fuck each other. (*Frank and Patricia enter,*) Frank! What is the matter with you? Are the Dutch people calling you a fascist again?

Frank (*a Dutchman sitting on the bed between Father's and Kathy's bodies*): I'm no goddamn fascist. I don't have any politics. I'm like an American.

Patricia (*also Dutch*): I'm thirsty.

Frank: I'm sick of moralists. For the first time their economy's going under and the Dutch are beginning to realize their posh ways of life might no longer be available to them. At this moment they're acting scared 'cause they'll do anything to avoid rocking the boat.

Father: Of course. I'm a good Frenchman.

Frank: . . . They've always worshipped anything that's safe. That's why they're Liberals. The Dutch Marxists in announcing themselves as the only opposition to this reaction have grouped and defined themselves so rigidly that they've got no political power. They're as bureaucratic academic and rigid as the Right-Wing.

Patricia: How long will we be as bloody and dirty as children?

Kathy (*masturbating*): Oh oh oh.

Patricia: For how much longer are our toys – the coffins of friends out on heroine – going to be the only things we can love? For how much longer will severed heads be the only people I place my lips upon? I love death. The Committee of Happiness better begin its work.

Father: Your statements are reactionary 'cause you can't so simply put ideals on top of what's actually happening to you. If this society in which you're living shits, you have to shit. (*He's such a big guy, he farts.*)

Patricia: But ideals can pick holes in the social fabric. 'True' and 'false'

313

are beside the point. Even if they did nothing, they're the only tools we've got.

Father: Look, I'm a musician: I know language like music isn't stating big things, but breathing. Otherwise, poetry opera art painting aren't only dead they also cause death. That's why Rockefeller sponsors them. Throw everything's that's dead up the assholes of those who're too tight to fuck in the ass.

Kathy (*stopping masturbating for a moment*): I'm too crazy. The only thing I want is feeling. Talking to friends.

Frank (*feeling up her cunt*): How're you going to do that? They either worship you or they despise you, but you'll never be human because you feel.

Kathy: This talk shits. Go crazy. We're going to cause a revolution. I tell you. I'm going to cause a burning revolution. (*Disappears.*)

Father: The hell with her.

2. *What my grandmother saw in London*

In America:

Tom (*barely audible and fucking*): Love.

My Grandmother: (*Can't stop herself from saying it*). I love you I love you. (*She starts coming and can't stop coming. Gradually they calm down physically.*) I have to go to Europe now. (*They kiss a lot.*)

In England:

My Grandmother (*phoning Tom*): This is Florence.
Tom: Who?
My Grandmother: Florrie.
Tom: Who?
My Grandmother: Florrie . . .
Tom: Oh. Florrie. Where are you?
My Grandmother: I'm drunk.
Tom: That's nice.
My Grandmother: I'm in London. (*Pause*). Am I disturbing you?
Tom: There's someone here with me.
My Grandmother: I'm sorry; I didn't mean to disturb you. (*She hangs up the phone.*) Oh, thank you. (*She looks through the window and sees the following scene*):

(*An outside street. The bright sunlight is evident mainly in all the colours which are so bright they're almost white. There are working- and lower-middle-class three- and four-storey tenements in back of and around the streets. There are groups of typical that is small and eccentric English people on the streets.*)

A Middleaged Housewife: You know those fuckin' uppermiddleclass women. They say a woman who's a whore is the pitfall and living cancer of human existence. I'll tell you something. No woman wants to be a whore. Oh maybe some bitch who went to Oxford and has to have daddy needs to be a whore or gets her thrills whoring. I have nothing to do with the rich. Most women who whore whore because you need to be supported. You, daddy. You hire fuck and arrest the whores.

A whore needs a pimp. A whore doesn't need a pimp because she's weak. A whore needs a pimp because a pimp controls the territory. To control this whore the pimp, just like a record company with its rock-'n'-roll stars, gets her hooked. Your daughter is now supporting two daddies and a habit. Who did this to her? I ask you, who did this to her? Is she doing it to herself? (*She turns to a Frenchman who's standing on the street.*) You think whoring is fashionable? You think women who're too young to come whore because it's heep? Being a whore beats being a secretary (*back to her husband, who we now see's a drunken tailor*) or a wife 'cause, for the same work, work 'cause there's no love, only a whore not a wife or a secretary gets paid enough she might be able to escape men.

Tailor: Our daughter doesn't love me.

A Middleaged Housewife: I used to have a fantasy you loved me. Then I had a fantasy some man could love me. Now I can't find any fantasy inside my head. I can't find anything.

My Grandmother (*to herself*): What do I want? I'm a woman too.

Tailor: It's natural it's a Law of Human Nature: My daughter has to whore to support me. Give me a knife so I can increase the pain.

My Grandmother: Give his daughter the knife 'cause it's the hurt, not the hurters, who feel pain.

Tailor (*to his wife*): I will increase the pain. I will go crazy. I hurt; let all of us hurt more.

A Middleaged Housewife: To you everything's your cock; you worship your pain.

3. Art-criticism and art

The office of ARTFORUM, Mulberry Street, New York City.

Situationalist With Italian Accent: I just saw an American film. The title of the film is *Bladder Run.*

His Girlfriend: *Blade Runner.*

Situationalist With Italian Accent: I think it is a real American film. In this film which is a film and not a real event . . .

Girlfriend: . . . but it's a real film . . .

Situationalist With Italian Accent: . . . the filmmaker proves to us the audience that robots are as human as we are. Since simulation can take the place of reality . . .

Girlfriend: . . . non-simulation. . .

Situationalist With Italian Accent: . . . we no longer need money to make germ warfare, lobotomy, and other weapons as does Mr Reagan, Inc.

Girlfriend: We don't want germ warfare, lobotomies, and Thylenol.

Situationalist With Italian Accent: We make fake germ warfare, fake lobotomy, and good medicine which doesn't hurt anybody and yet works very well destruction of governmental control.

Girlfriend: Destruction of corporations.

Situationalist With Italian Accent: Yes. Corporality.

Marxist Feminist: But how can I tell the difference between the real and what isn't real that is, for our purposes, between their disgusting weapons and our good weapons?

Situationalist With Italian Accent: You can't.

Marxist Feminist: I might end up a Right-Winger.

Girlfriend: For you that's better than ending up in someone's bed.

Tom (*who's an Irish artist turned American*): No, this woman's correct. There's definitely a problem with Situationalism as it now stands. I therefore propose we get rid of all judgements. No more you v. me v. Reagan or rich v. poor. We don't mean anymore. We Americans and our allies the British (*in thick Irish accent*) will give the world a fine example!

Marxist Feminist (*not understanding anything*): Of what?

Tom: Of the new politics: no politics. Everything. We can and do everything. We are theatre.

Murderers (*all dark, black. The skin. Murderer*): Why do you keep murdering?

My Grandmother: I have to, my dear.

Murderer: You're a shadow that murders the body that casts it.

My Grandmother: So then I'll be left with shadows. . .

Murderer: . . . different textures of blackness. . .

My Grandmother: . . . my skin. Where's Danton? Fiction. I tell you truly: right now fiction's the method of revolution.

Murderer: All this is talk. (*Sharpening his knife.*)

My Grandmother: To dream's more violent than to act.

(*End of my version of art-criticism.*)

II. ACTION. TEN SCENES.

1. On heroism: Robespierre decides to kill Danton.

Robespierre: Danton's getting too famous. Let's kill him. (*Rubs his hands.*) Hee hee hee. (*Robespierre's Polish. All Polish people are gnomes* *who run around in tiny circles and act in malicious ways.*) You think murder's wrong. I'm going to prove to you there's no morality (*a Polish proof*): My mind is capable of and thinks every possible thought. Therefore there's no morality in the mental world. A thought turns into an action by chance. Therefore there's no morality in the real world, only chance. (*A picture of Ronald Reagan's asshole with shit coming out.*)

Robespierre and St Just (St because today it's Christmas), being both Polish jump up and down rubbing their hands together clap monkey feet together: Kill Danton the Powerful! Kill Lacroix the Foolish! Kill Hérault-Séchelles Philippeau and Camille!

St Just (*reading a long piece of paper which he rolls up and unrolls while everyone chants or chatters 'Good' 'Bad' 'Good' 'Bad'*): 'Robespierre kills.' That's a disgusting slander. The media lies.
Robespierre: I'll kill you for lying.
St Just: I'm not lying. The paper's lying.
Robespierre: You die anyway. My friends only love me when they're dead.
St Just: Or when you're dead. This is true in London not only in New York City.
Robespierre (*changing his mind*): You don't have to die yet, Justice. I just wanted to frighten you.
St Just: You're frightening everybody to death. (*Walks off.*)
Robespierre: Who needs friends? I do everything I do only in accordance with myself: I act. I am the hero.

2. *Danton learns Robespierre's going to kill him and agrees to it.*

Danton (*sitting in his own room*): I don't care about anything except when I'm obsessed.
Lacroix: You think so much you're not going to be able to murder Robespierre. You're not only committing suicide; you're killing all of us. Stop thinking; slaughter the creep. I just heard he's planning to kill you. Worry about why you're murdering later.
Danton: I'd rather die than murder. I'd rather be fucked than fuck.
Lacroix: You're right: It's better to die than to die. (*All the Poles, bent over, shuffling around in circles, follow each other.*)
Danton: I don't care anymore if I die. The only thing I have is sex and I'm not so hooked on sex though the physical ecstasy keeps getting stronger. Maybe Robespierre'll kill me soon. (In London people can't afford to travel around the city. Kids place wires on the soft spots of their brains so hopefully they're lobotomizing themselves. The beards

of old men sitting in the pubs sit in their beers. The buildings of the rich overtower all.) We have to find our own pleasure.

(Pasolini died
by suicide.)

3. Back to school.

Kantor: I want you to tell me about the War of Roses.

Danton (*pre-school age*): The War of Roses occurred in 1481. The House of Lancaster who were known as the red roses fought against the House of York who are the white roses. The red roses won because they were bloodier.

Kantor: Correct. Now tell me whether or not you are going to die. You don't know, do you? You're going to have to go to school. Let's go to school.

Danton: I don't want to go to school.

Kantor: All little boys go to school. Little girls don't do anything. Besides this school doesn't have any pupils and needs pupils 'cause a school needs pupils to be a success.

Danton: I won't be a pupil because I have pupils. I must be a school.

Kantor: If you're not at school in an hour, you won't have any more pupils. (*Picture of Polish people putting little Polish girl into the earth.*)

Danton: OK. So I'll go to school.

Kantor: Let's go to school right now.

(*The Spirit of Death takes my hand and wafts me to school.*)

4. In school

All the teachers are female and all the boys are male.

Teacher (*gazing at little boys*): Boys! Boys! Boys! I need more.

Two other teachers talk to each other. (*This is a pastoral scene: people occur in clumps.*)

Teacher 1: I've already got herpes.

(*I'm standing hand in hand with the guy who's brought me to school. I'm abnormal and abnormally shy. My toes quake inwards. I turn my face away. I don't want to go into this nasty place because I don't know nothing. In there. The Spirit of Death who's now a patriarch my uncle who's keeping me these days away from my own money, shoves me forward into the School-mistress' face. The Schoolmistress is part ogre and part pig. She has a fake English accent even though she's English.*)

Me: My name's Johnny.

Schoolmistress: Well, here's little Johnny. (*Feeling my cock between my*

318

legs.) You certainly are a little Johnny. I wish I was teaching future criminal offenders in the South Bronx. I always knew it was better to live in America.

My Uncle: Leave the goods alone, Mrs Selby.

Headmistress (*correcting him*): They're virgin. (*Moving away to a beautiful grove of trees.*) Look how well all the students are coming back. They know how to walk. They all know how to walk. We have a very fine establishment here.

Beautiful Blonde: They ain't innocent enough. I always said, we don't get enough virgins and so they ain't worth anything to us, they's just used rags 'cause they parents gets 'em first, an' they ain't worth anything to the people we's sell them to. Now, you's a father. Do you know how hard it is for a teacher to make a boy fresh and innocent again? You can't do it with young girls which's why young girls don't go to school. There ain't no use for them to go to school. We have to be really highly trained and it takes a lot of the taxpayers' money to make an already rotting vegetable into a strong carrot. You wouldn't believe how much work 'cause you's a father.

My Uncle (*to himself*): Let 'em rot. At least these rotters are willing to stand up. (*To Beautiful Blonde.*) Madam, it is your job to train these young pliable minds to want goodness. These pliable minds will be the owners of the world and the world will rest on their shoulders. Goodness or godliness, you know, is a taught desire: the social caviar. You must persuade their frail wills to want goodness rather than coca-cola.

Boy: The only thing we want for our coca-cola is hard drugs. (*Shoves his ass in the Beautiful Blonde's face then runs away.*) *The Punk World.*

5. *Love scene*

My Grandmother: I miss you so much

Danton: I'm not near you. I'm in England.

My Grandmother: I wish you were next to me so I could lick your ears. The tips of your ears tip tip. Then into two eyes. My love. We've never said anything affectionate to each other. We don't really know each other.

Danton: We don't know each other.

My Grandmother: Shit. You're less capable than I am. I should forget about you.

Danton: A person should be as self-sufficient as possible, but I don't know what the hell for. Robespierre's coming to arrest me.

6. *Robespierre and his gang plan.*

St Just: In two hours Danton's going to announce his son's engagement 'cause he knows people love a wedding so that way he can keep them under his thumb.

My Grandmother: But George, the son, is a Siamese twin. Half a Siamese twin.

St Just: They just need this wedding to keep the people happy. They don't have to have sex.

My Grandmother: An advertisement wedding is as good as a real wedding and better than the sex I'm getting these days.

Robespierre (*looking her body up and down*): I hope you're speaking for yourself.

My Grandmother: You don't have anything worth speaking of.

Robespierre: That's why I like human blood. This semi-Siamese son is a human booby and basket phenomenon; the non-married semi-twin, Arthur. . .

My Grandmother: – he's the one who ruled Britain –

Robespierre: . . . is the one I want to use.

My Grandmother: What do you do in bed?

Robespierre (*annoyed*): I told you I like blood! Arthur's going to help us kill Danton.

My Grandmother: He won't commit patricide. He's too intent on fratricide.

Robespierre: If Arthur kills his father, the people'll decide Danton has to be a shit.

My Grandmother: I'll go back home and tell Arthur his other half's getting married. He's so dumb he doesn't even know it yet. He must have been born on the other side of the brains. When he learns Danton's marrying off George, he'll be pissed off enough to slaughter George but he can't because then he'd die too. So he'll murder his father.

Robespierre: A family scandal'll really kill off the Danton family. Murder advertisements always top wedding advertisements. The people'll know we're just as pure as driven snow. We can even kill a few more people.

My Grandmother: Due to that Watergate scandal – when even dumbies as dumb as the Americans had to know their leaders, Nixon and everybody else, lie steal murder cheat and take hard drugs – these same leaders simply gained more power. Don't throw your money into advertising. What matters is that you get all the political power.

7. Danton

Danton: I want to be less nothing. There are some thoughts that shouldn't ever be heard. It's not good if they cry out the second they're born a baby out of the womb it is good: they can blow up the world.

8. Robespierre's coming for Danton

Lots of battle scenes, small battles, all around. Only street fightings no more major characters.

9. Robespierre's Coming For Danton 2.

Make more and more like a painting.

My Grandmother: Do you know who I am?
Danton: How can I know who you are? I only fucked you twice. (*Lots of sunlight and little battles.*) What I believe is what I see. It's harder to live than die for what you see.
My Grandmother: What do you see? (*Lots of sunlight and little battles.*)
Danton: Last night I had this dream: I was fishing. I caught an eel. As the fish I had caught flapped on the wood dock, my hook slipped out of its mouth. This made me very upset. Surprisingly, when I put my hook back into its seemingly smiling therefore sly mouth, the fish readily accepted it.

(*The audience beginning to see Robespierre and his men advancing on Danton realizes Danton's faster and faster closer to his death, at the point of punk ecstasy, in the daylight.*)

My Grandmother: You have to say what you are. Tell me what you see.
Danton (*even faster no fighting against the speed at the same pace*): We are particulars. We are this world. (*Now the people are on him. A housewife digs her fingernails into his thigh.*) There's more and more world a proliferation of phenomena. How, you religious people and more important you politicoes who believe in your wilfully therefore violently changing this world who believe in your wills, how can you be apart from the world? And if you're not apart from the world, how can you be apart from the world? Who is doing the changing? All phenomena which include me being phenomena are alive.
My Grandmother: And it's OK that the rich maul the poor?
Danton: Hello, Robespierre. You're slaughtering me for being a revolutionary and I don't believe in anything I didn't choose to be the freak I was born into. (*As Robespierre's arresting him, in a weak uncertain voice.*) I would like to love Florrie.

321

Robespierre: I'm taking over this world because I'm strong and you're weak.

My Grandmother: The moments are gone: Tell me what you see.

Danton: Your eyes work the same ways mine do, you cunt. I see a three-storey brick building whose bricks the sun is wrapping, a blood-stain on a white collar, a black window frame. I'm hoping, my love, that you love me cause I'd like to live in love. Since I'm given I don't give, I can't create love I can only hope it's here. (*Robespierre leads away Danton.*)

10. My Grandmother.

My Grandmother (*alone on the sunlit street*): Today I've been deeply wounded in my sex: I've had two viral warts scraped off my clit. My cunt cut open at my clit.

III. THE AFTERMATH OF WAR. TWO SCENES.

1. My Grandmother talks to Danton.

My Grandmother writes a telegram. The telegram says:
I'M CRAZY I MISS YOU ARE YOU MARRIED I CAN'T WAIT SIX WEEKS FOR YOUR RETURN. She waits for the phone to ring. She waits for a return letter in the mail.

My Grandmother: He hasn't phoned me. There's no telegram coming back. There won't be any letters because letters from England take too long, a week, and by that time my memory's over and, besides, there are no letters in a revolution. I'll forget him. It's better to forget the people you care about. Being free: that's what I know. I hate this fake freedom. This fake freedom's being in prison. It's social; all psychological is political. I hate.

I'm strong. I need to be part of a family and this world; and when I have to feel needs that are unsatisfiable, needs are only anguish.

(*Her phone rings. To phone.*) Let's go see 'Line.

Phone: 'Lina? Lisa Lyons? What's she doing?

My Grandmother: 'Line. She's fucking some white guy on stage in the middle of the poorest Puerto Rican section. Maybe there'll be a riot.

Phone: Sounds like a riot. There're riots all over the place. Let's go.

My Grandmother: Pick me up at 8:30. If you don't get killed on the way. There're already two corpses on my doorstep.

Phone: They're dead. Dead junkies can't hurt me. How long will she be?

My Grandmother: How long does a fuck take? Ten minutes?

Phone: Five minutes?

My Grandmother: How the fuck should I know?

Phone: It takes longer than a death.

My Grandmother ((*immediately hanging up phone retaking it off hook and dialling*)): Melvyn. I'm desperate. Just listen to my story. It's about this guy I saw in England. Now I'm going to tell you exactly what happened so you can give me advice. I met him by accident in England. The next day we fucked. I wasn't expecting anything to happen. I was too busy. I could barely sandwich him into my life. We didn't talk about anything. All we did was fuck. The minute we saw each other we fucked. It wasn't that we didn't have anything in common. We really like each other's work. We just fucked fucked. I'm a real dope I didn't ask him if he had a girlfriend. We didn't say anything to each other. The next day we saw each other in the afternoon, but I had to see the TV people that night. And the next day I had a dinner date and couldn't take him along. You know how it is. But we see each other all the next day. It was really great. We really got along. That night I was upset I couldn't say anything well what do you expect? I had to leave England. At the end I asked him, 'Am I going to see you again?' 'I'm coming to New York in February.' When I got back to New York a few days later, there was stuff about the magazine he works for, I phoned him. It was all right to phone him. We said we'd work together on an art piece. I said I couldn't keep phoning him cause it cost too much so I'd blow all my money. He said he'd phone me. Robert, the woman who actually runs the magazine, was supposed to be here last week but she won't be here 'till next week. I haven't heard from him since I phoned. I sent him a telegram. He didn't reply to my telegram. Now, I want to know if this means he doesn't like me.

Melvyn: There's obviously something between you. When did you send the telegram?

My Grandmother: Fifteen minutes ago. Five minutes ago.

Melvyn: Maybe he's not in town.

My Grandmother: That could be.

Melvyn: Look: You're very far apart. Let him know you keep caring and at the same minute, protect yourself: don't obsess. (*They both laugh.*) Fuck someone else.

My Grandmother: It doesn't work like that. (*She hangs up phone.*) You're not around me and even if you were around me, I'm just dealing with my own desires. It doesn't matter if I name these desires because every desire acts the same: Either, if I let myself be overcome in desire I'm being sentimental so not letting the mind have a resting place I should take every desire which rises up in me and shove it; or, I should be dumb passion! Let desires and revolutions act! The last choice makes me happy because it's true there's no will.

Where are you? Please call me.

2. Everything is gone.

Paul Rockoffer (*in mourning*): Shut up, bitches! I'm returning to Art
 I'll be an artist and now I'll be happy. I'm an artist I'm an artist! I
 don't believe in breaking traditional form.

Ella (*a pretty eighteen-year-old girl*): You're 46 years old.

My Grandmother: I'm 22.

Ella: Well, you're fat enough to be 46.

My Grandmother: My body doesn't matter. It's always trying to die
 anyway. The hell with it. My mind matters less. It's a conditioned
 piece of shit. Keep your mind on what matters, girl.

Ella: What matters?

Paul Rockoffer: Tell me please, what is life really?

Ella: Now I don't know anymore so I feel dull.

Paul Rockoffer: Don't force me to make speeches. I could tell you
 things, beautiful and horrible deep and drastic, but it'd be just more
 lies.

Ella: Now the artist's talking sincerely.

Old Man-Teacher: Now, Cleopatra's nose . . . Cleopatra. Cle-o-pa-tra.

My Grandmother-In-Old-Age: What about Cleopatra's nose? C'mon,
 fellers, what about it?

The Other Pupils: The nose, the no-o-se, her no-o-o-se. Cleopatra's
 nose!!

My Grandmother-In-Old-Age-As-The-Good-Student: It's the nose of
 Cleopatra, her no-o-se. (*She sits quickly down.*)

Old Man-Teacher: And the foot of a mountain. . .? (*He's clearly at the
 point of losing his self-control.*) Well, the foot of a mountain?

My Grandmother-In-Old-Age-As-The-Good-Student: Foot. Foot foot
 foot foot. (*Epileptic fit.*) Footfootfootfootfootfootfootfootfootfootfoot
 (*drooling*).

**Old Man-Teacher-More-Anxious-Cause-He's-Realizing-The-Dumb-
 ness-Of-The-Kids:** And what about Achilles' heel? Quickly. Achilles'
 heel, Achilles' spiel, heel and toe around is woe, don't show your cunt
 bare, bear. (*The Man-Teacher's penis now becomes real for the Man-
 Teacher a thing of flesh and blood it grows and grows.*) Heel! Heel!!

My Grandmother-As-A-Young-Child: Out of love.

Convict: Get me vittles. Pork pie and steak 'n' kidney pie 'n' tomatoes
 'n' cabbage. I got a young man with me and this young boy eats up
 children like you for supper. If you don't get me those vittles, this
 young man will eat up your nose, then part of your cheeks, your eyes.
 He likes big chunks of young girls' thighs. (*Grabbing her nose.*)

My Grandmother-As-A-Young-Child: I'll get you your vittles! I'll get
 you those vittles you want!

Convict: I'll tell you something. You might run away, but you can't run away. A child might be warm in bed, he might pull all the covers over his head, but my young man gets into the house, he gets under your covers, he gets at your toes, your legs. There's nowhere you'll be able to escape him! You can never run away.

My Grandmother-As-A-Young-Child: I'll get you the vittles! (*Running away.*)

Convict: Remember, child, remember.

My life

1 Childhood: Catholic blatherings

1 THE SON

(to Charlotte Bronte in
Brussels)

Dear Charlotte,

I don't know how to write with you, but I can for you.

I'm holing up like a bear now. I'm cuddled up in my sofa and here, under the endlessly heavy ocean, I peek eyes, two eyes round peer beep beep, our mother she was warm she was a warm person. Her big breasts sagged low and the flesh on her skin was thick. She wasn't warm to us because we were children and she was a child and wanted to be *the* child: she was warm to her mother. Childhood was green. The house's hall's walls were green and our bedroom's walls were green. Green was the colour I hated.

Father (*my* father, not the man who adopted me and had you) was really a murderer. I haven't found out who he is. He left mommy when she was three months pregnant with me because she was pregnant with me. Mommy adored him so since then she's shut herself off. I've shut off myself. He's our family ghost: Among all the things we and especially I can't touch, he's the most untouchable. When ten years old I asked Nana about him. (This was the first time I had ever asked anything.) Nana answered, 'He's sick. You can't see him.' 'What's he sick with?' 'He's dead, Emily. . .' 'Oh.' 'He's a murderer, Emily. You can't have anything to do with him.' This sentence made me know she was lying. Three years ago I traced his family. His first cousin, meeting me, propositioned me then told me his daughter fucks Soho bums and my father's mad. A year ago he murdered someone who was trespassing on his yacht. It might be dangerous to meet him since I'm his daughter.

It was the end of winter. It was one of those London days when the rare snow's melted and grey wetness is overlaying our eyeballs. The air stinks that the end is almost over. And the wind blows, wind so strong it was more powerful than a human being, it was the dog in our building who knocked us off our rollerskates every time he said hello to us.

In those hours the hours of not knowing just before we went out on the streets to play with other children, just feeling. Air pink satin hot air lots of time anxiety about the gigantic mother being left alone is peace glory from words in books. All the emotions are violent. I say to you, 'If you enter my life and who am I kidding you're already in my life which is the heart, I'll care about you there and want you there. I don't let people go easily. The more they're wedged in my flesh, the more I get sick screech when this skin's torn apart.' Everything is the body. Disease is just apparent pain. I can cry with all this life. I used to run around and fly, it was like running down mountains, the stars made my ecstasy the other side of anguish. I ran into the school library and dumped all the books on the floor. That didn't take much time. I told the girl they had ordered to room with me if she roomed with me I would knife her. From then on I lived alone. What are colours? They taught us names, but there are no names but impressions and connections. Our drawings were full of cruelty, pitfalls and aggression.

(*next day*)

Mother ordered us, 'You can't stay home all the time. you have to go down to the street to play with the other children.' We were kicked out of nothingness. There was no more nothingness. There were no ways we could fight her orders. She was absolute. We went downstairs, though we didn't want to. Outside (the sixth floor) was alien that is known. A thing is alien because I don't want it. We walked outside into this cold grey-brown. I held your hand. In front of the apartment buildings equally-sized squares divided the sidewalk. A bunch of girls played handball against the building walls which lined the street. Each girl owned a line of squares from the street to the wall. Whenever a pink rubber ball was in her territory, her open palm had to hit it once down on the sidewalk then into the building wall. If she didn't, she lost her territory. The girl who usually had the first territory or the head of the line was the most powerful girl.

Maggie, the most powerful girl, is my friend. We don't talk to each other. I don't know whether other people talk to each other because I only know how people act when they act around me. I'm not comfortable with language. I have nothing to say to anyone. Now I'm second-in-command to Maggie even though I don't have anything to do with language and other people. Language for me is private. If someone gives me the allowance to play then I can use language. My best game is when Maggie and I walk up to the whitest oldest most distinguished-looking guy we can find walking down our block:

: Excuse me, Sir.

The gentleman barely notices us. Then, bending down his crane's head: Yes?

: We want to know Sir, . . . (breaking into giggles).

The Gentleman, very kindly: What can I do for you?

: We want to know what (can barely get word out) a pee-nus is.

The Gentleman: Do you really want to know?

Bopping our heads: We really want to know. (Giggle. Giggle.) The gentleman: A penis is a part of the body every man has. It is long and straight and. . . (We run away giggling.)

Now our world where language isn't communication our world now, there is sex and masturbation but have nothing to do with communicating anymore,

I can talk by plagiarizing other people's words that is real language, and then. . .then I make something. Tonight I don't fuck someone who has a girlfriend anyway cause I want to be in this nothingness.

Dear Charlotte,
   For those who live in silence: to sing.

Dear Charlotte,
   1968 is over. 1981 is over. Future is between my legs ha ha.

Dear Charlotte,
   So people do come here in order to live. I thought everyone just died. Today I went out on the street. I'm just a mouse. R___ because he poisoned me tells me I'm crazy. If I'm crazy, what's sane? That is it's impossible for any person who likes herself to believe she's crazy. Today R___ told me I'm crazy so did the Dyna-Vent man because the Dyna-Vent isn't working because I make it not work, but when the Dyna-Vent man is here the Dyna-Vent works. Today I walked outside this room. When I'm outside this room, I become well. I think writers make themselves sick to write. I spent today crying. In a movie on TV an-English-earl-giving-a-little-boy-everything-he-wanted was my mother, but I wasn't included in this circle of giving because my mother gave me nothing. Whenever I don't do anything, I cry. I have to work as much as possible. I was crying because I was feeling the pain my mother felt right before she suicided. Or am I making this up? Is my picture of her pain actually a picture of my own loneliness? I want to talk about loneliness. Lonely people stink. I constantly think: I'm not talking to anyone these days. I've cut out all my friends. The less I talk to people the less I want to, so this wanting solitude or being solitudinous is a sickness. The next thing I say to myself is: I've lots of friends. The next thing I say to myself is: the reason all the parts of me don't fit together is that I'm not fucking enough. Whenever I talk to one of my friends I perceive my friend is even lonelier than I am because he's less willing than I am himself to see the loneliness horror and awkwardness: solitude: nothing: what I call 'the actual state of existence'. These people have to act normal to avoid seeing what really is, because if they did see like my father the day he was dying they wouldn't be able to bear it because it's not bearable.

Dear Charlotte,
   I'm thinking about loneliness again. All you think about is sex. You say it's love but it's not: it's cunt. I think: I have to meet my loneliness

face-on right now. Love I mean sex doesn't matter. I am alone. Melville says love does matter: we can be kind to each other: sweet your flesh why are you staying away from me?

You describe your acute physical horniness for me yet you're staying away from me but I'm not staying away from you. I become physically sick when I sexually want someone and I don't get that for an extended length of time. You write that also in you sex is almost death because when someone whom you sexually want rejects you you come close to physically dying. So I want, instead of death, flesh in the nose, waking up, sniffing, smelling, surcease ease. Now there are two times: no time and slow time. No time isn't the capitalists' substitution of commodities for values, as you say it is; no time is loneliness and the absence of love. The other time, slow time is touching someone.

Love, Emily

Dear Charlotte,

Black hole black magic. All so tragic. . . Sus (I can't read this word) fantastic. An anti-hell.

Dear Charlotte,

Today three English spies violently died. The first died in New York City; the second died in the Caribbean; the third died in New Orleans. Who killed these spies and are their deaths connected? The Circus tells James to find out.

A fortuneteller predicted James' arrival. 'He's coming here to ruin us! The devil. The world's going to end!' In New York City there are many cars and most of the cars, driven fairly equally by whites blacks and Puerto Ricans, are following each other. This is one of the reasons we can't live together. When James' in his taxi driving from the airport, a sniper shoots but doesn't kill him.

James walks into one of the voodoo shops. In a corner of his eye an amazingly fat black guy is disappearing behind a curtain. James follows this edge of vision to where the car in which the sniper was sitting stands. Two black men're driving this car and James', as they've planned because they're now controlling James, following them. In this way the blacks lure James into Harlem where every black's one of them. James' new taxi driver's one of them. The newspaper vendor is one of them. This is one of the reasons we can't live together. Because he's white, James is a dope and dopeiness is his intelligence. He walks into a black bar in Harlem which every white man knows is a dumb thing to do. Of course the wall against which he's sitting flips around so he's down in black bestial animal hell voodoo in where black man says 'Mr Big gonna take care of you woo.' James cause he's stupid tries an identity bluff. The fortuneteller whose territory is identity answers James, 'No cause and effect, baby. Voodoo. Nominalism. The blacks cause they know reality'll take over this world.' Mr Big: 'Hey, baby James. I is big so I take over you and this world only cause.' Mr Big wears white which is the colour of Jesus Christ the conqueror as every good voodoo person knows. His steel arm shows the union of human and nonhuman and of life and death within this living world. In a typical abandoned lot on to whose rubbish floor and graffitied rat and roach walls the sun daren't penetrate, this is one of the reasons we can't live together, a black CIA man cause there're only blacks in this land stops James from being murdered. That is: the whites are trying to set blacks against blacks.

My only question, darling, about reality is: Why does Mr Big want to knock off English spies?

Knanga is an important black diplomat but I don't know from where cause I never read newspapers. He is heading for San Monique. Innocent now-plucky-instead-of-dumb James is taking a bath in his luxurious San Monique hotel when a black-and-white snake jumps for his jugular. Wham! James since he's white has super-technology to burn up this snake energy. A black hat sparkling a bloody white feather.

Where in San Monique was the English spy offed? James' CIA (that is good) cohort is a black (that is evil) female (that is suspect). Having smartened up in matters of the world James tells her, 'You're evil. I'll fuck you anyway 'cause I have to fuck.' Fucking dissolves all evil. So in this voodoo land as she fucks she becomes white. Now vulnerable to voodoo, she sees big one-eyed voodoo mask in which life and death are inseparable. White people say: 'Too dangerous to be between good and evil. Got to be all good or all evil 'cause we want war.'

White people got love and black people got sex. (Except if you're like me you fuck everyone but your friends, but I'm kookoo.) Not like the dead black slut the beautiful female fortuneteller is white (that is good). James understands even though she seems to work for Mr Big she's good 'cause he knows understands that this world is only appearances and that these appearances are real only symbolically. Since the only reality of phenomena is symbolic, the world's most controllable by those who can best manipulate these symbolic relations. Semiotics is a useful model to the post-capitalists. White man say: Voodoo is power. Fortune-teller is pure white virgin. If you make her red, she die. James makes her red so she's no longer black (that is she can no longer tell truth, fortunes). Mr Big is going to kill her.

Everyone on this black island is black therefore after me. Everyone I see. Motorcyclists policemen washingwomen actors. I've got to run away. No matter how fast I'm moving, I can't move fast. I've got to get away from dying. Voodooland is dreamland. White people, if you can cut out your dreams you'll never lose your power. James can run fast. James can get away: 'Voodoo doesn't exist. It's just a cover-up of the real stuff, the heroin trade which is the only liquid-money business left in this world.' Evil versus good has become unreal versus real. 'I can protect you,' James tells his red and dead girlfriend, ''cause I'm all-powerful.'

The next world is New Orleans. In this total dream or belief the same taxi driver who drove James to Harlem is now carrying him to Mr Big. Cause every thing now means something James' black funereal mourners though James hasn't died yet are whooping it up. Our deaths are their lives. James walks into the same bar. The same wall, rotating, seats James in front of Mr Big who's wearing one white mask one black mask and whose real face is our death. 'James, did you make this girl red?' 'Yes Sir Mr Big I rape all girls.' 'Ha ha. Eyes' no voodoo man. You know reality. I'm just a little ol' drug man. I use white and black masks only to make money. My plan to make money is to give away the two tons of heroin I'm growing in San Monique through my American soul food restaurant chain. The Mafia won't have any business left, then I'll take over the stock during the lowest point of its depression. I learned my lessons from the American stockbrokers and CIA.' All blacks are whites. There's nothing unknown. 'You die, girl,' so the girl dies. They send James to the farm to rehabilitate him. This world isn't dream, but death. Alligators eat you up. Crocodiles even eat each other. Africa's the land of predatory animals. Dank jungles the tops of trees and bottom foliage so high and thick through which no sunlight can penetrate. Black people are black 'cause they live in perpetual night. During night there's no possibility of rationality.

James burns up Africa. He rationally knows why the English spies were murdered.

Dear Charlotte,

I know what evil is. I've known what evil is ever since I was three days old though it took self-consciousness to realize evil happens in this world. Evil is human and not natural cataclysm; I see a huge fire for hours murder people; well human mind refuses to accept (understand) both of these. Childhood is dumb senseless world there aren't distinctions so open to everything. But at the edge: outside. When does this outside begin to happen? The strange world like sex surrounds the child. Or everything is strange: banks tall buildings too many turds all around the head and there is no friend anywhere. The child can't know how to make friends. Nothing nothing. The horror. No way given to make one's way. No way given in this society in which to live. Nothing taught. Rules that is lobotomies taught. And if you don't totally succeed where there's no possibility of succeeding, you die.

In a high and lofty loft, formed from iron pillars, whose walls are great black holes through which the thin gasps of available air are blowing back and forth: the echoes of the city, the sound bounces up down especially in the top next to the sky; the hammers' pounding up and down mingle with the hissings of subways creeping over dead rats through the below unused city. The fire rages. At its edges: gloom, through which, lost, moving like the living dead among flames and smoke, one of their faces peeps, dimly and fitfully seen flushed and reddened by the near leaping flames. And nearer the fire men wielding great towers work like ants. Others the bums who get their daily salaries by dancing filthy wipecloths in front of car windows then spraying those windows with a liquid which renders them opaque, others, thin girls who by the time they're sixteen have only half their flesh left out of this gloom draw forth, as mosquitoes throw themselves on light bulbs rather than on sources of blood, to the great sheet of glowering existence which is emitting an unsupportable heat and whose light is either beyond white or the deep dull red Jesus Christ dropped on the cross.

Through bewildering lights and deepening sounds, with thoughts such as this and other thoughts of Utopia and hope and peace and human love and human calmness and personal happiness, the child, absolutely knowing nothing (and not even knowing this) and thus having only belief (Utopia and hope and peace and despair and horror) walked farther forward into this awful place: the green plastic garbage bags appearing again again never disappearing caused the form of unbearable because unending repetition. The same dream appears in every possible form. You are trying everywhere and every way to escape and can't the poverty that's no longer only or mainly material that is no possibility of friendships no love between man and the genital he pays for the end of marriages not even cried over she has to get out. To make escape possible. The whore and the old dodderer had abandoned themselves to the mercies of a strange world, and left all the dumb and senseless things they had known behind. What do I actually remember was childhood?

It's not so much a process of remembering as of now being a child. Now I say to myself. Mommy. I don't like you because I recognize you're going to hurt me. You're outside me. I don't say to you because I say the truth. Right now I like Jeffrey because he is my friend because he isn't hurting me. I am all alone so I have all my time with very few intrusions from the outside world to mull over my thoughts, for they are my dolls, though sometimes they torment me or rather the thought that I might be mulling too much torments me. R___ can hurt and can not hurt. These people have nothing to do with me. Due to my fearing, my world is apart. How can another person penetrate this childish world?:

1956. The Cegielski metal factory was the largest factory in Poland. As a result of the city communications and Cegielski factory workers' unfulfilled demands, the Poznan riots broke out.

The first thing we see is men, standing under doorways, shooting guns. There're no other people on the streets. We therefore have no way of knowing at whom they're shooting. During a workers' march to Kochanowski Street to free some political prisoners from the secret police, a cop killed a worker. The rest of the workers dipped the Polish flag into his blood and rioted. In this perpetual war there aren't any functional nations: the functional political distinctions are military versus civilians. The Polish police fled the city. The army entered.

Now we see one man. He's shooting, like all the other men. We and he have no way of knowing at whom he's shooting. All the newspapers therefore everybody blame the lumpenproletariat because the lumpenproletariat as stupid immoral drools in their inabilities to know and act define civilian life's actual conditions. The newspaper deny the lumpenproletariat's therefore ordinary people's existences: 'All Americans are Reagan." "All Americans are impoverishing all other people because all Americans own toilets.' The man who's been shooting comes home. He has to flee Poland though he and we don't know why, it's not because he's evil because he's a good man because he's responsible to his wife and children. His wife and children won't flee with him we don't know why so love is broken up.

Since the new reformist officials supported the Poznan riots, the civilians thought they had won. But the officials quickly centralized the workers' councils and reduced them to decorations. Military versus civilian seemed to equal centralized power versus non-centralized power. They either corrupted or removed the popular worker leaders.

I am in school because I haven't learned anything. Maybe, a little, the cause of my suffering. Nothing matters unless it is right now. I see you so my heart is stopping still.

What is writing about; what is writing? If it is anything: Adorno 'Art expresses the individual, the unique, the utopian, the critical, the new, the innovative vision' and is the opposite of opposes media advertising commerciality or the market. If writing's nothing: it isn't presenting a story, it isn't presenting an expression of what's real, since it's present it isn't even this (time past); it is; going back to beginnings. childhood beginnings.

Begin childhood from the very beginning. I have a great deal of difficulty beginning to write my portion of these pages, for I know I am not clever. Whether I shall turn out to be the hero of my own life, or whether that station will be held by anybody else, these pages must show. Among other public buildings in a certain town, which for many reasons it will be prudent to refrain from mentioning, and to which I assign no fictitious name for there's no need for fiction anymore, there is one for many many many years common to most towns, great or small: to wit no wit, a workhouse; and in this workhouse was born – on a day or date which I need not trouble myself to repeat because it isn't known and of course doesn't matter to you, the reader, at this point, at least at this point – the item of mortality whose name is prefixed to the head of this chapter. My father's family name being Pirrip, and my Christian name Philip, my infant tongue could make of both names nothing. In these times of ours, though concerning the exact year there's no need to be precise because it isn't known because everyone's a heroin addict, a boat of dirty and disreputable appearance, with two figures in it, floated on the Thames River, between Southwark Bridge, which is iron, and London Bridge, which is stone, as the wetness of life is closing in.

All Polish students think about is sex. I know my parents were some kind of revolutionaries right-wing or left-wing I don't know which back in 1958. The only thing I care about is how to get the boy at whom I'm staring to fuck me. Adam Mickiewicz in his play DZIADY shows that the kids who plotted against the Russian Tzar were heroes. The Russian ambassador closes down Kazimerz Dejmek's production. The boy doesn't want to fuck me because he wants nothing to do with sex. When the students protested the Russian-Polish censorship by occupying the university, students in Warsaw Poznan Krakow Wroclaw and Lodz supported them. For any revolution to succeed nowadays, the media liberals and those in power have to experience the revolt as childish irresponsible alienated and defeatist; it must remain marginal and, as for meaning, ambiguous. The Polish workers didn't understand why the students revolted, but gave them food. *His* older brother is the hunk of the school and the main revolter. The cops, acting normally, beat us all up. Some of us get physically gaoled. None of us no matter how well-educated or whether our families are rich or poor are going to get jobs. In San Diego: Marcuse lived in fear of his life. Whenever we were in a car, the cops stopped the car because, they said, we were bank robbers. Now the cops no longer bother us because we don't exist. My life doesn't exist. What did I learn in school? This music isn't non-music; it's violence. *This text is violence.* The ruling elite stuck its own people into the now vacant university positions. Boy, you're not only going to fuck me, you're going to make love The whole Department to me of Philosophy and that of Sociology You has disappeared. do. There's no hope; there's only romanticism.

Well the main thing is to fuck only people you dislike, says the older brother, – that is if you want to save your friendships and ability to love – 'cause sex is the rampant disease. In my family, my mother never talked to me 'cause mothers are above their children: they don't have to love their children and their children have to worship them. In this way my parents taught me love is an expression of power. Sometimes mom blabbed to, not with, me 'cause none of her friends were around at the moment with whom she could talk. Mom was the first person to teach me the world is other than me and that I live in silence. I don't talk to anyone: I talk to myself; I either play images with other people or do whatever they tell me to do. Grown-ups and kids are my enemies. 'Mom,' at the dinner table, 'I'm getting married.'

'Kathy. . . don't tell me.'

'Tell you what? I told you I'm getting married.'

'You are.'

'Are what, mom?' I know.

'We can get you a cheap operation.'

'I don't want a cheap operation.' My parents were always as cheap as possible with me; my mother spends every cent she can get her tootsies on even my allowance on gawky Gucci jewelry; 'I'm not getting married because of that.'

My mother has the usual look on her face of 'this stubborn girl'.

My father helps out my mother whenever she's too angry to lecture me: 'You're not going to have the baby?'

'What baby?. . .There are other reasons to get married!'

'You might as well tell us if you're in trouble.'

'Yeah, I'm in trouble.' I shoved my right inside wrist covered with razor scars over the dining-room table. 'Now don't ask me any more questions. I'm not going to tell you anymore.'

My mother turns her face to the left. 'Oh, Kathy,' my father as my mother instructs me, 'don't do disgusting things at the dining-room table.' Each time I slice the blade through my wrist I'm finally able to act out war. You call it my masochism because you're trying to keep your power over me, but you're not going to anymore. This is the beginning of childhood.

Now there is no possibility of revolting successfully on a technological or social level. The successful revolt is us; mind and body:

Theory: The separations between signifiers and their signifieds are widening. According to Baudrillard, the powers of post-capitalism are determining the increasing of these separations. Post-capitalists' general strategy right now is to render language (all that which signifies) abstract therefore easily manipulable. For example: money. Another example is commodity value. Here Baudrillard differs from Marx: according to Baudrillard, political power is determining economy. In the case of language and of economy the signified and the actual objects have no value don't exist or else have only whatever values those who control the signifiers assign to them. Language is making me sick. Unless I destroy the relations between language and their signifieds that is, their control.

Christ is rising on the cross. In the nineteenth century truth and beauty were. In the twentieth century use determined. Bohr, Werner, etc. Now destroy the twentieth century. Is use value a post-capitalistic construction? The value of this life is what I make or do. I live in absolute loneliness. What's the value of this life which is painful if it's not what I make or do in the world? Assumption of this question: I am the subject of the making and doing. I make (my) values or meanings. *I do* means *I mean*.

Given this syntax and grammar, functionality is the only possible value: I'm a Puritan; I write; I don't love; *I*.

But what if *I* isn't the subject, but the object? If the subject-object dichotomy is here an inappropriate model?

(Note: the war is now, further than the body or sensible fact, on the language level.)

I don't mean. I am meant. That's ridiculous. There's no meaning. Is meaning a post-capitalist invention?

The shits have made me. The shits have determined the sick bad relations of these parts sexually to each other. What I'm trying to say is that I can't just say, well human lives have always been miserable pain is just another event like shitting. Be above it (no meaning).

I buy lots of dresses. I don't need lots of dresses because I own lots of dresses. I have to buy a dress like I did today because buying it makes me into, one, a person who can buy and, two, a person who's buying a frivolous thing. By buying (eating) I'm bought (eaten). *I* am the commodity. The commodity buys me.

Take this formula farther. According to Marx: when I work, there's the actual value of my work and the market value of my work; the problem is that the market value is increasingly, now fully, the determinant of the work's total value. When a file clerk for Texaco, I spent all my working time in alphabetizing varying pieces of paper. Texaco could have had this work done more cheaply and quickly by computer. Why do they still hire file clerks? So we'll have the money to buy their products. So we'll have the money to be bought up. Marx's definitions of work value don't apply to my situation: I don't work. I am worked. On the one hand I'm in prison.

On the other hand everything's possible and is 'cause there's no more eye there's only romanticism. Romanticism isn't fucky fuck because at the end of the movie the older brother who's totally political runs away from Poland which I know's useless where's he going to run to, the USA? Even though your brother ran away, you're coming back here to me in Poland because you love me and you know your action is meaningless and useless too this is what I call romanticism not love never just love.

Descent into not talking to anybody, only romanticism.

Dear Charlotte,

The first time I met you, the next night we spent fucking, after two nights fucking we couldn't see each other again. I want to I want to be loved so desperately I've made myself invulnerable to love though not to fucking fucking has nothing to do with love. My mentality is a horror of burns and scars. By saying this I'm making you guilty for not loving me. You have a number of girlfriends. Your father has sent spies to separate us. Given all of the above, and the following consideration, that the pain when two people who have pledged their souls to each other and are brother and sister separate is disgusting: I can't even mention sex because it's too explosive. This scared running away from you is my running away from my memories: I'm being sexually hurt. I won't have anything to do with myself. I can't exist in such violence and also work. I want us to love calmly (the only impossibility). Now we're separate. If it happens you'll have nothing to do with me for the next two weeks or for ever, which I know might well happen 'cause human desires stop and no will can dictate desire, even though any contact with you is pain I won't stop writing you. I write you who I really fuck and when I'm celibate, though I know when we're physically fucking we're not so honest with each other. What is writing? This is writing. When I write you I just blab at the pen so I tell you all my grotty faults the awful despair: the French men I know acting as if they want to fuck or are fucking me whenever they're alone with me no matter how they feel about me, my hatred of the intellectuals who live on the upper west side of New York City, walking down black Orchard Street, Vivian Westwood's dress, President Reagan's using AIDS to control the American populace. These writings are the fuels of love. Each statement is the absolute truth – and an absolute lie – because I'm always changing. So, despite all changes, despite and due to all our emotional fluctuations and all the times you and I have to be in different parts of the world, these writings, this work will fuel our love. Only actors and actresses stably love.

That passionless Finlandia who's sticking her cunt in your face is a lesbian but keep on fucking her in London 'cause it's good in London – lots of energy in the clubs and on the streets 'cause the media doesn't control the streets there, yet, as they do here. Dream in your deepest bed about me but don't tell anybody you really know me, 'cause it's dangerous. Your father if he finds out is going to murder you. And don't wake up in your own bed, groin, and yell out to your nanny, 'She's got cancer again. She died. She jumped right off the Alps. A man ran a sword through her body. I saw blood come out of her fallen body.'

Wish me better luck. It was enough for me once to have had your lips and arms on me. –

Dear Charlotte,

What is this thing: human? What is the measure of human?

In his early twenties John Donne was a fashionable brilliant law-student, avid for every kind of pleasure and worldly advancement, not a debilitant, tidy, a ladies' man, a playgoer a theatre afficionado, and a great poet. Though he struggled and slaved, he wasn't a worldly success.

When he was thirty years old he had his first chance. Sir Thomas Egerton, Lord Keeper of the Great Seal, made him his private secretary. Donne was happy for the first time. His poems aren't sentimental – he doesn't care about beauty or love – and sex fascinates him: he can use sexual arousing as a tool by which to rebel against everything's that given. At the same time he secretly married his employer's second wife's niece. When her father found out, he got Donne imprisoned. On Donne's release, he made Egerton fire Donne. Because of his romantic passion Donne had to return to his former life of starving and grovelling in front of the knees of rich moneybags only now he had a wife and kid.

Dear Charlotte,

I want to tell you how miserable I am 'cause you're not here. The only thing that interests me about this situation is that you're able to make me miserable even though I don't know you and 3,000 miles separate us. When I or anyone writes paints (makes). . .that person is controlling. I make your body on top of mine. This isn't enough for me. The pain you write you feel and the pain I feel 'cause of this separation are just the unfeeling tools by which we're both making our new world. Like America. I bet the first Spaniards who sailed to America were scared. The first time a boy touched my naked flesh I was scared out of my mind. I thought I'm entering a new world unknown territory. Scared out of my mind, literally: this' what I like. What is this thing: human?

One day I want you so badly I'm going to die if I don't get you. The next day I'm absolutely uncaring about your existence. The weathers rage over the ocean; natural catastrophes happen. So known territory is the same as unknown territory. The world when I alone write (imagine) is the same as the world that we're writing and that's publicly happening.

This writing we're doing is the fuel of love and of indifference and of hatred and of the wish to destroy and of greed and of admiration.

Love, Emily

Dear Charlotte,

The more violent these weathers, this fearsome ocean hovering above my head (when I was a kid, once I had crawled into the triangle between the pink satin folds around the sides of my father's and mother's matching twin beds, two curled-at-their-tops bodies of ocean hovered above me. In that trough I was safe.): actual impersonal love. I'm safe in violence. To live in the realms of emotions though this might be too dangerous.

Taking this idea further: The main saying of the young boys I met in Haiti who knew that a third of them were going to die that fall 'cause the drought was ruining the avocado crop was 'Pas de problêmes'. The only words out of the only-rich-guy-I-know's mouth are 'The world's about to end' (just like the *Village Voice*) and 'All my friends do junk'. He hates himself more than anyone else I know, not that I know any other rich people (the only people in the world). Why are poor Haitian boys happier than rich American men? Obviously love matters, not wealth. Fuck parental stability. Fuck parental security.

Take this theory of emotions further: When I was a child everything that happened (to me) was either totally good or totally evil. Now I'm adult, events are partly good partly evil even institutions. The United States of American government can't be all bad. Its organizing and administering are defective and so am I. Only unlike me it hides everything. Now I've been saying a lot of bad stuff about this government so please, understand, I'm just exaggerating certain imperfections. These imperfections in terms of the overall historical imperative don't matter; they just affect, here and there, now and then, a human life. True example of this: Once the CIA heard a gang they were after would be in a certain Baltimore bar on a certain day. At the correct time the agents bust into the bar shot everyone in the place. Two old hookers, one junky, one fat bartender, etc. The gang was in another bar. Logical example of this: A perfect 18-carat gold watch. Each tiny exquisite watch part has cost a fortune and is perfect. Two tiny parts don't properly fit together. It's a tiny unimportant flaw that makes this watch disfunctional. When something matters to me, I return to my feelings. You and me.

Love, Emily

No Babylon love affairs no more.

3 CHRIST FUCKED THE WORLD

Dear Charlotte,

These last few days this MAN's been staring at me. He's ugly and he has only one eye. His eye is this hole which white drool comes out of.

His mouth his very lips are thin thin-lipped people have no emotions these lips are wrapped into a snarl. The beard is grey. His colour doesn't matter 'cause all beards stink 'cause they're snot. I remember when that Frenchman french-kissed me in France, his smell made me want to vomit though I was coming. Today, the house doorbell rang, though we can no longer afford a real house 'cause we're so poor; I opened the door 'cause I wasn't thinking I was day-dreaming as usual about this romantic theatre guy who absolutely doesn't want to fuck me. It's The Drool. I was so scared, I was surprised. Uncle's footsteps were coming all over through the floor, as usual wandering around, looking for his glasses. The Drool says: 'Don't you know me?' I recognize you. Uncle's voice yelled, 'Emily, I can't find my glasses.' All rapists who come to my door are lovers. I passed out of this world. When I came to, my love, I was lying on auntie's satin, the maid (I'm sounding like my mother who always said 'The girl' or 'She') *the slut* was in the room, so I said through my weakness to her, 'Slut. Please find this drool who has one eye and looks like a mass murderer. Beg him not to love me, leave me alone,' because you don't really love me and I've been physically sick 'cause I've wanted love so much, but now I'm recovering, a samurai. I serve only I don't know who I serve.

Love, Emily

(no heading)

The last letter I was talking about my health. I haven't told you the whole truth. I'm weak. It's hard for me to say this. Big farts are always coming out of my ass. My other disease is that I need love so badly – this is proof that either physical and mental are the same or that they're inextricably joined – when I fuck the wrong person I get sick and if someone I love leaves me I die. This situation's result is that I'm going to be an old maid. How can anyone be an old maid? I know the most horrible thing in this world is to be sexless. At the same time I know society's taught me to believe this 'cause men who don't marry aren't sexless, useless, and old maids: Men don't need sex to be real. It's better to be an old maid than to die. I'm being very serious now. Though I know I don't sound like it. I think I'm becoming an adult. But the thing that happened next amazed me. I was all set out to be an old maid. The Slut told me you had told her you're not a starving actor. Who the hell are you? I know we've never fucked. Worse: I don't know if you want to fuck me. Is my night-time ending? She also, excuse me, the Slut said you have lots of money. I don't care about money; I do. So now we can marry each other. Do you want to fuck me? I think so. But I'm stupid. Slut has forgotten all the details of everything you've said so I have no way of knowing what's real and what isn't real. I haven't seen you since all of this happened. I know you're just lying, you're being romantic cause the English are romantic and they don't mean anything by their romanticism.

What is the truth? Everyone's totally apart in this city. Everyone is madly 'cause unsuccessfully trying through success to stave off fear. Is this true? How can I know what's true? I don't even know if I eat 'cause I'm hungry or lonely or nervous. Now: I know you don't want me because I'm not wantable. That's a belief. Another belief which I think at least once a day is that without a man's love I have to shit. If some man would love me, a miracle would be happening. I'm really good to a man I love; no, I'm a real shit: everything I say false and yet, I love this life very much I know it isn't mine,

Yours: I love you!
sklare wer wird dich befreien?

Dear Charlotte,

I don't understand what you mean by what you say 'cause you're English. I don't have a girlfriend. As for Miss Blacker (you keep mentioning her) (I should say Ms cause I wouldn't want to offend you), I see Ms Blacker now and then you see a number of women too. No one talks about you as if you're married – the women you've been with say quite the opposite. To go by what they say between the sheets, you have a lousy reputation. So either we're husbands or we're fuckfaces. Or are you agreeing with their dumb ways of seeing things?

This Blacker, though she's trying to blacken and end our friendship by drooling with lips meant for better past-times, is a friend. You say she's pregnant *enceinte* with child, etc. If this' true, it probably is my kid. I'm enormously fertile. Fertilities-in-action, that is pregnancies, are like cats: cats jump on to and paw the laps of people who're allergic to them. She's one girl who should be pregnant: her reputation stinks so badly anything could clean it up.

I'm thinking about this matter further: I'm probably not the father. I always get my sexual genders confused. The snake publisher made her pregnant just so he could get back at me. He knew my reputation's so poor, I'd get blamed. Men act like this (women are more dishonest than men because women know how dishonest men are and can't fight back any other way). In other words these people with whom we're living are degenerate – 'degenerate' isn't a word I usually use and, when I do, I don't usually do it pejoratively – but in this case 'degenerate' means 'lives wasted in psychological dramas'. Let them all get each other pregnant and gossip nastily about who the father is: If she says the baby's mine, she can have it and throw it into the garbage of the East River. I will not take part in wastefulness. If I have to, I'll send her fifty dollars. Why, I don't know. I'm not a total pig. Give her the enclosed fifty and keep my name out of it; otherwise the bitch'll think

I'm guilty therefore responsible for her idiocy or idiot or shit that's why I'm giving her the money. Women don't understand they have to be responsible for their own actions.

The only person who visits us is M. the Abbé, the sole true grand family friend.

Dear Charlotte,

My uncle's best friend, the publisher (whom I mentioned in the last letter) Quinn, today semi-pissed in the steam-room though how anyone can be pissed enough to piss in a steam, told my uncle, 'Living would stink in his nostrils if he didn't steep it in Scotch.' My uncle and this man have been friends for years cause they never listen to what each other is saying only to themselves. His limbs were loosened; for love and longing and passion and pine were sore upon him; desire and transport got their hold on him and he turned pale. Such a political philosophy would avoid all war.

Love, Emily

Dear Charlotte,

Last night at my aunt's hotel, the Hotel Dorset, my aunt asked Gus the waiter for fresh cream she could take up to her room and then for a sixty quid meal tipped sixty pence. 'I saw you in *Hamlet*,' she says to Quinn.

'I'm not a ham, ma'am,' replies the jokester.

'Of course not, I'm paying for your ham. It's much too expensive. You were a perfect ghost you look like a ghost now, and your cock was huge.'

'That was a play cock, ma'am.'

'Whether real or not, his size's just what I need. If I could get hold of him after the play ends, he'd be able to fertilize my roses.'

'He tastes pretty good too, ma'am.' The cocky word-slinger is always thinking of himself.

'Sister,' my uncle, waking up from his alcoholic stupor, 'this man was never a ham. You're confusing him with Nell Gwynn.'

'I'm not a sexist,' my aunt in her confusions gulps down her seventh glass of wine. 'Whenever a man tells me he's a feminist, I tell him I'm a faggot.' Being drunk she turns the conversation to a less *entertaining* channel. 'Are you a richie, Mr Quinn?'

'I'm a sink of profligacy and extortion, ma'am.'

These are the men I keep meeting.

When mom was three months big with me, auntie was fond of soldiers. She even bought a few. She didn't care about money like nasty Americans. 1947, then right after the war, so a lot of soldiers didn't know what to do with themselves and how to earn money now that they

347

weren't killing. (Of course by now they've learned how to kill in all sorts of ways.) As soon as she ran out of money, 'cause even then the military was economically the largest and most costly profession in the world, she went on to the priesthood. They're the oldest militia and they know how, the Jesuits have taught them, to wait for their money. Within the confines of the confessional netting, the priest asked my aunt her sins. Gradually, within her recital, she let in sexual sins. Then a few descriptions. 'He put his cock into my ass.' The descriptions had more details. 'His cock was almost too thick for my asshole', to personal details, 'and I felt, I. . .I. . .' 'Priest, I'm masturbating.' 'Priest, do you want to know how I'm masturbating?' 'The third finger of my right hand which is covered with red nail polish is touching a tuft of my wet cunt's hairs, oh, above above, as I'm. . .talking to you, I. . .' The priest is in the booth with her 'Like this, baby?' 'Do you want to hear more?' Priests and bums probably because both are Irish (I love the IRA) being the most moral people in the world, quickly bore nymphomaniacs like my aunt. A nymphomaniac is someone who wants constant attention. To get help my aunt ran to her doctor. The sicker she could get, the more he'd treat her like a baby. She was so love-starved – 'cause in any of its serious that is violent stages even physical sex is always really love – she went so far out as I am, she lay on her deathbed and almost moved from the doctor back to the priest. Now she wants to get married. I want to get married too, but only for love.

Love, Emily

Only in nighttime I see you. In darkness, I feel you. A bride by my side. I'm inside many brides. Fuck the mothers, kill the others. Night Shift sisters, await your nightly visitor.

Der Charlotte,

Language begins in joy. Today I saw my publisher. He said to me, 'All the phenomena in the world are just signs for other truths. Our job as humans is to find out what each thing represents.' I think he was talking about my writing. 'One of the truths,' he continued, 'of human existence is a malignancy. Malignant because it's real and we can't understand it. I hate this truth which manifests itself as the fact that human life is suffering. People have and do live in pain.' He pounded his fist against the table until he bled in order to prove this point. 'I won't accept this!' Pound. 'That this is true!' Pound. 'I will fight against what really is!'

'How will you do that?'

'In the same way you females are fighting against male hegemony.'

'In the same way? Right now either a female dies of exhaustion cause she can't be a male and a female and live without love or else she's still in prison only now she knows she's in prison. Fighting against what's unchanging –'

'Are you with me, boys? Are you going to fight with me, down to the death, the dungeons of existence, to fight for our own impossible possibilities more and more?

breaking into joy

'Yeah! Yay!' Our blood was boiling with his blood. My scarf fell over my bad eye.

'Drink.' He raised the bottle. 'Drink the wine that is the only blood we can drink until we halt this flow of cannabilism this greed and diarrhea that's now coursing through our world. Help! Help!' he cried.

'Captain,' the second mate dared to interpose, intervene out of his strong beliefs about human identity and will that are common to New Englanders. 'Don't you think you're willing too radically, and by doing so, by ignoring or going against all that is given the world, you're endangering not so importantly yourself as all of us your men?'

'Your blood must be my blood and your eyes must be my eyes.'

The stubborn second mate continued, 'You have given yourself over to your work. This' what's generally happening all over the American eastern seaboard, for there's no other pleasure anyone can find. Your goal or job has transformed you. You're now a monster: all your energies're against what's given; you're Walking Death; you're going to destroy us men.'

'I will kill what is evil,' the man who choses isolation screamed. 'If I destroy part of them, it's for freedom.'

'The main characteristic of my American life is fame. Everyone wants media fame that is total isolation. For Americans, human identity has to be being against the world. What are the ramifications of this situation?'

Dear Charlotte,

I live alone. Anything else I write is nonsense. There's no other sentence except about knowing. I must tell you – I'm frightened. I must tell you – it makes me shiver.

What are the relations between pain and knowledge? Sometimes I'm lonely and I feel that that loneliness' painful. How can I deal with this pain? When I feel pain, I say to myself, since the pain I'm feeling is the same as any other occurrence I'm distant from it. Through analyzing and understanding I persuade myself I'm not in pain. But I know I'm in pain cause I feel it. Knowing (the cry, pain) isn't describing or analyzing or understanding.

How do I know I'm in pain? This isn't understandable.

Pain, or a cry, is primitive.

Any statement beginning 'I know that . . .' characterizes a certain game. Once I understand the game, I also understand what's being said.

The statement 'I know that . . .' doesn't have to do with knowing. Compare 'I know I'm scared' to 'Help!'

What's this language which knows? 'Help!' Language describes reality. Do I mean to describe when I cry out? A cry is language turning in on its own identity, its signifier-signified relation.

'To of for by' isn't a cry or language-destroying-itself. The language has to be recognizably destroying itself.

All of the above's description.

Cry: the incurable illness is the rule not the exception. Hiroshima is our rule, not the exception. Hiroshima was a historical instance of a meeting between two cultures, pre-industrial and post-industrial; my reality, between post-industrial and computerization. Today, the most interesting art is coming out of those countries in which political and cultural violence is the heaviest.

Cry: I want, above all, to avoid 'doing something about' my life, and when, from time to time, the obligation is put to me to make some sort of career for myself, and to prepare for my future, I try to meet these demands and always fail.

Don't, don't go. You must stay with me now. It is the last time. Be with me always – take any form – drive me mad! Only DO not leave me in this abyss, where I cannot find you! Oh Jesus! it is unutterable! I CANNOT live without my life! I CANNOT live without my soul!

Emily

Dear Charlotte,

There was an air-raid warning.

A ball of blindingly intense light shone in the sky. Then all of Hiroshima became dark.

A light brown haze took over the sky. Finely ground-up chalk seemed to be falling from the sky. Most of the houses were flattened to the ground.

There were some upright building foundations. the finely ground-up white chalk lay over the surfaces. All of the skins of all of the people bled. They felt pain. Layers of human skin peeled off from layers of human skin. People felt thirsty. Some of the peoples' faces were swollen to double the size. Fires starting in a dozen places moved from left to right. The railway ties blazed. The railway poles smoked either at their tops or halfway down.

In the sky there was a great an enormous column of cloud. This cloud trailed a single thick leg below. Its top flattened as its body below the top swelled opening like a flower. The cloud seemed motionless. Its head blew first to the east then to the west then to the east. Each time it changed its direction, part of it shot out an illumination that was reddening purpling lapis lazuli-ing greening. Its insides boiled. Its stalk twisted and grew. It was bigger than Hiroshima.

The sky was an almost oblique mass of tiny particles. The cloud grew towards the southeast. On the Yokogawa railway bridge track a long freight train lay on its side. On one side of the Yokogawa railway bridge thousands of people squatted.

A loud noise happened. It shook the ground. Immediately a column of black smoke rose to the sky in the northwest. Another loud noise happened. This happened again and again and the columns of black smoke. Fires in the forest above Futaba-no-Sato roared downward and threw red-hot stones.

Many of the inhabitants were jammed around the train station although the trains didn't work.

A man's back flesh hung limply down from the lower part of his back and the flesh on the back of his hands was loose like pieces of wet newspaper. Broken tiles covered the road.

Out of the city's centre a tremendous funnel of flame shot into the sky. The column of fire, growing, sucked in all the other fires burnt up the Fukuya Department Store, the Chūgoku Power Supply Corporation, the Chūgoku Newspaper Office, and the City Hall. Several human bodies floated in the water below the Miyuki Bridge.

Outside Hiroshima, the country floor was black. The thousand-year-old camphor trees burned and carbonized in the shapes of trees lay horizontal on the country floor. Silver drops of melted power cable lead dotted the sides of the roads. Live wires dangled from their iron poles. Most of the dead bodies lay on their stomachs and were naked scorched black and in a pool of shit. The corpses were many. Round black balls lay in the sand. Bodies floated down the river. A child tried to get milk out of her dead mother's breasts. The smell was nitrogen. A woman was carrying her dead baby. Many living people were diarrhoetic and vomitted.

Dear Charlotte,

The main thought in the morning is that I need to shit. Only as soon as I shit do I feel good. If people telephone me before I shit, I grudge at them on the phone. Today I grudged at my English boyfriend he's not my boyfriend he is English 'cause he hasn't fucked me. I don't know whether he wants to fuck me. I don't fall in love with those males I haven't fucked in order to protect myself only now I haven't fucked him and I have a crush on him. After I shit, I keep thinking about the size of the shit. Shit and rings are my main things. When I was a child, I was safe (happy) if I had a ring. Every week with my friends I stole a new wedding ring out of Woolworth's. If I let out a turd that isn't a bunch of hard little pellets (the worst) or watery disintegrating (I can live with this) and I have a ring, I can talk crap on the phone which I love to do.

I just found out my English boyfriend's very rich. Is this a problem? I don't think so. I think I can love him even though he's rich. My uncle, who used to hate his guts (I shouldn't use such a word) when he was a penniless actor, is now in love with him and will do anything to get us married. It's nice to get along with uncle; I don't care about the fact that I despise his feelinglessness and materialism, for I'd rather get along than not get along with the people who're in my daily life even if I hate them.

I've decided to not think about my shit due to my overwhelming interest in love. The guy on whom I've got a crush might really be interested in me 'cause he's been following me for the last three months. So I think we're going to get married. Today I'm going to my friend Rhys' wedding party. I'm going to drink a lot of champagne and never lie again, especially to him, or to any boy; I'm not going to pretend I'm not in love with him. It's a lie: pretending to be feelingless. All these emotions and interest unclog my blood valves, unknot my muscles, let the shit move through my guts. I've been shitting a lot more since I started this regime (no regime).

Last night Brandon died.

This is a turkey, *this* is a wild duck, *this* is a pigeon. They put pigeon's feathers in the pillows. In my sleep I don't die because my pillow has pigeon feathers in it. Tonight, when I go to bed, I'll throw it on the floor. Here is a moorcock's; and this – I can recognize it in a big pile of feathers – a lapwing's. Birdbird, whirring whirling over our heads in the middle of the moor. It wanted to get to its nest, for the clouds had touched the swells, and it felt rain coming. It dropped this feather on the heath; we didn't shoot it. That winter we saw its nest and its nest was full of little skeletons. H__ set his trap over it: the mother was too frightened of the trap to get to her dead children. I yelled at H—. I made him promise to never again be cruel to a non-human. Here are many lapwings! Did he kill those lapwing children? Are their bodies red? I will look at every bruise myself.

Love, Emily

Dear Charlotte,

Everything in the novel exists for the sake of meaning. Like hippie acid rock. All this meaning is the evil, so I want to go back to those first English novels: Smollett, Fielding, Sterne: novels based on jokes or just that are. Masculinity.

Love, Emily

Dear Charlotte,

When a young man was a child, his parents starved to death. A Buddhist priest found the abandoned child. He brought up the child.

Japan

The child, now a young man, meets a famous wise old man who says he knows something. The young man tells him he himself hasn't learned anything. The old man tells the young man to go to Buddhist school.

As the wise man and the young man are conversing, policemen and the prisoners cufflinked to them, walking by, chant that President Reagan is the best ruler even though Reagan'll be ending some of the prisoners' lives.

Two years later the wise man knows that the Reagan government's out to get him because he's wise and the Reagan government's ignorant. He's wise because, unlike most of us nowadays, he can touch what's really daily happening. The police arrest him.

While the cops drag the sage ignobly through the streets, a group of young novice priests stick a sacred chalice over the head of the young man who's now a priest. They can't get the chalice off his head. They ask the chained wise man to help them. The wise man can't help the young man who's lost his head because the young man, though he's in Buddhist school, doesn't know anything about himself. The young man can't change himself or anything else. The wise man tells the other dumb Buddhists that the young man will find his head only when he dies.

An unknown man tries to kill Reagan but instead drops William Casey. Reagan becomes more paranoid about his power. He and the sage plan to kidnap, bring up in secret, and if necessary murder the remaining Kennedy children. They have to act, as the wise man says, in accordance with the overall historical imperative.

Right now our main historical imperative is to preserve our imaginings, dreams, and own actings which Reagan is trying to decimate. The wise man says, if you government officials surrounding Reagan assassinate him, you'll save human civilization. We can't successfully revolt against our government because they control technological, military, and psychological information and power. But: there's one human power who's more ruthless, greedier, and stupider than Reagan. This power lives in the far East.

An essay on the relations between government and morality: A presupposition of any government is that humans need social rules to curb their innate greed, angers, lusts, etc. Rousseau said that, to the contrary, social rules make us act in the ways we have to in order to destroy these rules. If this is true, why do we need to be governed? This solution is idealistic therefore useless. How can a government whose nature is power be good? Only if the governor knows what's good for his people. Human beings don't know in this way. A governor has to be in a morally impossible position. He has to become who his position says he is, just as an artist is exactly what is given.

This powerful stupid yellow ruler who lives in the far East can only speak broken English. Missionaries who dared stormy seas to enter this foreign land converted his first wife to Christianity. At the present time the United States needs missionaries more than the foreign land does. Since she's only yellow and slant-eyed, George Bush tries to fuck her while the sage and the yellow monster are planning to overthrow the government of the United States of America.

Yellow people are taking over the United States of America. They own the vegetable groceries, golf courses, fashions, technological designs, and car manufacturing plants. Unlike us, they believe in wisdom. They're going to make the sage the American vice-president and instil desperately needed anti-materialism.

For the last six months the American people have been reacting to the constant political nausea, fluctuating economy, and social breakdown by returning to their only memories of social and political stability: the McCarthy era. They are worshipping various post-capitalist phenomena such as the nuclear family. Such contents are now hollow or formal; only the forms are sacred, thus the hypocrisy of the middle class; no American believes in anything. If nothing's real, how can anything be real and is this hell? Yellow gooks are infiltrating our civilization and now they're destroying it. They wear two feet high purple hats trimmed in fur. Their eyes are the eyes of insects. Their men have tongues which move up and down a hundred miles an hour. Their men like whips better than cunt hair. They are, one, stopping the freedom of our civilization; for instance, artists in their country have to do exactly what the government officials tell them to do. They are, two, eradicating all Western anti-social heroism individuality and weirdness, all blackness, all our civilization is really depending on. The yellow gooks are taking away our selves. 'Without white minds, white people be much happier.' Wise men says, 'If white people can be lobotomized white people want lobotomy: white people have no dreams.'

Actually beyond our cliches which are beliefs, actually outside our cliches which are beliefs.

President Reagan.

What is Japan?

Wittgenstein: Can I describe (know) anything truthfully? No.

I: For me when I love I don't know and this is Japan.

My love, the quality of love.

My love, pain's within rather than is love.
Solitariness.

As for solitariness, the great forests of the north, the expanses of
unnavigated waters, the Greenland icefields: still the magic of their
changeable tides and seasons mitigates their terror. But the special curse
of the Encantadas is that to them change never comes; neither the change
of seasons nor of sorrows. Finally ruin itself can work little more in this
place. They were cracked by an everlasting drought beneath a torrid
sky. Man and wolf alike disown this land. Little but reptile life is here
found: tortoises, lizards, immense spiders, and that strangest anomaly
of outlandish nature, the iguana.

The yellow men have captured Reagan. They bow to him and say,
'We are not original. We take what is given such as American know-
how, do it better, then send the products – such as clothes, machines –
back to America. We adopt everything. We adapt to everything. We
adapted to Hiroshima. (Bowing.) Hiroshima was the way we adapted to
your non-adaptable civilization. Now we give Hiroshima as a reality
back to you. (Bowing.)' Reagan's head appears stuck on a white pole
yellow with dog piss. Blood drips down the pole's sides. 'Reagan's head
appears stuck on a white pole yellow with dog piss. (Bowing.) The self
is the object, not the subject. We don't adopt; we are adopted. We don't
know who our father is and our mother hates us because our father
abandoned her because she was three months pregnant with us.
Language knows only when it cries. (Bowing.) A child who's been hurt
is the devil and must cause social pain. (Bowing.) How is it possible to
govern? (Bowing.) During Pearl Harbor, not as in *The Winds of War*,
the white people screamed the yellow devils were going to decimate
them and the yellow people, who like my mother were very sensitive,
killed themselves. (Bowing.) Somewhere there has been a breach of
honour.'

Love, Emily

Dear Charlotte,

As far as I can tell, both Nietzche and Wittgenstein thought their
lives were painful.

Ludwig Wittgenstein was born into the midst of all possibilities
including great art and wealth. When he was a young man he gave all
his family wealth to his siblings even though they despised him. He
wanted nothing or he had turned against himself. He turned to studying
mathematics then philosophy with Gottlob Frege then Bertrand Russell.
He left his graduate studies to live in Norway as alone as possible. He
wanted nothing or he had turned against himself. In the end of World
War I he wrote his doctoral thesis in an Italian fascist prison. He had

given away so much money, he couldn't afford the travel fare to return to Russell. When he asked Russell, Russell sent him the money.

I think he hated his body rather its demands, for he was celibate except now and then there would be two or three weeks of violent nights, fuck every young boy by the river, the body pleasures until the desire for love and friendship turns around and vomits. As in me the fierce longing to unite affection and sexual desire or the mind and body is the basis of living pain.

He loved his job teaching just-adolescent boys in southern Austria. The hicks took away the job from him 'cause they thought he was corrupting his students though he probably wasn't.

I say I'm in pain. Is my pain hidden from you? Can you see my pain? Say, there's a group of people who don't know what pretended pain is. If one of them says 'I'm in pain', the others cry. Someone teaches these people the phrase 'to simulate pain'. A beggar says, 'I'm in pain so please give me money.' Now: Is simulated pain a kind of pain? (By analogy, if I accept the model of analogy, I'm asking about the relation of falsehood to reality.)

I can only be in pain if I know what pain is. I'm in pain so I know what pain is. If I know what's pain; when I'm pretending pain, this false pain can't be pain.

Now take the example of 'hidden pain'. Example: when I feel pain as I am now with this ulcer, I pretend I'm not feeling it so you'll keep believing me and so you might still love me. Hidden pain is the same as simulated non-pain. Therefore simulated pain is overt pain. This kind of logic's useless 'cause it has nothing to do with human intentionality.

'Your inner self is hidden from me.' This means: I'm unsure how to describe your words and acts. I can only guess at your feelings. I am burnt and cry out. I wouldn't call this 'pretending'. We teach each other language. We don't teach each other to cry out. What, then, is 'pretended pain'? Am I pretending to cry out to you?

Nothing is hidden from you; if I were to assume something's hidden, I would be assuming a psychology or description less interesting than your intention, the cry. I affirm life and life doesn't need affirmation. I am lying down for you, Charlotte, and spreading my legs.

Emily

2 Teenage Macbeth

The English Are The Good Guys and The Irish are The Bad Guys

Note: All the characters can, obviously, be played however the actors and actresses want. Total schizophrenia or freedom, including any distance between player and character, reigns.

All the English characters are either upper- or upper-middle class or identify themselves as such.

Macbeth: Repetition one

ACT I

1. The two sides

As yet there's no language. These words, therefore, must just be shown: what is war? War happens when one side fights another side.

Side One (*still no speaking*): Nothing given to or understable by humans. **Nothing's Appearances In The World** (*still no speaking*): In geographical terms, the desert. In psychological terms, those who aren't rational logical or understandable to humans: the witches. In epistemological terms: not-knowing. In verbal terms: prophecy. In temporal terms: only the future is reality.

(*There are huts made of earthen sods, or of mud strengthened with straw; the rank reek of the wet turf on the heath; the smoke that blinds the eyes as one creeps into the interior: ((Rain brown-dripping through the thatch; in this webbed murkiness men and women and children and animals huddle. Human beings live like this. Description of nothingness.))*)

Side Two: Something: We English who are honourable and just. In geographical terms: our stronghold in our empire: Ireland. In psychological terms: reality is only and exactly that which appears. We aren't liars. In epistemological terms: we understand reality, therefore define good and evil. In verbal terms: simple declarative statements. In temporal terms: the past which we're naming or history is the present.

2. The two sides have identified themselves. Now war can begin. Each side starts fighting by trying to lay out its territory.

Let's say that the English or Side Two is White and The Irish or Side One is Black:

England: The past is the present. Ireland challenged our natural hegemony. We own all that's natural or the world because we're upright and honest. (They do stand very straight.) The rebel Macdonwald, though he was a Protestant being a Mac-, fought us and we, because we're in the right, have defeated him. The Irish who identify with us are English. The Porter who though Irish is English killed the traitor Macdonwald. Therefore, The Porter will be allowed to be Protestant, really English, and noble.

The Irish Bitches. (*They don't wear anything. Neither shoes nor stockings,* nor any covering whatever on the head and have no churches but unnatural ones their own. Some shreds of flannel which might have once been a slut's underpants. One tattered shirt of unbleached linen ties around one old crone's waist. Another sports a rotted blanket over her bone-thrusting-through-flesh shoulder. The final bitch has made herself out to be, at least in her opinion, feminine. Her hands have shoved her hairs so filled with filth they can be moulded like clay into the shapes of birds.

(Pride, passion, and disdain dilate their eyes' pupils.

(Human beings are these Bitches' drudges, slaves, horrors, and conveniences. The ruling idea or the only perspective they want to communicate is that no event fits into its context and, at the same time, necessity compels every event.

(The Second Bitch's a child. Passions predominately avarice're owning her mind and therefore actions): We're malicious and cause causeless revenge. In this world Nothingness' chaos. We'll make The Porter and his friend Banquo, who're coming here, our territory by convincing them our Irish future's more real than their English past.

(The Porter and Banquo arrive in front of The Bitches.) Porter, you will be our leader therefore you're our leader.

The Porter: I believe you not 'cause I've any reason to believe you, only 'cause I want to believe you. This world's desire.

Banquo: I never believe in cunts or holes. Females always lie 'cause all they do is talk from feelings. All of my friends, 'cause all English are, are male. (The Porter and Banquo, once friends, glare at each other. Civil war begins.)

3. Nothingness or the Irish uses the Porter to advance its territory.

The Porter (thinking alone in the maze of the forest): I believe the Bitches: I'm going to rule Ireland. But how can I rule a country that belongs to another country? England owns Ireland. England'd rather start World War III than give up her favourite colony, the economic portal to Western Europe. England's more powerful than me. I can't fight such power. I can only fight by being devious. Deviation is my war strategy.

Now: Our Irish Prime Minister – ours? – is relying on trusting me. I'll murder him. The Irish character isn't straightforward.

4. Nothingness extends its territory not only through the Porter but also through his wife.

Mrs Porter: I'm confused. On the one hand, I'm human just like my husband; on the other hand, I'm unnatural because I'm female. Females are those beings who only want revenge. My humanity has tempered infinite revenge into caused revenge or ambition. Irrationality, Animalism, and Night: own me. Since I can't know, I don't want clinging to my thoughts fucking up my mind.

5. *The other side, something, defines its territory.*

In the Porter's castle

Duncan (*the Irish Prime Minister. Very properly*): We English are good, honest, and kind. Natural owners.

Mrs Porter: We hope our hospitality'll reflect at least half Your Kindness.

Duncan: I'm sure you're as good as Us.

6. *Nothingness repulses something by rejecting something's goodness.*

The Porters talking to each other in their castle.

The Porter (*pondering*): Either events are caused or rational, or else there're no causes no morality no justice. If the first is real, I should keep being a fake or English. If the second's real, the Irish must control Ireland. Since I'm ambitious, babe, I'll opt for the second. This reasoning's circular. So I've no reasons for choosing nothing.

Mrs Porter: You're back in the 19th century! How can your reasons or so-called rationality be separate from you? And if your reasons're you, there's only desire and will. Therefore there's no morality in the 20th century: there's only ambition.

So either play at being a good boy like the English and as the English want you to do, or by recognizing who you are and being responsible for it, be adult.

The Porter: You mean: 'Kill the Prime Minister'?

Mrs Porter: In this century what we know as 'natural' our conquerors have invented as their identities and use as a tool to control us.

The Porter: I'll destroy this human malignancy to our land by acting hypocritically and spying.

Mrs Porter: You'll take over the rule of Ireland then?

The Porter: It's evil to want political power.

Mrs Porter: In this century the only way a human can't be a slave is by being evil.

The Porter: You're arguing rationally for irrationality.

Mrs Porter: I guess I'm nuts.

The Porter: I guess we've chosen to be mad rather than good and knowledgeable... (*It's nothingness' advantage.*) ... OK, Voodoo, since I can't know anything: I don't know this body therefore this body's dead; I don't know anything therefore language is all lies. (*In uppitty English accent.*) Welcome, Your Highness. (*Bowing.*) We're so proud to have you here. May we eat the scraps of filet mignon off your plate? That's better food than we usually see. Your spit is our blood. Are your mummy's polo ponies teething properly? Perhaps they would like to teeth on our corpses? Here a corpse's bones're supposed to be full of calcium. (*Pauses. Now in a very lowly peasant's tone as if his mouth's full of shit.*) I'm not sticking this knife in your back, Sir, 'cause I'm ambitious. You've already made me a Caw-tholic or Protestant or whatever the Hell religion is. I'm killing you, Shit, in order to kill you. I choose to be the head of the IRA.

ACT II

1. *Having repulsed the first English attack the Irish, getting courage out of nothing, try to extend their territory to the Porter's friend Banquo and to everywhere or nature.*

In the same castle.

The Porter (*blurting it out*): Banquo, what d'you think's more important? Friendship or political morality?

Banquo (*standing up very straight*): Political morality. (*Not taking The Porter seriously.*) Do I grade correctly?

The Porter: You *are* English (*Aside*). So I'll murder you and your children. I choose political morality too. But I'm not pretending I'm not contradicting myself. (*Looks at Banquo to see if he notices anything.*) Jesus Christ! The sky's so fuckin' beautiful: Masses of clouds on clouds bluer than the sky. This' the first time in months I've felt happy: the sky's making me feel space. I'll never sleep again. Every human must become space all the time! I will space! So I don't have the time to relax. If I had the time to relax, I'd fuck men by the score 'cause having a man love me's the only event that relaxes me. My life's without rest; my life's now made; my life's now hollow. Goodbye, life! Goodbye, ambition! I had to die anyway because all humans die. I'm dead: I'm unnatural: I'm alive only because I make. The hell with wanting to fuck. Let Banquo be his natural naive self. The English might rule the world, but they're more innocent than us.

(*Outside the castle.*)

A Tree: They're against us because we're natural.

A Baby Bird: I'm not natural. I'm full of cancer cause they stuck hypos full of carcinogens into mommy's eggs before I was even able to fight.

A Tree: You have to be natural: you're Nature. . .

The Water: I'm polluting my brothers and sisters.

Reality: The Irish don't have to destroy us because they're so full of self-hatred and hypocrisy we, being out-of-balance, are reacting. The pendulum'll swing more and more violently 'cause there's no way out of Nature.

(*In the castle.*)

The Porter (*all alone*): Morality makes a-morality and a-morality makes morality. Human will makes causality; causality destroys my ability to perceive. (*Screams. His wife runs in.*) I want a lobotomy. (My main nightmare: that of wanting one.)

Mrs Porter: To Hell with you. To Hell with you.

The Porter: I'm already in Hell.

Mrs Porter: They've been lobotomizing me for years. I'm more of a man than you are.

The Porter: You could win out over anybody. You're like Mike Arguello.

Mrs Porter: Who's he?

The Porter: A fighter.

Mrs Porter: I don't approve of macho shit sport. (*Her egoism wins over her good judgement.*) How's he like me?

The Porter: He's the greatest bantamweight cause, not only has he fought at every different weight, but he gives and takes an unbelievable amount of punishment.

Mrs Porter (*spreading her legs and throwing them over The Porter's blood-smeared mouth*): Is that why you won't fuck me now?

The Porter: I'm about to murder. Go away.

Mrs Porter: You know you're a sadist only your sadism isn't confined to your bed. All I want to know is how conscious are you of your obsessions?

The Porter: If I'm going to be a good artist, I have to judge myself as little as possible. (*So The Porter must even get rid of human knowledge.*)

Mrs Porter: I think I'm falling in love with you cause you won't fuck me anymore.

The Porter: Unnatural has become natural: You love me only cause you're repeating your father's unwanted rape. Cause you said 'No' to him, you can only say 'Yes' to a man who doesn't want you who's rejecting you. Victims like you, not the victimizers, suffer; or the victimizers are victims.

2. The IRA kills off the Irish Prime Minister

Macduff (*an Irishman who loves the English 'cause the English have enrolled him as Chief of Police*): Knock. Knock. (*Knocking.*)

The Porter: Who's there?

Macduff: Ida.

The Porter: Ida who?

Macduff: I don do anything

The Porter (*still not opening the door*): What *do* you want?

Macduff: I wanna fuck you.

361

The Porter: Oh then, come in. (*Opening the door, sees Macduff*) Shit, you're going to hurt me.

Macduff: Our English Lord is dead! Our English Lord is dead!

The Porter: Cut out the capitals: you're not Caw-tholic.

The RUC (*entering and shouting*): Treason's somewhere in this castle!

Mrs Porter: Alas.

The Porter: I don't want to be fucked anymore.

Macduff (*to The Porter*): Give a damn.

(*The Irish Prime Minister's sons, Malcolm and Donalbain, one who's ten and the other who's twelve years old, enter.*)

The Porter (*to these two boys*): Give a damn. This' Hell. Your father's been murdered. Don't make a sound.

Donalbain (*the elder*): Is it suicide?

The Porter: Absolutely not. The evidence points to unknown causes.

Macduff: Let's go to war! The Falklands! Who killed him?

The Porter: The butler, of course. (*Mrs Porter, who's been fucking the butler, faints. The Porter kicks her*). Ignore her. All she wants is attention because she's a failed actress. Women can't go to war to get what they want.

3. The English fight back by arranging their defence.

Same room

Donalbain (*to his brother in secret*): Keep your trap shut. It's better to have neither your own language nor identity these days. Just like Arguello, be reservedly polite continously until it's time to come out: Then, kill.

Malcolm: I'll retreat to England. England's peaceful cause she's making her colonies, especially Ireland and Scotland, fight civil wars.

Donalbain: I'll retreat to America who learned imperialism from England.

Banquo: I don't know.

4. Because the Irish are beginning to control their territory, they're wrecking their territory. 1845.

Outside The Porter's castle, the tips of the potato stalks wither. The decayed tubers' stench flies into the hovels and turns the air into gas. Thousands of people are starving, but the Irish don't care about their own people.

Young Irish Lad (*tousled-haired and freckled*): This fall I'm probably going to starve to death. So what. My mother's starving to death now.

Daniel O'Connell (*the famous Irish leader who uses language to lie to the Irish*): We've conquered England, babes. Robert Peel our main

English enemy, has just slit his own throat 'cause he won't back down from opposing the repeal of the Corn Laws.

Robert Peel (*in haughty British accent*): You're right. I'm resigning from the English Cabinet. The Cabinet's all yours, Lord John Russell.

Lord John Russell (*even more haughtily*): Excuse me. I can't form a Cabinet because I'm an aristocrat.

Robert Peel: OK I'll take back the political responsibility. The English people'll have cheap corn. The Irish colony'll have no corn. And there'll be an Irish Coercion bill.

O'Connell: Death by fighting for our country's better than this slow mass-murder of the Irish. (*O'Connell, because he chose to deal effectively politically lost his human judgement of human beings. The non-IRA Irish, who know the English bring order to Ireland, have to retreat from this wreck.*)

Macduff: I'm going to hole up in the Belfast.

Ross: I'll go with you. We'll fight from there.

ACT III. IRELAND IN ITS YEARS OF SELF-INDEPENDENCE

1. Political power as a living existent to stay alive must expand. Nothingness keeps trying to extend its control to Banquo.

Outside the IRA stronghold

Banquo: I know who killed our English master. The Porter who's now the Thane of Cawdor Glamis and the head of the IRA offed him. (*Now Banquo considers.*) Since The Porter acted against the English, he became politically successful. Should I do the same?

(*At the same time, inside the IRA stronghold.*)

The Porter (*to Mrs Porter*): We have to make Banquo one of us.

(*Outside.*)

Banquo: In a corrupt political society if you fight that society by the opposites of corruption, you don't get anything accomplished. In a corrupt society to fight society you have to be corrupt. I'll stick with The Porter and be Irish. It takes an Irishman to hate an Irishman. I'll be corrupt.

(*At the same time, inside the IRA stronghold.*)

The Porter: I'll murder Banquo. It's the easiest.

Mrs Porter: What about his children?

The Porter: I'll murder them too.

Mrs Porter: How many terrorists do you think we need?

The Porter: Two.

Mrs Porter (*going for the phone*): I'll get two. I'll get two who are so autistic, they don't care what's going on.

The Porter: They'll be easy to find. Murder solves my fear.

Mrs Porter: Murder some more. You're a whole country and if the English don't care about the Irish, why should you?

2. *The Irish territory.*

Same scene continuing.

Mrs Porter: I'm unhappy.

The Porter: Don't lay it on me. I can't handle my own problems.

Mrs Porter: You don't understand. I don't know what to do. Even thought hurts me. It hurts me to think.

The Porter: You'd be better off dead.

Mrs Porter: considering: If I was dead, I'd be really asleep. I'm dying to sleep.

The Porter (*whose egoism has to override her*): Everything I do's out of fear. I hate this kind of existing. How did I start living this way? (*She tries to answer*). You, shut up. We're all going to die anyway. Why's my whole life governed by fear of the one event that has to happen to me? Then if I'm not scared of death, what's there to be scared of? Why am I still always scared? The life which I know which is anxiety and fear is a prison. I want to be out of prison: I want to be dead. Why should the one thing we want most scare us the most?

Mrs Porter: You're not going to kill yourself so you might as well consider your ambition. The IRA isn't, to say the least, in the solidest of positions. Let's grant what you're saying's true: this living isn't worth considering cause it's just a prison whose director is fear. Therefore: There's no morality here. No causation for us. We can do whatever we want. Anything including hypocrisies and lies are just tools. Every event's unreal and separate from meaning. If this' all true, why am I feeling so much pain?

The Porter: My mother trained me to always kiss my elders 'Hello' even if I hated their guts. I hate hypocrites. I will say 'I hate'. I will go for ambition. All that's so-called 'natural' is neurotic. I'll tell you what's really natural: sex. . . (*He doesn't fuck any more 'cause he has so many political responsibilities.*). . .holocausts, murders, any extraordinary events, peoples'-fingers-getting-cut-off, sexualities that make people crazy always: these're natural.

3. *The IRA lose a battle.*

The two Terrorists Mrs Porter phoned plus one other who isn't recognizable it might be The Porter, in black masks, stand inside an office building. The fluorescent light is even.

A Terrorist: Are they coming?

(Banquo and his children enter the building. He wears a businessman's hat. They're regular little boys. The Terrorists jump them. Just as Terrorist 1 has his left hand holding one of the son's hands at the back of the son's neck and, in his right hand, a knife two inches in front of this same neck, the lights go out. In the black.)

Terrorist 2: What happened to the light?

Banquo *(gurgling in blood)*: Murder. . .

Terrorist 1 *(as Banquo's son gets away)*: Where'd he go? *(Scuffling as he looks for the child.)* The lights went out so the kid's escaped me.

Terrorist 2: Who turned out the lights?

Unknown Terrorist: This' the first time our side's failed.

4. The Irish territory's insecurity.

A grand IRA feast's taking place in The Porter's castle which, of course, is a hut. The food is potatoes and nettles. Irish people eat all the time. They eat only with their hands. Their noses're red. Terrorist 1 and Terrorist 2 barge their ways into the unruly drunken mob.

Terrorist 1 *(to The Porter)*: We got the father.

Terrorist 2: But not his son.

The Porter: The son's more important than the father.

Terrorist 2: How come?

The Porter *(hitting him)*: How dare you question your leader? This' military rule. *(Aside)* The son's the first human I haven't been able to murder.

Terrorist 1 *(being Irish; quickly)*: We'll do whatever you want, sir. For money.

The Porter: Do you think the IRA has money? That's why we use terrorism. *(Looks behind him, starts back in terror.)* Blimey. What the hell's going on here?

Banquo's dead body: Hell. You know that, dumbie.

The Porter: I know that. I killed you. *(Looks around to see if anyone can hear him. The Porter's scared of his own mother.)*

Banquo's dead body: Death isn't your business.

The Porter: What *is* my business?

Banquo's dead body: The Irish don't have any business. Give up, Porter.

The Porter: I can't give up nothing. I won't give up nothing.

Banquo's dead body: Shh. Someone might hear you. Don't you have any social sense? Look: *(A scene of The Porter getting married. He's very happy.)* Is a man who fucks English or Irish? Look, Porter. *(Shows him two long very thin snakes like paper strips who, as they rise* *out of the African river, grow. The snakes rise to The Porter who, then climbing upward, they begin to reach because each time they rise they grow. The Porter's about to scream in the land of Apartheid.*) Is a man who lives according to fear Irish or English?

The Porter: I don't know what to think. I'm the IRA leader and I'm as confused as Hell.

Banquo's dead body: Englishmen're never confused 'cause they don't concern themselves with death and they know to not think. Stop murdering, Porter.

The Porter: I'm not murdering: I give the past present and future Irish their self-control.

Banquo's dead body: No person can give another person power.

The Porter: I should give up. (*Banquo, having won, disappears. The Porter turns to his IRA men.*) Stop eating as if you've the ability to be hungry and go on home.

Tousled-hair and freckled lad (*who's now anorexic*): We don't have homes.

(*Outside the IRA stronghold, before the humans begin to dribble back somewhere like tiny black figures.*)

Morning: I'm the secret man of blood. I have to fight. Let all the mourning in this universe come out.

(*Back in the IRA stronghold.*)

The Porter (*to Terrorist 1*): Now. Where's Macduff?

Terrorist 1: You won't be able to get at him. He's holed up in his home in Belfast.

The Porter: I didn't get Banquo's son and I can't reach Macduff. (*decides.*) I don't care if it's useless, I'll fight for the Irish. Now that I've made my decision, I won't think: I'll plan. (*Calls all his men to him.*) This' guerrilla fighting. Don't think. Follow orders.

5. *Sex lies under power.*

Eleanor Courtenay's public memory.

Eleanor Courtenay (*to O'Connell in his Merrior Square home*): Sir. I hate to bother a busy person like you. Everyone says you're more than kind and I don't know where else to turn. My father, he just died, left me a small estate in County Cork.

O'Connell: You were here before, weren't you?

Eleanor Courtenay: You asked me to return.

O'Connell: I did? Oh yes. What can I do for you?

(*End of Eleanor Courtenay's public memory.*)

Eleanor Courtenay: Vain were all my struggles, all my prayers, all my cries for sustenance: the man O'Connell descended into the brutality of the monster and wouldn't leave me to sink into apathy until he had finished and finished and finished the most amoral remorseless and revengeless atrocity which humans have ever perpetrated on each other.

Priest: (*masturbating behind the confessional's bars*): What happened next, child?

Eleanor Courtenay: I had a bloody kid.

Priest: Why was it bloody? (*Suspiciously.*) Was it conceived unnaturally?

Eleanor Courtenay (*properly*): Of course not, father. Rape's very natural these days.

Priest: I simply meant that you had no money.

Eleanor Courtenay: A woman who doesn't have any money has to get money out of a man. After O'Connell raped me, he put his right hand on The Book and swore by the Virgin Mary he'd support me.

Priest: Does he know you had his child?

Eleanor Courtenay: You bet your ass. Sorry: fathers aren't asses. I gave that bloody nuisance up to Major Macnamara. . .

Priest:. . . O'Connell's political agent. . .

Eleanor Courtenay:. . . who put the son who had been torn out my soft feminine arms into one of those charitable institutions in Dublin that are favoured with many of Mr O'Connell's illegitimate offspring.

Priest: Are we going to share the booty?

Eleanor Courtenay: We're going to destroy O'Connell.

6. *The English're strong because they don't engage in double-dealing. From this strength they start their second attack against the Irish.*

England, the land of perfect goodness.

Malcolm: We know the head of the IRA offed your Irish Prime Minister.

King Edward of England: A land that needs to murder isn't a good land. Ireland needs Our help.

Malcolm: You'll help us to attack the IRA?

(*North London.*)

Macduff: Uncle, we need assistance against the creep Porter.

Siward (an English general who's Macduff's uncle): I could use a little war.

Northumberland: The Empire could use a little war. There's a bit of poverty going around these days.

Macduff: In this place of safety, let's start cautiously slowly planning our attack now so we don't take no chances in keeping England safe.

ACT IV *While the Irish army violently rages, the English're building up their attack: active versus potential power. Which is the stronger?*

1.

The Irish: We are nothing. We talk nonsense. We hate human beings. We write poetry.

(*The Porter again comes into this area of nothingness. The world is horror and screaming if you see it that way. There are huts made of earthen sods, or of mud strengthened with straw; the rank reek of the wet turf on the heath; the smoke that blinds the eyes as one creeps into the interior*:

((*Rain brown-dripping through the thatch; in this webbed murkiness men and women and children and animals huddle. Human beings live like this. Otherwise there're just soap operas and there's also pain.*))

The Porter (*in pain*): Bitches! I know I can't know the future. You have to tell me the future. I'd give myself to pure evil in order to enable the Irish to realize their own self-control. I know as an Irishman I don't have the power to order around anyone. I'm ordering you to obey my wishes.

The Bitches: We love you and'll give everything you want.

The Porter: I am the *violent one* who sets forth into the un-said, who breaks into un-thought, compels the unhappened to happens, and makes the unseen appear. . .

Bitch 1. . .another ego artist. . .

The Porter: The *violent one*'s the adventurer. Ireland risks dispersion. . .

Bitch 2:. . . is dispersed. . .

The Porter:. . . instability disorder mischief.

Bitch 2:. . .etc.

The Bitches: If you want to know the future, boy, we'll show it to you: (*Visual: A big brain and war weapons.*) You're going to die, boy.

The Porter: My personal fate doesn't concern me. Tell me what I'm dying to know.

Bitch 1: You're dying to know: (*Visual: Blood covers children.*) The Irish children're covered by blood. . .

The Porter (*getting fed up*): That's not what I need to know: that's what I see every goddamn day. Instead of children we Irish have abortions. I want to know how to make Ireland self-independent!

The Bitches: You still think you can know abstractly? An unnatural child'll kill you, boy: (*Visual: A blood-covered child is wearing a crown and holding a tree.*)

The Porter: Is that me? That's not me. Who's that?

The Bitches: Who isn't you? We love you.

The Porter: My wife's had five abortions. Is that one of her abortions? Abortions're alive. What's this have to do with Ireland? Oh Ireland, where the hell are you? You're cut up and bloody. You don't exist. There's an open stomach, cut, the blood gushes out. Is the bloody child coming out of this? Can something be born out of nothing? If I don't make something out of nothing, if I don't make a self-sufficiency where there's now, if anything, chaos and blood: there's no possible Ireland. Is this what you're telling me, bitch-holes? We can make something out of nothing?

The Bitches (*masturbating*): Still too abstract, boy. When Birnam wood comes to Dunsináne hill, you're gonna die.

The Porter: Why're you always harping on my personal death? Is that all there is? (*Understands.*) I'm going to die, bitches, aren't I? (*Visual: Banquo's dead body's the Prime Minister of Ireland. The English're still controlling.*) Something can't come out of nothing. Who the hell're you to tell me what's true?

The Bitches (*laughing*): (*As he rushes at them, they burst into nothing.*)

The Porter: In wartime the only possible females're whores. (*Changes his mind*) OK. The English're so powerful, they'll always control Ireland and eliminate the Irish. I don't care. I'm still going to fight.

Lennox (*an Irish pro-English lieutenant, entering*): Porter. Macduff's now in England. He's working with the English against you.

The Porter: Is Macduff a bloody child? He can't hurt us. Nobody can do anything relevant in this world of Hell.

(*The Irish, cause they're stupid, are disintegrating their own territory.*)

2. *The Irish fight back against Macduff and win.*

No visuals.

The Porter (*reconsidering*): Macduff's working against us in England. I'll stop him. . .the only way I can. . .indirectly. I'll go after his territory here.

(*Now visuals.*)

Mrs Macduff: Macduff lied to me. He told me he loved me, he was going to take me to England where it's safe, as soon as we were safe he'd be able to fuck me again: they are all lies because he was all the time planning to go to England by himself. By abandoning me and our son here, he made every part of our former life together a lie. Memories're hurting me.

Ross: How can a man love in a world that's humans knifing humans?

Mrs Macduff: I think you have to love.

Ross: You can't love by yourself. You can't trust anyone anymore you can't believe another person. It has to be every man for himself. . .

Mrs Macduff:. . . 'Man'. It's worse: it's the abandonment of love. . .

Ross:. . . so, what is there?

Mrs Macduff: We don't use each other, but we're scared. (*With understanding.*) Macduff ran away from us out of fear. The only thing I know is how to be scared and that stinks.

Macduff's Child (*picking up her fear therefore screaming*): Mommy!

Mrs Macduff (*looking at her child*): I don't want to live always by fear.

Macduff's Child: We can be animals.

Mrs Macduff: They say the poor're eating dogs. There can be nothing as natural as a human or an animal anymore.

Macduff's Child: Why do you call 'human' such a small thing? When an animal's hungry, it does everything it can to eat. I've seen Flopsy do this. Animals've always been eating each other. Isn't this how the world is?

Mrs Macduff: Oh my baby. Should I eat you? If it's natural to eat you, human motherhood must be unnatural. Humans've always been unnatural.

Macduff's Child: You taught me, mommy, to lie, not to care if I lied believably, and to use other humans. Do you love me, mommy? Is it natural for a mother to love her child? If it's natural, why do you lie to me and really not give a damn about me too? Humans're all things.

Mrs Macduff (*obsessed by the memory that a man's lied to and abandoned her*): Humans are criminals. (*The Terrorists enter and start murdering Macduff's Child.*) There's only my will. (*They murder Macduff's Child.*) Since there're no more people, I don't have a life. Since there're no more people in my life, it doesn't matter what I do. (*She runs away, but the Terrorists murder her.*)

3. The English keep building up potential force. Does the Irish active side attack on the Macduff territory succeed in weakening the English Macduff-Malcolm build-up?

Malcolm and Macduff in a pub in England.

Malcolm: The Porter's after you. You might have to play ball with him by giving me up to him.

Macduff: Forget it, kid. I don't act like the Porter.

Malcolm: You live in this Porter's world. Are you the only man who's honest?

Macduff: Then what's the use of fighting? We can just stay here and drink.

Malcolm: Because when reality's horrible, there's no way you can get out of horror. Are you honest? You just abandoned your young wife and child to our enemy. In order to sit on your ass and swill Scotch? That makes you less human than a pig. Oh shit. Who'm I to judge? I'm horror too in this horrible world because I'm not trusting anyone so I don't know what people mean by what they say. Are we totally conditioned by this world we live in? Are we zombies? Yes: You betrayed your love. I rely totally on my brains and I know my brains're deficient. We'll assassinate the Porter. We'll get rid of thinking: You a traitor and I an idiot'll run Ireland for England.

Macduff: How can a traitor and an idiot govern a people who don't yet exist?

(*The English have the possibility of trying to figure out why they fight 'cause their backs aren't every moment against the wall. On the other hand, the Porter can only think actively 'cause he has to act every moment.*)

Malcolm: I can damage anyone. I'm more of a fighter than the Porter. I wouldn't get near me to fuck me or even with any intention of being nice.

Macduff: You're just self-centred. You're not anywhere near as evil as the Irishman what he's now doing to Ireland.

Malcolm: I'm more vicious than the Porter: I've endless bottomless hunger. When there's just a hint an inch a speck of hunger in me, that hunger's the only thing in me. I or my will is hunger; else, I'm empty. I'd do anything to fuck you. It's only cause a certain level of me is scared that I seem one level below my surface honest and trustworthy.

Macduff: Every human's hungry in this same way. Why do you think you're different? You have to learn to control these hungers which're energy, like you work your muscles.

Malcolm: Repressive and hypocritical.

Macduff: Hypocritical only if you call these attributes 'you'.

Malcolm: What else are there? I love being evil.

Macduff: On one side of the coin you're good; on the other side, evil. On one side of the coin this world's good; on the other side, evil. You don't know anything 'cause all you see are your attributes, so you say there's nothing and no one else.

Malcolm: If I'm not English and I'm not Irish, what am I? I see: I'm twenty-two. I'm an Irishman who's pro-English. I'm going to assassinate the Porter so I can run Ireland for the English.

Macduff: You're OK. At least you've stopped being an intellectual. Use Siward and the ten thousand men under him.

(*Outside.*)

King Edward of England (walking over to a crowd of Pakistanis, rats, sailors who lost their legs in the Falklands, and self-lobotomized kids): No more poverty.

371

(*Inside the pub.*)

Malcolm (*through the window, watching King Edward*): The English King is good.

Ross (*entering the pub, to Macduff*): The IRA burnt down your house and slaughtered your child and wife.

Macduff: No. I've no life left. Not the IRA, *I* killed my wife by running away.

Malcolm: You told me I wasn't my attributes. Are you your attributes? Does IRA terrorism control you?

Macduff: No. There's no causation. I'm giving my life away to defeat the IRA.

(*Irish active force doesn't defeat English potential force. English potential force's secure.*)

ACT V DIRECT BATTLE

1. The Irish defence's weak.

Mrs Porter (*holding her hands in front of her, a bloody white cloth hanging off of these hands, and stumbling over everything*): I've got to get to sleep. When it becomes late at night, I feel sleepy. I go to bed. When I'm in bed, I relax. All these thoughts I've been keeping out of my head now my defences're down infiltrate my head. All the thoughts're alive. Where's sleep? The more I can't sleep, the more painful I become.

Doctor (*overlooking, to The Porter*): She can't get to sleep.

Mrs Porter: Every thought, no matter what its content, 's pain. The only way to run away from thinking is by sleeping. And I can't sleep.

Doctor: Her disease's mental. We can't cure schizophrenia.

The Porter: We can by killing.

Mrs Porter: If I can't will sleep, at least I can will death.

2. The English extend their territory into Irish territory.

The English army march through the Irish countryside (no seeable country-side). Malcolm, Macduff, and Siward are in front. When they reach Birnam Wood they meet the RUC, UDR, UDA, and the UVF.

Siward (*saluting a young man*): Son.

Siward's Son: Our ex-Irish Prime Minister's younger son, Donalbain, is missing.

Siward: Bad manners. Nowhere to be seen.

(*All the English and the Irish soldiers shake each other's hands.*)

3. The Irish territory that's left is Dunsinane.

Dunsinane.

The Porter (*to the IRA soldiers in the room*): Don't think the English can hurt your leader cause our witches and mad women and prophetesses say no living man can touch me.

Young Soldier 1 (*to Young Soldier 2*): He must be closet.

Young Soldier 3: The Irish language and madness're holy.

The Porter: The English can't hurt you because they're pansies and've been lobotomized by their culture.

Young Soldier 4: Our culture is madness and drunkeness.

The Porter (*aside*): This life's hollow. Is this really a life? Everything's now war and I'm a soldier. What's ambition? What's success? There's certainly no fucking. Am I descending into sentimentality? Adult living is making decisions. I've made my decision. You don't go running to a doctor to cure your decision. You don't judge a decision. This violence's life.

4. The English further extend their territory to IRA defectors and by decimating the Irish land.

Malcolm (*to four mixed English and Irish-Protestant Soldiers*): Cut down this wood to use as camouflage. In that way approach the Irish stronghold. I know you think the Irish don't fight according to agreed terms.

The IRA're turning against their head 'cause he's a drunk.

5. The Irish territory or the Irish language further disintegrates into meaninglessness.

The Porter (*talking to himself*): The good-for-nothing Irish're revolting against me. We're slaves.

I'm all alone in the room. My wife she killed herself out of loneliness. Why can't women go beyond their personalities? Is it cause they're dependent on men? Slaves. I won't be a slave to the English. I'm all alone in this room and everywhere else. I'm beyond thoughts, needs, and emotions.

I'm no exceptional person to follow. I'm the same as any other human: phenomena come and go, become and die. Phenomena: you see outward; you don't see inward.

If every phenomenon no matter what it is comes and goes, how can there be any value? Fuckin' human life's worth nothing. This world should be war cause all human living is is useless.

IRA Soldier (*shivering against the wall*): Trees're coming at us, sir.

The Porter: So what? Nothing's real and nothing matters. There're just different events. That's all there are. That's what I see: phenomena; that's the only thing I can see. My business is with becoming or phenomena, not with Platonic ideals. We soldiers're realists.

We soldiers're brutal realists. My business' this country's actual conditions. First and foremost I'm not a social revolutionary: I'm a political revolutionary. Political change or war first: social change later. (*yelling*) Men! Men! Let's arm against the English! (*The Porter alone arms himself.*)

6. *The English begin to fight to control the last Irish territory. . . .*

Dunsinane

Outside Dunsinane.

Malcolm: Siward and young Siward. You lead the first attack. Macduff and I'll clean up behind you. We should kill the Porter.

7. *. . .Which's now only The Porter.*

The Porter.

The Porter versus Siward's Son.

The Porter: Since you're normal, you can't kill me.
Siward's Son: I'll kill you.
The Porter (*after knifing him*): I killed you.

(*Outside The Porter.*)

Macduff: I'll kill him off and then we'll control everything.
Siward (*to Malcolm*): We own everything else: The Porter's lost the IRA. He's all alone and soon won't even be a man.

8. *The Irish territory.*

The Porter: I believe in witches. Nothing's real and nothing matters. The witches base their reality on the lack of causation. How does one phenomenon relate to another phenomenon? The Irish language and madness're holy. I have to die. Should I commit suicide or kill? I have to give meaning. Since there can be no safety for Ireland without a repeal of the Union, I'll kill.
Macduff: Turn around. I'll kill you first.
The Porter: It's not worth it. Neither life nor death matters. It's not worth killing. Why'm I always concerned with absolutes? I don't want to be a slave while I'm alive. I don't care, Macduff, whether you're alive or dead.
Macduff: I'm gonna kill you whether or not you fight back 'cause the only thing I want in the world's to kill you.

The Porter: No normal man can kill me. I can't die. The Irish prophetesses predicted this.

Macduff: I'm not normal.

The Porter: You're English.

Macduff: They ripped me in gushing blood out of my mother's womb 'cause she not wanting a kid but for medical reasons got pregnant aborted herself.

The Porter (*realizing absolutely*): I'm gonna die. I don't want to die.

Macduff: Fight, goddamn you, fight. You're still looking for reality which doesn't exist.

The Porter (*fighting*): Since there can be no safety for Ireland without a repeal of the Union, I'll kill. (*Keeps on fighting.*)

9. The World.

The English Soldiers're all talking to each other.

RUC Lieutenant: Which leaders do we have who're still alive?

English Soldier (*saluting*): Sir. Siward and Malcolm.

Siward: My son died like an English gentleman.

(*Macduff enters, holding The Porter's head on the tip of his sword.*)

Macduff (*giving this head to Malcolm*): You're our head and the new Prime Minister of Ireland.

Malcolm: Our only purpose'll be to negate. (*Hail falls.*)

Macbeth: repetition two

1.

The Witches: Now we'll start the world. Bang. (*Nothing happens but this noise and a string of blue grass beads.*) The first phenomenon's power or territory. (*A frightful human skull on stage. A heart like a jewellery heart not a human heart hangs out of its mouth.*)

Witch 1 (*walking to the right side of the skull and writing a black dot where the skull's right ear should be*): This is good or being born or the world. (*Walking over to the left side of the skull and painting a black snake where the skull's left ear should be*) This' evil or lack of humanity or nothing.

Witch 3 (*walking over to Witch 1 and holding a mirror so the skull can see itself in the mirror*): Reality or the relations between something and nothing are: Something comes out of nothing and nothing disappears.

(*The world fully appears: air as a nail-polish bottle full of Orlane Vermillon 18; fire as a black burning candle dripping red; water, a red plastic Cassio watch; earth, a string of brown similar-to-shit beads.*)

Witch 2 (*a child*): Humans, appear!

(*Two Ulster Defence Association officers who're friends, The Porter and Banquo enter.*)

Banquo: Now we own the world, old chap (*in thick Irish brogue*). . .

The Porter: (Everyone always disappears.)

Banquo: . . . we English. The head just raised our ranks for killing that lousy IRA rebel.

The Porter: That's not enough. I want what doesn't disappear. I want to know what's real.

Witch 1 (*to Witch 2*): This' the nature of these humans.

Witch 3 (*answering The Porter*): You're the ruler who does a lot of damage to a lot of people. (*Rubbing her clit.*) You like that one, boy. (*To Banquo.*) You're not the ruler; you're the father.

Banquo: You're not telling me anything!

But how can he be ruler when we already have an English leader?

The Witches: We're starting Ireland as best we know how.

2. Reflection of Scene 1: The skull looks on.

In The Porter's castle in Ireland.

The Porter (*repeating*): The only way I an Irishman can rule Ireland is by terroristically assassinating the English Prime Minister. I have to cause terrorism.

(*Two of The Porter's henchmen, now IRA Terrorists, dressed in black trenchcoats, black hats slung over their eyes, assassinate the Prime Minister of Ireland. There's lots of blood.*)

The Porter (*in shock*): What'm I doing?

Mrs Porter (*who looks like The Porter*): You've caused destruction so now you're destruction. I'm tied to you by the heart. Lemme give you a heart. We have to cause the death of the world so there's only passion. May blood be matter. Blood's matter.

The Porter: I'm responsible. I have to cause the death of the English world.

ACT II IRELAND: THE BALANCING OF BLACK AND WHITE

Inside The Porter's castle, all in black and white stylized shadows.

The Irish Prime Minister's sons, Donalbain and Malcolm, who're very tall teenagers, running around; their arms flap the air: Our father's dead! Our father's dead! What're we going to do now?

Donalbain: Since he was good, whoever murdered him's bad.

Malcolm: There's evil in this fair land. We must find our where it is. . .

(*Outside the castle, The Irish're drunkenly rolling around. They look like swine.*)

The Porter (*to Donalbain and Malcolm*): I can tell you how your father died. All the gays're dying from AIDS.

Donalbain and Malcolm (*murmuring to themselves*): Oh dear. We have to defend ourselves.

The Porter: Man's main psychological defence or immunity system is identity and his principal political defence, centralization. Any breakdown is madness and death.

Donalbain: We have to restore society.

Malcolm: Who's causing this breakdown?

The Porter: If there's no identity, how can anyone be guilty?

Donalbain (*turning back to The Porter and whispering to Malcolm*): I don't know what's going on in these portals of hell. I can't tell anything here.

Malcolm: We have to get out of here. I'll go to England where it's safe.

Donalbain: And I to suburban America. There we'll be able to be good.

The Porter (*aside*): I can't get out of my bed in the mornings. My only real life is that hour I'm not supposed to have – between waking and getting up – when I can be obsessed by a private figure, when I've a private life. Otherwise I want to die. That's a cliché. Now I've died. What's possibly natural about this life? My life's only what I make. So any event other than my will is murder: sleep, falling in love, being drugged. If I'm going to be happy, I can only be my will. Donalbain and Malcolm made up their *good versus evil*; I make up *natural versus unnatural*.

I rule Ireland because I decided to rule Ireland. But the witches said I'd rule Ireland. So maybe I'm not making, but seeing. I've got to find out what being human is.

Donalbain and Malcolm (*whispering to each other*): Let's escape from this evil.

Macduff (*whosever he is*): I don't know anything and I don't have any power. Ross, disappear with me. I don't want to be real anymore.

Ross: Yes, sir.

ACT III RED AND WHITE

A portrait of Ogu the God of War

The IRA stronghold.

Banquo (*The Porter's childhood friend*): Harsh homeland, the falsest, the most miserable imaginable. I'll never return to you hatred. With these eyes closed: enveloped in the blurry ubiquity of sleep, thus invisible, but nevertheless cleverly and subtly suggested, foreshortened and far in the distance; with even the tiniest details recognisable with such scrupulous activity as to border on the maniacal: an insolent light, a perfect sun: your loved memory and memory of love bring pain and sorrow to anyone who holds you; your name is forever cursed by those who mention it.

The Porter: Don't be ridiculous.

Banquo: You assassinated him.

The Porter: Ireland?

Banquo: Our Prime Minister.

The Porter: Yours? If Ireland's going to become its own country, it needs men such as you to find your own power.

Banquo: By following you?

The Porter: No. By following Ireland. By doing what Ireland needs.

Banquo: I presume you're Ireland.

The Porter: If someone doesn't do provisionally what's necessary, how else's Ireland going to exist?

Banquo: You're presuming you know the future.

The Porter (aside): Ride me, horseman. 'I rule, then his child rules.' The Witches said so. We, we Irish, mightn't be real, but we've real ways of knowing and being: bitches wild behaviour winds. So Banquo'll never believe the Witches. I'll have to off him and his son.

(*Pacing*) That's going against the Witches' prophecy.

(*Still pacing*) Those Witches're more powerful than me 'cause women don't make sense. Ireland doesn't make sense. Ireland's a hypocritical cunt bitch. (*Holds himself in.*) Since I'm responsible for our lives, I don't have the luxury of considering. I've taken my course, so now the curse runs itself.

(*The Porter and his Terrorists in the stronghold.*)

The Porter: I've a job for you, boys.

Terrorist 1 (*counting money between his fingers*): What d'you want?

The Porter: Murder and a half.

Terrorist 1: Who?

The Porter: Banquo and his kid.

Terrorist 1: OK.

Terrorist 2: Banquo's your friend.

The Porter: I don't have to explain anything to you.

Terrorist 1: We have to eat.

(*Terrorist 1, Terrorist 2, and a third Unknown Terrorist who be The Porter getting his kicks at the crossroads. Baron La Croix watches.*)

Terrorist 1: He'll be crossing soon.

Terrorist 2: Jesus Christ.

(*As Banquo crosses, they kill Banquo, lots of blood, but're unable to kill his son.*)

(*The Porter's holding a dinner party Irish-style that is lots of potatoes for his friends. Everyone's drunk therefore swine. Terrorist 1 knocks on the portal. The Porter opens the door.*)

The Porter: Come in. Over here. (*His eyes're rolling red from drink.*)
Terrorist 1: It's been done. There was lots of blood.
The Porter: Enough.
Terrorist 1: Not enough: We didn't get the kid.
The Porter (*eyes wide open*): The kid was the main one. You didn't obey my orders. (*Terrorist 1 looks at him as if he's disobeyable and mad.*)
Banquo's dead body (*as Irish Prime Minister, sitting in The Porter's ricketty wood chair*): Hey, boy.
The Porter: You calling me, sir? (*Catches himself. Looks around. Sees no one has noticed him cause they're all drunk. The Porter's not drunk, now he's crazy.*)
Banquo's dead body: Shine these shoes, boy.
The Porter (*walks over to Banquo's feet, kneels down, and sticks his tongue out. Looking up*): Sorry, sir I's can't do this for free, sir. No, sir, I's a free man now.
Banquo's dead body: I'll free you. (*Kicks him hard in the belly.*) Here's your quarter. (*Tosses a quarter into a piss pool.*) Go lick that up.
The Porter: Better than licking whites. I want to lick your blood.
(*For a second catches himself. But he's beyond caring about people.*) In anticipation of the great and not too distant day when a world will dawn in which a slave will be the equal of a king, in which the lambs of God who've been last'll be first: the niggertrash – dogs, that bite, leash them tight! – have accepted whatever comes their way. In anticipation of the great and not too distant day on which you say you'll give me your love, man, I now eat all the shit you give me and say, 'This violence's my sexuality'. No longer, king, does your future murder my present. (*His sword slashes through Banquo's dead body.*)
Drunk RUC 1: He's murdering Our Holy Mother Mary.
Drunk RUC 2: Your mother's not supposed to be holy, only a hole.
The Porter (*screaming*): Having depopulated whole regions, you swept away your now unprofitable slave trade like water in hungry sand. Since we wouldn't work for you, zombie-like, your taxes simply bled out our money. Our nobility, our foremost warriors have become trivial art-world power-mongers. I'll sing the history of all slaves.
Filthy Prostitute: I think he's trying to kill himself.
The Porter: Not far from the bodies of the countless children of ours

you've aborted, the gaping entrails of women gasping in the agonies of death shot forth seventeen fetuses. The raped females hated themselves so much, they suicided themselves. One of the women's brothers was watching. The scene of his sister killing herself erased some of his fear. Does human exist? (*Turning to the Orderly.*) Where's Macduff?

Orderly: He went back to Belfast.

The Porter: I have to kill him and I can't kill him. I can't kill Banquo's child and I can't kill him right now. My power's gone. My power to know's gone.

(*White*:)

(*The English court in London. A bunch of poor people sit on the streets. Across, inside a rich room.*)

Malcolm: You are good. You have to help us save our country.

The good King Edward: We'll help you.

(*The English countryside. A small pub in the country.*)

Macduff (*to Siward*): I'm glad you're going to come to Ireland with your army and destroy The Porter.

ACT IV MY PSYCHOLOGY

(*Dream 1: Visual of me fucking. The man with whom I'm fucking's a friend of mine. Though it's real hard, I come and'm happy I do. As soon as I come my phone rings.*)

The Porter: This means 'I want to fuck'.

The Witches (*preening themselves and showing spread shots*): I'm beautiful.

(*Dream 2*)

The State: I need terrorism to keep a good front. I either use my own agents, or better, 'cause I'm cheap, infiltrate and use my enemy's organizations' members. Your hierarchical organizational form, Left, makes this easy: your autonomous clandestine militant cells, being separate from and ignorant of each other, don't communicate with each other. Since you function from blind discipline, not out of knowledge and questioning, you can be infiltrated. If you ever suspect one of our infiltrators, which you're usually too stupid to do, we have him arrested, get the media to play up the arrest, then let him 'heroically' escape so he can re-infiltrate. In this way, we destroy your ability to distinguish between good and evil.

The Porter: This means 'Blood's gushing out of my body'.

(*Dream 3: A visual of Banquo's child with a crown on his head and a huge tree trunk, ten times his size, in his right hand.*)

The Porter: That's the child I couldn't kill. His mother wanted to have an abortion but was too scared so had him instead so he's a living abortion. Now all children who're freaks rule.

The Witches: This means 'When unnatural's the only nature we've got, you're going to die.'

The Porter: Since unnatural's the only nature I've got, I'm going to die now.

(*Scene change.*)

I (*in Ireland*): Fear motiviates all my actions. I act only with regard to my memories so I won't be hurt again or so I can avoid the horror which's outside my home (my physical extension). I've three memories: 1. My mother hated me. 2. My husband left me. 3. My mother suicided. These memories're history or myself. If I don't act in accordance with them. I don't have any identity and certainly no nationality. No wonder Ireland's either a horror populated by ghosts or a non-existent country.

(*To my child, a girl.*) Macduff's left us. I'd kill myself because I can't live without him, but I'm not going to.

My Child: How're we going to live, mommy?

(*The Terrorists're lurking in the trees.*)

I: However I have to live. There's no such thing as 'natural' anymore. (I mean 'love'.)

My Child: Animals who live as they have to live're natural.

(*The Terrorists kill me and my child. There's lots of blood. Unlike classical Greek drama, this play displays more blood and violence than's necessary.*)

(*Macduff, in England.*)

Macduff (*to Malcolm*): I guess I killed my wife by abandoning her.

Malcolm: You can't be responsible, man, for another person's life.

Macduff: I did evil by abandoning my wife. She didn't do anything but good. She's the one who died. What can justice be?

Malcolm: You killed your wife in order to fight the IRA. Your methods're as inhuman as the IRA's. You're a pig.

Macduff: I'm Irish.

(*The skull's looking at the skull.*)

Malcolm: Who'm I to judge? I'm horror, too, in this horrible world 'cause I'm not trusting anyone so I don't know what people mean by what they say. Are we totally conditioned by this world we live in? Are we zombies? Yes: You betrayed your love. I rely totally on my brain and I know my brain's deficient. We'll assassinate The Porter.

We'll get rid of thinking: You a traitor and I an idiot'll run Ireland for England.

(*The skull's looking at the skull.*)

Macduff: If we're all fascists, why should I do anything but drink? Did I kill my wife and kid for fascism?
Malcolm: How can I act? All this' idealism. How can I act?
Macduff: What's an appropriate action now?
Malcolm: To kill our controllers.
Macduff: Kill the controller.
Malcolm (*walking over to the skull and splitting it*): Ogu. I'm a warrior.
Macduff: It's hard for me to say 'I love you'.

ACT V THE IRA'S DEATH

1. Death

In bed,

Mrs Porter: I'm a horrible person: I want power so much I've disregarded every friendship and love in me and I can only see my point-of-view. I confess to myself, like Catholics have the health of confessing to someone else, so there's no world but me. Since there's nowhere for this energy to go, I have to live with too much energy. I no longer want to be alive.

2. Animal life.

Marching to Birnam Wood.

Malcolm: The time's ripe to smash the Provisional IRA.

(*Malcolm, Macduff and Siward with five other soldiers meet the Irish Protestants, parts of the RUC, UDA, UDR, and UVF. They shake hands.*)

Protestant Private: Kill 'em. (*shows his teeth.*)
Protestant Lieutenant (*to the English imports*): Our army and the local security forces've been released from their years of low-profile and're going on the offensive.

3. Humanness.

The Porter (*very big-eyed*): I'm going to die.
His Butler: Sir, your wife just killed herself.
The Porter: Tell her not to bother me. (*Back to himself.*) The news' Birnam Wood is moving here, to Dunsinane. I know I'm going to die.

Not only the Protestants, now even my Catholics're supporting an anti-terrorist campaign. I've no support. I'm up against the wall. (*These cries come from unseen: 'Mrs Porter's dead!' 'Mrs. Porter's dead!*) Another person has died because people die. I'll fight.

4. Death

Inside the closed IRA territory.

Siward's Son (*very young so cocksure. To himself*): Me. I'm gonna kill that son-of-a-bitch Porter. (*When he sees the Porter, runs at him.*)
The Porter (*turning around*): What a child! (*easily kills him and wipes the blood on his sword off on his pants.*)

5. Animal life.

Goat: I'm gonna tear the Porter's brains out of his head.
Jaguar: His men've abandoned him so it'll be easy to kill him. Just kill him.

6. Life and death're fucking each other.

The Porter (*all abandoned*): I'm going to die. I'll kill myself. I'll kill other people.
Macduff: Either you're going to die or you're going to kill me.
The Porter: You can't kill me.
Macduff: Then kill me.
The Porter: No.
Macduff: That's not possible. You either have to kill me or I'm going to kill you.
The Porter: I'm not going to die. (*He fights Macduff.*)
Macduff: Either you're going to die or I'm going to die.
The Porter: No, neither of us're going to die.
Macduff: Either you're going to die or I'm going to die.
The Porter: Do I have to be human? Do I have to be in this world?
Macduff: You who're a slave: aren't you every slave who's ever existed? What do you call 'human'?
The Porter: May the spirits of the living and the dead help us to laugh at our slave human beliefs. I'm going to either die or kill you, cause I'm the hero. (*They fight.*)

7. Ireland.

Macduff, walking out of the Porter's castle, carrying the Porter's cut-off head, gives it to Malcolm.

Malcolm: I'll tell you how to stop the slavery. Kill all the slaves.

Macbeth: repetition three

The English are the good guys and the Irish are the bad guys.

ACT I

The Irish world begins in and as nothing. The Irish fortunetellers who're nothing foretell the beginning of the world. In this beginning which is the hope for power and about power because the Irish don't have any power or the establishings of territory because the Irish don't have any territory, the nothing of the Irish equals evil, and anything 'cause the Irish're so desperate equals good. Everything because it must come out of nothing will die, the Irish will always lose the war, or, as Ireland really is nothing, so evil or Ireland has to win.

The English overrun the stage.

The King of England: Who's that bloody man over there? The English are taking over the world for once and for all. A bloody man can tell us what the real state of the world is.

Man Dripping in Blood: Thanks to The Porter and Banquo we cut off many Irish heads.

The King of England: Oh valiant cousins! Worthy gentlemen!

Man Dripping In Blood: Now we own all of Ireland.

The King of England: Porter and Banquo, I dub thee Knights.

(*The world's nothing again. Dust and smoke and penicillin swirling around the stage. Don't bother with stage props because it's too difficult. Kind of blabbing noises.*)

The Porter and Banquo enter the scene.

The Porter: Here we are in nothing to learn about nothing.

Banquo (*to nobody*): Who're you? You should be women because the only people I talk to're women only I don't feel any desire to fuck you.

Females (*to the Porter*): You'll become evil and by becoming evil powerful.

Banquo: But what about me though I don't give a shit about you, females?

Females: You won't become evil that is Irish. Your child'll be powerful.

Banquo: Does that mean my child'll be good or evil?

(*The Plan*)

(*In the Porter's southern Irish castle.*)

The Porter: I hate the English! I'm going to assassinate the King in order to save our homeland. (*It is night. He kills the English King.*)

The Porter's Irish Wife (*to the Porter who comes bloodily out of the English King's bed not 'cause he actually murdered the King but 'cause his hands touched the arms of the young punks he had paid to murder the English King*): I'm glad you murdered that upper-class snob. I'm part of your blood, my husband my love, because genitals when they touch make the blood flow together so my blood's your blood. Like you I'm Irish. Like you I'm nothing and want nothing: not Knighthood nor any other baubles the socialized English uphold. We're prophets and evil. We don't want to own our own country.

The Porter: We don't want to own our own country. That's not enough. We want to destroy the world.

ACT II THE PORTER HAS A CONVERSATION

The Play's Writer: A definition of this world's a portal.

A definition, my first, of this world's AIDS. AIDS' the breakdown of the body's immunity system: the body becomes allergic to itself. At this moment in New York City fags Haitians and hemophiliacs're all getting AIDS. I just heard this heterosexual garbage collector got AIDS.

What's AIDS? A virus. A virus' seemingly unknowable who gets identity by preying on an entity, a cell. Writers whose identities depend on written language're viruses. I'm trying to break down the social immune system. Even this sentence's false.

If there're no identities, there're hallucinations. The first portal of this world's hallucination.

The Portal: Knock. Knock.

The Porter's Voice (*still in sleep*): There's no reality. Go away.

The Portal: Knock. Knock.

Morning.

The Porter (*in his bed, sheets knotted around his body with the sweat that indicates he fell asleep drunk but couldn't sleep*): You hate my guts. You hate me, so I'm nothing. Your lips are the most wonderful things. I don't care if this fantasizing is you rejecting me, I still want to stay here.

The Portal: Knock. Knock.

The Porter: I don't want to get up in the morning because I want to die.

The Portal: Knock. Knock.

The Porter: I don't want your fraternity pin. Is he talking about us, Tad? Oh, Alfred, you're breaking my heart.

The Portal: Knock. Knock.

The Porter: Amanda, come on in. Oh, you brought that book of essays they assigned you in English class. The teacher's cunt's a set of falsies.

Oh no, you're at the portals of Hell only I'm drunk. But I'm out of booze. Hell, this place's too boring for Hell. Try another city. (*He knocks himself.*) Knock. Knock. Well, I'm going to make a new resolution. I just murdered the King of England. I've got blood on my hands. I'm gonna wash it off. Out, out, bad blood. Life's just a walking shadow allowing everything. I'd pee on life only coke's made my cock too small. Oh horror horror horror. Who's going to alter my blood-stained hands? I'm more courageous than you, big boy. Who thought that a human contains so much blood?

The English princes, Malcolm and Donalbain, they're about eight and ten years old, run in and start screaming: Daddy's murdered.

Malcolm: I'm going back to England where I'll be safe 'cause the only dirty Irish there the English kill or starve.

Donalbain: I'll go Brazil. Let's not tell anyone where we're going 'cause now the forces of nothingness Ireland're ruling the world.

The Porter (*in his bedclothes*): I smell sex. (*Smelling old blood.*)

Macduff (*to Ross*): Even though we're really Irish we can still act English by retreating.

The Porter: Here are the manipulators who manipulate everyone but God.

ACT III THE PORTER TALKS TO THE GHOST

Banquo's dead body: Porter, this's your cock.

The Porter: I don't feel sexual desire.

Banquo's dead body: I'm Banquo.

The Porter: Fuck you. I killed you. Where's your cock?

Banquo's dead body: I'm not a cock; I'm a ghost. You know why you can't get it up, don't you? You're guilty as hell.

The Porter: If I were guilty as hell. I'd be the Devil.

Banquo's dead body: You killed our King. That's the same as killing God.

The Porter: Your *King* said she was female.

Banquo's dead body: That's why you can't fuck.

The Porter: Then no Englishman can fuck.

Banquo's dead body: It's called 'The English Disease'.

The Porter: As long as I can't fuck, I might as well be social. (*Throwing open his arms in a royal gesture and indicating his dining-room guests.*) Everyone gets ahead in their top-level jobs the most possible by being social.

Banquo's dead body: Well, be social with me, honey. (*Patting the chair.*) A ghost like me needs company. (*Crossing his legs.*) Now, tell me something. I've got this thing for Mrs Porter. Does she. . .put out?

The Porter: She's Irish! Listen, Ghostie, I've done so much fuckin' shit to this land by fighting the English, if I make the slightest mistake now that is if there's the slightest flaw in my territory, I'm a dead duck.

Banquo's dead body: You're worse than that, honey. (*Again patting the chair.*) You might as well admit what you really are. You've lost everything anyway.

The Porter (*sadly looking down*): I know. (*Changing.*) I will not lose! My will will keep going! Now I'll kill Macduff.

Banquo's dead body: That's like asking me to slit my own throat.

The Porter: I suppose you want to slit mine. You can't. I'm alive. I have to get back to the living.

Banquo's dead body: I never heard anything more perverted in my life. You're just going to learn to feel guilty, and if you can't feel guilty, then scared.

The Porter: I suppose this's the way of the world. Oh please, ghost, don't hurt me. (*Runs away because he's sacred of what he knows, only now he doesn't know anything.*) I don't know anything.

(*In England*)

Siward (*an English general*): I've so many soldiers, Ireland has to be decimated. Fuck the IRA!

ACT IV

1. The Porter talks to the hallucinations.

A woman is having an abortion. This has to be real. *Her aborted gook is seen and placed next to children. Red blood is covering the children. This' the place of desolation.*

The Porter: Since I'm not going to hurt anymore, I'm not going to hurt anymore.

The Bloody Children: Die. We're killing you because you aborted us. (*While they stick sticks into the Porter's body*)

The Porter (*dying*): Ireland has to succeed! In accepting the job of Prime Minister of Northern Ireland, I do so in and with the hope that the British army goes back to England dead.

The Child Who Has No Blood (*appears. This child is crowned King and holds nature in his hand*): Die, Porter. When Birnam Wood walks to Dunsinane, we're going to murder you. The Great Commonwealth of Britain must take over because Britain's natural. It's your fault: You Irish by trying to go against our good sweet naturalness have forced us to be as unnatural to you as we are in your minds. When you get killed, you want to be killed. We're freaks in this world only 'cause you are.

The Porter: Being a child's just another hallucination or ploy.

The Child: The only non-hallucination you've got is the fact of your own death.

The Porter (*croaking in an old man's voice*): I'll tell you what we've got against you: Since from 1921 onwards the Irish people freely have not wanted the British to govern them, the government of Ireland has been a government without consensus. When you have a situation like that, you have a situation of permanent instability. Permanent instability means recurring acts of violence. Ever since 1921. What does one life matter?

2. In the middle of war, the English're being murdered too.

In England

Malcolm (*to Macduff*): Our soldiers, in Ireland that poor place, have fallen in the trenches. Flies sit on their lips. Pus comes out of their nostrils. Those who come back to us alive have hollow eyes, are zombies, need or are, simply, hooked on heroin the only substitute for life.

Macduff (*dead now that love's abandoned him*): I've decided to be dead. Rather: these muscles that no longer work, these continuously wandering eyes, this throat that stops up rather than issues forth language, the life now in Ireland, are same as a war which no soldier can understand. The Irish led by the Porter have plunged their heads into an all-destroying dream called self-sovereignty and so make maddening confusion and the deafening music of tanks. . .

Malcolm: Why should I trust you? You ran out on your family so your family died so you're as perverse and evil as any Irishman.

Macduff: There's no such thing as purity in these times that shit. Since I'm as dumb as any Irishman, I have to refuse who I most desire.

Malcolm: No. (*Thinking.*). . .

3. Those who're murdered become fascists.

Malcolm:. . . Where am I? Run. Walk. Get away. Hunger. No matter. Live. Run. Breathe. Survive. My guns. What can I chew? My ankle. Ragged nerves plunge me into hallucinations. Hallucinations're my perceptions. I look at my life (I remember). The worst things that've happened to me I in no way caused: cancer, my mother's hatred of me the instant I came out of her womb so I have no mother, my marriage's break-up, my grandmother's desire to die right after her only daughter suicided and her subsequent death. Likewise, the fortunate events. There's only chance. Or else I can't know causes. Good doesn't lead to good, evil doesn't lead to evil; and I can't tell the difference between good and evil. What're my categories?

Unfold my dreams:
In a rectangle which is also Africa through which a body of water runs I am travelling and there're snakes. As I rise up from the river, the snakes're after me. When two long snakes resembling broken rubber bands lift up, I grab on to the ropes though attached to the walls I cause them to swing and so climb up to the ceiling. But the growing snakes more ferocious can climb almost as far. An inch from me.
I'm fucking with you.:
If the categories are wills and desires, what's fascism?

Macduff: In Nakem-Ziuko the winds of emancipation've brought demands for reform. Our Prime Minister has explained to us that England's main concern at this moment is the headlong political development of its colonies such as Ireland, Scotland, and British Africa. Let war and fascism rage. I love war and fascism.

Malcolm: There'll follow six months of bowing and scraping, of correspondence and council meetings at which the griots'll review the political development of the sorrowful Nakem-Ziuko.

The King of England: If our people nominate half-whitened Pakistani, servant sons some who have cocks that are still unreddened, they can't write, the best of them managed to stay in school till age thirteen by controlling their teachers and classrooms, if you nominate these men: they'll win twice as many votes as anyone expects. The niggers're refusing to go back to their holes unless they are our political candidates.

Macduff (*to Malcolm*): Let's follow him.

The King of England: Right without might's a caricature. Might without right's an abomination. Admit it.

Macduff: The triumph of might is the triumph of its right. We'll have to win out over the IRA.

ACT V THE ENGLISH AND THE AMERICANS OWN THE WORLD

1.

Mrs Porter: To bed, to bed. (*Still masturbating.*) Here's someone at my gate. He's bald and his hair's so blond it's almost nothing; his eyes are the pale blue of ghosts. Get him out! Get him out! But I have to do it. Here's a doctor. He's French too. He carries big whips around his waist and tells me I'm sick. I know who I, female, am. And another: A face as screwed-up and old as a bull-dog's. You're the foul coke-fiend. Come come come. Don't take eight hours.

2.

In the war-time.

War music: Boom boom boom.

(*Malcolm, Siward, Macduff, the good English, enter with English soldiers.*)

War music: Boom boom boom.

(*Now it's wartime. Only one army's advancing, the only army* (English).)

Menteith: Partition is resented but the present generation knows that if partition is ever to be ended it must be by peaceful arrangements. The few young toughs who make up the tiny remnant that will now lay down its arms uses a grand and famous name for their organization, but the *Irish Republication Army* belongs to history and it belongs to better men in times that are gone. Let's put a wreath of roses, a bloody wreath (*laughs*), and move on.

Caithness: With the English bombing campaign at a dead end by the 1939 autumn, Sean Russell and the other like-minded militarists who comprised IRA's depleted inner circle decided to seek assistance from Nazi Germany.

Lennox: The Irish've driven all the Protestants, whom the Irish call 'unbelievers of their faith', like swine into the surrounding seas. By force by knife and by poison. They are trying to cut them down like a farmer hews down a mahogany forest. They use any method of deception in order to destroy all Protestants.

Menteith: They're planning to advance the Priesthood and Catholic faith until the Pope rules the entire world.

Caithness: I've reached the stage where I no longer have any compassion for any nationalist: man, woman or child. After years of destruction murder intimidation I have been driven against my better feelings to this decision: the Irish nationalists or us. Why haven't don't we hit back in the only way these nationalist bastards understand? That is: ruthless indiscriminate killing. I'm going to roast the slimy excreta the Irish that pass for human beings.

3.

Malcolm: Of old time priests of high degree with their hands strained on the rack the limbs of delicate Protestant women; prelates dabbled in the gore of their helpless female victims. The cells of the Pope's prison were paved with the calcined bones of men and cemented with human gore and human hair.

Menteith: We doubt it nothing.

Siward: There's a fuckin' Irishman.

Menteith: An real Irishman cause he's drunk!

(*The five men rush at the old man. One soldier beats his hands against a tree. Every time the old poop collapses, the same soldier along with a second soldier beats the insides of his feet at his ankles and his hands until the old man has to again stand up. This happens numbers of times.*)

Menteith: Get up!

(*The old man crouches on the earth and weeps. He doesn't know why. They kick him back and forth until he's able, standing, to have his hands again thrust against the tree.*)

Siward: How large is the IRA? (*Behind the old man a soldier sticks a knee in his spine and shoves the head back.*) What does it matter? Most of the Catholics we have to murder're innocent of any involvement with the IRA.

The Window Cleaner: I'll murder Catholics as they sleep in their beds.

Malcolm: You just want to run off and kill the first Catholic you find. You're like a roamer looking for a teague. I feel we have to be more selective. Let's kill their heads.

Macduff: They don't have heads.

Siward: We're not trying to have any specific effect on the Catholics. I suppose we just want to tell them they can't force their views on us. The IRA is anti-Protestant most certainly. They're haters of everybody: the British, their own people. They'll have to be stopped.

4.

The Butler (*to the Porter*): Your wife's dead.

The Porter: I'll tell you a story. It used to be the only way a Catholic could enter the middle class here in the North was by running a pub. Owen McMahon was my father. He did just that.

In those days the Ulster Defence Regiment was partly coming from the B-Specials. The B-Specials were a group of men who helped out the Belfast cops by murdering and spreading anti-Catholic bigotry as much as possible. The Catholics had just gotten their shit together in those days, 1922, and started to off the pigs who were decimating them. No one else. They weren't killing civilians. I want the Irish to survive. They had to off two B-Special murderers. They did so. As reprisal, the next day, the B's broke into my father's house on Antrim Road. Grey early morning. They line him, my five brothers, and the barman who was working at my father's place up against his living-room wall. Then they shot them in the front. Two of us didn't die. I didn't die because I had been hiding under the couch. Hiding under the couch, peering up to where the only light was. In the light a bullet enters my father's chest. He falls to the floor. I hear the sound of the body as it hits the floor. The next bullet goes into one of my brothers. Blood bursts out of a hole in his right cheek. His eyes are wide open. Simultaneously there's the noise of my youngest brother's body hitting the floor. Suddenly one of my brother's screams, the first scream, runs forward as a pig-cop catches my brother in his arms his knee goes up to my brother's tiny delicate cock. At the same time, the rifle turned, the rifle butt smashes in my brother's head. I see white worms quivering come out of this skull. I'm screaming now. Who can fight my egotism? The barman, stunned, lets them kill him and dies.

The Butler (*interrupting*): Your wife's dead.

The Porter: There'd be time to react to this if I lived in another world.

5.

Macduff: There must be a change in security tactics. The army and the local security forces must be released from their present low-profile: we're finally on the offensive again. I'll kill the Porter. Both the Northern Irish Protestants and the Catholics're supporting our determined anti-terrorist campaign. The time is ripe to kill the Porter.

Malcolm (*entering*): Due to the IRA's terrorism, the Irish have turned against the IRA.

6.

Malcolm: Sixty-six per cent of the Catholics in Ulster are unemployed. That's not enough.

Siward: It took Bobby Sands sixty-six days to starve himself to death. We should have starved him more quickly.

Malcolm: We killed Constable Victor Arbuckle in 1969: the first man in our security forces to die.

Ross: We now control and'll always control Ireland 'cause it's the port to Europe. We'll give up any of our other colonies before we give up this port.

Siward: Are the Catholics dead?

Ross: Aye, in Belfast in February 1982 we arrested so many creeps and confiscated so many of their arms, we neutralized the Irish National Liberation Party. When the Sinn Fein and Irish Republican Socialist Party ran for election in all twenty-six counties the next month, none of them became TDs.

Siward: Is it a crime to be Catholic?

Ross: What does it matter? They can't win.

(*Macduff, holding the Porter's cut-off head, enters the battlefield.*)

The Porter's cut-off head: What O'Connell gave us is hard to tell:. . .

(Dedicated to Sean O'Faolain's book on Daniel O'Connell.)

The Porter's cut-off head:. . .he taught me to have pride. He taught me the one word (world) I have is *no* and that word isn't a negative but allows the world. He almost killed truth back in the early nineteenth century. He exposed the life of the Empire. He gave the Irish discipline and tolerance. He accepted duality as the basic fact. (*Blood pours out of his mouth.*) The Union was a manifest injustice, and continues to be unjust to this day. If the Union continues, it will make crime hereditary and English justice perpetual. We've been robbed, my countrymen, most foully robbed of our birth-right: our independence. Alas, England that ought to have been to us a sister and a friend – England whom we had loved, and fought and bled for – England at a period when out of the 100,000 seamen in her service 70,000 were Irish – England stole upon us like a thief in the night and robbed us of the precious cherry of our liberty. Here, England: (*He looks up at Macduff who's holding him.*)

All: Hail, King of Ireland! (*Macduff gives the head to Malcolm.*)

The Porters' cut-off head: While we believe the English, while we believe in this religious dissension, while we're lost in this stupor of insanity: the English have and plunder us of our country. Hammer my brutal reality – my loneliness and hollowness and fear – into an ideal: the struggle of the Irish.

3 Adult now

For Arabia

Preface

The Evil: Shylock R.

Shylock R. on why he's demanding a pound of flesh out of Antonio:

Shylock R.: There's pain in this world. I feel pain. God doesn't feel pain. Considering this: This world's always been this way. This world stinks and always has stunk. Strung up. It must be God doesn't give a shit about human beings.

The Good: Portia

Morning light comes through the curtains. Translucent white curtains, parted as they hang from the high wood bedframe, through which, glimpses of white stain quilts guilts huge white pillows. The laughter of the first morning sun, white, yellow. The flesh is white not because it's white but 'cause it's ease. Riding light laugh always. See.

Portia: I've seen a vision. It's the vision of freedom or of wild space. 'Fuck' rhymes with 'stuck'. The one nightmare: I'm stuck. I'm stuck in this brain which defines (makes?) the world spacially and temporally. I'm stuck in these returnings. The circles, moving temporally faster, are making me nauseous. I'm stuck in my own world: I can't meet anyone new; I always know what's happening.

    The vision: infinity. Whatever can't be counted or is alive. I saw livingness and it made me laugh and then simultaneously there's no more knowing and this makes me laugh. There's only fucking.

(All the black people hate all the white people. All the people're black except for Shylock R., the British armies, and Julius Caesar.)

(In summer it's so hot that emotions burst out:)

ACT I THE SUN

A poor young mercenary named Bassanio falls in love with a woman. Since Portia's beautiful, intelligent and self-independent, the man feels he needs money. He hits up his friend, Antonio. Antonio doesn't know why he's always sad and can lend his friend money only by borrowing cash from Shylock R. who's tight-assed. Since Shylock R. hates everyone who isn't himself or Jewish, he gives Antonio the dough under forfeiture of a pound of Antonio's bloody flesh. All Antonio cares about are his friends.

1.

: You must be mad 'cause you're in love.

Antonio: I've nothing anymore to do with sex so I can't be in love. I'm sad for another reason.

: You're sad because you're not in love. I guess you're losing all your friends.

Antonio: I guess I am. Bye-bye friends. (*His friends go away. Yells after them.*) Let's have dinner together.

: O.K.

(*Two new friends enter.*)

: What's the matter, babes? You look like the pits. You care too much about things—

Antonio: I know nothing's real.

: You're too attached to things of the world. That brings trouble.

Antonio: I am trouble.

: Get a sense of humour. At least you'll live longer or, even if you die, enjoy every moment you live. You're going to die soon the way you're going.

Antonio: So are you. Well, I'll leave you to your dinner. My stomach hurts I'm so hungry all the time.

(*Antonio alone with Bassanio.*)

Antonio: So how're you in love? Who you in love with, boy?

Bassanio: I'll tell you something. 'Cause I've bought too many clothes, I've no money left and I owe you the most.

Antonio: Don't worry, honey. If you need it, I'll lend you more.

Bassanio: I'm always in need. If you lend me double what I now need, I'll pay your first loan back. I don't want to owe someone.

Antonio: Money's an easy problem. I'm sad.

Bassanio: I'm in love with a rich cunt.

Antonio: She must be upper-class. Forget it. That class' women's cunts have teeth.

Bassanio: That's why I need your money in order to get her.

2.

Portia (*who looks exactly like Bassanio*): My father said marriage's a state affair.

The Maid (*the only person who loves her in the world who's still alive.*) I thought you've never known your father.

Portia: That's the only thing he ever said to me.

The Maid: Well. . . Anything lasts longer than sex and love: (*Thinking.*) Governments're lasting a long time these days 'cause they're all becoming one.

Portia: True marriage.

The Maid: This' why you're supposed to get married.

Portia: This' precisely why I don't want to get married. Real men don't exist anymore.

The Maid: Of course they exist. There're still people in the world. The most romantic men're in France.

Portia: Who'd ever know? The French – by 'the French' I mean Frenchmen – the French're so provincial, they look down their noses at the rest of us and don't mingle. They're snotty cause their economy's been stable for years and even though they talk politics all the time and now and then have tiny political revolts nothing never changes in France. . .

The Maid: . . . Stability's good for a marriage. Have you decided to marry France?

Portia: I'd prefer England to France. England looks very proper, but its people're starving to death. Money may not be everything in life, but it certainly buys dresses. As for the English colonies. . .

The Maid: . . .You can go scumming without having to get married. There's only one country left.

Portia: What a description of this world! Who's that?

The Maid: Germany. A solid stolid economic giant.

Portia: What good Hitler did! May we learn all our lessons from politics. The only problem with Germany is their diet. . .

The Maid: . . . The Diet of Worms. . .

Portia: By the end of the day the Germans have so much sausage in them, their guts're red meat. In the nighttime they're little better than beasts.

The Maid: Better animal than human. . .

Portia: . . . red than dead. . .

The Maid: . . . in your bed.

Portia: Except the beast's too drunk on beer to do anything but piss in its sleep.

The Maid: It's more civilized to sleep in separate beds.

Portia: I sleep in my own bed now. Why should I have anything to do with the world?

The Maid: What about Bassanio? He's smart as hell and mercenary. Excuse me, a mercenary.

Portia: He's cute. (*Sighs.*) I wouldn't mind his weight.

Servant (*some old cutthroat*): Excuse me, Miss, another man's knocking on your door.

Portia: I hope he's a locksmith and giving me a chastity belt: I hate men and I don't want their hard world.

3.

Shylock R. has a thick Jewish accent.

Shylock R.: People have been dumping on me all my life and I never had a chance. I'll tell you what it's like to grow up in The South: If you talked to a Black, you were scum you were Black! If you liked a Black, you were scum you were Black! If you dared to read a book, you were scum you were Black! If you wanted to go to a play, you were a fag!

Antonio (*pouring himself some of Shylock R.'s wine*): So you had no choice: you were Black or a fag.

Shylock R. (*screaming*): I had no chance: there was nothing I could do!

Antonio (*bored*): Why didn't you run away?

Shylock R. (*quietly*): Columbia University accepted me. I came to New York for the first time. A black man on the street spoke to me hostilely. Me; hostilely. My childhood love was a black man shooting me up with junk. It's the first time I tasted junk. And then this black kid on the street speaks to me like I don't know who blacks are.

Antonio: He spoke to you from where he was. That's how people are in New York. It doesn't mean anything.

Shylock R.: How was I to know about New York? I was so freaked-out by the city, I didn't even go to Columbia, I left after two weeks. Do you know how scared I was? (*Screeching.*)

Antonio (*shaking his head 'cause Shylock R.'s so mad*): Let me get to business for just a minute.

Shylock R.: Who are you?

Antonio: My name's Antonio. I hear you're a coke dealer. I don't mean that. I mean, I hear you dabble, you know, from no one. . .

Shylock R.: I don't deal coke. I just put people in touch with people.

Antonio: It's not my business. I just thought you might be able to lend me money.

Shylock R.: I don't have any money. I have to work for a living.

Antonio: Your girlfriend's rich.

Shylock R.: Are you insulting me? I might be able to lend you what you need.

Antonio: What do I need?

Shylock R.: So what do you need? (*Thicker Jewish accent.*)

Antonio: I need. I need thirty thousand dollars.

Shylock R.: Who has that kind of money? Arafat. Go to Arafat.

Antonio: OK (*Starts walking away.*)

Shylock R.: Wait a second. I'll be able to borrow the money from a friend, but I'll lose money doing it. I'll do it for you (*staring at Antonio's tits*), because I like you.

Antonio: I'll give you your money back in three months with 300 per cent interest.

Shylock R.: Interest? (*Aside.*) Does this man think the Jews're interested only in interest? Is he so prejudiced? Doesn't he know we have hearts and souls? (*to Antonio*) I want flesh.

Antonio (*shrinking from fear*): I think you're human.

4.

Roughs on the street.

A Welfare Worker: Here's your new home, ladies. Well, what's the matter with you? Think you have a choice of where to live?

Black Prostitute: As long as we put out.

Welfare Worker: No one lives for free in a democracy. You no longer have one of your brutal pimps above you.

Black Prostitute: You government're so powerful, you don't need to indulge in individual brutality.

Welfare Worker: Me? Do you think I make the rules?

Black Prostitute: No, you live by them.

(*Portia dressed as a leather boy, walking along the street and kicking whatever she sees.*)

Gratiano: Portia!

Portia: What d'you want?

Gratiano: I want to go along with you.

Portia: I don't know. I don't trust you. You don't hold yourself in: you're wild rude unsocial. I have to be with men who adjust to all social classes.

Gratiano: What should I be: a woman?

Portia: I'm sick of men who worship their machoism as the be-all and end-all.

Gratiano: I want my way as much as you want your way.

Portia: I'm going to get as drunk as possible.

5.

Isabel: Daddy, you want to know about politics. I'll tell you about politics. The United States' overrunning El Salvador and Nicaragua. You say you want to devote your whole life to stopping this inanity but of course you're not going to waste your time going to Nicaragua. 'What can I do?', you pound your fists tear out your hairs scream desperately, 'What can I do?' First, you say, you need to disseminate information because when and only when the people receive accurate info, whatever the hell that is, they'll know how and more important want to stop the US infiltration of El Salvador and Nicaragua. 'How can I start this first step?' you scream. 'How can I get this information to the people? We need a large media group. There's no organized group. What can I do? I'm helpless.'

You're accepting the US government's version of reality: you say you need a commercially-acceptable organization or a beaurocracy in order to act functionally. My reality's mercy.

Shylock R. (*looking at his fingernails*): I told you to get out of here.

Isabel (*alone*): Even though I'm Jewish, I can fall in love. My father terrorized me because he hated my guts because my mother whom he adored left him before I was born. Are we always to be governed by our parents' fucked-up lives? Rebels're as slavelike as toadies. Me: I hate everyone: rebels and toadies. But Lorenzo. I'm running away to him! Out of this hell! He's promised to marry me which means love me for ever even if he doesn't love me. Being without a mother and my father's hating me's carved bloody ruts unable-to-heal below my flesh before I was old enough to have the power to run away. (*Running down the street.*)

My father knows nothing about my treachery and'll disown me if he finds out. (*Still running.*)

(*The sun's very bright and almost white. I'd burn up my flesh burn up so white it turns to black.*)

ACT II FLESH

When Antonio can't return the money to Shylock R., Shylock R. intends to cut out Antonio's flesh.

1.

A castle in bright sun. Army enters, flags, horses, approaching castle. Henry Hereford, Edmund of Langley, the Duke of York, and the Earl of Northumberland lead the soldiers. Hereford turns around on his horse to talk to Northumberland. As he does, Northumberland's son, Henry Percy enters from bottom right centre.

Percy: The castle's guards're strong.

Bolingbroke (*quickly turning to Percy*): Against us?

Percy: The King's there. He's established his stronghold. His (*pointing to York*) son, Salisbury, Scroop and a non-cock're with him.

York: That must be the Bishop.

Bolingbroke: They're all in the same place. Good. This' how I'm going to break down the defences. You all three of you (*to Percy, York and Northumberland*) by truce tell the King I'll bow to Him if He lets me go free and gives me back my ancestral territory. If He does, I'll be faithful to Him. If He refuses, I'll kill everyone in sight and turn this summer sun and all that it's nudging, red.

Percy:. . .Life 'n society're red. . .

Bolingbroke (*ignoring the younger male*): Tell Richard I don't love blood. (*Turns around to the men.*) Shut up on the music; walk gently, not with aggression. By giving up, we're trying to avoid more blood.

Percy:. . .Life is blood. . .

Bolingbroke: King Richard and I, we are equal powers; neither of us'll be less than the other: I'll play passive and He can play owner because we both have to play something so we'll go to war.

York: Does He know this?

(Martial music blast. King Richard and York's son, Salisbury, Scroop, and the priest on the castle balcony as the white sun blazes around them.)

Bolingbroke: Obviously Richard's scared to death.

Percy: He still owns the power.

King Richard *(to Bolingbroke)*: You. Don't you know We're the one power? How dare you approach Us except by crawling? Down. Down, all of you. Down down down.

The only way a man touches Our dreadful power is illegally. You're less than Us. How dare you try to pretend you're anything else? Crawl, because that's natural. If you at any moment forget to crawl around Us, we'll make you crawl because We're stronger and smarter than you.

In the past you've gone against Us. Your petty stinky rebellions. Even if no one likes Us even if We've no friend in the world and everyone believes We're a freak, We shine more and more strongly until Our blaze is the only worldly sun who exists. Our power's so strong, We're your only possible seeing light. Try going against Us. Ha.

And tell that snivelling wivvle-worm Bolingbroke over there: If he dares make one more move that isn't in open adoration of Us, We'll simply step on him as We walk crush him to bloody pulp. His little bit of blood fertilizes Our milk thighs.

Northumberland *(answering King)*: Hey, wait a minute. We don't want to touch Your power. We know You're all-powerful. *(Stepping back a few steps.)* Bolingbroke adores You: he's lying around You; he's tonguing Your lavender-coloured nipples. He's a faithful slave. Bolingbroke swears, by all he holds dear which is blood, he's approaching You not with a military intent but just to beg You to let him be near You. He begs You not to banish him. As long as You don't banish him, he'll give You his arms. As long as You don't banish him, he'll give You his blood and romanticism.

King: Tell him We accept this. *(The couriers leave. Turning to the Duke of York's son.)* If we don't accept these terms, he'll fight and kill Us.

Duke of York's Son: Be hypocritical until You're strong enough to bash in his head.

King: That's a good idea. We're honest. We use hypocrisy honestly. Wartime. Here's that ghost Northumberland again. *(Northumberland enters right, stands in front of castle. Looks like a ghost.)* We're a liar. Because We're social. We've given away purity. Because We're the

head of society, We've given away joy. Because We're the head of your society, We've given away Ourselves. We're none. We'll be truthful and become a nun. (*Putting on a nun's habit. In high drag,*) If we fuck again, We'll get AIDS. This girl isn't going to do anything more dirty. Let their feet trample on Our head. Their hands with knives in them're cutting apart Our heart. Rip. Our sex is strips of shredded skin. We can't find where to masturbate. Oh, the habit. Women. We know, We can tell, feel sorry for Us, but We know that tears and sex and all such psychological dramas're unimportant: (*Going back on this.*) Oh We feel sorry for Ourself, that's why We're a poet.
This world stinks and everybody in it stinks.

Northumberland: Especially when it's this hot. (*Turns around and leaves. Faces Bolingbroke.*)

Bolingbroke (*to Northumberland*): Can I stay in England or do we paint our people even redder?

The King (*entering, behind Northumberland, answering Bolingbroke directly*): There's no war.

Bolingbroke: I must remain a man: I have to have rights.

The King: You have Us, Our blood. We'll have war only in those countries we control. (*The Duke of York's son's crying.*) Why cry? Why cry in this world? Why cry for this world? Cry for another person if you must be human. Or cry because you don't know what else to do. Anything but action's useless and We've no actions left.

The Duke of York's Son (*as Bolingbroke's men're binding him prisoner*): That's not true.

King: We're Bolingbroke's prisoners.

Duke of York's Son: It matters what we do cause it matters what we believe cause this world's belief systems.

King: In gaol We'll be able to believe whatever We want. Like women.

Bolingbroke: You've always lived in gaol. I act don't moralize. I'm killing you because I, unlike you, am the power.

2.

The Irish criminal and the Slave arrive at The Thames. The Slave is the beautiful slave of the Arabian Nights of Pasolini. The Thames' full of garbage. The female Slave says the Irish Criminal's raped her. She kills him.
She talks of paradise which was her childhood.

Slave: Now paradise to me is war.

Modern British soldiers arrive by helicopter to kill her. The British killed Pasolini in order to keep control of their Empire. We always knew the British upper-class're embarrassed of their homosexuality. Caesar and the British Army meet and shake hands.)

Caesar: We're restoring civilization cause culture 'n' writing are great things and this stinkin' writing's plagiarized.

3. The scene of my marriage.

Bassanio (*to Portia*): You're the cause of everything. (*Looking down at her cunt.*)

Portia: Are you going to hurt me? (*Both fright and delight in her eyes.*)

Bassanio: Are you crazy, Portia? What're you talking about?

Portia (*realizing he's not going to get it, lies*): You don't know much yet. I'm evil. (*Has no other way of saying it.*)

Bassanio (*totally ignoring what she's saying cause he has no way of understanding what she's saying*): I want to smell you. (*He thrusts his face into her cunt and smells, hard. Lifts his dripping face, dripping.*) You're wet.

Portia: Let me taste. (*Draws her hand across his face. Then licks her insides. Wrinkling her face, surprised.*) It's not that bad.

Bassanio: I like Camembert.

Portia: I'm always so frightened I taste bad I don't want men to lick me.

Bassanio: I could lick you all night.

Portia: You could? OK boy. (*To herself.*) At least it's something.

Bassanio: Dead fish smell and the desirousness of a cunt're allied just as death and love.

Portia: You want something, but I can't tell what.

Bassanio (*looking at her*): I'm gonna murder you.

Portia: S & M's unnatural. (*Looking at him closely.*) You're really upset. You don't love me. Did I do something?

Bassanio: Stop talking.

Portia: OK. I did something.

Bassanio: You slept with Tim.

Portia: I haven't fucked Tim.

Bassanio: You shouldn't lie because I'm gonna murder you if you're lying. I own your cunt.

Portia: Then you're not going to kill me. Yet.

Bassanio: In a few minutes. It doesn't matter what you say. For the hell of it tell me everything you've done against me.

Portia: I've always loved and always done everything I could to be good to you. If I've judged badly, please know I've tried.

Bassanio: You hurt me. You wouldn't sleep with me. You slept with other men besides me. I'm going to hurt you for ever. I hate your guts.

Portia: I've always wanted to please you and to be however you wanted to be pleased.

Bassanio: You fucked Tim.

Portia: We were always fucking other people. You wanted me to fuck other men so I wouldn't get too close to you 'cause I depend too much on you.

Bassanio: Since I can't say it, I'm going to murder you.

Portia: Divorce me and I'll kill myself. Don't murder me right now 'cause I'm scared. I love you.

Bassanio: Get down to the floor.

Portia: Let me spend one last night with you.

Bassanio: Get down.

Portia: Just fuck me once more.

Bassanio: I can't talk. It's the moment. Get down.

Portia: Your kiss' my life. (*Her fingernails're red.*)

Bassanio: I can't talk. No more. (*Sticks a knife across her throat so there's lots of blood.*) I murdered her.

ACT III MARRIAGE

Portia and Bassanio hastily marry. All day it's been as hot as hell. So hot the people are animals. While they walk around, dioxan sweat pours out of their skins. They don't think anymore. And now this night, that makes us forget our agony:

ACT IV

Portia disguises herself as a boy. She also gets rid of all her feelings so she can go to Venice to judge the Antonio-Shylock case. She gets Antonio off by deviousness and trickery and takes all of Shylock R.'s money. She wants in payment only her cunt which smells of rotting fish:

1.

Lorenzo: On such a night as this the light of your fingernails ran over the muffin main. The pirates have left their shore. Shall we start moving? Now, given the strength of our wills, we shall not fall into despair again.

I(sabel): On such a night, the music is lullabyes noise the regular beat that makes us not think voodoo house zebra I can now now. Rowing to their main boat, they could glow at a moon beginning to exist because everything's in consonance with everything else.

Lorenzo: This night which'll never end the night'll never end. Here we dangle our knees over the wooden wharf; there're invisible fishingrods in hands, which stretch over across to that boat for which. . .

I(sabel):. . . We no longer want to go anywhere. . .

Lorenzo: This night here's our ease and our freedom. For light, love, Puerto Ricans throw down, and no tension; we have abandoned your father the Jew.

I(sabel): There're no more parents.

Lorenzo: There'll be no more parents.

I(sabel): Make love to me.

Lorenzo: Make love to you how?

I(sabel): There's only night.

Lorenzo: Or just like when suddenly you've a tiny purple lump at the base of your spine that's growing so fast in size and pain you have to nuisance-like see the doctor and suddenly he tells you you're going to die in a month or when you're lying late at night in a cot plumped in a large hollow living-room and something bursts inside your right hip then in temporal waves keeps bursting and you decide you're haemorrhaging so you call an ambulance: then, when you find out you're not going to die, since there're no more causes and effects: There're no problems.

I(sabel): I want to give myself away. I'm not what you think. I'm dumb. I've developed myself. I'd give away all I've developed my world, if some man would take me. I'm trying my best to give away everything even though I don't have a boyfriend, because for me giving away's the only life that is. I have to have living life or blood.

Lorenzo: Then your blood's mine.

I(sabel): You're my blood.

Lorenzo: I don't know what's happening anymore. Can this be happening? All I know is life's blood and death's everything else.

(The beginning of sexual desire.)

I(sabel): I haven't been able to want to fuck for a long time.

Puerto Ricans: They want us out of here.

Puerto Rican: Mayor Koch's giving money to the real estate entrepreneurs to chase us Puerto Ricans out of the Lower East Side so they can buy up all the buildings then make their investments worth as much as possible.

Puerto Ricans: We going bye-bye.

Puerto Rican (*rich from dealing*): I get rich, boy, so I buy-buy.

White: Thass a lot of scare-talk. I say that 'cause I'm white.

(On Eldridge Street in New York City.)

Anorexic Prostitute Who Works on the Corner of Forsyth and Houston: I never seen cops come into this neighbourhood an' these last three weeks, every other day there's some cop car on the block. I don' know what they think they're doing. They jus' sit on the fuckin' street corner. Then last night around five in the morning I'm lookin' for a John these two fuckin' cops have their cuffs around a bum. A bum! What d'they think they're doing? Cleaning up my neighbourhood? They gonna arrest all the bums? Then they just be more bums. Want some bum, mister? (*Lifting her skirt, showing an ass too skinny to be an ass.*)

Prostitute 2 (*slapping her*): No way. I'm not gonna get your AIDS.

Anorexic Prostitute Who Works On The Corner of Forsyth and Houston: My aid? I got no aid. Sarah 'n' I're just watching these fat farts put their manacles around this has-been; the needle boys're jus' watching; none of us're gonna run; we know the cops can't penetrate our territory. What're they gonna do: blow up the whole Lower East Side? This place's a jungle down to twenty feet down.

Prostitute 2: Money does everything.

Anorexic Prostitute Who Works On The Corner of Forsyth and Houston: Money's made us into graves. (*with a needle in her arm.*) There's no water 'n air anymore.

I(sabel): I don't feel sexual desire anymore. What's going to happen to me? I want to be human.

    I'm gonna fight.

    Who?

    Koch's hirelings.

White Cop 1: You crazy? What you doing that for?

White Cop 2: Everytime I see one, I beat him up.

I(sabel): And meanwhile, this life's so nothing: how can I speak of anything? For how long do I have to scream?

White Cop 1: OK. OK. (*Two more White Cops enter.*) We don't want trouble here.

Bum: I live here.

White Cop 3: No more. This' private land. (*Four White Cops haul off the bum. I(sabel) remains behind.*)

I(sabel): You made little drops in my hair. Sperm within the night.

Another Bum: Don't go yet.

I(sabel): Marry me.

Another Bum: Wait a little while.

I(sabel): I want you to love me. (I(sabel)): a shrivelled puppet. My head nods like a doll's. My face's white.)

White Cops (*returning*): We've finally driven her mad.

I(sabel): ha. . .yer.

       Why. . .yer. . .yer.

       Ha. . .m. . .m. . .b.

       T. . .t. . .b. . .w.

       B. . .b. . .w. . .w. . .

       L. . .l. . .

       g. . .g. . .

Were the day come, I should wish it dark
Till I was fucking and stealing against your flesh.

Lorenzo: On such a night as this the light of your fingernails ran over the muffin main. The pirates have left their shore. Shall we start moving? Now, given the strength of our wills, we shall not fall into despair again.

I(sabel): On such a night, the music is lullabyes noise the regular beat that makes us not think voodoo house zebra I can now now. Rowing to their main boat, they could glow at a moon beginning to exist because everything's in consonance with everything else.

Lorenzo: This night which'll never end the night'll never end. Here we dangle our knees over the wooden wharf; there're invisible fishingrods in hands, which stretch over across to that boat for which. . .

I(sabel):. . .We no longer want to go anywhere. . .

Lorenzo: This night here's our ease and our freedom. For light, love, Puerto Ricans throw down, and no tension; we have abandoned your father the Jew.

I(sabel): There're no more parents.

Lorenzo: There'll be no more parents.

I(sabel): Make love to me.

Lorenzo: Make love to you how?

I(sabel): There's only night:

Lorenzo: Or just like when suddenly you've a tiny purple lump at the base of your spine that's growing so fast in size and pain you have to nuisance-like see the doctor and suddenly he tells you you're going to die in a month or when you're lying late at night in a cot plumped in a large hollow living-room and something bursts inside your right hip then in temporal waves keeps bursting and you decide you're haemorrhaging so you call an ambulance: then, when you find out you're not going to die, since there're no more causes and effects: There're no more problems.

I(sabel): I want to give myself away. I'm not what you think. I'm dumb. I've developed myself. I'd give away all I've developed my world, if some man would take me. I'm trying my best to give away everything even though I don't have a boyfriend, because for me giving away's the only life that is. I have to have living life or blood.

Lorenzo: Then your blood's mine.

I(sabel): You're my blood.

Lorenzo: I don't know what's happening anymore. Can this be happening? All I know is life's blood and death's everything else.

When Bassanio returns to Belmont Portia demands to see the ring she gave him:

Portia: I've come home: In arms: In his arms: This is a message to you: This whole book isn't a message to you, but I know that the whole book does revolve around dark red dark brown cerulean the sensuality of your fleshs' our only made value:. . .

Bassanio: Be clearer.

Portia:. . . I refuse: I refuse to give up sensuality for anything:. . .

I(sabel): It's Portia's voice.

Portia:. . . So it's my heart I give to you. It's too soon to say this. It's too soon to say anything. My whole life's changed.

I(sabel): Have our husbands come back?

Portia: I'm not going to marry again.

I(sabel) (*laughing*): Here's your husband, bitch.

Bassanio (*to Portia*): I want to fuck you and I want sensuality 'cause I love the sun.

Portia: Are you really saying that?

Bassanio: Yes.

Portia: Here's my cunt. Tell me we'll go on for ever even in our graves we'll fuck.

Bassanio: I swear our corpses'll fuck to death.

Portia: I'm telling you: you don't even know me.

Bassanio: So I'm giving you nothing and promising you nothing. I don't want to live with someone.

Portia: Where's the ring? The ring I gave you.

Bassanio: What ring? I never phoned you.

Portia: I won't fuck you again unless you get back your ring 'cause I won't have anything with which to fuck. Because of you, I'll never fuck again.

Bassanio: I gave your flesh to a doctor.

Portia: Just 'cause I don't want to fuck 'cause I don't want to get hurt, doesn't mean I need a doctor. Is the doctor cute?

Bassanio: He's civil.

Portia: Who cares about civility in the bed? I want my cunt back.

Bassanio: He's a civil doctor.

Portia: Doctors aren't civil: they're murderers. By inventing penicillin, they've caused AIDS.

Bassanio: This goes to show that doctors heal the soul, 'cause this society's a sole.

Portia: No. Your flesh, no, more precisely, your wanting me and your real fingertips' touching me 'n' my not sleeping all night're my health and my disease.

Antonio: Then you need a doctor.

Portia: I'm the doctor. Don't you recognize me? I've always made everything myself. I'm self-independent. I don't ask anyone for anything.

Bassanio: And I am my own world.

Portia: I need you like an eye to see needs an object to see. Last night we fucked all night and today I walked through the winding streets of the West Village, blind. So I'll give my cunt to a doctor.

Bassanio: This doctor ain't civil.

Portia: Your wanting to touch me restores my health. For this reason genitals bleed red life.

This book is for Pier Paolo Pasolini

THE END

Edmund White
A Boy's Own Story £3.95

'This is not exclusively a homosexual boy's story. It is any boy's story, to the marvellous degree that it evokes the inchoate longing of late childhood and adolescence, the sense that somehow, someday, somewhere life will provide a focus for these longings, and the agonising length of time that life seems to take in getting around to this particular piece of business. For all I know it may be any girl's story as well . . . we are in the hands of a superior craftsman. I can say with conviction that it is one of the two or three best novels I've read all this season' THE NEW YORK TIMES

'A whole young life, abstracted and vulnerable as a Picasso acrobat, on its highwire between invention and total recall. The style can take your breath away' JAMES MERRILL